Valley of Dragons

BOOK FIVE OF
THE SECRETS OF ORMDALE

CHRISTINA BAEHR

For my last dragon.

For there is nothing covered, that shall not be revealed; neither hid, that shall not be known. Therefore whatsoever ye have spoken in darkness shall be heard in the light; and that which ye have spoken in the ear in closets shall be proclaimed upon the housetops.

The Gospel of Luke, 12:2-3

Prologue

JULY, 1899

The Russian novelist says that all happy families are alike, but that each unhappy family is unhappy in its own way.

I do not believe it for a moment. On the contrary, it is my observation that unhappy families share very specific habits. One, in particular.

They keep secrets from one another.

"You're his father, aren't you?" I asked Forrester, rather abruptly.

I was still so dazed by my rapid ascent from the underworld—indeed, my escape from the very jaws of death in the form of an indignant Quetzalcoatl—that I did not fully consider what I was saying to the shadowy retainer of the Drake family.

The colour drained from his face. I could see the truth of it there. Not only in his reaction to my unpardonably rude question, but in the very lines of his features.

How had I not seen it before?

Forrester sat on a rock and put his face in his hands. "You mustn't...you mustn't say such things, Miss Edith..." he faltered.

"I—I'm sorry. But you see...I love him too."

He looked at me, and then he nodded. The colour slowly returned to his face.

Meanwhile, it was beginning to dawn on me how awkward it would be to know this important detail about Simon when Simon himself did not.

"Don't you think he ought to know, Forrester? I mean, when he comes home. A man ought to know who his real father is, surely?"

"Ah, Miss. I've never been *that* to him. I gave up that right, a long time ago." His voice was taut. "Whatever I am to him, I'm not that."

I heard shouts. The children were scrambling up the ravine towards us.

I brushed gritty earth from my scraped hands, wincing. Forrester sprang up to help me to my feet.

"Miss, you won't—"

The look on his face was so desperate that I spoke quickly to reassure him.

"Of course not. I'll keep your secret, Forrester," I promised rashly. "Your secret—and Mrs Drake's. But you must tell him, Forrester. You simply must."

His face sagged a little in relief. Then I thought there was a flicker of something—confusion? Alarm? It was too late to inquire because people were running across the great pavement to embrace me.

CHAPTER ONE

SEPTEMBER, 1899

"One and a half minutes, miss," Lily said, referring to the watch she held, as the rat that ought to have been dead picked itself up and began nibbling at a bread crust.

We had administered the experimental antidote made from the scales of the *varanus salvator*—more commonly known as Frances—on a dragon-poisoned rodent.

"Eureka," I breathed, clutching Frances closer to me. I had made sure she was in the room for this epochal event.

It was mid-September in the laboratory at Wormwood Abbey, located in the old muniments room at the top of the octagonal tower. It had been odd at first to see beakers and burners mixed up with dragon bones and bundles of herbs, but now it seemed like a symbol of how quickly Ormdale was changing.

"We have to repeat it," cautioned Janushek.

"I know. But do you have any idea *how* it works?" I asked Janushek.

He pointed to the old mortar and pestle he had used to make the mixture. "Rusalka, I am here crushing dragon scales in a medieval tower to save your lover, who is being held hostage by Arthur Pendragon. Please, let us not fool ourselves with scientific terminology. Such words do not fit our situation."

"Magic, then," I whispered with a smile.

Once, as a child, I had broken off a twig of a tree and carried it home with me in my pocket. When Mother found it, she dipped it in honey and pushed it into a pot of earth. I watered it whenever she told me to and the following spring it put forth shoots of green life.

Since becoming a dragon keeper less than a year ago, my entire perception of the world around me had changed. It wasn't that the magic hadn't been there before, it was that I had not seen it.

"It works on animals," said Lily with her good sense. "But will it work on people?"

Janushek cleared his throat and started to speak.

"No," I cut him off. I knew what he was about to offer. "We're not going to poison you, Janushek. I've been experimented on myself, and I've watched Farley experiment on Hanna, and I won't have it. It's bad enough doing it to these poor rodents, though I suppose it can't be any worse than being eaten by Frances, which seems to be their natural fate." I turned to gaze out the window, which we had opened to let in some air. "If we are going to be in the business of magic here at Wormwood Abbey, it will be utterly light."

Something in the landscape below us caught my eye. It looked to be a shepherd coming down from the fells, slowly approaching the abbey. His gait was dogged and awkward, and he leaned heavily on his crook. I had not noticed that any of our shepherds walked with a limp.

I leaned and peered out. What was that ungainly protuberance just below his knee? Could it be...?

"Lily," I said, suddenly filled with hope, "send Thomas to Embsay with a telegram to Ogwen Cottage. Tell him we have what Pendragon wants. Janushek—follow me with the antidote!"

I snatched up my Dragon Keeper's belt, which clanked with useful items, and ran out the door and along the roof walkway in the autumn-mellow air, careful of the crumbling masonry.

I ducked through the low doorway into the abbey. On my way through the dim passages I almost collided with Gwendolyn.

"You saw him?" I asked, fastening the buckle at my waist.

"Yes," she answered.

I yanked open a door and we were outside.

We ran round the corner and there he was, waiting. He was approaching old age, wore the traditional smock of a shepherd, and had a mud-brown dragon the size of a badger attached to his leg.

I stopped short. I'd seen this kind for the first time during the sheep clipping. The sheep shearers called them 'groundlings'. A sett had been discovered that extended under the wool sheds. We had spent a good many days relocating them, as the last thing we needed was to send off a bale of wool to auction with a clutch of baby dragons inside.

"How far did you walk?" I asked the man, crouching down on the gravel walk to get a better look. The beast was latched onto him like a limpet.

"From Cleasby's pens," he answered.

Gwendolyn gave an exclamation. "Why, in heaven's name? You could have gone to Drake Hall sooner than here."

He gestured at me with his chin. "I wanted to see the abbey Mercy," he said, using the Dalefolk's name for people who could heal dragon bites—a local corruption of the foreign word *Marsi*. There were two in the Dale—me, and Helena Drake.

"How did it happen?" I asked.

"Foot went through into the sett," he answered.

I glanced at his stout staff. "And you couldn't beat it off with your stick?"

He looked horrified. "I don't want to be sent out of Dale, Mercy."

"Sent out of the Dale? Whatever for?"

"For destroying one o' them." He indicated the creature currently attached to his leg.

I told myself I would investigate this later.

"I'm going to try and make it release you. Gwendolyn, would you please offer this crook as a substitute for the leg?"

Gwendolyn took the crook and held it ready.

"And shepherd, if you would just be ready to move your leg well out of the way as soon as it lets go."

I took a bottle of artemisia out of the little satchel that hung from my belt and unstoppered it. Then I carefully dribbled a few drops of the greenish liquid into the side of the creature's mouth. The beast recoiled, causing the shepherd to breathe in sharply, then released the man's leg and convulsed with a retching sound, its tongue rolling about wildly.

The shepherd drew quickly back and Gwendolyn slid the crook where his leg had been an instant before. The groundling snapped onto it savagely. Gwendolyn let go. The groundling stumbled, righted itself, then ran off, carrying the shepherd's crook with it.

The three of us stared after it.

"I'm sorry about your crook," I said.

"I mun make another," he said simply.

"How do you feel, Jacob?" Gwendolyn asked, and I felt instantly ashamed for addressing him as 'shepherd'. How did she manage to remember the names of every old man in the Dale? They looked embarrassingly similar to me.

"Fair," he answered, but his breathing was laboured, and his eyes were too dilated for being outside in the sunshine. Gwendolyn had taught me to check for this.

We exchanged a glance. My heart beat faster with mingled hope and fear.

"Jacob, we need to take you inside so Miss Gwendolyn can clean and dress your wound," I said. "By then I'll be able to tell if you've been envenomated. We'll see you right, don't you worry."

The shepherd took off his hat and followed us inside, limping.

Gwendolyn attended to the shepherd's wound in the room we used as a sitting room. The shepherd leaned back and gazed at the ribbed ceiling, his leg propped on a chair. This had been the Chapter House, in the days when a community of monks lived here instead of a family. The ceiling still bore traces of colour: blue, studded with gold stars.

Had Jacob never been inside the abbey before? Why didn't we ever have people like him to tea, I wondered?

"He's ready for you now," Gwendolyn said.

I sat next to him. Though deeply weathered from decades of exposure on moor and fell, his skin appeared pale and clammy, and his hand trembled.

I paused.

He hadn't fought back when the creature had threatened his livelihood and attacked his very person. It was clear the shepherd would do whatever I wanted.

Part of me identified this with everything that was wrong with Ormdale, and hated it. But the ease of it tantalised me: at last, getting Simon back was within our reach.

I knew I ought to ask his permission. But did he have education enough to understand what I was asking? His only tutor had been the pitiless Yorkshire skies. What could he know of science and progress?

The thought made me bite my lip in shame—it was exactly how Farley had thought.

"Jacob," I said quickly. "I'm quite sure you have been envenomated. You already know I can heal you." He nodded. "You must know we've been trying to find a way to cure dragon bite. I don't suppose anything that happens here in the Dale is much of a secret from you. We've been trying, but now we think we've found it. And if we have, it means the Dale can always be safe, even if one day there's no Marsi here to heal people. But we haven't been able to finish testing it yet. This would be the last test—on a human being, not an animal."

"Tha'd try it on me?" he asked.

"Yes—right now, but only if you'll let me."

"Tha coulda done it without asking, Miss," he said, and the knowing look in his eyes made me reassess him—the deep lines around his eyes from squinting into the sun after straying sheep, and the scar on his temple that must have been a close scrape with death.

"No," I said firmly. "I'm *asking* if you'll do this. Freely—with no fear of being bullied or sent away if you say no. I've had my full share of people doing things to me without asking. It would be rank hypocrisy for me to do the same."

"Aye, Mercy," he answered softly.

I looked up and saw Janushek in the doorway, with Lily behind him, watching over his shoulder. I was suddenly very glad that I had asked Jacob's permission.

I was not the only person here who had suffered at the hands of someone stronger.

I took the vial out of my pocket and pulled the stopper out. Inside, flecks of gold danced in a blackish sludge. It smelled faintly of smoke.

"Heaven help us," I murmured, and dribbled some onto the wound.

"Will tha na sing for me, Mercy?"

He must have heard of me singing to Talbot's little girl when I healed her, and thought it was some kind of ritual.

I laid my smooth hand over his knobbly one.

"Of course I will," I said, and sang.

Praise God from whom all blessings flow
Praise him all creatures here below
Praise him above ye heavenly host
Praise Father, Son, and Holy Ghost.

Jacob revived within ten minutes, though we made him rest there for an hour more, while I sat with him in a sort of numb amazement, and Gwendolyn took his pulse and scribbled notes.

It was done.

Ormdale would be safe now—without Helena, and without me. In a profound way, I was not needed as I had been only moments before.

It was a strange feeling of lightness and loss mixed together.

"Take this, Jacob," I said, pressing my bottle of artemisia into his hand. I had more in the muniments room. "Wait for a dry spell and then sprinkle it about Cleasby's sheep pens, to discourage the groundlings from hibernating there. They'll have enough time to find alternative accommodations before the cold sets in."

"Aye," he said. "I'll see m'self out, Mercy," and with a backwards glance around the room and a respectful nod at Gwendolyn, he left.

For a moment, no one seemed to know what to say. Gwendolyn broke the silence, turning unexpectedly to Janushek, of all people.

"Janushek, thank you. The laboratory, the experiments—we couldn't have done this without you. I don't need to tell you what this will mean to the people of the Dale. And I suppose that's who you did it for. But I want to tell you what it means to me, all the same." She took a deep breath. "I grew up bearing the burden of guarding these creatures, and dreading and hating them at the same time. Now, there's nothing to hate anymore.

There will be no more lives on my family's ledger. I owe you a great, great debt. I can't imagine how I might ever repay it."

I could not imagine how he might respond to this surprising speech. Gwendolyn had once told me she believed Janushek would never think of her as a friend, and certainly the two of them had always seemed more like uneasy allies.

"A debt?" Janushek repeated quietly. "I came here as an enemy, and I was made welcome. It has been—what do you call it?—a twist in my story. Do not speak of a debt. Not between friends."

And he stretched out his hand to her.

Gwendolyn's eyes flashed with astonishment. She took his hand quickly, as if afraid the moment might escape her. Janushek shook her hand firmly.

"And Lily," said Gwendolyn, clearing her throat. "I did not think it possible that you could surpass your own service to this family."

Lily shook her head, blinking. "If you'll pardon me, miss—it's not just *your* family's place. It's mine, too. This is the only home I've ever known. I want to see it safe as much as you."

If this went on any longer, I thought, we'd all burst into tears—and Janushek would be the first.

"Edith," said Gwendolyn briskly, forestalling any such regrettable display. "What do we do now?"

I took her hand and gripped it. "Let's go fetch Simon, shall we?"

CHAPTER TWO

The telegram instructing us to meet at Ogwen Cottage for the exchange was folded up very small in my glove. The faint crinkle of it in the palm of my hand all the way to Wales reassured me that Simon would soon be within my reach.

As our train went through a tunnel, a memory from my last journey to Wales came back to me with breathtaking sharpness.

"When in disgrace with fortune and men's eyes, I all alone bewail my outcast state..."

Simon had quoted Shakespeare's famous sonnet. My mind supplied the rest now.

Haply I think on thee, and then my state,

(Like to the lark at break of day arising

From sullen earth) sings hymns at heaven's gate...

With every rotation of the train's great wheels, with every mile that brought us closer to the mountains of Snowdonia, I felt my own heart arising like the lark in the poem.

There was only one thing that worried me—I had no idea of what I would say to him when we met again.

Ours had been a curious courtship. While Simon had never made a secret of his feelings for me, he had also never forced me to confront them. I had found it all too easy to turn a blind eye to his quiet devotion and treat him as a friend.

But then, during that last fateful meeting, I had told him to leave me in Wales, and certain tender sentiments had escaped me. Sentiments that must surely have made it clear to him how much my feelings had changed during our perilous sojourn in the mountains.

I flattered myself that I was generally able to chart a course of behaviour appropriate to even the most unusual of circumstances, yet I felt wholly unequal to these.

Young ladies were supposed to be impervious and tranquil of mind about their young men until the moment they declared themselves—at which point a flattering surprise was the agreed-upon response.

But when it came to Simon, I was neither impervious nor tranquil of mind. Which left me with a conundrum.

How ought I to behave towards a man whom I had fallen thoroughly in love with *in absentia*?

"Edith?" prodded Gwendolyn, across from me, her brow wrinkled.

Janushek was next to her, mumbling derisively to himself over a Fabian tract by G.B. Shaw—*The Impossibilities of Anarchism*—much to the alarm of the other occupants in the compartment, who clearly feared the appearance of a bomb at any moment, and might be about to inquire if Janushek hadn't found his way to the wrong class of rail travel. In fact he had offered to travel third, but Gwendolyn and I much preferred to have him with us.

Gwendolyn plucked the pamphlet out of his hands with a show of familiarity that surprised the whole compartment, including myself.

"If you've quite finished with my pamphlet, dear brother, you took it when I was in a most exciting passage," she said distinctly.

Whether anyone could truly believe the rumpled Pole with the picturesquely scarred face (which was not the result of an anarchist's bomb, but rather a laboratory experiment gone wrong) to be the brother of my patrician cousin, I did not know, but it seemed to cause the mood in the compartment to mellow.

"Edith," she said doubtfully. "You are quite alright?"

"Everything will be all right as soon as we have Simon back with us," I said.

We arrived at Ogwen Cottage in the gloaming. It lurked at the edge of the crag like something on the border of fairyland, with far fewer people about than when we had visited it in high summer.

Impatient for the morning, Gwendolyn and I repaired early to our room after supper. We had not yet undressed when there came a knock at the door.

Thinking it Janushek, I called out, "Come in."

When I didn't hear his voice, I looked up.

A silent, hooded figure waited in the doorway, lacking only a scythe to represent Death himself. A horrible chill fell over me, and the figure threw back his hood, revealing the bearded steward of Gwynedd.

"Emrys!" I cried in relief.

During my visit to the Dragon Keepers of Wild Wales, I had thought him perceptive and kind, a possible ally. But in the end he had disappointed me by being too much under Pendragon's thumb to assist in my escape.

"My lady," he said, with an awkward bow. He didn't meet my eyes. My first intuition had been right—something was wrong. "Mr Drake needs your help."

I was already on my feet. "Where?"

Gwendolyn slipped away to get Janushek, who had the antidote in his room.

Emrys went down the passage with me at his heels, then paused with his hand on the doorknob.

"Please believe that I did not know of his plan," he said hoarsely, and opened the door.

The shadowed room was lit only by firelight. I looked about for Simon. There were three other men in the room, standing about with an uneasy watchfulness. But none of them were Simon.

Then one of them stepped aside, and I saw him.

Simon was lying on the bed in his shirtsleeves. He had grown a short beard, and it was very black against the pallor of his face. Perspiration stood out on his forehead.

I ran to his side and took his face in my hands, turning it to the firelight. The pupils of his eyes did not contract when the light fell on them, and there was no sign of recognition in his eyes.

"Where? When?" I demanded of Emrys.

Emrys answered. "He was bitten before we left our valley, this morning."

"This morning!" I stared at him.

"I did not know until we left. Lord Pendragon instructed me not to tell you until the meeting tomorrow morning."

Had he obeyed, Simon would have died in the night.

Janushek and Gwendolyn came in now with the case of antidote. Gwendolyn gasped when she saw Simon. Janushek—quickly assessing the situation—shifted so that he stood between her and the Welshmen.

"Where was he bitten?" I demanded.

One of them stepped between me and Simon.

"The antidote—show us," he said.

I stared at him. "That's what this is about? You think we are lying?"

Emrys looked at the floor.

My voice rose. "Emrys! Show me where he was bitten!"

The three Welshmen braced themselves, and Janushek adjusted his stance, ready to fight.

Emrys spoke quietly in Welsh to his men, and the feverishness in the room ebbed a little.

He pulled up Simon's sleeve to reveal the bite. I grabbed hold of Emrys's arm, which made him meet my eyes.

"I will prove to you that it works, though you had no right to ask it of me," I said in a low voice.

I knelt down and poured the whole vial of antidote on the bite.

Emrys murmured something in Welsh to his men, who moved as if to leave.

"No!" I said. "I want them to stay. They should see every bit of suffering this has caused."

Emrys nodded at them.

When I looked back at Simon, he was so still and quiet that I thought for a moment he was dead, and I remembered the way Emrys had appeared at my door.

Then I remembered the Talbot child. I had thought her dead, too.

I laid my cheek on Simon's chest to find his heartbeat.

And there it was.

Eyes shut, I sang softly, the pulse of the song matching his slow heartbeat.

Oh may my soul on Thee repose
and with sweet sleep mine eyelids close,

Sleep that may me more vigorous make
to serve my God when I awake.

I imagined the thread of my song knotting itself around his heartbeat and teasing it faster. A stanza later, I was sure his heartbeat was quicker. My cheek lifted and fell with his breathing.

And his face was warming to its familiar sun-browned colour.

Hardly knowing what I did, I took his face in my hands and brushed a kiss on his lips.

Wake up, my love.

He gave a great, shuddering sigh, and his eyes closed, as if passing from nightmare into dream.

I held his wrist to my cheek. His pulse was now strong and regular.

Dazed, I turned to my friends. Gwendolyn was sniffling softly into her handkerchief. Janushek had an arm around her shoulders and was murmuring something suspiciously like a prayer. At any other moment, I would have quizzed him about it.

"It worked," I said, though my lips felt like cotton wool. "He's asleep."

Gwendolyn gave a great gasp. Janushek swore. The Welshmen murmured to each other and looked at me in awe.

I suddenly felt myself back in a forest clearing in Gwynedd, with the smell of the sun-warmed pines in the air, and Arthur's ailing little boy surrounded by a crowd of people who were powerless to help him.

Anger at the memory supplied me with strength.

"Come here," I said.

Emrys obeyed, and he and the others stood before me.

"He did this to your prince's child as well, you know," I said. "His own grandson."

They looked at Emrys, and there was an exchange of Welsh. They appeared shocked at what he said, shaking their heads.

"I've been among your people, Emrys," I said. "They deserve better than to be bullied by a man like that, who puts himself in the very place of God."

He flinched at these words. Had I touched a nerve at last?

"Look at me, Emrys," I said softly. Reluctantly, he obeyed. "I want you to know—even if you had killed Simon—I would have given you the antidote, for their sake."

Emrys dropped to his knees and put his face in his hands.

I picked up the case and held it out to the men with him. "Take it. I give this freely to your community, as a gift, asking for no payment."

They took it, looking in confusion at Emrys.

"We've no right to this kindness, my lady," he said, his voice muffled.

"Kindness leads to repentance, and repentance leads to change," I said—so easily that it must have come from some sermon of Father's. "But if you and your people allow Pendragon's rule to continue, he will keep doing harm, and he will not be the only one who is judged for it. You know that, don't you? You've known it for a long time, Emrys."

"Yes," he whispered.

"I'd like you to leave now," I said.

They did as I asked.

Janushek was the first to recover. He pulled a chair up to me, and I fell into it.

Gwendolyn checked Simon's pulse. "He *is* sleeping—you're right."

"I'll stay with him," I said.

Gwendolyn looked at me doubtfully. "We could take turns."

"You sleep. I've waited so long."

Janushek banked the fire and Gwendolyn tucked a woollen blanket round me, dropping a kiss on my cheek.

"You did it, Edith. You saved him," she whispered.

After they left, I sat and watched him and listened to his breathing and the sound of the fire. I thought I would never in my life hear a more lovely combination of sounds.

Everything was well.

CHAPTER THREE

I had not thought to draw the curtains, so I woke with the cry of a rooster in the yard, in the grey stillness before dawn. My neck was sore.

Simon's eyes were open now, focused on me with the utmost gravity. The lines of his face looked less boyish than I remembered.

"You kissed me," he said at last.

Simply hearing his voice again would have been enough to throw me into utter confusion, but the words he said were almost too much for me to bear.

"I—I'm sorry." My voice came out horribly small.

He raised his eyebrows. "You're sorry?"

I wasn't really sorry, but what else could one say when one had kissed a man unbidden?

"I thought you were dying."

"Ah," he said. "You remembered."

"Remembered?" I echoed, bewildered.

"The first time you saved my life. In the abbey church. Gwen said it might help to kiss me."

"Did it help?" This was an idiotic rejoinder—I had kissed him because I loved him, not because I thought it would help a dragon bite—yet Simon considered it seriously.

"I was trapped, as if I was under a lake of ice. When you kissed me, it was like breaking the ice, and your singing—it was like the sun warming me. Thank you, Edith."

Why was he thanking me? All I wanted to do was fall at his bedside and sob.

"I'm so dreadfully sorry, Simon," I said, holding back tears with difficulty.

"For what?"

"For everything! For not listening to you when you told me we were in danger! For lying to you about *why* I was stay-ing—but most of all—for abandoning you! I didn't mean to—I thought you'd gone home already. How you must have hated me for it."

At this, his brow furrowed, and he was about to speak when Gwendolyn burst in.

"Simon! Welcome back to the land of the living! No—don't try to get up yet. Give *me* a chance to do something, for once. I can't let Edith have all the fun, saving people and what-not!" She got out a stethoscope. "As for you, Edith—shoo and get ready to leave. Get yourself a little loaf to eat on the way—I don't want to stay here a moment longer than necessary."

I was only too glad to make my escape. I flung myself on the bed in our room and cried a little. Then I tidied myself (a boy brought hot water up), changed into a clean dress, and, displeased at how pale I looked in the glass, pinched my cheeks for colour.

How absurd to be crying when Simon was safe and everything—absolutely everything—was well!

After I had sent my bag down with Janushek, I went back to Simon's room to look for Gwendolyn, but when I got to the door, I hesitated outside it like a schoolgirl.

"Edith? Is that you?" Simon called. "You can come in if you don't mind that I haven't put my jacket on."

Well, I'd seen Father and George often enough without a jacket and had never been shocked by it, so I ventured in. He turned from the washstand mirror, putting down a flannel.

"Are you really quite well?" I asked, to cover my confusion at that fact that Simon-in-shirtsleeves was an entirely different beast than my father or brother.

And how could I have forgotten how tall he was? He positively dwarfed me!

"Perfectly, it seems," he said with a smile. "Did you really heal me with an elixir—which *you* discovered?" Then his smile dimmed suddenly. "Gwen has been telling me that you went through a very bad time to get it."

"What else could I have done, Simon? After I abandoned you like that! Were they cruel to you in Gwynedd?"

"Cruel? No! It wasn't pleasant to be a prisoner. But I learned a lot about their dragons. And being out of the Dale for the first time gave me time to think."

He took a tentative step towards me and my heart gave a jolt.

"And you?" he asked. "Are *you* quite well?"

I felt like my insides were whirling about outside of me.

"I think I must be hungry," I said. "We're to breakfast on the train—Gwendolyn is determined to get away. Are you ready?"

"Nearly." He rubbed his chin and gestured to the washstand, where I now saw to my dismay that a bowl of hot water and a razor waited. "I thought I'd get rid of this first."

"Oh!" I exclaimed. He looked surprised. "Never mind! I'll meet you downstairs," I blurted, and fled.

Simon followed soon after, beard intact, which made me flush.

Gwendolyn's merriment covered my nervous mood on the way to the station. She excitedly told him about going to London for her entrance examination to medical school in two weeks. Janushek leaned back and watched us with sharp eyes.

Once on the train, Simon was lifting our things onto the storage rack when Janushek spoke suddenly. "Did *you* try to escape, Drake?"

"At first, yes. I made a complete hash of it." He winced. "But then it was made clear to me that I was there in Edith's stead. And so I gave my parole."

Simon sat down. Gwendolyn stared at him blankly. The last whistle sounded.

"My word of honour as a hostage," he explained. "And they let me have the run of the place after that."

The train began to pull away.

Gwendolyn went pale. "You gave them your word not to escape? And you *kept* it? Oh, Simon!"

Janushek laughed. Gwendolyn sprang up, seizing her walking stick.

"Well! I must say, after all Edith's been through to try and save you, you might at least have gotten yourself *wounded*!" She hit the floor of the carriage with her stick indignantly. It looked as if she would have preferred to use it on Simon. "I'm going to the dining car."

With that, she left, and Janushek followed her with an enigmatic backwards glance at me.

Now the two of us were alone.

After a moment, I offered apologetically, "Gwen was very worried over you last night—I don't suppose she *really* wants you to have been wounded."

"I'm not so sure," he said drily. "I grew up with her. She wounded me a few times herself. What about you, Edith? Do you have a sudden desire to wound me?"

On the contrary, I had a sudden desire to kiss him. It would be quite different to kiss him when he was awake. I quelled this urge, which was so unseasonable in one of single state.

"I hope never to see you hurt again, Simon," I said. "Last night was horrible. Do you remember it much?"

He shook his head. "It was like a dream. It gave me quite a start to see you sleeping in that chair when I woke up. I had begun to wonder if you had ever really existed outside of my dreams—if such a legend could really exist." A smile played on his lips. "The bards sing about you. The mothers tell their children bedtime stories about you."

"Why on earth would they do that?" I exclaimed.

"Edith! You charmed the *addanc* with a song. You climbed onto an unbroken dragon and flew it out of the valley. You snatched a child back from death."

"Oh. Well! I suppose I did."

He laughed, that deep laugh that came out at the oddest moments and made me feel warm to my toes. "Yes, I understand it's nothing to *you*. Just another day being Edith Worms."

I flushed. Did he still see me as a saint? Surely not, after Wales. "Nobody would call me a legend if they'd seen all of the mistakes I've made in the last two months, Simon."

"Did he hurt you very much?" Simon's voice went oddly hollow.

"Do you mean Farley? It was frightening, more than painful. I'd be happy never to see a hypodermic needle again." I touched my neck. Simon's face went still. "It's only a small scar," I added to reassure him, and turned so he could see.

He leaned close and brushed a curl away from the place as gently as one might shift a butterfly from a leaf.

"Can you ever forgive me for putting you through all of that?" he said quietly.

"Forgive *you!*" My head snapped back to face him. "What do you mean?"

"Edith, I told you I had time to think while I was in Wales," he said, staying rather close to me.

My heart was pounding—was it out of fear or joy? "And?"

He leaned back in his seat, giving me a sharp pang of disappointment as the warmth of him retreated.

"Ever since I met you, I've been terrified that you might not...need me." He looked at the floor. "That I might find myself needing someone so deeply who would turn out not to need me at all. And while I was in Wales, I began to see it differently."

"What do you mean?"

"I love you enough to want the very best for you." The entire world tilted. Was this it? The moment when we would finally declare our love? "The very best of everything. And the best—it isn't me."

At that moment, I felt like I had been shoved into a pit.

"But—what if I *do* need you?" I managed.

"You don't." His certainty unsettled me. "Edith, look at me. What good am I? I can't even ask the woman I love to marry me."

"You can't?" I whispered.

"You said it yourself, that day in Wales. How could I ask any woman to make Drake Hall her home? How could any woman be happy, joining herself to my family? A man must put his wife first in everything. I oughtn't to marry if I can't do that. What kind of husband would I be?"

Every word was a fistful of dirt landing on my coffin.

"You asked me to forgive you, but it ought to be the other way round," he continued. "You said something I did not want to hear, and it shook me—so much so that I left. You seem to have forgotten that I abandoned *you*, Edith. That's not the man you should marry."

I was confused, my eyes hot with unshed tears.

All at once, I became convinced of one thing—that crying in front of a man who had just told me he wouldn't marry me would make everything much worse.

So I rushed out of the compartment.

I don't know where I would have gone had I not bumped into Janushek in the passage. He pulled me into the next compartment. The woman occupying it glared at us.

"Do you mind?" he asked her coldly.

"Well!" she exclaimed, and stomped out.

Janushek patted me while I choked out an apology through my sobs.

"Oh, not again! I promised myself I wouldn't make a habit of this."

"It is necessary to cry sometimes. Otherwise, you become like that one." He indicated the departed woman with a shudder. "And it is better to cry in company." I removed my damp face from his shoulder and fished about for my handkerchief. "However, in this country, I usually cry alone, lest I cause dismay."

"Yes, I suppose you might succeed in startling even Dugdale if you were to cry in public places."

"Would you like to cry more?" he asked, offering his shoulder amiably. I noticed there the collar of his shirt needed mending.

"I don't think so."

I had found my handkerchief by this time, so I sat down and applied it.

He looked at me narrowly. "It's the mother, isn't it? Would you like me to get rid of her for you?"

"Get rid of her!" I repeated blankly. "How on earth would you do that?"

"She is confined to her bed, yes?" he mused, sitting down. He looked up with sparkling eyes. "A pillow would be the easiest way."

"A pillow? Janushek! You can't *murder* Mrs. Drake!"

"And you think if you married him, she wouldn't put poison in your tea?"

"I think...I think I would insist on making my own tea if I lived at Drake Hall," I said soberly.

"Ha! You see?"

"Stop joking—it's appallingly bad taste. The fact is, I won't live there. Because he hasn't asked me. In fact, he's just told me he won't ever ask me!"

"Has he?" He sat back and looked at me thoughtfully. "I hate to say it, Rusalka, but if he won't do something about the mother, then he's right."

"Of course he is!" I wailed. "That's why I'm here, crying with you, instead of staying and arguing with him, you dreadful anarchist!"

"Poor Rusalka! You've fallen in love with someone as good and serious as you. It is hard for such people to smooth their way."

"Is it easier for people who are less good and serious?" I wondered, sniffling.

"We shall see," he shrugged, then offered by way of explanation, "I expect I will fall in love again soon."

I stared at him. For myself, I had fallen in love reluctantly, fighting it even when I had no pressing reason to do so. And here was Janushek, talking of losing his heart like I might speak of ordering lunch.

I wasn't sure I had the moral fibre to watch him fall in love and be happy for him when everything was going so badly for me and Simon. The smallness of my own soul was suddenly loathsome to me, and I felt as empty as a pillarbox.

Everything was all wrong.

"You should eat something," he declared. "There's an old Polish saying: Trouble in love makes one hungry."

I squinted at him. "Is that really a Polish saying?"

He stood up and took me gently by the elbow. "Perhaps it is, perhaps it isn't. And perhaps we have been friends long enough that I know how much you like eating."

As Janushek led me to the dining car, it occurred to me that I had been rather naive to suppose that everything would simply fall into place for my own happiness.

We had rescued Simon, but all wasn't well. Because he was still trapped in a deeper captivity—from which I had no idea how to free him.

Chapter Four

"Edith, when your father comes, you will explain to him about the rents, won't you?" Gwendolyn said to me a week and a half later.

"Yes, Gwendolyn, I will," I said patiently. I had said it so many times on the way to Embsay Station to see her off for London that the words had almost become nonsense. Gwendolyn looked at me expectantly as she waited for her ticket.

I sighed and repeated my lesson dutifully. "The rents are due on Friday. Dugdale will tot up all the figures and be on hand to assist in receiving the rents, but my father must sit in the Great Hall as Squire on Michaelmas to represent the family or the tenants will feel slighted," I repeated.

"Hurt," she corrected, taking her ticket. "I said *hurt*, not slighted."

"Of course."

In my town life, I had not mixed with rural people such as they—farmers, shepherds, cottagers. I found the Dalefolk to be an unexpected mix of pride and humility, wisdom and superstition.

"And whatever you do, don't pick blackberries after Michaelmas," she said as an afterthought as the porter wheeled her luggage to the baggage car.

"Yes, Gwen—" I stopped. "What did you just say?"

"Just—please don't. You'll upset everyone no end if you do."

"But why?"

"Because the devil—well, he did something unspeakable to them when he fell from heaven. No country person would dream of picking them after that."

"Wait a moment—do you mean that they really believe that Lucifer falls from heaven *every* Michaelmas? And stops in Ormdale just to spoil the blackberries?"

Gwendolyn sighed. "I don't know that they think about it in such modern terms, Edith. Just—please. Don't do it."

"All right!" I said.

"And as for Simon..."

"What about Simon?"

"He will help with anything. He knows everyone in the Dale. But don't forgive him too soon for being such a dunderhead in Wales." Her brow furrowed. "And don't leave it too late, either."

If only it were a matter of forgiving Simon as Gwendolyn supposed! I had hinted to Gwendolyn that all between us was at an end, but with her head full of the entrance examination to the London Medical School for Women, she had either misunderstood or simply disbelieved me.

"Now, haven't you got any advice for me?" asked Gwendolyn as I embraced her on the platform.

"No," I said quietly. "Because I think that passing this exam is going to be one of the easiest things you've ever done."

"Easiest!"

"I oughtn't to say easiest—I know you've worked terribly hard—only it's different when it's something you really want to do, isn't it? It's not drudgery then, no matter how difficult the work is."

Gwendolyn's eyes lit for a moment. She hugged me again fiercely.

"It's all you, Edith," she whispered in my ear. "I wouldn't have done any of this without you."

Then she got in her compartment quickly.

"Make sure you write to me," I said through the open window. "I want to know all about your modern life in London! You know, indoor plumbing and omnibuses, and Miss Rivers's radicals."

And then she was gone.

Gwendolyn had said it herself—she wouldn't have done any of it without me.

I felt dreadfully alone as I walked back along the main road of Embsay, feeling almost as alone as I had when I'd stumbled along it after escaping Wild Wales.

A kind voice penetrated my melancholy.

"Miss Worms! What a surprise!"

It was Mrs Worthing, with a basket on her arm, inviting me to come and have some tea at her house ("I have just bought some crumpets") before I started back for Ormdale. I liked the doctor's wife and welcomed the impromptu invitation.

It was agreeable to shake off some of my melancholy in her parlour, under the influence of tea and hot toasted crumpets. Mrs Worthing had relatives in Ormdale and knew something of its isolation. She had played a small but important role in Gwendolyn's medical career, and must have sensed how hard it was for me to let Gwendolyn go.

We talked about the charity bazaar Mrs Worthing was organising at Christmas and the difficulties in finding enough people to mind the stalls. Weakened by the generously buttered crumpets, I was rash enough to commit myself to the wretched business.

One of the most blessed things about living in Ormdale was escaping the sort of mind-numbing social obligations which I had done my best to avoid as a clergyman's daughter.

When it was time to go, Mrs Worthing brought out a worn volume in an absent sort of way. Despite this, I had a distinct feeling that this was no postscript, but the reason she had invited me in the first place.

"Miss Worms, I have just been going through my husband's predecessor's records of his attendance on families in the area. Dr Dunstable was very elderly indeed when he retired, you know, and he left these with the practise when my husband succeeded him. I found some interesting references to your family, as well as to the Drakes. I thought perhaps...for family history purposes..."

"Oh, I'm sure my cousin will be very interested. What a shame we missed her."

Mrs Worthing made a neutral sound. Did she wish me to know that the journal was meant to be of interest to me, not my cousin? I couldn't imagine why.

I took the volume from her with a smile. "Thank you, Mrs Worthing; I'll keep it for her."

On the way home in the carriage, I glanced at it—just enough to ascertain that it was a very thick volume filled with exceedingly small handwriting. I wondered why she had thought it would be of interest to me. Unable to make sense of it, I decided that probably she was just tidying up and didn't like to throw it away.

My parents and the children arrived a few days before Michaelmas, to fine weather. No one ever wastes a fine day in Yorkshire by spending it inside if they can possibly help it, but my saintly father and stepmother had already spent most of it in the confined spaces of train and carriage with three children, and they looked distinctly pinched.

"Come, children, put on your oldest clothes and each of you get a stout stick, for we are going blackberrying," I announced as soon as greetings were over. "We must go at once. We have only a few days to forestall Lucifer."

"Lucifer?" exclaimed my brother George.

"Yes. Now go and see if Pip can come with us. He's likely to know some good places and can tell you more about the involvement of fallen angels than I can."

We soon set off merrily with our pails. Violet took up the lead, tapping on her pail with a stick and loudly singing 'With Catlike Tread' from *The Pirates of Penzance*.

Frances trundled behind us. George looked back at her thoughtfully.

"Is she slowing down yet, do you think?"

"What do you mean? Reptiles live for years and years, and dragons even longer. I expect she'll outlive us all."

"No, I don't mean getting old. I was wondering if she was slowing down in this cooler weather, preparing for winter."

I stopped still. "George. Do you mean..."

"Well, don't all the dragons here go into hibernation?"

I was filled with deep dismay. How stupid of me not to have thought of it! So she, too, would leave me for months on end, just like Gwendolyn! What on earth would I do with myself, the long winter months at the abbey? It was too bad! I looked away to hide my unexpected emotions.

"Steady, old girl," said George gently. "If you keep her very warm, she might not, you know, or not for a while yet, anyway."

"Thanks, George," I said. "Oh! Here we are! What beauties!" I exclaimed, trying to be cheerful as we came to a thicket of brambles that had climbed up from the riverbank, now heavy with black fruit.

As we began to fill our pails (some of us were more intent on filling our mouths) with the fat berries, I heard a familiar, friendly bark. A few minutes later, Pilot's muzzle poked out of the undergrowth as he scrambled up the bank to join us. Thankfully, Frances had made friends with him over the summer, as I'd kept Pilot with me at the abbey.

I crouched down to rub his ears and pick brambles from his coat.

"Hello," came Simon's voice.

I damped down my involuntary rush of delight—it was not conducive to my now-likely future as a spinster.

After the avalanche of excited questions from the children about his captivity had settled, he joined them at their task, helping to push the thornier sprays out of the way so they could reach the best fruit. A shout from one of them sent them all rushing to look at a hedgehog, leaving the two of us distressingly alone for the first time since his homecoming.

The thud of berries in my pail were suddenly loud.

"You saw Gwen off?" Simon asked at last.

"Yes. I was surprised you didn't come to say goodbye," I said. I had hardly seen him since he returned home.

"Gwen told me not to. She hasn't forgiven me yet for my lack of heroic exploits." There was a pause. "You will miss her a great deal, I'm afraid," he said at length.

I nodded, not trusting my voice to be steady.

"My mother has asked if you will see her," said Simon. "She wants to thank you for bringing me home."

I winced, catching my sleeve on a bramble.

"Don't move," he said, and coming close he began to carefully unpick the thorns from my jacket. "Will you see her?"

"Are you really asking me?" I asked in disbelief.

He was close enough that I could see the muscles in his jaw tighten in concentration. I focused on a distant cloud instead.

"No," he said lowly. "I have no right to ask you for anything. I already owe you my life twice over." His eyes shifted to mine. "You are free."

His words hurt more than the bramble thorns. I stepped back and turned away.

"That's not how it works, Simon." I turned towards home. "Tell the children I went home."

"How what works, Edith?" he asked.

"Love," I whispered to myself, though he couldn't hear me.

I kept walking. Although I did not look back, I imagined his face lined with perplexity.

I had begun to realise that for Simon, love was something that had never been free.

CHAPTER FIVE

After depositing my pail in the kitchen I went looking for Mother—she was, of course, in the cloister garden, looking thoughtfully at the herbs as if they were having a real conversation with her.

"There you are, Mother! Where would I find knitting needles? I'm going to knit a woollen waistcoat. For Frances," I said, gesturing to where the dragon was creeping up one of the cloister arches.

Mother absorbed this information with admirable poise. "Just look in the work box, dear, in the sitting room. You will find some lovely wool. The Talbots spun and dyed it for me."

I retrieved the necessary supplies and settled on the seat in the garden in case I needed assistance.

A moment later, the children trotted by on the way to the kitchen, gory with berry juice. George stopped dead when he saw me engaged in my uncharacteristic pursuit. I tried not to fumble it too much under their astounded inspection.

Violet was the first to make a guess, in a loud stage whisper. "I know! She did something naughty and Aunt Emily has given her something useful to make for the poor."

Mother made a sound that politely turned into a cough partway.

So far, the fruit of my labour looked more like a net than a garment. Perhaps that's exactly what it was: a net to catch Frances; to stop her from leaving me. Perhaps I ought to knit them for everyone I loved before they slipped away.

I would have to knit a very big one for Simon.

"It is not for the poor," I said mournfully, looking at the crooked thing. "I don't think the poor would want it."

"Oh, Eddie," said George, in a tone of pity. "It's not for *Frances*?"

"Off you go to the kitchens, children," Mother interrupted, "and wash hands and faces under the pump, please. And soak those pinnies while you are at it."

They thudded away.

"How is Simon?" asked Mother, as if she heard my thoughts.

"He seems well."

"Seems?"

"I see him so seldom."

Mother looked at me for a moment. "Things have gone awry between you."

"Yes. They've gone awry," I said as I attempted to stretch my ridiculous garment into shape, wondering if I would have to start all over again. "And I don't see how that will ever change."

"People change, Edith," she said softly. "You have."

"Ah, but I don't have *semper eadem* as my personal motto," I pointed out a little bitterly.

"I'm not much of a classicist, but... *Always the same*?" she guessed.

"Well, that's one way of translating it. The other is, *I never change*." My tone made my frustration evident.

"Fidelity in a man is nothing to scoff at," she observed mildly.

"It depends on what you are being faithful to, doesn't it? What if change is the very thing that's needed? What if you're caught in a horrible web and you think it's a virtue not to struggle?" In my agitation, I dropped a stitch. "*Cholera*!" I hissed under my breath, fishing for the loose stitch.

Mother calmly cut flowers. "Sometimes, if one is stuck in such a web, one needs to be cut out."

Snip, went her little clippers.

"Am I to do everything for him, Mother?"

"No, of course not. He has to do it himself. But you might hand him a knife." She looked up. "Here's your father." She smiled fondly as she saw him coming down the cloister passage.

"Shall I leave you?" I offered.

"Oh, no, it's you he wants. We've been crammed together in a train compartment all day. I'll go and make sure the children have soaked their pinnies before they're only good for the rag bag."

Despite the aforementioned train journey, they paused as they passed each other in the cloister, and I saw them brush hands—a common enough motion of affection, but it brought a lump to my throat.

They did not keep record of everything they had given each other in the way Simon had spoken, measuring out obligations to each other. With so much given and so much received every single day, how could they? They had shown me that love was both the most free and the most costly thing in the world.

How could I explain all that to Simon? Was it a language one must learn when young? Was he doomed to always speak it haltingly, even if someone did manage to teach him?

"Edith, my dear," Father said cheerfully. "There are a few details that you might just fill in for me, as regards your most recent escapades."

"Oh, yes?" I replied faintly.

He settled into the space beside me. I felt as if I was eight years old and had a loose tooth that was about to be dispatched. "Which escapades interested you in particular?"

"Whichever ones you weren't telling me about in your charming but opaque letters."

I put the knitting down and sighed. "Well. If I'm going to tell you about London, you must promise to pretend for a little that it all happened to someone else, and not your daughter."

"Shall I pretend I am hearing your scheme for a new work of sensational literature?"

"That precisely," I said.

About an hour later, Father had a few probing questions for me about the Chinese dragon I had liberated in London, and its astonishing feat in rescuing me from a tropical constrictor.

"And the creature hasn't done anything unusual since?"

"Well," I reflected, "*unusual* is rather the name of the game here, isn't it? But no ponds have come leaping at me, if that's what you mean. The plumbing at Wormwood Abbey is non-existent, as you know, so I have no way of repeating the experiment. Not that I'd want to repeat near-strangulation. At any rate, Oolong is living at Drake Hall for the moment, with Mrs Drake's oriental dragon. I was too busy with the laboratory to take another dragon on, and the two of them get on well."

"And you've heard nothing at all about Farley's fate?"

"I've seen nothing in the papers. But I assume the War Office might want to keep it rather quiet. I don't like to ask Stephen about it—I was careful not to leave any evidence that I was connected to the affair. I thought that best for all of us. And of course, I still don't know who the mysterious Barrington is—the man who hired Rivers, and whether he's connected to Farley at all. So many things remain unclear."

"And what about you, Edith?" asked Father.

"Me?"

"You said you gave yourself time to mend. Have you? How is it with you?"

Reluctantly, I considered myself. "Well, I was cross-grained today, but now I'm just tired and tender—like a snail that's lost its shell."

"You've had enough adventures this year to make anyone tired and tender."

"I've let my heart out of a box, Father, and I've found the results are even more perilous than adventuring." My eyes roamed about the garden. An idea struck me. "Is that why...is that why Mother has been cloistering herself in this garden whenever she's here? Because of people, and how tiring they can be? Perhaps *I* ought to take up gardening—one can do things to flowers one would never allow oneself to do to people. Whacking off a bunch of little rose heads with a really sharp knife would probably do me a world of good."

"Perhaps that is a sign that you should confine your sharp knives to fiction, my dear." Father laughed. "Dear Emily. I don't know how she weathers it all. The life of a clergyman's family is often harder than that of the clergyman himself."

Something in his voice roused my suspicion. "Is something going on? In the parish? Are *you* being opaque now?"

"I don't see eye to eye with my bishop on the affairs of this world. It's nothing to worry over, Edith." He turned and looked me over thoughtfully. "I thought we'd let you take on too much here. But you've grown up, Edith. You've put off childish things."

I glanced doubtfully at the ridiculous garment I was knitting. "Then I must have been very childish before now! Was I?"

"One grows up in different ways at different times. You've always been determined and knowing for your age. But now there's something else."

"What?"

"I'm not sure." His eyes searched me. "Love?"

"Only now?" I exclaimed. "What a clanging cymbal I must have been. How *could* you live with me?"

"There's more than one kind of love, Edith. There's the love we have for those who nurture us when we are young, because we have need of them. Then there's the kind of love we give as a gift, regardless of need. A love we choose, though we could have got on tolerably without it. I suspect that is what you have now, and what has changed you."

"Is it wrong to need someone?" I asked, thinking of the longing I felt for Simon, and how much I already missed Gwendolyn after less than a day. And here in my lap lay my net to keep Frances close.

"Not at all. It's simply that when you can choose to love someone freely, without needing something from them—then you begin to understand a little about the love God bears towards His children."

In that case, perhaps helping Gwendolyn get away from Ormdale had been the most loving thing I'd ever done. Far more loving, in its way, than my attempts to rescue Simon. I'd told Janushek I wanted to save him for Ormdale, not me, but perhaps that had not been true. Perhaps I wasn't so different from Simon after all. Did I, too, speak love with a foreign accent?

I gave a shiver. "To love like that—it's hard, Father."

"Oh, yes! But it is worth the effort—worth more than knowing the tongues of angels."

I laughed and slipped my arm through his. "Well, that's saying something, coming from you. I imagine you'd give a good deal to philologise with the heavenly host. Oh! Speaking of angels—here is Michaelmas, almost upon us. I'm told it's rather big around here. St Michael throws Lucifer out of heaven on schedule every year. There's usually a feast, but the family and the tenants eat separately."

I paused. Suddenly, the thing struck me as all wrong. Perhaps that *was* how it had always been done, but what if there was a better way?

"What if we feasted together this time?" I said, thinking quickly. "There's plenty of room for everyone in the Great Hall. We ought to let them see what sort of people we are, don't you think? What else is a great room like that for, if not for filling up with people?"

"Filling up with people?" Father smiled at me. "Edith, you *have* changed."

I laughed ruefully. "I'll go make sure Martha has everything she needs. I expect she'll burden me with silent curses, but at least she has a bit more help in the kitchen now."

CHAPTER SIX

Father spent Michaelmas afternoon seated in state with our estate manager Dugdale at his side in the Great Hall, a hefty ledger open in front of him, as the tenant farmers came in with their families to pay the annual rents. I was surprised to see Simon slip in and wait in a shadowy way near the tapestry. It was, I realised, the precise spot where I had first seen him. I had been so suspicious of him then—a premonition of all the terrible trouble he would bring me.

Father was enormously pleased to see him and seemed to visibly relax. Of course the two of them *would* get on famously—they were so alike in so many ways. How irritating of them.

I was just about to slip away when the atmosphere in the room changed.

Two villagers came in, flanking a third. The one in the middle had his head bent in an attitude of complete dejection. A woman carrying a bundled baby followed. She had a wrung-out look, as if she had cried all her tears away.

I caught Simon's eye across the hall. He gave me a slight nod, as if to tell me this was why he was here.

"How may I help you?" Father asked.

One of the villagers spoke. "It's Sowerby, sir." Indicating the wretched man. "He's broken the commandment."

My Father did not react outwardly to this startlingly imprecise accusation. "Which one? We have all broken the commandments," he went on in a gentle voice that still carried throughout the cavernous room. "Have you not heard, *let he who is without sin cast the first stone*?"

In the utter silence, Simon stepped forward. "They are not speaking of a scriptural commandment, sir."

"What other commandments have they?"

On of the villagers supporting the man spoke up. "Sowerby killed one o' *them*."

I remembered the shepherd, and put my hand on Father's shoulder. "Father, I think this man has destroyed a dragon."

"What response is customary from the squire in such a case?" he asked me quietly.

Simon was now close enough to hear this. There was a tightness around his eyes as he answered my father in a very low voice.

"Anyone who destroys a dragon, accidentally or by design, is to be sent out of the Dale, and never permitted to return."

"I see." Father's eyes hardened. I knew that look. Simon and I both stepped back instinctively.

"Mr Sowerby," said Father. The man still did not lift his eyes, but he was clearly listening as if his life depended on it. "Can you tell me what circumstances drove you to do something that might carry such a grave penalty?"

It was his wife that answered, in a hoarse voice. "He found one o' the beasts in the bairn's cradle, sir. 'E weren't thinking. You're a father, sir. What mun you do?"

Her arms were tight around the child that her husband had defended.

Father nodded his head gravely to her in thanks. He then gestured for Simon to approach.

"Drake, you are the magistrate here. Tell me, is there anything in English law that condones exiling a man from his parish for the destruction of an animal?"

"No, sir. A fine would be payable, if the owner of the animal demands it."

"The owner in this case being whom? Myself?"

Simon nodded.

Father now stood and addressed the room.

"I find that Mr Sowerby killed the beast for no cruelty or gain, but rather to defend those whose lives he had a duty to protect. Under English law, Mr Sowerby is liable to pay a fine to the owner of the animal. That is myself. I will arrange the details of the fine with him privately. The matter is now concluded. I hope you will abide by my decision as squire in this matter."

He sat down decisively. There was absolute silence in the room. Nobody moved. Nobody did anything. Dugdale took charge.

"Aye up, now. No dawdling. If you've had your business with Squire, go 'ome. We've plenty of business to do without folk mitherin' here."

At that, the people who had gathered at the back of the hall to listen to the case left. Sowerby seemed to be in complete shock. The two men near him left with backwards glances. His wife came and stood close to him. When they were the only ones remaining, Father spoke.

"Dugdale, a seat for this man and his wife."

Dugdale pulled up two chairs and the two of them sat, dazed.

"Now. Mr and Mrs Sowerby. You may be aware that before I was a squire, I was a clergyman. I am still, in fact, a clergyman. As such, I confess that I know more of the laws of the ancient Hebrews than the law of my own land. This beast that you killed, is it the kind that has caused deaths in the Dale?"

They looked at each other. "It were a groundling, sir," said the woman.

"Aye, it were," muttered the man.

Father looked at me for assistance.

"Yes, they are venomous. I treated a man only this month who would have died from such a bite," I explained, recalling the shepherd. "And he was a grown man, hale and strong." My eyes met Father's. "He told me he dared not fight it off because he was afraid of being sent out of the Dale."

"The groundling was likely only seeking warmth in the child's cradle," Simon put in. "But if the child had startled it, it would have bitten."

"Then it seems, by any reasonable judgement, Sowerby was justified in dispatching the creature," concluded Father.

At this, the Sowerbys went utterly still.

The man shook himself a little. "The fine, sir—if you can give me time to pay—"

"Yes. The fine. How much do you think, Simon, would be just and fair, for me to pay?" Father looked at Simon, then Dugdale. Everyone's eyes were now large. "It was my animal, was it not, that endangered the life of a child?"

Dugdale cleared his throat. "Squire, will you explain a bit what you mean by it? Dalefolk are not used to such ways."

"As the law of Moses would have it, an owner is responsible for his beast. As I see it, *I* am culpable for the state of fear these good people live in." He turned back to the couple. "You have been in great distress. You might even have allowed your child to be endangered, for fear of losing your home, Mr Sowerby. I am glad you proved to be a braver man than that."

"I'll not take anything from you, Squire," said the man with determination. I had thought the woman drained of tears, but I was wrong.

"That is very gracious of you," Father said with perfect sincerity. "Now, my daughter and her friends have made an antidote which is very effective against the venom of these animals. As Squire, I intend to provide antidote to be kept in every home in the Dale. I hope this will do something to alleviate the peculiarities of your situation. But should you find yourself in the same situation again, you must not hesitate to protect your family. Now—go home and rest. You've had a nasty shock to recover from," said Father.

As they went out I intercepted them long enough to put a vial of antidote into their hands. "Just a few drops on a bite, and if they don't improve straightaway, come here to the abbey or to Drake Hall."

"Aye, Mercy," whispered Mrs Sowerby, and she kissed my cheek.

Until today, I had failed to really believe in Father as Squire of Wormwood Abbey. But I'd been thinking about it all wrong. Father as Squire was the same person as he was as Rector. And that was exactly what Ormdale deserved. They'd had autocratic and tradition-bound squires enough; squires that guarded their rights first and every else's second.

Perhaps they had never had someone with the heart of a shepherd, not since the Dissolution had banished the monks with their calling to pray and serve.

Today, it was not I who had acted the part of Mercy—it was Father.

CHAPTER SEVEN

We feasted that night—roast goose and trimmings, potatoes golden with goose fat—in the cavernous Great Hall, at old trestle tables brought out for the occasion, laid with dragon-engraved silver.

The tenant farmers had all accepted our invitation to dine with us. I recognised the Talbots, their six children looking starched and combed within an inch of their lives. I doubted they would thank me.

At my request, the servants had removed the tapestries so that everyone could see the frescoes of Ormdale's history. I had been a little worried that the ancient abbot would appear as a spectre at the feast, but he seemed quite jolly in the firelight with his wyvern footstool.

I noticed Pip gazing at it in fascination.

According to tradition, the servants also ate in the hall, at their own table. There were a few new faces amongst them. Besides Janushek and Hanna, there was a little tweenie woman from the village, and a young man, whom Dugdale had brought in to rehabilitate the long-neglected kitchen gardens.

But it was Hanna and Janushek that drew my attention. Janushek had lost most of the impudence he habitually wore as armour, and his posture was carefree. Hanna had woven daisies into her crown of braids and wore a brightly embroidered blouse, her small waist belted tight. She had made no attempt to blend in with her peers, and I noticed a few of the farmer's sons' couldn't stop looking at her.

The fire blazed at times as tall as a man in the huge fireplace. Frances got so close I wondered if her scales would become molten. I thought that she might plunge in and grow before our eyes, as she had done before, but instead she gazed into the flames as if seeing visions.

Was she remembering the day of her hatching, in my study fire—or the time she had thrown herself in the fire of a London kitchen and come out suddenly larger? I wondered if it hurt to grow like that—like a refiner's fire, with the dross being burned away.

We were all contentedly pushing away plates stained with blackberry pudding when a mournful downward scale sang out across the hum of voices and clatter of crockery.

It was the kind of beauty that hurts and heals at once. It was Janushek, playing his fiddle.

All talk ceased. Hanna rose. She strode across the room, head high. All eyes followed her. Slowly, she began to dance, stepping from side to side to Janushek's pulsing melody. Her hair sparked in the firelight, and the flames crackled behind her.

Something was present that was quite new—something that flashed like a jewel against the backdrop of the faded tapestries of the declining abbey and the weathered faces of the Dalefolk. Hanna had brought something from faraway Odessa, on the shores of the Black Sea, and was offering it to us.

Was Ormdale ready? Was it ready for change in such a degree?

Then Hanna danced closer to the servants' table and stretched out her hand to Lily. For a moment, Lily hesitated.

My heart gave a lurch, and the fiddle music faltered. At the sound, Lily thrust her hand into Hanna's. Hanna smiled a smile that would melt any heart. Lily was on her feet, tall and lissom, her eyes flashing their amber light, and she held out her hand to Mrs Talbot, then Violet came next, and Mother and Una. Then I had to get up myself.

It was a circle dance, so simple that to join it was to know it. I looked around the ring of women and felt the tightness in my heart loosen.

It was like and not like a dance I had taken part in once before in Wales. This time, I did not lose myself. All around me were people—people who had changed me. But each of them had made me more myself, not less.

As I swept past Janushek in the dance, he grinned his familiar crooked grin at me. The thought darted into my mind that I ought to have offered to mend his collar. My eyes caught on the place where the tear and been—but it had been mended already.

The music ended and everyone applauded. Janushek bowed and passed his fiddle to a farmer, who began to play Yorkshire airs.

I headed back to my seat, breathing fast, my cheeks hot. I passed Hanna, chatting happily with Janushek. She straightened his collar absentmindedly.

Something fell into place.

Hanna and Janushek.

I think I may fall in love again soon, he had said on the train home.

A picture came into my head, of Hanna and Janushek at a candlelit table crowded round with rosy infant versions of themselves, learning to say their sabbath prayers like the families I had glimpsed through the windows in London.

It felt like a handful of cold earth tossed on me. Instantly, all the warmth and joy I'd felt from the dance shrivelled into nothing.

Frances hefted herself onto my feet under the table.

"Oh, you want me now, do you?" I muttered. "But for how long?"

I looked up to meet Simon's dark gaze across the table. All evening, he had let me alone and talked with Father, for which I'd been grateful.

"You're afraid Frances is going to hibernate," he said.

His perception annoyed me now. How could he understand so much about me, and yet not quite enough?

"I must admit I'm jealous of the Welsh," he said. "Their dragons are warm-blooded—they don't hibernate."

A flash of bright saffron in my mind—the colour of a dragon much bigger than Frances. Warm-blooded? Of course! Otherwise, they could never have kept their dragons closed in those dark buildings, away from the sun. George would have understood it at once, but I was slow with such things.

"Cariad does miss you—in case you wondered," Simon said.

I stared at him.

"Arthur said you named her before you left," Simon explained.

I briefly wondered how honest Arthur had been to Simon about his attempt to stop me escaping. If Arthur had any real qualities at all, honesty was not one of them.

"She was...in good health, when you left Wales?" I ventured to ask.

"Her kind bond deeply with their first rider. He couldn't do anything with her after you rode her. He certainly tried."

"But what will happen to her now, if they don't ride her?"

"They will use her for breeding. She's small for her age—not ideal for riding anyway, except as a lady's mount."

I remembered how joyously she had winged her way across the sky. Then I recalled her dark stable in the forest. Even if she did not need the sun to warm her blood, she needed it to lift her spirits.

"Have I said something to upset you?" Simon asked.

"I didn't realise she would be locked up—because of me."

"I'm sorry, Edith," he said heavily. "And I'm sorry for bearing the message from my mother. You don't have to see her ever again, you know."

The way he said it—with a sort of emptiness in his voice—reminded me of the sacrifice he had made to protect me from his mother. The sacrifice of our future together.

Perhaps I was being too hard on him.

"I'll go," I said suddenly. "I'll come and see her. But I won't pretend that everything's all right."

He looked surprised. "I don't expect you to ever be anything but truthful, Edith."

Violet's voice broke in on us, "No, I said that the Devil piddles on them tonight. He does it when everyone's asleep. George, do stop bruising my shins!"

Father engaged Simon in conversation about the leak in the vestry of the Ormby Church. Relieved, I drew in upon myself, like a snail drawing in its horns.

When everyone had gone home, I invited Father to come out and see the abbey ruin with me. There was no need to take a lantern, as there was a full moon. Frances accompanied us. Father was silent on the subject of the unprecedented garment which I put on her to shield her from the cold night. I was grateful for his tact.

When we got outside, we could see lights twinkling through the empty windows of the ruin.

"Come and see," I whispered to him. "Gwendolyn told me about this."

We stepped into the ruin, and it was prickling with light. Where the sanctuary once had been, under the empty rose window, there were lit candles. They were concentrated around the feet of one statue, even more chipped and weathered than the others. What remained of it was an armoured and winged figure, pinning down a gaping serpent. There were bunches of wildflowers and Michaelmas daisies near his feet.

"Gwendolyn says they used to do this every night from Michaelmas right up to October tenth."

"That is the date of Old Michaelmas," said Father. "Traditions like that hang on in these parts of England."

"But what does it mean?" I asked. "Gwendolyn didn't know."

Father took a deep breath, seeming to recall something.

"*And there was war in heaven,*" Father quoted sonorously. "*Michael and his angels fought against the dragon; and the dragon fought and his angels, and prevailed not; neither was their place found any more in heaven. And the great dragon was cast out, that old serpent, called the Devil, and Satan, which deceiveth the whole world: he was cast out into the earth, and his angels were cast out with him.*"

"Oh," I said. All of a sudden, these little offerings of light and flowers were no longer charming, but tragic. "You said once that the church had been a comfort to you when you were young, Father, because it mentioned dragons. But aren't they a symbol of evil in the scriptures?"

"A symbol, yes. To say evil is like a dragon is to say evil is deadly and long-lived. It is in our best interests to not underestimate evil, Edith. That is a protection. But not all of the dragons in the scriptures are evil. What of Job's leviathan? You will not find a passage more full of wonder than that. Everything was good when it was created."

Frances stood on her hind legs and grasped at my skirts with her claws. I picked her up and held her close,

"When I look at the dragons, I see something beautiful—something worth protecting," I said, dropping a kiss on her head. "But the people of the Dale, they see something fearful. Something only an archangel can save them from."

"God made both people and dragons, my dear. What we must find is a way for us to live together peacefully—as He intended. Your antidote is the beginning, Edith," Father said encouragingly.

"You make it sound almost easy!"

"Do I? I don't mean to. Blessed are the peacemakers, for they shall be called children of God—there's no suggestion that peacemaking is anything other than extremely hard work. God works very hard Himself, I believe."

"So I must work harder?" I asked, trying to quell the feeling of panic that rose at the prospect.

"No, my dear, on the contrary, I think you need a holiday. Even the Almighty rested on the seventh day, you know."

I stared at him. "A holiday?"

"Hasn't it occurred to you that your invention of an antidote leaves you relatively free?" he probed. "You can be quite sure no one will die because you're away."

It had occurred to me. But something else had occurred to me—I wasn't sure there was anywhere else I'd rather be than Ormdale. And that frightened me, too.

Now that Ormdale no longer needed me, what if I needed it?

"Where would I go?" I said.

"You might go to the seaside."

"But what if everything—falls apart here without me?"

Father pointed out a piece of fallen masonry. "Things have been falling apart at Wormwood Abbey, regardless of you, Edith, for generations. Wherever you go, you ought to do it soon—if only to cure yourself of this belief that everything will fall apart without you. Then come back and see it all with fresh eyes. Now, your mother will be waiting for me, so I will bid you goodnight."

He left me. I lingered to pray for a little in the church, and then went outside. Frances and I were silvered with moonlight. She shut her eyes and basked. I followed her example. I had a sort of suspicion that Marsis and moonlight went together. Perhaps it might strengthen me for whatever decisions lay ahead.

Frances wriggled in my arms. A birdlike call pierced the stillness, and my eyes flew open.

There on the grass in the moonlight were three—no, four!—figures. It was my old friends: the tame wyvern and his mate, now joined by progeny. The two juveniles appeared to be in the same awkward stage of development which chickens pass through in adolescence—all scrawny necks and legs.

"Well done, you two!" I said, remembering my injunction to them to go forth and multiply.

On my way to bed, I heard Janushek's voice, coming from the cloisters. Why was he at the abbey at this hour? He should be at the lodge, which he shared with Dugdale. Curious, I made a little detour to investigate.

"And that one, the bright one, is Sirius," he said. And now I could make out two figures on the bench in the cloister garden, faces tilted upwards. One of them was a woman, a shawl pulled over her hair against the cold.

Quietly, I slipped away. I should be glad for them as I'd been for my little wyvern family.

But I wasn't, and it was no good pretending. I was lonely, and with my friends pairing off, I was only going to get lonelier still.

Shivering, I got into bed and pulled Frances close. It was a very cold night. Did she even know how to hibernate? Where would she go?

I fell asleep clinging to her.

Chapter Eight

I woke the next morning to the first hard frost of the season, and to find that Frances had vanished.

She wasn't anywhere in my room. I had no idea how she had left. My door was still shut. Had she climbed up the chimney? The waistcoat had been chewed off and abandoned in a pathetic puddle on the counterpane.

Somehow, I knew that she was really gone. Gone—until spring. Would it be four months—five? And already the abbey felt so empty without her.

I sat down and cried a little, and prayed to the God who knew the fall of every sparrow to be as watchful towards my salamander.

And then I felt better. Frances knew how to hibernate. She would be all right, and she would be back.

Everything wouldn't fall apart without me.

Perhaps the only way to truly believe that *was* to leave for a while, just as Father had suggested. A holiday from the fretful tension between Simon and me—and from observing Janushek and Hanna's charming courtship—seemed suddenly just what I needed.

Perhaps when I came back, I would see things with fresh eyes, as Father said.

Maybe I would even start writing again.

It was at breakfast that two things happened.

Father was handing out the letters in the mailbag. "Here, Emily, a letter from the bishop's wife—it will be all about my faults, I imagine."

"Well, since I know them quite well already, I will not bother to open it," said Mother, piling jam on a piece of toast for him. "Do pass the toast, Edith."

Meanwhile, I was imagining my future as an opinionated spinster, and remembering how confidently I'd told Miss Falconer that I'd be happy with a single life—*pride goeth before a fall*—when all of a sudden I remembered someone I should never have forgotten.

"Miss Birtwhistle!" I exclaimed.

In Wales, I had asked Miss Birtwhistle to visit us, in the midst of my dramatic escape, but I ought to have written formally so she knew I really meant it.

"Who, dear?" asked Mother, as I passed her the toast rack.

"I forgot someone, that's all. How dreadful to be always forgotten! That makes it worse. Never mind, I'll write to her today and ask her here for Christmas." I had an idea that Christmas with the Falconer family might be something anyone would be glad to miss.

"There are some people who are better off forgotten now and then," Mother said, in the direction of the unopened letter from the bishop's wife.

Father picked up another letter and went still. It took a moment for us all to notice.

"George," said Mother. "Is there something wrong?"

"Oh, Father," I said with a nervous laugh, remembering the last time he had looked like that at the breakfast table. "Please don't say it's another long-lost relative begging us to take up a grand house somewhere. We don't need any more mysterious inheritances!"

To my dismay, he did not laugh. "Edith, it's for you."

The letter was passed to me. It was on very thick paper. The handwriting was beautiful, confident. The sender was The Honourable Irene Belmonte.

Never in my life had I received communication from anyone of the name of Belmonte. That had been the name of the woman who had given me life, and then died when I was a baby.

In a daze, I took the letter opener from Mother and slit open the envelope, releasing a warm fragrance of roses.

It all rushed back to me: the lady in tangerine silk. She had sat with me under the orange trees at Lady Battersea's. She had asked who my mother was, and her face had been solemn. Her name was Irene, and she had smelled of roses.

I read the letter, then handed it silently to Father. He read it, then handed it to Mother.

"Well! It looks as if half your guess was right, Edith," said Mother. "They *are* estranged relatives, but they don't seem to be offering you a grand house. Perhaps we can be grateful for that."

"Please excuse me," Father said, and left the room. Mother and I looked at each other.

"Eddie, what on earth is it about?" George burst out.

"It's my mother's family, George. They want me to visit them."

"Whatever for?" asked George indignantly. "You belong to us."

"Why do they want you now if they never wanted you before?" Violet asked. "What's their game?"

Mother gave both of them a look of gentle reproof. "Now, children. This lady, who is Edith's aunt, says that they didn't know about Edith before. They've only just found out about her."

"Oh," said George, then mumbled into his tea cup, "pretty cheeky of them, if you ask me."

I got up from the table. Una made a small, panicked movement—her hand was holding tight to the folds of my skirt. I looked down into her tremulous blue eyes.

Was this a picture of myself? Fearful of being left behind by those I had come to love?

"I'm just going for a walk, Una," I said as cheerfully as I could manage. "I'll be back presently."

I took the letter from Mother, kissed her, and went out.

It was cloudy but dry, so I walked for longer than I had intended, the letter in my pocket.

My dear niece, it had said. I could remember her voice easily—my aunt's voice, all silk and roses.

Your mother Miriam was my husband's beloved sister. He still mourns her sudden disappearance.

I felt light-headed and odd. I found myself crossing the stepping stones across the river and winding upriver. Soon, I heard the sound of the waterfall known as Bess's Foss, named for Queen Elizabeth. Approaching it along the bridle path that Simon often rode, I sat myself down on a rock, close enough to feel the spray in the air, but not close enough to get damp.

Then I read the letter again. And again.

They had not exiled my mother. They had looked for us. They had wanted us.

They had wanted me.

I watched the water creaming into the pool, then dissipating into a deep stillness. The rowanberries were scarlet now; some had fallen into the pond and spun about there in the current.

Everything in Ormdale was changing, and perhaps I was changing, too. Perhaps my dross was being burned away.

Perhaps Ormdale didn't need me anymore.

I heard the crack and bend of saplings being pushed out of the way. Simon emerged from the bushes in his shirtsleeves, carrying a small hatchet.

I blinked in surprise—he looked very agreeable in such an active role, like a humble but heroic woodsman.

Simon stopped when he saw me. He gestured at the hatchet a little sheepishly. "The paths became overgrown while I was away."

"Oh," I said. "But you can find your way about the Dale blindfolded."

"They aren't for me," Simon said.

Of course they weren't.

Simon knew my defective sense of direction, and he was maintaining paths for me, so *I* didn't get lost.

Oh, Simon, I thought, *it isn't me who is lost in this place!*

"Is something wrong, Edith?"

"Look," I said, and pointed into the pool. A heavy branch was damming up one area, causing it to fester with dead leaves and mud. He put down his hatchet and pulled it out easily. The water swirled free, carrying the dead leaves down stream. Together, we watched the water run clear.

A scaled neck, trailing with long wispy fins, broke the surface and then disappeared again.

"It's almost as if she was saying *thank you*," I said.

Simon smiled, and for the moment, we were simply fellow Dragon Keepers once more.

"I've had a letter," I said. "It's from my mother's family. It's the first I've ever heard from them, you see. They've asked me to visit. And I suddenly realised—the Dale doesn't need me anymore. I could leave. I could try something different for a little."

There was silence for a moment between us.

"Would that—would that hurt you?"

"I told you once before," he said carefully, "I would never wish to keep you trapped here."

"Yes, you've always wanted *me* to be free, haven't you?" I said, allowing my tone to betray some of my exasperation. Simon hadn't even wanted me to know I was a Marsi until I'd freely chosen to stay in the Dale. "But what about you? Why don't your freedom and happiness matter? Why shouldn't yours matter to me as much as mine matter to you?" I demanded.

He exhaled heavily and crossed his arms. "I wish that it did not matter to you, Edith. Mother needs me. And with what's left over—I don't have enough of myself left to give. I have to do my duty, Edith. I wouldn't know myself without it."

I stiffened. "So that's why you came with me to Wales—because it was your *duty* to follow me and keep me out of trouble."

He kicked at a root with the toe of his boot. "No. That wasn't it."

"What was it?" I asked sharply.

"It's not to my credit, Edith." His voice was especially low.

"I haven't put you on a pedestal, Simon," I said softly.

He looked at me. "No, you haven't, have you?" He took a deep breath. "My mother told me that you didn't like me—in that way—and that you never would. She told me that you would meet someone more—*eligible* in Wales and never come home."

I took a quick breath. "Then you came along for yourself? Because you—wanted something?"

He flushed and looked ashamed. "Yes."

"You didn't come because you thought it was your duty?" I persisted.

"Why are you *smiling*?" he asked, astonished.

I was beaming. "Because it means that you *can* change! You're not frozen, not *semper eadem! I never change?* My sainted aunt!" I scoffed. "Or rather, my aunt is Jewish, it turns out. So I suppose she can't be a sainted aunt. They don't have saints. Though they do treat Abraham rather like one. And Jacob, though I can't understand why, since he was such a sneak!" I stopped and took a much-needed breath. "I mean, Simon, that I haven't given up hope. Like all of those irritating suitors in all of the novels when the heroine turns them down the first time. What is it they always say? Ah, yes! *Will you allow me to hope?*"

Against all odds, he started to laugh. And kept laughing until he doubled over. Finally, he quieted.

"*Edith!*" He gave a shaky sigh. "What can I possibly say to you?"

"Exactly!" I said approvingly. "The heroine usually says something just like that! But there's something more I need to ask. Don't laugh. It's not pleasant, and it's very important. When I told you that your mother intended to trap me in Wales, did you believe me?"

This took the laughter out of him completely. "You are intent on uncovering all of my worst features, aren't you?"

"Oh, yes," I replied. "I'm assessing them as impartially as I can."

His jaw tightened. "All right. I didn't believe you at first, about my mother. I couldn't. It wasn't rational, and I'm ashamed of it. But after I left, I realised."

"What did you realise?"

"That I trusted you more than her."

His answer made such a difference to me, I could hardly take it in. I shut my eyes for a moment. My pulse was galloping.

He went on, hoarse with emotion. "But none of this matters, Edith. *Your* family is happy. Mine is not—or at least, not happy like yours is. I've seen what your family is like now. I can't ask you to make that change. I won't. I won't watch the light die in your eyes, a little more each day. I won't spend every day thinking how much happier another man would have made you—someone who could give you all of himself and not just a little."

We gazed at each other for a moment. How very paradoxical it was that we both loved each other, and had come to understand each other, and yet—here we were.

"So," I said. "We are at an impasse."

I wouldn't fight with Helena over Simon as if he were a bauble. But Simon? Perhaps I could fight Simon himself.

"All right," I said at last, and held out my hand to shake, as if at the commencement of a sporting match.

"What do you mean, 'all right'?" He looked doubtfully at my hand.

"I'll give you a year," I said, still holding out my hand. "To change. Or to convince me that you can't, because I still don't believe it. And if you don't—I'll give up and stop trying to convince you. We have until the rowans are red again. Do you agree?"

He glanced at the rowan, went a little pale, then grasped my hand for just a moment longer than he really had to—though I wasn't about to complain! A moment for me to think about how my hand felt in his, which was very nice indeed.

"Agreed," he said.

"And may the best man win?"

"Oh, Edith," he said, his voice very low indeed. "I'm quite convinced the best man is you."

"I'm not," I whispered, and for a moment, I thought his resolve might break, and he might just lean forward and steal a kiss from me. Only it wouldn't be stealing, for I was quite willing to give it. In fact, I had an idea that if he did kiss me, the game would be up for him and he'd *have* to marry me.

To my disappointment, he shook his head with another low laugh, and picked up the hatchet by the head, tossing it to catch it lightly by the handle.

Then he went back the way he had come.

Chapter Nine

I found Father in the library, praying at his desk. I sat down near him, and he put a hand on mine while he said his prayers, as he had done since I was a child.

"Father," I began, as soon as he had finished. "I met Irene in London, without having any idea who she was. I liked her. I liked her very much. It's sudden, but I think...I think it would mean a great deal to me, to see where my mother came from." I paused. "Would you rather I not go?"

He looked at me searchingly. "I trust your judgment, Edith."

"But if they treated you badly..."

"Don't refuse out of loyalty to me. We must all forgive as we hope to be forgiven."

"Father, I've never known *you* to do anything that required very much forgiveness."

"All of us require forgiveness, Edith," he said very quietly, checking my flippant laugh.

Very studiously, he began to arrange papers on the desk.

Had the letter brought back the grief of my mother's death to him in some unbearable way? I thought of Janushek's opinion of crying in company. It would probably do most of the Englishmen I knew a world of good to have a decent blub now and then.

"All right, then," I said awkwardly. "I'll write to her now."

I left him to his memories and went to Mother with my plan. As usual, she was in the cloister garden.

"Mother, I'm going to take a holiday."

"Really, dear? What an excellent idea! To the seaside? I have a school friend who lets a cottage—Robin Hood's Bay—I'll write to her for you, if you like."

"No, Mother, not to the seaside."

Something in my voice made her look away from pruning the spent rose blooms.

"You're going to accept the invitation? From the Belmontes?"

"Yes. Does that trouble you?"

There was a flash of movement in the birdbath.

"Have you spoken to your father about it?" Mother asked.

"Yes. He says he can see no reason to decline. And I've decided I'd like to marry Simon, but he won't ask me, because he thinks his mother and I will not make for a happy family life. I think absence will help him see things differently. You know. Pining."

Her clippers had stopped their rhythmic clipping.

"Well, you *have* had an eventful morning, haven't you?"

There was a splash from the birdbath, and Gilbert Sullivan slid over the edge and whisked across the grass to vanish behind a bush. Exchanging knowing glances, we stepped to look round it.

Violet was lying on the other side of the bush, staring up at us over the binding of Nelly Bly's *Around the World in Seventy-Two Days*.

"Oh, Violet," said Mother, "we didn't see you there. What have I said about making your presence known?"

I went back over everything I'd said in the last few moments. I'd said rather a lot.

"Don't worry!" cried Violet. "If I see Simon pining, I'll encourage him on. With the pining, I mean."

"Ah. Thank you so much." I tried to imagine what it looked like to encourage someone to pine but found I couldn't. I especially couldn't imagine Violet engaged in such an activity.

"Though I don't know why you don't just have Janushek instead," suggested Violet, "if Simon is so much trouble."

I went quite red. "I can't just *have* Janushek, Violet—he's a man, not a sweet in a sweetshop!"

"Well, he's been sweet on *you* for ever so long," she said, looking pleased at her own pun.

"Well, he's sweet on someone else now!" I snapped. "Good luck civilising this barbarian, Mother," I said, making my escape before I became the object of any more impudent remarks from the younger generation.

I looked up the Falconers in Burke's Landed Gentry and wrote to Lavinia Birtwhistle at Falconseat, Derbyshire. The letter was sent along with a padded case of antidote and instructions on how to administer it. We did the same for the Tallantires at The Scalehouse, Renwick.

"We'll need to make more, you know, if your father is serious about putting it in every cottage," said Janushek, as he took the packages from me.

"He is," I said.

Janushek was right. Frances had disappeared. We still had a couple of skins we had retained from her last two moults. That would not be enough to keep up a fresh supply. We were not yet sure how long the antidote lasted. Did it fade in potency over time? Janushek believed it would.

"Wait here," I said, and ran up to my bedroom.

Standing on a chair, I felt carefully about on the top of my wardrobe for Frances's eggs, which had waited there since I had come back from Wales.

Goose eggs, I thought, as I drew them down from their hiding place, remembering the story of the cook who had thought to boil them for dinner. Arranging the three of them in my skirt, they really did look like goose eggs. Creamy porcelain in texture, ovoid. Not blue-veined like the river dragon eggs, or black and globe-like as the quetzalcoatl's had been.

Globe? I caught my breath.

When I had seen the giant black egg the first time, I had thought it was a globe. I must go back to Drake Hall to look at that portrait of Bartholomew Drake again. Perhaps I'd missed something else, some other clue hiding in plain sight.

I took the eggs down to Janushek in the laboratory.

"Now, last time, I did this quite by accident, but I think I can do it on purpose." I stoked up the fire until it was blazing. Gingerly, I tucked the eggs between the logs. "Wait a minute." I was remembering it all in detail now. "I think it's important who it sees when it hatches, like ducks, you know. Fancy being a father, Janushek?"

He crooked an eyebrow at me. "As a matter of fact, I do. But I have particular ideas about who the mother will be."

"Well, run and fetch your lady, then," I said, "because you are about to have babies."

Janushek moved pretty quickly at that. I crouched behind the sofa and peered over it.

Janushek came back flustered, although Hanna was with him.

"I can't find her," he said helplessly.

"Never mind, go close to the fire, both of you. Quickly!"

Janushek hustled the bewildered Hanna onto the hearth rug, and not a moment too soon. She gasped and pointed into the fire.

"*Zmej!*"

Janushek grabbed the poker and flicked two glowing sala-mander bodies out of the fire: one dark, one light. The third and final egg shell appeared empty.

"Very good!" I shouted. Though at present very small indeed, these two creatures' frequent juvenile moults would provide all of the scales necessary to make more antidote for the foreseeable future.

Hanna went down on her knees, making a soft clucking sound. Janushek poked at one of them tentatively with the toe of his boot. The larger of the two salamanders knew a good thing when it saw one: it went straight to Hanna, who stroked it and spoke sweetly to it.

"Mind you keep him warm—perhaps even in your pocket. We don't want him disappearing into hibernation, too!" I instructed from my hiding spot.

The smaller one gazed up at Janushek uncertainly. It was oddly pale, with pink instead of black eyes.

Janushek looked at me helplessly.

"Go on!" I urged. "Take your child!"

Janushek bent down and offered his hand. It ran onto his palm and clung there, the tiny forked tongue whisking at Janushek's wrist. Janushek looked startled.

"I'm afraid you'll have to forgive me for making you a father so unexpectedly, Janushek," I said.

Janushek looked at me, mild revenge in his eyes. "Rusalka, those are not words I ever expected to hear from *you*."

Thankfully, I was near enough to a hot fire to get away with the colour that painted my cheeks at that remark.

The fact was that over the past months the suspicion that Janushek had once entertained a sort of *tendresse* for me had settled into a certainty. I had not recognised it until it was all over, so friendship had survived unaltered. I felt cross at him for making a little joke of it, all the same.

Lily rushed in at that moment.

"Mother said you— *Oh!*" She stopped upon seeing the infant salamander perched on Janushek's hand.

He quickly began stroking it tenderly.

Lily came closer, reaching out a finger to touch its pink, babyish scales. Similarly occupied, Janushek's finger met hers. There was such a jolt that even I heard it.

Lily jerked back.

Hanna let out a small and knowing gurgle.

"It's only electro-magnetism," explained Janushek quickly. "Nothing to be afraid of, Miss Dugdale."

"I'm not afraid of *that*," returned Lily, a little scornfully.

"Then what?" returned Janushek, his eyes locking with hers. "What is it that you are afraid of?"

I stood up straight now and gaped at them. How long had *this* been going on?

Lily saw me and went red. She rubbed her hand on her apron and turned away from Janushek without answering him. "Was there something you were wanting, miss?"

"Me?" I almost squeaked. "No, no—never mind. But as you see, we'll be making more antidote. Let Martha know you'll be needed again."

She nodded and went out without another look at Janushek.

"Janushek!" I hissed, when she was out of earshot. "It's Lily, then?"

Now it was his turn to turn red. "Of course it is."

So it had been Lily in the cloisters that night. Somehow, this coupling gave me the sort of feeling one gets when a book slips into precisely the right place on the shelf.

"But why—" I stammered.

"Why?" he repeated. "Because she is brave, and beautiful, and kind. Is that not enough?"

"It's more than enough! I meant—I just thought—why don't you take more notice of Pip?"

"Because it wouldn't be fair," he said with a sigh, looking at the salamander. "I like Pip. We are friends, the two of us, but I don't want him to see me as a father—not yet."

"But why?"

"Because then—Lily might choose me for *him*, not for herself," Janushek answered. Hanna nodded in agreement. "And what of Pip himself, Rusalka? Is he only to matter because I wish to court his mother?"

"Ah," I said, sitting down slowly. "And you say *I'm* too good and serious?"

"More like proud and stubborn," he said, with something between a smile and a wince. "I must know I am the right man for her. I would not be happy otherwise, Rusalka."

It was the day before I planned to travel into Hertfordshire that another letter came for me. It was from dear Cousin Stephen in Bloomsbury. I opened it in the cheerful expectation of receiving news of his son, Crispin, of whom I'd become so fond during my London visit, and perhaps something about the publisher's soirée he had arranged and which I had promised to attend. Heavens—was it only a month away?

As soon as I opened it, my eyes fell on a name that made my blood run cold. The passage ran thus—

The evidence that was brought to light against Farley ought to have been enough to end his career. However, Farley gave crucial evidence which allowed Scotland Yard to break up a notorious ring of white traffickers. This has, I fear, put him on a better footing with those who govern us than he deserves.

It is entirely possible that you may meet him socially in London. I thought you ought to be informed of the possibility. I am sure you will know how to act.

Did I know how to act? My first instinct was to cancel my trip and curl up in the abbey as if it were my shell. I had written to Lady Battersea, urging her to have nothing more to do with him, but Stephen made it sound that if I went on with my plan to appear at a social event for my publisher in a month's time, there was a possibility we might meet.

Unless I meant to retire to my tower and live as a trembling recluse, I ought to continue with my plans. It would be in Farley's interests to stay away from me. My reason told me this, but something deeper and wilder than reason warned me that my story with Farley had not ended.

I shook myself. There could be no danger of meeting the mad scientist in Hertfordshire, as he would not know to look for me there. I would be safe at the Belmontes' summer home.

As soon as I had come to this decision, I sensed that someone was outside my door—someone very quiet and small.

"Is that Una? Do come in."

The door opened and Una wavered on the threshold, all forget-me-not eyes and cornsilk hair. She reminded me of a porcelain doll left behind on a park bench after a picnic.

"Thank you for coming, Una. I wondered if you'd like me to bring anything for you when I come home? I'm bringing your sister lemon drops, though she asked for a motorcar. I think she's got the wrong idea about how much money writers make. Not to mention the roads in Ormdale!"

Goodness, the silence of this child always turned me into such a chatterer. Give me Violet and her indiscretion any day! I waited, but Una only looked at her shoes. I reminded myself that it had been mere months since she lost her father and brother.

"I was about your age when I met Mother," I said, suddenly reminded of it. "I had another mother, who died when I was very small, like yours."

Her hands tightened on her pinafore, and I remembered how she had clutched at my dress. Who knew what silent feats of bravery a normal day cost Una?

"Taking on Gilbert Sullivan—that was very brave of you," I guessed.

She shifted on her feet. "Violet's the brave one," she said quietly.

"No, I don't think so," I said. "Violet doesn't think about all the things that might happen. But you do. Don't you?" Una breathed in sharply. "When I took on Frances, I didn't think about the fact that I'd have to say goodbye to her one day. But you thought about that, didn't you, with your dragon?"

She nodded and let out her breath slowly.

"Here." Impulsively, I took the Prayer Book from my desk and held it out to her. "When I think too much about the things that might happen, I start with the prayers of Thanksgiving."

Una held it with reverent hands and a doubtful look.

"I have it by heart," I said, answering her unspoken question. "Perhaps you will one day, too. I'll be home soon, Una. Go on, now—go and keep Violet out of trouble. If that's possible!"

She disappeared. I'd never been without that book since my father gave it to me. But giving it away didn't feel like a loss. I felt I'd grown richer by it.

Chapter Ten

"Miss Worms?" asked the man in a footman's livery at the station in Hertfordshire.

"Yes," I replied. He glanced over my shoulder.

"Does your maid travel third class, Miss Worms?"

"I have no maid. It's just me," I said simply.

The footman damped down his surprise admirably, but I suspected this would not be the last time I was asked that question.

The carriage was just as grand as Lady Battersea's had been. I realised I did not have any idea how my mother's family had become rich. Were they bankers, like the famous Rothschilds? Was it dreadful of me to assume it?

The luxurious interior grated on me a little. Though I had been hardly more than a baby when my mother passed away from an unexpected illness, yet I still retained an impression of the grief and desperation in the house when the tragic event had occurred. I also remembered many very cold nights, which I later understood was due to my father's inability to buy sufficient coal.

Money, of course, could not have bought back my mother, but it might have made my father's mourning period less comfortless, or have made me grow into a less serious child—someone who hadn't set out to attain financial independence at the earliest opportunity, as I had.

After leaving the town and a stretch of pleasant countryside, we turned down a stately avenue of elms. Soon, a lovely Tudor-framed manor house came in sight, perfectly proportioned and bright with flowers. I leaned forward in anticipation. But the carriage did not slow down, and we left it behind us.

It was now dwarfed by the rambling palace that lay at the end of the drive. I had left my gothic home behind, but what lay before me now?

An architectural flight of fancy, with crenelations, buttresses, and turrets, and a leaping fountain at its front.

It might have been the abode of a Medici prince.

Irene appeared as I was deposited at the entrance, so I had no leisure to be intimidated. She was wearing a loose afternoon gown in warm tones, and as she embraced me, I was enveloped in layers of softness.

"Thank you, thank you," she whispered. "I'm so happy that you have come."

I swallowed, unsure of what to say. She took me into a hall where murals of figures from Boccacio disported themselves. There was a gigantic porcelain urn filled with late roses—the entire cloister garden at the abbey would have had to be de-spoiled to make one such arrangement.

"I've ordered tea in the conservatory—it's so lovely there now. David's orchids are at their best."

A servant took my outdoor things and then Irene whisked me through a succession of rooms. Everything was rare and fine. I glimpsed Venetian lanterns on the staircase, and Portuguese tiles about the fireplaces. We had arrived at the conservatory, where tea was to be served.

"We were in an orangery when I discovered you," Irene said. "Do you remember? How odd you must have thought my be-haviour! But I had to leave and speak with David and Sir Joseph. I didn't want to pounce on you in Connie's orangery—I was so worried I would frighten you!"

"Frighten me!" I laughed. "I'm not so easily frightened."

"No. I see that now," she said. "After all, you came, didn't you?"

There was a pause. Somewhere here, lost in the grandeur of it all, was something I wanted desperately, and I struggled to voice it. "Excuse me, but do you mind—I do so want to know—"

"Anything!"

"Is this where my mother grew up? Is it still how she knew it?"

Irene made a lacy sweep of her arm. "All of it. I wouldn't dare to change a thing. Belle Mount was Miriam's favourite residence. She spent every summer here."

Tears sprang to my eyes as I looked about me.

"You are tired from travelling!" She laid a hand on my arm. It sparkled with rings. "Forgive me—shall I take you up to rest?" said Irene.

"No. It's only that I have never had much to remember her by. And this is—so much. I feel she must be everywhere here."

"Oh, she is," Irene said softly.

I looked about, almost as if I expected to find a portrait or a photograph, which of course was out of the question in a conservatory.

"Come," she said, holding out her hand to me. "I've something of hers to show you."

A grand staircase later, Irene took a key from her chatelaine and paused at a small door.

"This was her own sitting room. Are you ready?"

Was I ready? I nodded and she led me in.

The room was perfectly round. We were in a tower room. My mother had chosen a tower room, just as I had at Wormwood Abbey. How odd to think that someone I had hardly known might still influence the daily decisions and personal tastes I had thought so entirely my own.

The high ceiling glowed with a sky out of Botticelli, celestial blue with clotted cream clouds. I half expected angels to peep out.

There was a beautiful Georgian desk, poised on delicate legs, that I would have given my little finger to write at.

"Irene?" came a man's voice from behind us.

He was her age, a handsome, sandy-haired man in his late thirties in clothes of the best cut, with the addition of a skull cap such as the ones I had seen worn by the Ashkenazi of London.

"David, dear. Here she is at last."

Irene put an arm about my shoulders while David gazed at me.

"You are Miriam's daughter," he said slowly. "I am your uncle, David."

For a moment, I thought he would embrace me, but instead he glanced down at his feet. So did I. The toes of his polished shoes were lined up at the threshold. He looked at Irene imploringly.

"I ordered tea in the conservatory," she said cheerfully. "Shall we go down and have it now?"

"It all happened while I was at school," Uncle David explained while Irene poured us tea amongst the palms and orchids. "I came home for the holidays and Miriam was gone. I think there was a note, but it wasn't shown to me. Father tried to trace where she had gone, but he never managed to find out who she'd run away with or to where."

I was horrified. This didn't sound like the sort of thing Father would do at all—snatch a girl away from her family and never send word to them!

Irene glanced at me. She seemed aware that I was hearing this story for the first time.

I shook my head in confusion. "I can't understand it. I knew that your family didn't approve of the marriage, but I never imagined..."

"Perhaps a letter went amiss," Irene suggested tactfully.

"I suppose it must have," I murmured. I looked at my uncle. "What a terrible shock it must have been to you."

"Yes, it was. She was everything to me then," he said. He looked at Irene, who was just now pouring us a second cup, and the connection was clear. His wife was everything to him now. Was it pleasure or just the steam from the silver teapot that made her colour slightly?

"You have no other siblings?" I guessed.

He shook his head. "She was the most wonderful older sister. I could hardly believe that she left me alone like that of her own free will. But she did. To elope."

The word sounded discordantly frivolous in the face of his hurt.

"And there was never any letter?" I pressed. "Not even...in eighty-one?" One letter might have gone amiss, but surely Father had succeeded in notifying them of her death.

"None." He had gone pale. "Eighty-one, you say? That was when she died?" I nodded. "That's strange. My mother became very ill in eighty-one. She had to be sent to a sanatorium on the Continent for treatment." He looked into the distance.

"Do you remember Miriam?" Irene asked me, obviously wanting to give David a moment to regain his composure.

"Only a little," I said. The few memories I had were too precious to speak of on such short acquaintance, and I was grateful that they did not press me.

"I always hoped she would come back one day, you know," David said in a level voice. "Year after year. I had an idea it would be at Pesach. That was her favourite festival. It would have meant a great deal to me to have sat *shiva* for Miriam. It's all wrong not to have done it."

Irene took his hand and then turned to me. "Sir Joseph will want to meet you, of course."

"Where is he now?" I asked, glad for a change of subject.

"He is on the Continent at present."

"He's meeting someone in Brussels, I think—what was it this time, Irene?" asked David. "Mines in Africa?"

"Oh, I can't keep up. Sir Joseph is very active in the family business," explained Irene.

"What is the business?" I asked, seizing the opportunity. "Banking?"

"No," said Irene, with a little smile. "Contrary to popular literature, those of us who are of the Hebrew religion are not only pickpockets or bankers."

"Of course, forgive me," I said, ashamed.

"Father is a financier," said David.

"Oh," I said, but my face must have shown that I had no idea what that meant.

"That means he helps people who have more ideas than money turn their best ones *into* money," explained Irene.

"Oh! That sounds a little like philanthropy."

Irene laughed. "If only everyone thought so!"

"But what about you?" asked my uncle. "Irene says you are an author, and very clever."

"Then she is very kind. Which you already know, as you are married to her."

"I've read all your books since we met," Irene warned. "So you needn't be modest about them. I read them all this summer—and not out of kindness! I've seldom enjoyed myself with a book more."

I could not resist a smile of pleasure.

"I'm afraid I'm too stupid to read novels," admitted David ruefully.

"Too stupid for novels? How refreshing!" I laughed. "Usually, people say they aren't stupid *enough*."

"I take everything so literally, you see. Books of information are better for my dull wits. I know exactly what they are trying to say."

I didn't believe for a moment he had dull wits. But there *was* something about him; I could sense it in the way he looked at me after he spoke, as if he wasn't quite sure how I'd react, or how he ought to react himself. And the way his wife smiled and touched him, now and then, as if she kept him in balance.

After that, I asked if my mother had had a favourite place about the grounds. Uncle David showed us a hidden place, screened by hedges, with a seat hardly big enough for two. This was a place she had liked to sit and read, he said, and where they had shared cakes in secret.

The gardens were even more extensive than I had imagined. There was a hot house, a banana house, orchards, a sunken rose garden, a grotto, an Italian garden, and others. David introduced me to the head gardener, with whom he seemed to be on the best terms, and directed my attention to all of the rarest plants. In his insatiable fascination with the natural world, he reminded me strongly of my brother George.

It was disconcerting to think that David could have no warm feelings at all towards my family—towards the stranger who had stolen his sister away, as he thought of my father.

Could such vast discrepancies in the story of my parents be explained away by nothing more than a lost letter? I thought of the desk in my mother's room. Had she kept any journals, I wondered, which might throw a light on her frame of mind before she left?

I thought of my father, as I had seen him in the library in Ormdale, praying silently, speaking of his own need for forgiveness, but I shook the memory away.

Whatever the case, there must be an explanation that absolved my father from any wrongdoing.

At dinner, I learned more about the family's habits. They were soon to repair to their London residence for the commencement of the social season and were only waiting for my grandfather's return from the Continent to do so. I got the impression that the couple would have happily remained in the country year-round, had it not been his fixed habit to go up to London at the end of summer.

"Perhaps I shall see you there," I ventured.

As soon as I said it, I regretted it. It was likely they wouldn't want to acknowledge the connection publicly. The Belmontes had risen higher than I had dreamed. Even though the Worms family pre-dated William the Conqueror, it was clear to me that any social advantage to be had would be entirely on my side. I had nothing of value to offer them, save whatever peace of mind meeting me had brought to my uncle.

"Oh, will you be there?" Irene asked eagerly.

"I've promised my publisher I'll attend a soirée. It will be a sort of debut, I suppose. I've not appeared in public as an author until now."

"How terribly exciting! What will you wear?"

I stared at her. What I would wear had not once crossed my mind—I had been too busy crushing up dragon scales and chasing errant groundlings.

I really did need this holiday.

"See, Irene, it is not only me who doesn't care about clothes," Uncle David interjected. "Irene goes to Paris to get hers," he explained. "I can't tell the difference."

My eyes widened. I had thought Irene uncommonly well dressed from the moment I met her, but I had not imagined her finery exceeded that which England could supply.

"The difference is that the Parisian tailors are true artists," said Irene. "And I like to reward true artistry wherever I see it."

"More philanthropy," I replied with a smile, then caught myself. How would Irene respond to teasing?

Her eyes sparkled. "But it does have personal rewards. Perhaps...*would* you let me dress you for your soiree?"

I was about to decline when I saw something in those eyes. This—getting a dress for me—was significant to her.

"Well, I'm sure you know much more about it than I do," I admitted.

"Ah! Then it's yes!" She clapped her hands. "We can stay at the Hotel de Paris and have it done in a week—ten days at most. Pierre will grumble, but for me he will do it. Especially as I will tell him you are a very famous woman of letters."

"Stay at—oh! No, I can't possibly go to Paris...for a dress!" My head was whirling at the very idea.

"No?" She looked a little crestfallen. "Ah well, then it will have to be Redfern's. One week in London, then?"

"All right," I said weakly. "I think I can manage that."

Before and after our meal, David cleared his throat and recited a short foreign prayer. Irene folded her hands and listened with a pious expression. Both of them seemed to escape their surroundings in some real way for a moment.

Night had fallen, but the house blazed with electric light.

What a surprising mixture of ancient and modern these new connections of mine were!

When I remarked upon the dazzling quality of the light, David nodded.

"Would you like us to switch on the big chandelier for you?" he asked, as if this were a perfectly routine thing to do.

"The chandelier...?" I faltered.

"Her Majesty asked to have the electric chandelier in the ballroom illuminated no less than four times in succession on her visit," Irene confided. "As you can imagine, that alone has made it something of a feature."

"Oh!" I exclaimed. "Far be it from me to second-guess Her Majesty!"

And we all laughed.

After I had marvelled suitably at the spectacle, I asked, "Is there a library here?" That might be a place my mother had cared about—at least, if she was anything like me and Father.

Irene's smile faltered for an instant. "Yes, of course," she said lightly. "I'll show you tomorrow, shall I?"

When it was time to say goodnight, I turned to Irene in the passageway. "I was wondering if I might see my mother's room again?"

"But of course!" she exclaimed, without hesitation. She unhooked a key from her ornate chatelaine and handed it to me. "We are so glad you have come," she murmured, and leaning forward quickly, she kissed my cheek. Was there a slight catch in her voice?

I had to pass by my mother's room to return to mine. I hesitated, then unlocked the door. I switched on the lights. The room seemed as bright and carefree as an Italian summer under that painted sky.

How could the owner of this fairytale room ever have had any secrets at all?

But you did have secrets, Mother. Father was one of them, wasn't he?

My heart beat a little faster with anticipation as I approached the rococo desk. I traced the curling designs with a finger, then slid my fingertips into the crack to open the desk to see within. But it held fast.

Miriam's secrets, it seemed, were not so easily discovered.

With a disproportionate sense of disappointment, I made a little search for the key in the various boxes and jars on the dressing table but found nothing.

I would ask for the key tomorrow.

Chapter Eleven

Irene made no mention of the library until I reminded her of it after breakfast.

"Of course," she said again, and escorted me there, telling me about the pictures on the way.

At Wormwood Abbey, I didn't think anyone had bought anything for the house since the Regency. Everything there was inherited—along with a lot of dust and obligation, and a sense of inevitable decline.

In contrast, Belle Mount felt almost too lush, like a pudding with too many plums. The staff got about on noiseless feet, anticipating our every whim. I had grown used to knowing my domestic help intimately, as fellow persons, and I had to force my gaze to slide over these people as if they were part of the furnishings.

A footman appeared and eased open the heavy library door for us. The furniture was all walnut, and for all that it was heavily carved in a neo-gothic style, it gleamed with newness.

The books stood in their ranks behind glass; the most expensive editions, all matching—and all looking as if they had come fresh from the printers that day.

Irene seemed ill at ease here, and chattered about something inconsequential. I reached out for a volume of Sheridan but found the glass door locked and the keyhole empty.

I turned to her in astonishment. "But these books—does no one read them?"

"No," she said. "This is Sir Joseph's library. He is very proud of it. It is one of the house's showpieces."

"But where are the books that people *read*?"

She smiled. "I have a sitting room of my own. It is quite full of well-thumbed novels, though there is nothing handsome or valuable there."

I shuddered as we left the room. Something about all those books, forever unread behind glass, made me feel oppressed.

It quickly evaporated as I sat with Irene in her own charming room overlooking the rose garden.

"Irene, why are there no pictures or photographs of my mother about the place?"

Irene's smile faded. "I asked David about that once. He said that when he got home from school, not only had his sister disappeared, but all traces of her were gone. Except for her room, that is. And David only ventured in there upon one occasion."

"What occasion?" I asked.

"It was the anniversary of the death of their mother. Judith died in Switzerland, away from the family. She had tuberculosis, you know, and was sent there for treatment."

"And what happened?"

"He said he found his father there, sitting at Miriam's desk, with his head in his hands, in a most despondent attitude. Sir Joseph told him never to enter the room again."

I remembered how, when I first met him, David had stood on the threshold of the door of my mother's room, frozen to the spot, and the memory chilled me. I began to feel a little wary of this unknown gentleman. But perhaps I was being unfair—perhaps my grandfather simply did not wish to cry in company, and had startled his son, who had taken the command over-seriously. I could see that David might do such a thing.

Irene went to the window and looked out. Her next words startled me a little. "I'm afraid I used to rather resent your mother."

"But why?"

"David loved her so very much. When I came here as a bride, it was as if her memory haunted every room. Even without pictures. It is always difficult for a young bride—there is so much to learn about one's new family, and often no one to tell you the rules. And when there are so many rules..."

"I'm sorry." I didn't know what else to say.

"Don't be," she said firmly. "Those days are past now, happily. Shall we go for a drive today?"

She began to adjust the drapes, and I could tell she wanted to change the subject.

"If you like," I said. "And I was wondering if I might have the key to my mother's desk. It's silly, I know, but somehow I'd like to see where she wrote letters and things. It's that sort of everyday that says so much about a person."

"Yes, of course it does," she said. "But I'm afraid I don't have the key. The desk has been locked since I can remember. I've never seen inside it. And I looked for it very thoroughly myself, I confess. She was such a mystery to me! To leave all of this!" She waved at the prospect out the window, then turned to me and looked me up and down. Finally, she smiled. "But now that I know you, Edith, all that is over. The mystery doesn't matter anymore."

I could not say the same.

"What is this place?" I asked as the open carriage approached the lovely house on the avenue.

"Ah, the dower house. It's very neat, isn't it?" said Irene.

"Does anyone live here?"

"Your great-grandmother, in fact."

"My what!" I cried out. "But may I meet her? Would she see me?"

Irene hesitated for an instant, then tapped on the driver with her parasol, who slowed the horses to turn into the driveway.

She turned to face me, rather solemn. "Now, Edith, Nonna is very old. And she doesn't always know who is visiting her. That will not distress you, I hope?"

I shook my head.

A few minutes later, we were taken into an airy parlour with engravings of Italian views on the walls. A tiny woman, beautifully dressed, was bent over some handiwork.

"Well, Nonna, how are you today? Oh, you are getting on so well with your design!" Irene went to sit beside her. "I've brought someone to see you. This is Miriam's daughter, Edith. You remember Miriam?"

The tiny woman looked up at me, wincing at the movement of her neck. I quickly knelt at her footstool to ease the strain.

"Miriam's daughter?" she repeated, squinting at me, and her jaw slackened in amazement. "No! It can't be!"

"Yes. She has come from Yorkshire to—"

"I told you to leave!"

The old lady's eyes burned at me so that I flinched.

"No, Nonna, no—you haven't met Edith before," Irene corrected gently. "This is Miriam's daughter. We've only just met her, you see."

To my dismay, the eyes now brimmed with tears, and her harsh voice trembled. "Did he find out? I told you to go before he found out." Irene rang a bell and a uniformed nurse came in. "Why did you stay? I told you!"

"Yes, dear Nonna, she is going now, exactly as you told her—don't distress yourself. I'll see she goes myself."

Nonna abandoned her handiwork and gripped my hands in hers. They were small, but strong as steel. She leaned close. "*Mia cara!* You must go now!"

Irene kissed her cheek, gently extracted my hands from hers, and led me out of the room in a daze. Behind me, I could hear Nonna speaking in urgent Italian to the nurse.

"Some days are better. We will try again," Irene said soothingly to me, putting her arm round me.

I had promised Irene I would not be distressed, but I was shaken.

You must go now. A message from the past—but how urgent it felt!

"I'm sorry that I distressed her so," I said as we got back in the carriage.

"You mustn't blame yourself, Edith. Who knows what scenes from her long life she revisited today."

"What do you suppose she meant by it? Did she mistake me for my mother?"

"How could we ever tell? If one could open the life of a woman as one might open her workbox, one would find enough heartache to fuel many such warnings, I suppose."

I glanced at Irene in surprise. She had said something like this the day I met her—something that hinted that her life had not always been roses and electric chandeliers.

As the carriage began to roll away, I tried to rid myself of the burden of Nonna's warning. After all, the warning had not been for me.

At the end of the day, we went out into the flower garden to cut flowers for the house.

I took the opportunity to ask about Irene's own upbringing, of which I'd heard nothing. "I can't help but notice you never speak of your own family, Irene. Do they not get on with Sir Joseph?"

Irene shook her head. "It's not that they don't get on. Sir Joseph doesn't pay court to anyone; he prefers to bring people into his orbit—or not."

"And yours wasn't?"

"I wasn't sorry about it in the least," she said crisply, selecting a spray of roses. "Not to put too fine a point on it, they are spendthrifts, rakes, and wastrels. My brothers never noticed I existed until I attracted David's attention. It was poetic justice when they found themselves roundly rebuffed in their attempts to get anything out of Sir Joseph."

This gave me a little hope. If Sir Joseph shunned Irene's family for being grasping and unprincipled, then time might heal wounds enough to admit a truce between our houses. My family was universally admitted to be delightful, after all.

I came upon a wide bed of lilies edged with box. The lilies glowed pearlescent in the twilight—the air thick with their scent. I filled my basket with them, avoiding the pollen-rich stamens as much as possible.

"Ah!" Irene exclaimed softly, when she saw the contents of my basket. "These were Miriam's favourite flower."

I looked at them with new eyes, searching for the meaning behind them. For Christians, they represented Christ's mother—who had also been a Hebrew woman named Miriam.

Even as I longed to find the key that would unlock her secrets, I suspected I would never truly understand her, because I had not lived her life.

The mystery of my mother was like a double-shot fabric that showed different colours as I turned it to the light.

That night, I woke to the sound of voices in the household. Throwing on my dressing gown, I ventured out to see what was going on, and almost ran into Irene, who was on the way back to her bedroom.

"Oh, Edith! I'm ever so sorry you were disturbed."

"Never mind, what's happened?"

"Sir Joseph has come home from Switzerland. He took the late train and arrived before we got any word. It's nothing to worry about," she assured, but her words did not convince me. There was something different about Irene's manner already.

"Does he know I am here?" I forced myself to ask.

"Not yet," she replied. "We'll speak with him in the morning." She must have sensed my tension, for she pressed my hand. "I told you—he will want to see you. He loved Miriam just as much as David did, you know."

As I lay trying to sleep, I recalled the date. October the tenth. What had Father called it? Old Michaelmas, he said, before the calendars changed.

It was hard to believe, in this modern place of hot running water and electric lights, that I usually lived among people who worried about Lucifer falling upon them on a particular date.

How absurd, I thought, and went back to sleep.

I took extra care in my dressing the next morning and went down a little late for breakfast. I wanted to be sure that my grandfather had been warned of my presence. I had no idea how he might react to me. Just because my aunt and uncle had been so kindly disposed towards me, did not mean he would feel the same. Would he dislike me, belonging to my father as I did? Would he interrogate me as to my upbringing and situation and religion? Or would he simply dismiss me as someone of little interest to him and his important affairs?

When I came into the breakfast room and saw my aunt and uncle's faces, my fears were confirmed.

"Oh," I said. "I'll go directly. Don't worry, it won't take me long to pack my things."

Irene blinked. "Edith? Oh! No, it's not that...it's—"

She gestured at the newspapers which were spread out on the breakfast table in front of them.

"War," David said flatly. "It's war."

"War?" I gasped. I snatched up a newspaper quickly.

War in the Transvaal.

The Next War, it seemed, was already upon us.

I swallowed. A footman pulled out a chair for me and I took it.

"I'm sorry, Edith, if we gave you a shock," said Irene. "But I assure you, whatever dreadful looks we had on our faces, it had nothing to do with you. Your grandfather would like to see you in his study after breakfast, if that suits you." And she smiled encouragingly.

My head was spinning. "Yes. Thank you. It does."

Irene got up and served a plate for me herself from the covered dishes on the buffet.

I wasn't being banished. My grandfather—*my* grandfather!—wanted to see me.

Chapter Twelve

I tried to read the newspaper; if my country was at war, I ought to make an effort to understand it, but my mind was selfishly taken up with my own affairs. Besides, the causes behind this particular war seemed particularly impenetrable. Hadn't Father said something about disagreeing with his bishop on current events? And hadn't we had it all out with the Boers already? It seemed rather appalling that two Christian peoples could not resolve their differences without going to war with each other like this every few years.

At least, I thought with satisfaction, *there won't be any of Farley's poisons in this awful business.*

I ate and excused myself from the breakfast room. Once out in the passage, I felt a little lost. Where was Sir Joseph's study? A footman found me and escorted me to the correct door. I knocked, squaring my shoulders and telling myself not to behave like a little lost urchin. A voice invited me in.

The room was large. On the other side of a heavy carved desk, an elegantly dressed man with greying hair stood. His back was to the window, so I could not quite make out the details of his features, but he held himself with as much grace and command as any aristocrat.

I advanced a few steps, then hesitated. How should I address him?

The room was very large, and I was very small. My grandfather, on the other hand, was not small in the least, which kindled a spark of irritation in me. If only I had inherited my dimensions from this patrician man, and not from my diminutive great-grandmother!

"My dear," he said. "I have been waiting for you."

His voice was rich—it made me think of an old madeira wine I had been given a sip of once, which had rather gone to my head—and he spoke in a tone of playful remonstrance.

"I beg your pardon, sir," I replied, discomfited. "I was told to come see you after breakfast."

He came round the desk towards me, very slowly. "I have waited longer than that. I have waited one and twenty years."

He came closer and closer until I had to stop myself from stepping backwards out of instinct. Then he gently tilted up my chin with his hand. I felt as if I was being held to the light, like a jewel, so that he could better judge my value. If he saw a flaw in me, I wondered, what would be his reaction? Would he cast me aside as something beneath his notice?

"Look," he said, withdrawing his hand to show me an ornate ring on his finger, something a Renaissance prince might have worn. He pressed it and a lid sprang open, revealing a coiled lock of flame-coloured hair within.

He held it up for a moment, comparing the shade to my own. I didn't move.

"You are every inch a Belmonte," he said.

The wave of feeling within me left me shaken. Had I really wanted to hear this so much?

"Sit," he said, and guided me to a chair. He was surely in his late sixties, but with the vitality of a man much younger. Then he leaned against the desk and crossed his arms. I could study his face in detail now, and I did it eagerly. Was there something about the jaw that had made its way to my own face? Some sharp edge of determination?

While I was studying him, his dark eyes danced over me in return. "Now, what is to be done with you?"

Despite myself, I laughed. "Will you send me to my room, sir?"

"Perhaps. If you do not behave like a good child."

"I'm afraid I sometimes don't," I confessed in a whisper.

Now it was his turn to laugh. "Oh, I have missed you, Edith."

Missed me? How could he, when he had never even known I existed?

There was a knock, and the door opened a discreet crack. I glimpsed a surprisingly handsome young man wearing a suit and an expression of modest competence.

"Excuse me, Sir Joseph, I thought you should know that Sir William has arrived."

The young man's eyes fell on me and blinked. I had that unmistakable sense every woman has when a man has found her pleasing to the eye.

Sir Joseph's voice was cold. "Sir William can wait. In future, I don't wish to be bothered when I am with my granddaughter. Do you understand?"

The man gave a bow and left, without looking at me again. Not furniture, but still subservient. A secretary, probably. Well, I seemed to be passing muster with everyone. But I mustn't relax yet. The hardest thing was still to come.

I turned back to Sir Joseph. "You must have many questions for me, sir."

"Must I?"

"About the past—about what happened to my mother."

"The past," he said slowly. "I am older than you, Edith, and I have learned that the past must not be allowed to rob from us the joy of the present. It is enough for me that you are come back to us. Let us not sully the occasion with subjects that may divide us."

Was he really going to let it all just fade away? The elopement? My mother's death? I felt both disappointed and relieved. Until that moment, I had not realised how much I feared hearing what Sir Joseph might say about the man who had taken his daughter away from him.

"Thank you," I managed.

"I hope you will thank me for many things, Edith, in time. However, thanks seem unwarranted as yet," he observed.

I flushed. "I mean, for welcoming me. For not resenting me."

"I told you: I've been waiting for you." I did not understand how he could mean it, but he had said not to talk of the past.

Then I remembered that he had a visitor.

"There is a guest waiting for you now, I think," I said, getting up.

He waved his hand. "Never mind that. Come and see this." He led me to a landscape in a worn gilt frame. It showed a lake of dazzling aquamarine with a backdrop of mountains. "This is where your grandmother's people came from. The Lake of Fucino."

A chord chimed within me. The Fucine Lake region, in Italy. According to Father, the birthplace of the Marsi, the people the ancients believed could heal snake bites.

Sir Joseph touched the frame in a dissatisfied way. "I ought to have it reframed."

I had to stifle a gasp.

The old gilt frame was decorated with serpentine figures.

Could it be possible? Had my parents—with their star-crossed union—managed to combine the bloodlines of two Dragon Families, both English and Continental, without realising it?

"These figures...are they...significant?" I queried, trying to keep my voice light.

"Significant? In what way?"

"I only wondered—if there was a family connection. A heraldic symbol, for example."

"Ah, yes. The Fucine Lake was famous for its proliferation of serpents. I believe there were some folk beliefs. My wife's family came from there."

"Folk beliefs?"

"Their imperviousness to serpents. But that's all a thing of the past. The lake was drained in the seventies."

The words stung me strangely, as if I had personally experienced a loss.

"What a pity!" were the words that escaped my lips.

His eyes swerved to me. "Why do you say that?"

"Well—it was so beautiful." I gestured at the picture.

"It is far more valuable now as an agricultural plain. It was a great accomplishment—a credit to the engineers responsible. The ancient Romans tried to drain it, you know. It is something to think we succeeded where Julius Caesar himself failed, is it not?"

It was a discordant note, but this was a man of business I was talking to, after all. At least he was honest about it, unlike the other industrialist I had known. Pendragon would have talked cant about the Greater Good and What is Beauty. Thank heaven my grandfather was nothing like him.

"Will you tell me more about this place? About the family?"

His face went from steely to warm instantly. "I would like nothing better than that." His dislike for the past, it seemed, did not extend to family history. "The Belmontes came from

Portugal—we share the name with a town there. Ours was one of the first families to take advantage of Cromwell's toleration of Jewish migration." He considered me. "You write books. Successful ones."

"Yes," I admitted, a little startled.

"Then you understand the savour of success—of building something up yourself."

"I suppose I do." What I wasn't used to was talking of it so openly.

"Good. The Belmontes have never been content simply to stand where the last generation stood, like the English aristocracy. We ascend, Edith. Each generation. Whatever changes may come, we do not just weather them. We ascend."

"Much of the English aristocracy can only dream of standing where their ancestors stood," I noted wryly, thinking of our crumbling abbey. "Half of them are desperate to sell whatever remains to a rich American before it falls about their ears completely."

He laughed at this and seemed pleased. "You do understand."

My eyes went back to the painting. Had dragons swum unseen in that jewel of a lake? Had my mother's people lived at peace with them on the shore of this lost world? Had they been destroyed along with the lake?

"You are taken with it," he remarked. "Have it." He said it in a way which made opposition impossible. "As a gift from me. The first of many, I hope."

"You are too generous," I murmured. "I wonder..."

"Yes. Ask it."

"In my mother's room, there is a writing desk. I wondered if I might see inside it."

"Ah, but I'm afraid that key was lost long ago," he said. "Shall we go join your aunt and uncle?" he said, offering his arm to me. I took it.

As we left the room and went down the passage, he put his hand over mine, the one that lay on his arm, and it covered mine entirely. We were passing a mirror. How young and small I looked next to him, in my white summer frock, against the rich background of my grandfather's palace. I glimpsed the ring on his finger and thought of the Medicis again.

They would have put poison in it, instead of hair.

"Perhaps, my dear, the key may turn up yet," he said softly. "You will have to stay and see."

We now entered the parlour. A white-haired gentleman got to his feet as we entered. One glance at him put everything out of my head instantly. I stopped still.

"Sir Joseph," the visitor said with a wide smile, before he saw me. The moment he did, his face twisted. "*You!*"

I had told myself that no enemies lay in wait for me at Belle Mount, but I had been wrong.

Lucifer *had* fallen from the heavens after all—but he did not appear to me as an angel of light.

Before me stood the man I knew as Lord Pendragon.

"Sir William, may I present my granddaughter, Edith. Edith, Sir William Penrith. Though it appears that the two of you have met already."

Part of me wanted to make an excuse and rush out of the room. But I refused to be cowed by this man again.

Sir Joseph's hand tightened on mine—I realised I was shaking, and his hand was steadying me.

"How extraordinary!" Sir William gasped. He extracted a handkerchief from his pocket and mopped his brow. "I had no idea you had a granddaughter, Sir Joseph. How—charming."

It was not entirely unpleasant to see him in this state. He must be desperate for my grandfather's help in some way. I wouldn't have left the room now for anything.

"And how do you know each other?" Sir Joseph inquired, looking with interest between the two of us.

"We met—we met—" he scrambled.

"In Wales," I finished baldly. "In Gwynedd, to be precise."

Sir Joseph's eyes narrowed. "At the experimental community you are always talking about, William?"

"Yes," I said. I was not smiling. 'William' looked as if he'd swallowed a fishbone.

Sir Joseph stared at him. "I thought you said no one visited it."

"Well, you see—"

"I came by special invitation," I said to my grandfather.

Now I caught the gleam in his eyes. He was *enjoying* watching Pendragon—or Penrith—squirm. It was this realisation that egged me on.

"How is *your* grandchild, Sir William?" I asked—mercilessly, since both his son and grandson were illegitimate and unacknowledged in society. "I hope the medicine I sent recently was useful for ailments such as his. So awkward to call a good doctor there, in the mountains. Or at least, my cousin found it so."

"Oh, yes, very kind of you indeed, Miss Worms." He was very pale now, and his hand was twitching. I wondered if it were possible that he might have an attack of palsy right there in the parlour, in front of the Fra Angelico painting.

All at once, the fun had gone out of it entirely, and I felt terribly tired. I turned with dignity to Sir Joseph.

"Excuse me, sir, but I feel a headache coming on. I will go rest for a little."

He pressed my hand, then released me. I had the oddest feeling that I had pleased my grandfather to no end.

I stayed in my room through lunch. I had stood my ground against the cruel despot of Wild Wales in the parlour, but I refused to sit down with him to luncheon.

I found myself plagued with worries: what would he tell my grandfather about me? Would he try to prejudice him with lies?

The thought sickened me. Penrith must have done business with my grandfather, and he was obviously respected enough to be invited to his home, though I had detected no liking for him in Sir Joseph's eyes.

But the Belmontes knew almost nothing about me—nothing but the little I had told them.

All at once I felt the tenuousness of my position. How easy it would be, I thought, for them to see me as an opportunist. The prospect was unexpectedly bitter to me.

A servant tapped on my door. He bore a telegram from Embsay on a silver tray.

RECEIVED DELIVERY OF WELSH ANIMAL STOP PLEASE RETURN IMMEDIATELY STOP DUGDALE

Welsh animal! There was only one sort of Welsh animal that anyone would think to send me, and it wasn't the sort that would be easily sent by rail or post! But if it *was* a dragon—who would have sent one? Not Penrith!

When Irene came to inquire after my headache, she was appalled to see that I had packed my things. "Edith! What is this? Sir Joseph said it went so well between you!"

"Oh, it's not Sir Joseph. I've had a telegram, and I simply must go back to Yorkshire at once." I hesitated. I'd been learning to trust my friends with the truth—ought I to trust Irene? "And to be quite honest—it's that man." Irene stared at me blankly. "Your visitor—Sir William Penrith. I knew him under a different name, and under very unpleasant circumstances. I'm afraid to say he is a charlatan and a bully. He ought not to be at large.

I couldn't remain in the house with him, Irene," I confessed, a little shakily, "even without the telegram."

It felt hard but right to tell her all the truth I could. Perhaps I had learned from my mistakes with Gwendolyn after all.

"But this is shocking!" Irene exclaimed.

"I'm sorry. I don't expect you to take my word over that of an old friend."

"I would not call Penrith an old friend." Irene sat down. "I must first speak with Sir Joseph, and we never disturb him after lunch until we dine." She passed a hand over her face. "Dear Edith, my position in this household—I am not as much in charge as if my husband was head of the family. I cannot simply turn a business connection of Sir Joseph's out."

"Oh, Irene, of course I don't expect you to. I only wanted to be honest with you! Please—this visit has been quite, quite wonderful." I took her hands in mine. "Perhaps we may still see each other in London?"

Irene pressed my hands. "I will hold you to that, Edith. One week before your soirée, remember? And I will insist on the very best Redfern has to offer. You must have a work of art to wear—as much a work of art as your books."

I forced myself to smile back at her. "In that case, you must dress me all in yellow, and I shall carry a chloroform bottle—or a dripping knife!"

My voice wobbled between gaiety and despair, because in that moment, I could not believe I would see her again.

As I went down to get in the carriage, a jarring sight greeted me. A housemaid was removing the opulent arrangement of lilies from the entryway—the lilies we had cut only the day before.

"But these are still fresh!" I murmured.

The housemaid curtsied. "Yes, miss. I'm sorry, miss, but we never have lilies in the house when Sir Joseph is at home."

As they carried them out, I had to admit the smell was strong. Perhaps my grandfather was sensitive to such things.

The carriage was waiting. I was relieved not to see Sir Joseph. I had an idea it would be much harder to leave if *he* asked me to stay.

Irene embraced me as I left. "Until London," she murmured in my ear.

As the carriage wheeled past the little house where I had met my great-grandmother, I remembered her words.

I told you to go!

CHAPTER THIRTEEN

As the porter wheeled my luggage towards the street in Embsay, looking for a conveyance to take me and my luggage to the abbey, I spotted a familiar figure striding towards me from the other end of the platform.

"Dugdale!" I cried. "I *am* glad to see you."

"Not nearly as glad as I am to see you, Miss," he said grimly.

In the train shed behind the station, a huge crate shuddered, nailed boards groaning at the pressure from the creature inside.

"Dugdale, is there any vehicle big enough…" My voice trailed off.

"It's on the way, Miss. The biggest they have."

"Yes, of course," I said. "If we can only get it out of Embsay without *everyone* seeing."

It really was too bad to be expected to keep a creature of this size secret. Frances was one thing. This was quite another.

"I've put it about that it's a dray horse."

"Will anyone believe that?" I asked in amazement.

"Well, it's true we could do with one. Are these any good at pullin' a plough?" he asked dryly. "I thought not," he finished when he saw the look on my face. "Here's the letter that came with it."

Lady Edith,

What you asked has been done. We send this gift as a token of our thanks, and as proof that the tyrant no longer rules us.

Emrys

My mouth fell open.

No wonder the man whom I must now call Penrith had greeted me with such fury. No wonder he had been desperate for my grandfather's help.

Apparently, there really had been war in heaven, or at least in the closest place in Britain to heaven. And the warriors of light had cast out Lucifer at last.

But now that he had been cast out, what would he do? Would he come to trouble us in Yorkshire?

A fearful clawing came from the crate.

"Not much of a thanks, if you ask me," Dugdale muttered darkly, as well as something small-minded about the trustworthiness of Welshmen.

I stuffed the letter in my pocket and approached the crate. Putting my palms on the wood, I laid my cheek to it and breathed in the smoky fragrance from within. The clawing diminished, then stopped.

"Cariad," I breathed. "Is it you, dear one?"

An answering huff. Warm air gusted through a chink in the slats to touch my cheek, making me tingle all over.

"I'll get you out, don't worry," I promised.

When we arrived at the stables at the abbey, I was relieved to find the only person I could trust to help handle her.

Simon.

On our way through Ormby, I had spotted a boy with a pony and given him a coin to go fetch him.

Simon reached up to help me down from the cart, a question on his face.

"It's Cariad," I whispered as I hopped down.

A fizz of excitement seemed to go through him to me, and he gripped my arms for a moment, but the driver was watching us, and children and servants were spilling out of the abbey to see what was in the giant crate I'd brought home.

The crate had been very difficult to load on the cart with the help of several burly railway workers. It would be even harder to unload in their absence. The best plan must be to let the dragon out first.

I found Hanna in the crowd of onlookers and gave her a desperate look. She came up and tapped the driver on the shoulder.

"Kitchen," she said. "Cake." And she smiled.

Dugdale nodded. "Go on, lad. We'll unload it."

Hanna led him by the sleeve away from the scene at a brisk clip.

I grinned. Given his age and the way he had looked at her, it was possible he would return to Embsay talking about nothing but Hanna. And Hanna was one secret we could afford to let out.

Once he was out of the way, we quickly began. I remembered only too well how Cariad had snatched up Arthur and thrown him across a mountain glen. We cleared everyone from the area. The children reappeared at a window, watching with Mother.

Dugdale took the two cart horses into a stable stall and shut them in, then sensibly shut himself in another, and watched from over the top, chewing a piece of straw.

Only Simon and I were left.

He took off his coat and picked up an iron pry bar with astonishing ease.

"Ready, Edith?"

I positioned myself so that Cariad would see me first when the side came off, but not so close that she might strike blindly if she emerged in a rage. I made sure the slanting evening light would not be in her eyes. Everything hinged upon her recognising me right away.

"Ready," I replied.

The boards splintered and groaned as he pried, nails popping out. Finally, only a few remained. Simon paused and looked at me.

"Now," I said.

One movement and the side of the crate fell away.

I stepped back out of instinct. The light hit me in the eyes as an enormous golden creature, unexpectedly swaddled with restraints, burst out and ran straight at me.

I held my ground.

She stopped a mere hand's breadth away. She was muzzled, her wings bound. It felt wrong.

Slowly, humming a long note, I lifted my hand for her to smell. She did not toss her head or shy away. Her breath huffed out of the muzzle and whispered over my face.

Then she gave a low groan of discomfort.

I unfastened the muzzle and dropped it on the ground, then gently scratched the place where the muzzle had left an indentation.

She lowered her head in a gesture of relief. She shuffled her body round, presenting to me the wing restraints. I hesitated. What if she simply took to the skies, never to be seen again? What if I lost her too?

The double-lidded eye close to me blinked twice—once in one direction, then the other.

Her kind bond deeply with their first riders.

She had remembered me. She had defended me.

I thought of the restraints on Farley's laboratory table.

Holding my breath, I undid first one strap, then another. As the final strap released and it all tumbled at her feet, she gave a great sigh, and extended first one wing, then another, like I had myself upon occasion stretched my own limbs after napping in a railway compartment.

From Simon, I heard a soft exhale of relief. Cariad stiffened. Her head swerved round to stare at him. Cariad gathered herself like a coiled spring.

"Cariad!" I cried, and I flung myself at Simon. The blood was thundering in my ears but still I felt Simon's heartbeat through his waistcoat. It was beating rather quickly.

Slowly, I turned to face her, one arm holding Simon behind me.

"This is my *friend*," I said. "You are not to hurt him, dear one. Do you understand?"

I took Simon's left hand in mine and stretched it out to her, lacing my fingers with his. She dipped her head to our hands.

"She's getting your scent," I whispered.

Slowly, I extricated my fingers from Simon's so that Cariad could smell it alone. I was surprised to see his hand tremble. I could not recall a time when I had seen Simon tremble. Dimly, I realised that I had never touched Simon's left hand before—the one with the top of the thumb missing. I wondered if he minded me touching it like that.

Cariad gave him the same little huff of acceptance that she had given me, and then shook out her wings again.

I looked up to see the open-mouthed faces of the children in the window. George had a notebook in his hands and Violet was jumping up and down on the spot.

"Well," I said, "I suppose I'll have to do this for everyone at the abbey, won't I?"

Simon looked a little fuzzy. I walked to the drinking trough and Cariad followed, taking great gulps. I looked over at Dugdale, still watching from his stall. He tipped his hat at me.

"Simon," I called to him, stricken with doubt. "Do you think she'll fit in the stables?"

He came and considered it. "Just. She'll need frequent exercise, though."

Frequent exercise? I grinned at the prospect of soaring over the fells with her on a regular basis.

"Edith, I may have thought it impossible for you to surprise me further," said Simon, "but just how *did* you come to bring home a Welsh dragon from Hertfordshire?"

I gave him the letter. He read it and began to laugh.

"Kingdoms fall at your request now? They ought to get you to sort out that trouble in the Transvaal."

Dugdale cleared his throat, which startled us, as we had forgotten he was there at all.

"What about that cart now?" he prodded. "And these horses? They're getting right nervous, and I can't say as I blame them."

Simon and Dugdale hitched up the cart horses again and moved the cart out of sight of the stables while I waited with Cariad, crooning to her occasionally. Then I heard the jingle of harness and rumble of wheels as the cart driver left.

What was it Sir Joseph had said? *We ascend.*

I didn't want kingdoms—I would be admirably content with a dragon to ride and Simon to marry. Well, I was halfway there already.

Simon reappeared with a side of mutton from the kitchen. Cariad followed him into a stall, where he dropped it for her. While she was enjoying her mutton, I told Simon the story of meeting Pendragon in Hertfordshire, and of his real identity.

"I wonder if we should worry about Penrith," Simon reflected.

"Do you mean he might try to avenge himself upon us for his people ousting him? I'm not sure. He seemed terrified of my grandfather—which is very much a point in Sir Joseph's favour. And after all, it was his own people that threw him out, not us."

Cariad lay down in the straw like a giant hound, to gnaw at the remaining bones.

Simon shut the stall doors and braced them with a plank of wood. "I expect it may take her a bit to settle in. Is there anything I can do to help you with her?"

A plan had been forming in my mind over the last moments. "Haven't you guessed?" I said. "It's something I've always thought you were born to do."

His eyes went to Cariad. When they came back to me, there was a gleam in them that must have matched my own.

"Are you asking me to train a dragon for you, Edith?" he asked in his low voice.

I nodded, my heart beating fast.

"I may have disappointed you in other areas..." His smile unfolded slowly. "But I'll do my very best at this."

I felt a thrum of triumph. Perhaps I wouldn't need anywhere near a year to convince Simon.

Perhaps I might adopt Sir Joseph's motto for myself.

Chapter Fourteen

As tired as I was, I was not to enjoy an undisturbed night. I woke abruptly to the illumination of a full moon.

I didn't want to find Cariad's stall splintered and abandoned by morning, so I put on a coat and muffler over my nightdress and made my way through the dark abbey.

Cariad seemed to expect me. She was nudging the gate of the stall politely, though she could have forced it. I let her out into the stable yard. Then she sat and basked in the moonlight while I leaned against her warm side as I had under the rock in Wales.

"We're together now, Cariad," I whispered to her. "Home, and safe."

Penrith was no longer a danger to us, and the threat of Farley was so slight, I could not quite credit it.

I must have dozed for a bit, for I woke with cold feet and hands when the sky began to lighten. Cariad was meek and calm now, seemingly refreshed by her moon-bathing. I put her back in her stall and went to bed.

When Simon appeared later in the morning, I was already rubbing fennel ointment on Cariad's harness sores. Mother had made it for me from the cloister herb garden after I told her Topsell said it was useful for dragon ailments.

Even the air intoxicated me this morning—I didn't quite know whether it was due to Simon or Cariad. How lovely that I didn't have to choose between them, but that in some perfect way they went together.

"Shall we get the saddle from the muniments room?" I asked him eagerly.

"I think not," said Simon. "I don't think she will tolerate the sight of a saddle just yet. She'll remember it from Arthur's attempts."

His name was like a little shadow falling on us, but Simon was right. On our first day of training, we could go no further than introducing her to the weight of a saddle blanket.

Anything on her back was greeted with tail thrashing and hissing. Simon insisted we take off the saddle blanket and quietly wait at a distance every time this happened, until Cariad had completely recovered her composure.

Indeed, dragon training involved a great deal more waiting than I had expected, and impatience bubbled up in me like a shaken bottle of ginger beer.

"Arthur must have been cruel to her," I said indignantly as I stood at a distance with him.

"Not deliberately cruel. Impatient and demanding, certainly. For an animal, it is much the same."

By the way Simon spoke of him, I could tell that he did not know the worst of Arthur's behaviour, and I felt reluctant to extend Arthur's shadow any further over this day. All the same, I could not quite let this stand.

"Perhaps," I said. "Perhaps he was not *deliberately* cruel to her. But don't you think there is a kind of self-absorption that is the same as cruelty in the end, in its effect on others?"

He looked at me with dawning recognition. "Edith, I think I have tried my whole life to put that into words."

"You speak of your father?" I guessed.

"I was a great trial to him."

"How could you be!" I exclaimed.

But what if the man had suspected Simon was not his own child? That might have been a trial indeed, and no fault of Simon's. But I could not speak of it, because of my promise to Forrester.

"My father was—powerful. You forgot anyone else was there when he came in the room. He could command people so easily. The same is not true of me," Simon added wryly.

"Well, thank heavens it isn't," I retorted. "Christ said to take the lowest place, and then you may be asked to move up. I don't suppose Mr Drake ever took the lowest place, did he?"

"I don't suppose he ever did," Simon reflected.

The horrid Rivers had once compared Simon to a sheep farmer—an absurd comparison in one way, but quite accurate in another. To be a sheep farmer, I had discovered during my time in Yorkshire, required the steadiness of a rock in the face of storms and disasters.

Simon had a quiet authority about him that only an imbecile could overlook. Perhaps that's why animals *wanted* to obey him. It is easier, after all, to fool a human than an animal.

How would knowing Forrester as his father change Simon, I wondered? Would he think more highly of himself, knowing he had never been a disappointment to his real father? Or would the shame of being born outside of wedlock only damage his self-regard further?

"Do you ever wish that you had been born someone else? What if you were someone quite different than you thought you were?" I ventured.

Simon looked puzzled. "Have you found that you are someone different than you thought, after your visit to your aunt?"

I shook my head. "I don't think so. But there *is* something that was very different than I expected."

"Yes?"

"It's the story of my mother. I thought that by going to meet her family, I would understand her better, but it's more of a muddle than before. Their story is that Father spirited her away quite unfeelingly, with no word at all of her whereabouts or welfare. They didn't even know she had died."

"That doesn't sound like your father at all."

"No, it doesn't, does it? But he's never spoken of it much—how they got to know each other, I mean. I always thought it was grief, but...but what if..." I couldn't say it aloud.

"What if it's shame?" he said gently.

"Yes." I looked down. "And now *I* feel ashamed for even thinking it."

"Edith, perhaps I've no right to give advice in this matter, but I have begun to think that the happiness in your family is due in large part to the honesty with which you treat one another. That's a rare quality here in Ormdale, and it's something our families need more of. Don't lose it." He put his hand on my arm. "Write to him. Do it at once."

What would he think of my honesty if he knew I'd been keeping such a secret from him as the identity of his own father?

"Simon, I think that's only the second time you've ever given me advice. The first time, you advised me to run away with you."

"I've no right to advise you at all," he said abruptly, removing his hand.

I caught it in mine, almost horrified at my own boldness.

"I'll do as you say, Simon. I'm sorry that I didn't listen to you last time. I'm listening now."

Simon flushed and stepped away, extricating his hand with finality.

"Look," he said, nodding at Cariad, who had at last adjusted to the blanket on her back. "She's made great strides today. We'll try the saddle on Monday."

When he left, I felt as flat as a biscuit.

Would it really prove simpler to woo a dragon than Simon?

What had it been like between my own mother and father? How had Father convinced Miriam to run away with him? Had he serenaded her with Anglo-Saxon epics from beneath her tower window? I tried to laugh at this absurd picture, but I couldn't. David's grief had been too palpable.

Heedful of Simon's advice, I went to my own tower to write Father. It was an awkward jumble of a letter—words crossed out and ink smudged. I almost threw it in the fire. But I remembered Simon's words, and dutifully addressed it to the Rector of St Giles.

Janushek dropped in on me as I pushed the envelope aside in relief.

"Where's your dragon, Janushek?" I asked, looking round. "You haven't been neglecting it, have you?"

He lifted his cap to reveal the little salamander sitting on his head. Tiny eyes glinted ruby at me.

"Neglecting it?" he laughed bitterly. "It does not let me alone for five minutes at a time."

I chuckled. "What does Lily think of it?"

"She finds it charming," he said bitterly. "I did hope she would find *me* charming, without the assistance of an albino reptile."

"Considering how much she loathed you when you first came, I'd be thanking the salamander if I were you."

He looked startled. "Loathed me?"

"Violet told me she slept with a knife under her pillow."

"Ah! I don't know what I've done to frighten her."

He looked so sad at the thought that I ached to tell him it wasn't any fault of his. But the violence in Lily's past was another thing I was not at liberty to share.

"I think Lily is afraid for the same reason people usually are," I said carefully.

Our eyes met. He shook his head and put the salamander back on it. "Don't tell me any secrets, Rusalka. Not any that are hers. That is a gift I will accept only from her."

He replaced his cap and got up to go.

"I've become rather adept at not telling other people's secrets," I said ruefully. "Wait, Janushek." He turned. "If you want her secrets—you ought to tell yours. Tell Lily about your sister."

He blinked. "That advice is not bad. You should follow it yourself, Rusalka."

Then, putting his hands in his pockets, he strolled away.

Could he tell I was keeping a secret from Simon? And if that was the case, could Simon himself?

Chapter Fifteen

The leaky little church in Ormby was an unfailingly depressing place. The dreary curate always seemed as if he was counting the hours until he could get away from the village and back to Embsay. He seemed especially unnerved whenever Father was there—as if he expected him to arise from his pew mid-service and correct his theology.

There wasn't really much theology to correct. His homilies consisted of reminding the poor congregants to be content with their lot. I noticed he never looked at them too closely, so as not to be troubled by what their lot actually was.

After the service, I escaped to look round the churchyard. There was an old yew tree, dropping red berries, and a thrush singing in the branches. George and Violet were carefully stepping on the berries. They made a satisfying crunch.

"Careful," I said, taking Violet by the elbow before she went crunching across a grave where a bunch of fresh flowers had been laid. Most of the headstones shared the neglected air of the church, but this one had been carefully kept free of weeds and moss.

Sacred to the memory of Anne Forrester

Laid here with her infant son

1850-1873

It must be a relative of Forrester's. A sister, perhaps?

For there is nothing covered, that shall not be revealed; neither hid, that shall not be known.

The text chosen made me shiver for some reason—almost as if someone had stepped on *my* grave.

"Miss Worms?"

I turned to see the curate. As usual, he looked like he'd rather be anywhere else.

"I was told you wished to speak with me."

"Why, yes, I was curious to know whether there has ever been a Sunday School in Ormby."

"Not to my knowledge." His eyes darted away. "I'm afraid I really must go visit poor old—what was his name again? There's an old man dying in a cottage—somewhere. I'm sure you understand the irreplaceable comfort a clergyman can bring."

"By all means, don't let me keep you from your sacred duty—somewhere," I murmured, trying to keep my scorn to a deniable level.

He made his escape.

On the way home in the carriage, I reflected on the dire state of spiritual formation in Ormdale.

Father read Morning Prayers to the abbey household whenever he was here, but I had been glad enough of the extra quarter hour of sleep when he wasn't. I doubted whether the servants had ever been allowed to touch the books in the library, nor would they have found much there to help them if they had. Was there so much as a catechism there? I had not seen one.

I glanced at Mother, sitting across from me in the carriage. She was serenely reading a slim volume—*Gardening by Myself* by Anna B. Warner—while Violet and Una played cat's cradle next to her. She did not react when Violet's elbow bumped her.

George was next to me, nursing a jam jar with a bit of cheesecloth over it. It contained a chrysalis in it that he was much devoted to. I wondered if the curate knew that he had preached to an embryonic moth. It was the sort of thing, I suspected, that might make people think our family odd.

As soon as we arrived back home, the children spilled out of the carriage, leaving me alone with Mother. I wondered where Pip was. Oughtn't he to have attended church with us?

"Mother," I began deliberately. "It's come to my attention that we're failing at our duty and we're an irreligious blot on the upper classes."

"Oh?" she said, tucking the book into her bag and opening the carriage door herself instead of waiting for John.

"Yes. Why, we haven't done morning prayers with the servants since Father left! And do you know there has never been a Sunday School class in the village?"

"Really," she said as she stepped out of the carriage. "Well, I must say, Edith, I'm surprised to see you take an interest when you already have so much to occupy you, but I shall be happy to advise, if you find you require it."

"Me!" I exclaimed, almost tripping over in my surprise as I got out.

"Yes. You didn't mean to suggest that *I* begin a Sunday School, did you?" Her face was grave. I fell silent. "Good. Because as you no doubt remember, I have been in charge of one for the last eleven years. Not to mention the orphan committees, charity bazaars, poor relief, ragged schools, and sundry other good works which I have never asked you to assist with, dear." We were now inside the Great Hall, and Mother began to tug off her gloves. "Even the very fields themselves were to be left fallow every seven years, you may recall."

"And this has been your fallow year?"

She looked at me again and said rather more tartly than I was used to from her, "No, dear, it has not. This has been my year to educate a very active son as well as my two orphaned nieces, and to help your father through what promises to be a very trying time in the parish. Not to mention worrying over our usually responsible eldest daughter, who has shown a remarkable aptitude for attracting all manner of trouble of late. And just in case you were going to suggest I'm neglecting Pip's religious formation—he has toothache."

This list brought me up short.

"Well." I sat down on the settle. "I see. But what's all this about a difficult time in the parish?"

Mother sighed and sat next to me. "It's the war."

"The war!" And I had hardly thought of it again since the morning I saw the newspaper. "What's happened with it now?"

"Nothing yet, specifically. But you know how your father feels about such things."

"He'll be against it."

She nodded. "And there are many who say he has no business to be. You might remember your father in your prayers, Edith. He will always follow his conscience, you know, through the rough and the smooth. And of course, I wouldn't have it any other way."

I thought of the letter I'd written him, which I had planned to put in the mail bag tomorrow. How unkind of me to have doubted and questioned his youthful conduct at such a time! I resolved to wait until we were together again to bring up the matter.

I put my hand on Mother's. "Are you...are you *sorry* about the girls? I hadn't really thought how much it would be for you to take them on. Nothing has ever seemed too much for you. How stupid of me not to think of it."

"No, I'm not sorry about the girls." Her face softened. "I lost two children of my own. I'm grateful to have Violet and Una in their place. But it is a little harder, when one gets them so late. I'm impatient at times."

"You were never impatient with me, and you got *me* late, too."

"Wasn't I? Thank you for saying that." She gazed thoughtfully at the tapestry. "I know my enthusiasm for the garden amuses you. But I remember looking down at it, from the window up there, and it seemed like a neglected child that needed me, almost as much as the girls. It sounds absurd when I say it aloud, but there it is."

"No," I said, remembering the first time my heart had gone out to Ormdale, standing on the Great Rock and looking down at the abbey. "It doesn't sound absurd at all."

"It's not a bad idea, Edith—the Sunday School. But if you do it, make sure you're doing it for the right reasons."

"Are there bad reasons for starting a Sunday School?" I asked.

"There are bad reasons for doing anything," she said. "Now, if you don't mind, I'm going to put on my oldest clothes and potter in the garden before the weather changes."

The next day, Simon and I recommenced our training sessions. When we brought out the saddle, Cariad flared up like a schoolboy seeing a textbook during his holidays.

It took days for her to allow it to be placed on her back at all, and she submitted to having the girth strap around her belly with a reluctance that made me feel ashamed of asking it of her.

My hopes began to dim. I might have ridden Cariad bareback once when my life and liberty were at stake, but I could not do it regularly. And we had not even tried a bridle yet, with which I had hoped to direct her where I wished to go.

Was Cariad damaged beyond repair by her past? As for Simon, while unfailingly patient and gentle with my dragon, he was more and more formal with me, making me ache for our former friendly intimacy.

In the novels I had read, the hero was always able to convince the reluctant object of his affections to forgo her maidenly condition simply by his persistence and shining character, but literature had sadly little to say about such a situation in reverse.

I was growing impatient with both of them.

One morning after demolishing a particular tasty breakfast, Cariad seemed calmer than usual. We were able to tighten the girth strap sufficiently for the saddle to stay firmly in place.

I couldn't wait any longer. "Simon, I want to try," I said with a note of desperation that he could not miss.

He looked at me closely. "All right. But I'm going to tie you to the saddle just in case."

I nodded. The halter rope that tethered her to the stout hitching post in the stable yard would stop her from going very high, but it would still be high enough for a nasty fall.

I allowed him to get a rope and tie it to the saddle horn, then round my waist. As he finished, he paused, quite close to me, and said quietly, "I suppose there's not much use in telling Edith Worms to be careful?"

"Why, Simon!" I exclaimed in mock surprise. "I thought you hadn't any right to give me advice?"

He made a noise in his throat and then did the last thing I expected. He closed the distance between us, and taking my face in his hands, he placed a quick kiss on my hair—on the top of my head.

Then he stepped back and said gruffly, "Ready?"

I felt a little less ready now than I had a moment before.

"Y-yes!" I gulped.

He put his hands round my waist to give me a lift. I grabbed the saddle and swung my leg over.

I gained my seat just as Cariad lost her head.

She thrashed her tail wildly. I crouched forward and whispered to calm her, but it had no effect. Her wings beat like bright flags whipping in the wind.

Then she took off skyward, but I wasn't ready. Unseated and toppling head first, I groped wildly for a handhold. I found the girth strap at her belly and caught myself for a moment, then lost it and fell feet first. I tried to slow myself with my own rope but it burned and jerked at my hands.

Cariad reached the end of her tether about two stories into the air. I reached the end of mine four feet from the ground. The rope tightened about my waist, but the boning in my undergarments kept me from being squeezed unbearably. Instead, I dangled just above the ground like a puppet, while she strained to free herself upwards.

Simon caught me in his arms and quickly loosened the knot so I could slip out to the ground. He put a hand under my elbow to steady me as I regained my composure.

The whole debacle had lasted less than a minute.

"*Cholera!*" I exclaimed, stamping my foot in frustration, and stubbing my toe on a cobble stone for good measure.

Simon started to laugh.

"Oh, Simon!" I almost wailed. "And we haven't even started with the bridle yet!" I shook my head. "If only I had your patience."

"If only I had your boldness," he countered. "Are you sure you're unharmed?"

"Quite. Have I scotched it?" I asked ruefully. "Will she trust me again?"

He took a deep breath. "Give her a day. Give me some time to think. Then we'll try again."

The next day, I received three letters. One was from Gwendolyn.

*Dear Edith, I did it. **We** did it. I cannot believe it. I am terrified, and happier than I have ever been or ever dared hope to be.*

The rest of her letter was incandescent. I wanted desperately to celebrate her success, but my own heart was sick from deferred hope.

I moved onto the second letter, which was from Irene.

Dear Edith, wrote Irene, *Your grandfather was not pleased by your abrupt disappearance, and assured me he would have happily thrown Penrith out on his ear at once sooner than have him frighten away his only granddaughter. He asked me many questions about the matter, which of course I could not answer to his satisfaction. I warn you—Sir Joseph is used to getting his way.*

She closed the letter with a reminder of my promise to join her in London to have a gown made up for my London debut. I was relieved that they still wanted to see me again, but I could not look forward to the prospect of explaining my strange history with Penrith to my grandfather.

A glance at the third letter put this out of my mind instantly.

I sat very still, feeling as if I had just glimpsed the sword hanging by a hair over my very head.

Each stroke of the address was sharp and unyielding—I remembered the same hand that had formed those letters, slashing at me with a hypodermic.

Gripping the sharp letter opener like a weapon, I slit open the envelope with shaking hands.

Dear Miss Worms,

Congratulations on the success of your research into an antidote. Give it to me and I'll forget that you destroyed my own work. Withhold it from me at your own loss.

Nicholas Farley

How on earth had he heard about our antivenin? And what did he want it for? He had only ever wanted an antidote so he could make his own soldiers immune to the horrible weapons he was developing. An awful thought arose—was it possible he had begun to rebuild his stock of poisons once again? Had he persuaded the War Office to give him another chance? Could they be so unprincipled as to do so?

Cousin Stephen had told me that England had been one of the signatories to an agreement not to develop chemical weapons—but that had already been undermined by their negotiations with Farley.

No, I dared not trust in the promises of the War Office, not with the dreaded Next War upon us already.

But I had already given everything I could to stop Farley.

Chapter Sixteen

I woke to moonlight. The moon was waning gibbous, but still bright. I tried to go back to sleep but kept thinking of Farley's threat.

Withhold it from me at your own loss.

What could he mean by it?

This would never do! I dressed warmly and went to the stables. Again, Cariad seemed to be waiting for me. I led her out of her stall. She was utterly calm at night, hardly the same animal she was by daylight. She looked at me, and then nuzzled me gently, as if to say she was sorry for tossing me off her back.

Then she lowered herself to the ground, as if actually *inviting* me to get on her back. I hesitated, glancing at the saddle, which was hidden nearby under a saddle blanket. I went towards it, but she made a huffing noise at me that clearly said *No.*

I gazed into her eye.

Did I really dare try her now, alone? Did I trust her enough for that?

I thought of the bond I had seen between Simon and Portia. Perhaps such a bond could only exist if trust went both ways. And she had already risked so much on me. Perhaps I might risk something on her.

I got the rope from the wall of the stable and knotted it round her neck as I had in Wales. Then I tied the other end round my waist.

Next, I would have to get on her back without Simon helping me. As if she heard my thoughts, Cariad leaned her head at an odd angle, her horns angled towards me.

On an impulse, I grasped one in each hand, and she lifted me onto her back neatly.

"Clever Cariad!" I whispered in surprise.

Now there was something inside me like static electricity building up. I put my hands on the dragon's skin and almost felt a jolt pass between us.

It rushed through my blood like wine, like magic, like the sound of Janushek's violin, or the warmth of Simon's hand in mine.

I could not remember the word Arthur had used to tell his dragon to fly, but I didn't suppose that mattered. Arthur had not managed to train her. I would be the one to do that—I could feel it. It wasn't about the word itself—it was in this: this living flow of potential between us, which I hadn't felt since Wales.

I leaned low over her neck. "Fly," I whispered, and the word gave me gooseflesh. And then louder: *"Fly, Cariad!"*

Her ears twitched, she blinked, then her wings unfurled gloriously, elegantly. Her wings beat like a conductor beating time, and in two breaths we were above the jumbled rooflines of the abbey. The air stirred my hair.

All at once a gurgle of excitement bubbled out of me. Mother had always said I was too old for my years. What would she say if she could see me now, gurgling above the chimneystacks like a baby thrown in the air by her father!

Cariad was over the open land now, headed towards the fells. In place of the familiar landscape below me was a silver fairyland. The limestone crags in the distance glowed like the moon, and the rock walls below us made the fields look like a giant's chessboard. We passed over an owl in flight, hunting in the air beneath us, silent and white.

Cariad flew straight and true as an arrow, and as carefully as a nurse pushing a perambulator. We were above the great stone pavement, which looked like a dancing floor. Now for the first time she curved gently, altering her course. My body turned with hers easily.

Where was she going? Or was she flying for the sheer joy of it, like me?

Her kind bond deeply with their first riders.

Perhaps she had really wanted to be ridden by me all along, just on her own terms.

We were following the course of the river now. I realised with surprise that the sky was changing colour. Dawn was coming.

She flew toward the east, as if to greet the sun. We were skimming over a sea of fog now, and I lost all sense of our height.

It sounds quite mad in the retelling, but joy had left no room for fear. The sky began to glow pink, as the sun appeared on the edge of the moor. I had to squint against it, and tears ran down my face from its brightness as it burned away the fog, revealing the undulations of the coloured moor far, far below us. The heather was blooming in great streaks of colour.

Suddenly, we were surrounded by song. Skylarks! But instead of craning my neck to catch sight of one, I was among them!

I thought that my mortal body was not enough to contain the joy within it as the morning air rushed over me, and the sky blazed, and the heather bloomed, and my dragon glittered, and the larks welcomed me into their chorus of rejoicing as if I were one of them.

I thought that I would not mind even death itself, if I could die like this.

Perhaps we would have flown into the morning sun like Icarus and really died, but I heard the drum of hoofbeats below us. I looked down and there was a rider keeping pace with us, galloping as joyously as I flew.

I recognised that effortless grace: it was Simon! He must have gone for a dawn ride and spotted us. In the wide Yorkshire skies, a girl on a golden dragon would not be inconspicuous.

We raced each other, and I hallooed at him and he waved his hat at me, making me laugh.

Then Cariad turned and made for the abbey.

Some would say it is not very considerate towards the nerves of one's family for a young lady to come to breakfast on the back of a dragon.

Thankfully, Mother was made of sterner stuff.

As Cariad circled the abbey, the children ran hallooing out of the house into the stable yard. She put down rather more gently than she had on another memorable occasion, for which I was grateful. Instead of tumbling off her, I was able to hoist my leg over and slide off with a reasonable grace.

The children were shouting excited questions at me and crowding round.

"Wait a minute! Settle down! Dragon riding makes one dreadfully thirsty, don't you know? I'll tell you all about it once I've had a cup of tea."

I took off the rope with cold-numbed hands, put Cariad in her stall, and went in to have my breakfast.

Mother touched my hands and told me if I was going to make a habit of this, I'd better get some proper riding clothes. The children served me food eagerly if haphazardly (I have never seen so much blackberry jam on a single piece of toast, but I did not quibble).

The breakfast and the story were just ending when I glimpsed Simon arrive on Portia. My heart lifted. He alone shared my knowledge of the singular elation of flight. I told the others to let me alone for a bit and went out to join him.

"Simon!" I called out eagerly. He moved quickly to meet me, leaving Portia at the water trough. "You saw, didn't you?"

"I could hardly miss it!"

"I didn't mean to do it, exactly, only she was so calm..."

"Didn't mean to do it? Edith, don't tell me you *accidentally* rode a dragon!"

"I suppose I did! And oh, Simon—it was like the sonnet—the larks were all around us, *singing hymns at heaven's gate*!"

"I don't doubt it—you looked like something out of a stained-glass window, Edith."

Like children, we were talking at the same time, clasping each other's hands. Suddenly, Simon's brow furrowed and he dropped mine.

"Edith, I must apologise to you. I shouldn't have kissed you like that yesterday."

I laughed aloud. "Don't you think—at some point—we might *stop* apologising for kissing one another?"

He turned away. "Edith, I'll help you train Cariad. But that's all I can give you."

My spirits fell. I'd felt so invincible, ascending to the skies like that. Now he stood with his back to me, so close and yet, in spirit, so maddeningly far.

"Of course." I tried to pull myself together. "Simon, I've some bad news, I'm afraid. I got a letter from Farley yesterday." He turned quickly, alarmed. "He wants our antivenin."

"Well, what if we give it to him?" asked Lily, once we were gathered in my tower and I had shown them the letter. "It just heals."

"Janushek?" I prodded.

"No," said Simon suddenly.

We all—Lily, Janushek, Hanna, and I—looked at him in surprise. Hanna was stroking her dark salamander, who was growing tubby. The rats no longer stood a chance at Wormwood Abbey.

"I'm sorry," said Simon. "Please, go on. I'll listen."

"I want to hear what Drake has to say," said Janushek, crossing his arms.

Simon swallowed. "He hurt Edith and Hanna—and Janushek. Did he not?"

We all nodded.

"Then we give him nothing—ever." His voice was like steel. This was a side of Simon I'd never seen before.

Janushek nodded his approval. "I agree with Drake. Give him nothing."

"What do you think, Edith?" asked Simon.

"On the face of it, there's no harm in giving him the antivenin," I admitted. "But Farley deceived me once. I have trouble believing he has any good reason to want it. And he might have a bad reason."

Janushek grunted. "I do not like Farley knowing about it at all."

"Yes!" Hanna exclaimed. "How?"

Then they all looked at me.

"I have no idea. The only people who know about it outside of Ormdale are the people who were sent the antivenin."

"The Dragon Families," said Simon.

"Which implies that one of them is in communication with Farley. But I've no way of knowing which."

"Tallantire was in London," Janushek suggested.

"But Tallantire knew about our plan to raid Farley's laboratory, and he didn't tell him," I pointed out. "So I think we can strike out Tallantire as a suspect." Besides that, I could not believe such a transparent young man was capable of hiding anything.

"Miss Falconer?" asked Simon.

"Well, she's a bit of a 'dark horse', to borrow a phrase from Disraeli," I said, thinking of my uneasy truce in Wales with the formidable beauty from Derbyshire. "I don't doubt Meredith would join up with Farley—*if* it would do her any good, but I can't imagine any way they'd know each other, or anything good that would come to her from such an affiliation. I'm convinced Farley has a personal history with Ormdale, and I got the impression he didn't know there were dragons outside of Yorkshire. I think the evidence points elsewhere."

"You think it's Penrith?" suggested Simon.

"I think he's by far the most likely. And the one with the most obvious motive: revenge." I looked round the circle of faces. "And the most connections in the kind of circles Farley runs in. So. We are all agreed, then?"

"We are agreed on what we will *not* do," Janushek pointed out. "But what *will* we do if Farley comes looking for the antivenin?"

"Actually, I was hoping that you might have some ideas for us on that score, Janushek."

"Ah! At last, my criminal past becomes useful," he said with a low laugh.

"Not for the first time!" I corrected, and noticed Lily's quick glance at me. How much had he told her about his past? And what might she think of our friendship? "I seem to remember a lock-picking session that got me out of a tight place."

Janushek's eyes shifted thoughtfully to Simon. "Perhaps our local magistrate might have some ideas for us."

A thief and a magistrate. What more could I ask for, to defend Ormdale, than two such opposite and excellent fellows as Simon and Janushek?

"If only," I sighed, "we had a little more idea of who or what the threat might be."

"That's the thing with threats, Rusalka," said Janushek. "They make themselves obvious at last, usually when you don't want them to."

"But when they do," said Simon, raising his dark eyes to us with equal seriousness, "we will be ready for them."

Chapter Seventeen

Just when I most longed to banish my worries with the ec-
stasies of flight, it rained for a solid week.

There were leaks everywhere, and Dugdale went about with
a pencil and paper, making a list of necessary repairs.

I told him he might be served better making a map of the
few rooms that did *not* have leaks, damp, rot, or mildew. If there
were any.

In my heart of hearts, I did not think it would ever stop
raining.

Cariad did not seem to mind it, and I let her out for exercise
each day. But riding slippery wet scales into the heavens was too
reckless, even for Edith Worms.

Simon had made himself scarce. There were no cosy fireside
tête-à-têtes while the rain fell, and I kept remembering his last
private words to me: *I'll help you train Cariad, but that's all I
can give you.*

The children gave me little peace in the wet weather, and I prowled about the abbey like a sullen cat.

"How is it in the servants' rooms, Lily?" I asked, as I came across her in her duties. "You're all right up under the eaves. I expect you feel like Noah's family."

She gave me a granite stare—the kind of look she had not given me in months.

"That bad?" I laughed weakly. "I'm sorry."

She unbended. "It's not so bad for me and Pip, miss, or the new folk. We're still young, and a drop of rain here and there won't hurt us. But my grandfather..."

"Rheumatism," I remembered suddenly. "Janushek told me."

I tracked down Dugdale, who was looking thoughtfully at a patch of ceiling.

"Dugdale, what happens to the servants in a big old house like this when they get old—really old?"

"Well, miss, there are a few outcomes. If there's a grown-up child who's settled elsewhere, they go live with them. I expect my aunt will come to me, in a few years."

"What if they don't?"

"Some wealthy employers have a place for them on the estate—a lodge over the stables, or some such, for those who've served longest. Those would be the lucky ones."

"And the unlucky ones?" I was almost afraid to ask.

"The workhouse."

Our eyes met.

"Are they as bad as everyone says?"

"Worse, miss."

I remembered the East End. The workhouses were said to be a step down even from living in the slums. I swallowed. "What about the old cottage?"

"Cottage, miss?"

"Behind the abbey. I think it belonged to a gardener, in the fabled heyday of yore."

"What about it, miss?"

"If it's anywhere near repairable, it ought to be done up. John must be nearing eighty. And it should accommodate Martha and Thomas, too. If we are going to keep taking on servants to run this place, we must consider these things."

"Yes, miss," Dugdale said.

"Well, write it down." I nodded at his pencil, which had not moved since I began speaking.

"I won't forget, Miss Worms," he said quietly, and went back to his task.

"Oh! And Dugdale? I thought you might like to know—my cousin passed her exam with distinction."

Dugdale gave a slow, appreciative nod. "Aye. Thank you."

Before long, I was feeling sorry for myself again.

"Has Simon been here?" I asked Mother as I stomped into the sitting room.

"No, my dear," she said. "But why don't you come and sit with me for a while?"

She had all of her seed packets spread out on the table with a schematic of the garden and was busily making obscure notes.

I dropped into a chair and paged through a book of mother's—*Elizabeth and Her German Garden*. It seemed to be all about a woman hiding in her garden from her horrid Prussian husband. How could Mother bear reading something so dull?

"This weather!" I grumbled. "And there are no mackintoshes big enough for dragons. Wasn't there a French monarch who had a pet giraffe who wore a raincoat? All embroidered with fleur-de-lys?"

"That is a question for your brother, I think."

"Whom I have only just escaped—he was intent on delivering a lecture on the habits of the oleander hawk moth."

"It's called a narration, dear." Mother looked at me penetratingly. "The pining isn't working as well as you'd hoped, is it, dear?"

"It's working well enough on me!" I closed the book with a snap. "But Simon is being stubborn. So far, I can't convince him that his mother is an obstacle we can overcome together."

"Of course you can't."

This startled me. "Why 'of course'?"

"Well, it seems to me the obstacle in this situation isn't Helena at all. I'm very much afraid it is Simon."

I swallowed. "What do you mean?"

"I mean that while you might be happy to have him despite his current situation, unless he can actually believe he is the right man for you—how can *he* be happy? He'll always see himself as having done you a disservice by marrying you. That's no way at all to make a marriage."

The idea fell on me with crippling force. Even Janushek had said he couldn't be happy until he was sure he was the right man for Lily.

How had I not seen it from Simon's perspective before? After I told him I was listening at last?

I put my face in my hands. "Are you telling me I'll have to foreswear marriage and love him with a purely spiritual love from now on?"

"Oh, my dear Edith, no one who has ever seen the way you look at a treacle tart, let alone the way you look at Simon, would ever think you capable of such a thing."

I peeped at her through my fingers in horror.

"What! Mother, why did you never tell me this before? Are you seriously telling me I look at Simon like—well, like a greedy child outside of a sweet shop!"

"Some of us do not have the gift of celibacy, my dear, and it's best to admit it."

"But what good does it do to admit it?" I squeaked, cheeks reddening. "What good does it do the greedy child to say 'I want those lemon drops' when she hasn't any pennies?"

She put down a seed packet. "I think it might help you give him up."

"*Give him up!* But I thought I was meant to find the knife to get him out?" I almost wailed.

"I thought you might do that once. Helena is an obstacle. But it's not just a matter of removing her somehow. Because it's the effect she's had on Simon—on the man he is—that's the real problem. And that's not something you can mend."

I scrambled to find a flaw in this trenchant assessment of our problem.

"But you...you and Father...you said you had to tell him you really *needed* him before he would lift a finger..."

"You've told Simon how you feel, haven't you? And it hasn't made a difference?"

The look on my face answered her question. She laid down her pencil and sat next to me.

"There are some things that only God can mend, Edith."

I closed my eyes, an empty feeling in my stomach. "I've never wanted anyone else, Mother. I can't imagine ever feeling this way again. I'm not sure I'd even want to."

I felt her take my hand in hers. "Those are all things to consider, to be sure. But you are only twenty-one, after all. And you are no Marianne Dashwood, to worry yourself into a decline."

"Perhaps he'd change his mind if I did!" I said bitterly.

"Would you want that?"

I had to think about that one. "No. I wouldn't."

"Good girl," Mother murmured.

Chapter Eighteen

I had promised myself that I would stop going back for people who tried to destroy me. After all, I had already done that with Arthur, and again with Farley.

I did it once more.

My old nemesis, Helena, had sent me a note, begging me to come see her before I left for London. And if Simon wouldn't come to me, perhaps I might go to him.

Forrester met me at the door of Drake Hall. As he helped me remove my mackintosh and wellingtons, I seized this rare opportunity of speaking with him alone. "Forrester, have you given any thought to talking to Simon?" I lowered my voice. "About...what we discussed, up on the great rock?"

"No, miss," he said, going pale. "You were so good as to give me a promise, miss, upon the occasion to which you refer."

A few notes were struck on the piano in the library, and Oolong came padding down the passage towards me, wagging its lovely little amber tail. I bent down and petted it (I still could not be sure of the creature's sex).

"Oolong," came Helena's voice—from the library. Oolong galloped back, slipping on the polished floorboards.

Never having known Helena to leave her bedroom, I looked at Forrester in astonishment.

"Mrs Drake is feeling unusually well today," he said.

"So I see," I said. "Of course I'm bound to keep my promise." I touched Forrester's arm for a moment. "But please—think of *him*."

Forrester spoke very low. "It's him I think of, miss."

I followed the dragon into the library, where Simon's dark eyes met mine over the piano in a mute but unmistakable warning.

This visit was not turning out to be very jolly.

I turned to face my nemesis, Helena Drake. She was reclining on a settee near the fire, Mr Darcy in her lap. Her dress gleamed amethyst in the firelight.

During the time when she had served as a mentor to me, she had often been pleased to see me.

But this fragile gaiety was different.

At our last encounter, she had admitted to trying to exile me to Wales forever, to get me away from her son. Did she really expect me to behave as if that had never happened?

If I had become a snail without a shell, she was a shard of china, and I was all too aware of her sharp edges. I would not go any nearer than I had to.

Helena stretched out her hands to me. "Edith, how can I ever thank you? How can I ever repay you?"

I wished I could say she didn't owe me anything except honesty—which I had no expectation of receiving from her.

"Seeing Simon back home where he ought to be is all the thanks I need," I said, ignoring her outstretched hands. Her hands dropped gracefully, and she patted the empty spot on the settee.

"Please, sit with me."

I chose a chair instead.

The two Chinese dragons were sparring on the rug—Mr Darcy with the tolerance of an aging relative for a mischievous child.

"Simon has been so kind to me. He has been playing for me. You like Chopin, too, don't you? You told me once you missed the piano."

I looked at Simon. Was this what he had been trying to warn me about? Chopin?

"Would you like tea?" she asked, and she reached out for a little bell.

"No," I said quickly. "Thank you." (I'd had quite enough of untrustworthy people giving me tea.)

Simon hadn't said a word since I came in. His mother looked at him now, and I was certain in my bones that she was issuing him an order.

Quietly, he turned a page of sheet music and ignored her.

"Edith," she said, changing tactics, "wouldn't you like to play with Simon?"

Of course I wanted to play with Simon. There were a lot of things I wanted to do with Simon.

Simon flashed me a look of apology.

"I'm out of practise," I protested.

"There is an instrument for you to practise upon," Helena pointed out, "and a willing partner."

I don't know what spell was at work in that room, but all of a sudden, I to play with him. I felt desperately curious about what it would be like. To my own surprise as well as his, I found myself sitting beside him on the bench.

It was just the two of us, together in a safe little harbour shielded from the rest of the room. What did it matter whose idea it was?

"This one?" I asked, gesturing to the duet currently open upon the stand. I had heard him play only once before, but the impression of his beautiful command of melody remained. I would happily take the supporting part to hear it once more. "I'll play second," I offered.

"No, Edith," he said, so low that I felt rather than heard his voice. "You mustn't take second."

And then he got up and left the room.

I blinked, alone at the instrument. He had left the door open. A slight draft came through it. What was I doing here in this dim, sleepy room?

The spell was broken. Simon had broken it. I had been weak, and he had been the strong one.

There was a slight sigh from the settee. "You see your effect upon him."

"What do you mean?"

"He's not quite himself today. Won't you have pity on him? You might follow him now," she prompted softly.

Was she trying to bring us together now? Of course she was—if she couldn't get rid of me, she'd want me close.

Close enough to watch. Close enough to control. But she didn't understand that it was Simon who would never, ever consent to that plan.

"Not himself, you say?" I repeated, suddenly desperate. "How can he ever be himself when he doesn't even know who he is?"

Her face now became very smooth. Then she smiled. "Perhaps what he needs is you, Edith, to help him know himself. Won't you help him?"

I stood up and shook my head. "No. He doesn't need me. He *wants* me. What he *needs* is the truth."

"The truth? The truth is rarely plain and never simple," she quoted.

"The truth I am thinking of is an even harder one than what the playwright had in mind, I'm afraid, Mrs Drake."

"Really? What truth are you speaking of?"

I lowered my voice. "The fact that Simon's father has not died, but is living even now—here, at Drake Hall."

Her face went ashy. I couldn't look at her any longer. I looked down. I was standing there, in Helena's home, accusing her of betraying her husband and deceiving the world about her son's paternity. She would have every right to believe I hated her—that I wanted to shame her and threaten her.

I didn't want anything of the kind. I just wanted Simon to be free. To be himself at last—whoever that might prove to be.

A log in the fire burned through and hit the hearthstone with a thud.

"I'll let myself out," I said quietly, not looking at her. As I left the room, I heard the little bell ringing behind me. Forrester passed me, answering it.

I heard her voice, unrecognisably hoarse and weak, as I made my escape.

"Please, take me upstairs again. I am not feeling well."

I took a deep breath of air as the door shut behind me.

No wonder Simon had vowed never to bring me here as a bride. Something was desperately wrong at Drake Hall, and Mother was right—no matter how good I had become at breaking spells, this one was not mine to break.

I was just waking up and still lying in bed when I heard children whispering outside my door.

"I'm sure she's awake by now!" came a loud stage whisper.

"Well, I certainly am now, Violet," I responded.

At that, Violet burst in, clutching a package. Una hung back at the door.

"This is from Simon. He brought it at dawn. Look—it's not raining!"

I read the note she thrust at me.

Edith, would you like an adventure today? If so, look at the map. I've already started. And I've left something for you in the stables. S.D.

"It's a harness for riding your dragon! I've already been and looked!" Violet said excitedly.

Simon had sketched for me a rough map of the fells. I recognised the Great Rock and two distinctive peaks. On one of them, he had drawn some kind of tower and marked it with an *X*.

"What's a harness?" I asked in bewilderment.

"The thing he left you in the stables, of course! Do hurry!"

I tore open the package and a compass fell out, attached to a length of leather cord.

Trying not to look as eager as I felt, I dressed myself warmly, breakfasted quickly, and ran down to the stables, where Violet awaited me in an agony of impatience.

Hanging from a nail was an interesting piece of harness. It was a creation of leather straps and buckles, padded with lambswool. Violet showed how it would fit comfortably round my waist while keeping me snugly on Cariad's back. The straps fastened near her front and back legs without touching the sensitive part of her belly.

Simon must have been making this for me the whole week.

I took down the cloak of warm Welsh wool from its peg and hung the compass around my neck. It was very easy to harness Cariad, and it didn't upset her in the least. Simon had even designed it so that I could buckle myself into it without assistance, though on this occasion Violet helped eagerly.

"All right, thank you, Violet, now step back, I don't want her wings to knock you down!"

Violet obeyed wistfully. "Do you think she'll let me ride her one day?"

"Yes, I do," I said. "But you'll have to be very patient with her."

Violet nodded vigorously. "You've never seen someone as patient as I can be! How long do you think it will take?"

"Oh, Violet," I sighed. How alike we were sometimes!

Chapter Nineteen

The air smelt of rain, and birds were coming out to enjoy the sunshine. The sheep in their paddocks were clean from the deluge, as white as a string of pinafores pegged out on washing day.

I was able to keep Cariad on a northwesterly course. Now I could see a rugged peak in the distance—that must be it!

Then I spotted Simon, cantering across the ground ahead of me, heading for the same peak. I landed Cariad on a crag to wait for him.

From my vantage point, I spotted a lowering cloud, with dark streaks of rain descending. I looked about for shelter.

I gasped. The tower from Simon's map! It had fallen half into itself, and being the same colour as the limestone crags it sat on, I had mistaken it for a rock formation at first.

I might not have seen it at all, had not a solitary, wind-gnarled rowan tree stood near it, the few remaining red berries a shock of brightness. There were dead branches all round it from the harsh winds of this exposed place.

I ran across the plateau towards it as the rain began to fall and slipped into the arched doorway, pushing back the hood of my cloak. The timber floor above had half fallen in, but enough remained to protect me from a wetting. I was surprised to see a considerable pile of firewood inside.

I sat on a bit of interior wall that had fallen down and settled to wait for Simon. The arrow-slit windows provided narrow flashes of the fells.

"Hello," I said little later as Simon came in, his dark, great-coated figure filling the doorway. Though it was chilly in the tower, I was warmly dressed, and my blood was stirred from my flight. Another warmth spread through me upon seeing Simon again. "As you see, I did want an adventure."

"I thought you might," he replied with a low laugh. "Do you know what this place is?"

I'd made all sorts of resolutions about how I'd behave when I saw him again—a list of things that needed to be said—but now I struggled to recall a single one of them.

"No?" I looked around.

"It's called a pele tower. There are hundreds of them, all over England." His eyes were bright. "Every one of them had an iron basket at the top, and fuel ready for signal fire, night and day."

I drew a breath and sprang up. "The beacon. You've found it!"

"Well, you *did* get here before me," he pointed out.

"Bosh! You found it! I just followed your map." I peered up the crumbling stairs that spiralled up one side of the tower. "Do you suppose—would they be able to see it?" I asked doubtfully. "As far away as Derbyshire, or Cumberland? If we even knew how to light the right kind of signal fire?"

"I think a telegram would go faster and have a better chance of being seen."

Startled, I laughed. "You're right. Now that I'm here, it does seem fanciful."

"Fanciful?" With his gloved hand, he patted the exterior wall of the tower, which was at least five feet thick. "There's something solid here, to have lasted so long. They must have used them to communicate once, before they stopped talking to each other, out of fear, or envy, or whatever it was."

"Gwendolyn always laughed at me for wondering about all this. I suppose Dugdale would say it wasn't worth mitherin' about, after all."

He looked at me in surprise. "You're speaking Yorkshire now?"

"Don't you ever speak it?"

"Aye, lass! Happen tha's not 'eard me?" he said with a broad smile.

"I think it's lovely."

"That was something else my father didn't like," he recalled ruefully.

"He *was* cruel to you, wasn't he?" I suddenly needed to know.

His shoulders tensed, and he didn't look at me. "I probably deserved the whippings. Most of them, anyway. And Forrester was always there to patch me up, afterwards."

"Forrester? Not your mother?"

He shook his head. "I never told my mother. She was always—delicate. Even before her great illness. She'd have to go to bed for days, especially when something happened to upset her. When she was a girl, she wasn't allowed to ride or go out walking. I believe it ruined her constitution."

"That's why you never stop me, isn't it?" I asked softly. "Why you never scold me for my escapades?"

He looked at me for a moment, then swallowed. "It's not a life I'd wish on anyone. My father told me once...that my birth had damaged my mother. So some of it—at least—is my fault. She gave her strength to me, even though she couldn't spare it."

"Oh, Simon," I whispered. Then I noticed that he had one hand pressed to his side.

"Are you hurt?"

"No." He dropped his hand quickly. "It's an old wound. Sometimes it twinges."

"*Old wound*? You never had it before! Simon? What are you hiding from me?"

He gave a long sigh. "I did tell you I tried to escape."

The memory of a crossbow aimed at me in the Welsh mountains flashed through my mind. "They *shot* you?" I cried.

"The sentinel was only doing what he thought was his duty," he said apologetically.

I stared at him for a moment, then I burst out laughing. "Oh, Simon. Are you really worried that I'll think badly of the person who shot you with a crossbow?" I sat again. "And you're really perfectly all right?"

"It was a clean wound, and it healed well."

"But it might...that might have been the end..." I thought of all the times I'd imagined him dying in agony, far away from home. I had been closer to the truth than I had known.

Simon sat down next to me. "I'm here, Edith. I didn't mean to hide it from you—I just didn't want to boast about it. I don't mean to hide anything from you."

Those words stung me. I took a deep breath. "Simon, there is something—a few things, in fact—that I haven't told you—indeed, I haven't known *how* to tell you." He waited. "Do you remember how I joked with you, that I wouldn't feed your pet if you went away? Well, I did feed it. I very nearly became its dinner myself."

A look of horror came across his face. "Edith! You went into the caves? You—you *saw it*?"

I nodded. "I not only saw *it*—I saw *them*."

"Truly? How many?"

"I saw two, and an egg. The egg—it was very strange—but also familiar. Completely spherical, and black as night. Does that remind you of anything?"

He thought for an instant. "Bartholomew's globe!"

"Precisely! The dragon was hidden in the picture, after all—do you see?"

He passed a hand over his face. "But Edith…why?"

"Why put the egg in the picture? Well, I suppose—"

"No! I mean, what on earth possessed you to do it? To go into those caves again, knowing what was there?"

"Oh," I said. "I did it for the money, of course."

He stared at me in disbelief.

"That's how I paid for the lab to make the antidote. You landed gentry really have no head for money at all, do you?" I marvelled. "And what with the Americans buying up everything cheap, it's no wonder the entire class is turning their toes up…"

He was now shaking with laughter.

"Don't laugh!" I elbowed him gently—avoiding the crossbow wound. "There's more. Forrester helped me. In fact, he saved my life."

"He did?"

"And that was when I realised something about him. But I promised that I wouldn't tell you what it was."

"Oh, you mean, you realised who he is?"

He said this so calmly, it took the breath out of me.

"*What did you say?*" I whispered.

"That he's descended from the valet."

"The valet?" I repeated weakly.

Why was he talking about a *valet*, of all things?

"In the picture. Sir Bartholomew's man—the one who came with the quetzalcoatl, from the New World. He told me about it once, when I was a boy."

I stared at Simon, really seeing him, in a way, for the first time. His eyes, his complexion—he had never really looked English, had he? Of course, the foreign blood had been mixed with Yorkshire stock for three hundred years, but it was still there.

And his adopted father had beaten him—why? For being the child of someone else? For not being English enough?

Simon spoke quietly. "Yesterday—something happened between you and my mother, didn't it? After I left the room. Because since you left...she's been terrified. Why?"

My mouth went dry as I remembered the look in Forrester's eyes when I'd broached the subject. "It's not my secret. And, I'm dreadfully sorry, but I promised I wouldn't tell it, so please—please don't—"

"Of course I won't," he said, steadying me with a hand on my arm. "Not if you've promised. And I don't think I've met the man who could make you do something, Edith."

"No, you haven't *met* him. You are the only man who could do it, Simon. And you're much too good to take advantage of it."

His eyes were as dark as the globe in the painting. "It wouldn't be to anyone's advantage, Edith. I can't offer you what you deserve. I can't abandon my mother."

"You really think I'd ask it of you?"

His jaw tightened. "I think that is what it would come to, in the end, whether you asked it or not. She is not safe, and I would have to protect you. And I owe her more than that. I owe both of you more than I can hope to give."

"You think so much about what's owed," I said. "But love isn't like that."

"What is love like, then?" he asked hollowly. "Tell me. Because I fear I know nothing of it."

I took a deep breath and thought back to my conversation with Father. "Love is patient and kind. It keeps no record of wrongs. It doesn't hold things over you—obligations and debts. It isn't a ledger. And it has things it needs—but it isn't *just* need." I thought of the fear that lurked in Helena's eyes, that spurred her to control those around her lest they control her. "It isn't a hunger that can never be filled. It fills, and warms, and makes you *more* yourself, not less."

He looked dumbfounded. "I've never known a love like that. I've never filled anyone. I've failed everyone I've ever loved."

"Oh, Simon, that can't be true!"

"My father—I failed him every day of his life. Gwen? I tried to make things better for her with her family—tried to shield her from harm, but it never worked. Her father and brother even lost their lives because of my blundering. And then there's my mother. I can't make her well—and I can't be the kind of son she wanted." He paused. "And the very worst of it is how I've failed you."

"Simon!"

"Look at me and tell me that I'm not disappointing you now, Edith."

He touched my face with his gloved hand, pulling my gaze to his. I could smell the rain that clung to the oilcloth of his greatcoat.

I wanted to put my arms around him and tell him none of it mattered because we loved each other, but I didn't. Because Janushek and Mother were right, and I'd been wrong.

It hurt.

"So what now?" he said grimly, dropping his hand.

What indeed? What future awaited us? Furtive glances and melancholy sighs over the tea table?

"I don't have it in me to be a tragic romantic heroine, and pine away for you," I admitted, flushing as I remembered Mother's words about the gift of celibacy. "I'm an earthly sort of creature, really, not saintly at all. I like an adventure, it's true, but afterwards I want my crumpets and a warm fire and a good book. And...someone to put their arms round me."

"I know you do," he said, with a catch of affection in his voice. "And I want you to have all those things."

I caught a flash of crimson from the rowan tree outside, bending in the wind.

"I'm going to listen to your advice after all," I said trying to keep my voice steady. "I shall try to find someone else—in a year or so. And I'd like you to forgive me now, in advance, because I think it would be in dreadful taste to ever speak of it again."

Of course, I didn't know if it would really work—setting a date like that for taking my heart back, as if it had been lent out by a circulating library.

Perhaps I *would* become a tragic heroine, after all, despite my best efforts. Perhaps I'd never find anyone else I liked enough to marry. Perhaps I'd be a white-haired old lady, kissing a picture of my lost love every night, and telling my nephews and nieces about my great passion.

But I'd try my best to avoid it.

"I thought I could mend this, Simon," I whispered at last, "but I can't."

"You shouldn't have to," he said simply. "And I won't burden you with that."

I felt a gentle pressure, hardly a breath, near my ear. He'd dropped a feather-light kiss on my hair again.

He blotted out the light from the doorway for an instant on his way. "And there's nothing for me to forgive, Edith."

A moment later, I heard a whinny and hoofbeats.

It was awfully cold in the tower without him.

Chapter Twenty

"Here at last!" Irene's welcome at the Belmontes' London mansion at the western end of Piccadilly left me in no doubt of my standing with them, even if I still travelled without a lady's maid, to the consternation of the staff.

"Now, I hope you won't mind me showing you off shamelessly," warned Irene as she took me to my room. "Not one of my friends has a niece anywhere near as clever as you are, and I mean them to know it!"

I laughed. "Just how are you planning to exhibit me to them?"

"Don't worry, I won't step on your publisher's toes. I've planned nothing but a small dinner party—just intimate friends, you know."

"Not tonight?" I begged, aghast. I had hoped for a little more time to adjust to the world of the Belmontes before I was exhibited as belonging to them.

"No, no, no! I wouldn't do such a thing! Tomorrow night, of course—but only if you feel well." She gave me a closer look, touching my cheek with one slim finger. "Is something wrong? What has Yorkshire been doing to you, Edith?"

I let out a breath. What had Yorkshire been doing to me? Only breaking my heart a bit at a time.

"It *is* a little Gothic there at times," I admitted, smiling wanly. "London will do me good, I expect."

A less gothic setting than my grandfather's gilt and velvet city residence, which came with its own ballroom as well as two motor cars, would be hard to imagine.

"Never fear, I will make sure to wrap you up in cotton wool between the exhibitions," she assured, and then left me to take off my travelling things, inviting me to join her in the garden after.

As soon as she left the room, I sat on the bed and allowed the smile to fade. There were fine pictures and fresh flowers in the room, and a jar of biscuits by the bed. Perhaps here, in these soft surroundings, I might have a little time to adjust to the latest and most devastating way Yorkshire had tried to break my heart.

On my way to the garden, I passed by a door which was ajar. From it came cigar smoke and my grandfather's voice. Ought I to go in? Oddly, I could hear no answering voice. Was he speaking to himself?

"Yes—please make sure the invitation reaches him. Good-bye," came his decisive tones, and then a thump of something heavy set down. I hurried along to avoid anyone who might be leaving the room. I had reached the end of the passage when the same voice called my name softly. "Edith."

I turned to see Sir Joseph in the doorway.

"Welcome home," he said. I had forgotten the compelling timbre of his voice.

I opened my mouth to apologise for my hasty departure from Belle Mount, but he preempted me.

"I must make my apologies," he said. "I have a dinner engagement—important to the business, or nothing would take me from your side. You're not offended?"

"Of course not!"

He smiled. "Tomorrow, then," he promised, and stepped back into the room, while I joined Irene in the garden.

I ought to have felt relieved to postpone the conversation, but I didn't—it sat on me like a bad pudding. The time was drawing near when I must explain to my grandfather my connection with Sir William Penrith.

My plan to forget my romantic woes in palatial Piccadilly was ill-conceived. Watching Irene and David together felt like poking at a fresh bruise. And now, the conversation during our quiet dinner together had ranged to their idyllic wooing.

"David proposed to me in the Rothschilds' little Tea House, in the back garden just next door, with roses everywhere," Irene recalled. "It was perfect."

"I'm always amazed you could make anything out of that speech of mine at all. I thought I was going to faint," admitted David.

"And I tried so hard to make it easy for you! Nobody could have encouraged you more than I did—at least not within the bounds of propriety, and sometimes hardly then!"

"But it was asking a great deal of you, Irene, putting you in that position. And I knew it."

Irene laughed and changed the subject. But something had been touched on that was not a laughing matter—a bruise of her own, it seemed.

Later, when Irene bade me goodnight in the passage, I ventured to ask about it.

"What did my uncle mean?" I asked. "About the position he put you in?"

"Ah," she said, and something in her eyes became armoured. "Well, you see, my dear, I had to convert to marry David."

"You *had* to?"

"Yes." She smiled, but the smile did not reach her eyes. "Like your mother."

I hardly knew what to say.

"Shall I come in?"

I nodded. She took my hands and steered me to a settee, where we sat.

"Now, my dear, I do hope you will not judge me too severely."

"For following the dictates of your own conscience? I couldn't."

"I'm sure you couldn't! But, you see, it wasn't my conscience I was following, Edith. It was my heart. Perhaps you don't know yet what it is to really give one's heart away—so that one feels as if a part of you is missing. Or perhaps you do." She must have seen the look on my face. "I *was* afraid at first—leaving everything that was familiar, as far as religious customs...I confess it was hard. And there was so very much to learn, and I made so many stupid mistakes! But love carried me through it all, as I'm sure your mother's love for your father did. You have never seen, I think, a Hebrew wedding service?" I shook my head. "I hope you will—it is so beautiful!"

"I'm sure it is. I have found everything I have seen of the practise of the Hebrew faith to be very beautiful indeed." I was picking my words carefully, afraid of giving offence, but in this I was merely honest.

"As a bride, I walked in a circle about my husband seven times during the ceremony. It is an ancient tradition, and people give many origins for it, but the one I like best is that the bride revolves around her husband like the earth around the sun. He is her whole world."

I stared at her. Was that really how my mother had thought of marriage? Had she given up everything to revolve around my father?

"But you are tired from your journey. I will leave you now." She embraced me and went to the door, where she paused for a moment. "If you wish to speak of it tomorrow, then we shall—or not. As you wish, Edith."

Then she shut the door behind her. I let out a breath. I did not know what to think. Upon hearing Irene confess that she had once been a Christian, I had felt a jolt of betrayal.

Was that how the Belmontes felt when my mother left the faith of her childhood?

I had always believed that my mother had followed her own conscience when it came to changing her religion. That was something I could understand; something I could respect.

But laying down everything at the feet of a mere mortal? I felt resentful towards my father for accepting it. His marriage with my stepmother was nothing like that—they were equals, companions. One did not revolve around the other.

Then I thought of Irene and David, who seemed so happy together. Janushek had said Simon and I were *too good and serious* for things to be easy for us.

Perhaps if I'd been less serious I could have used his mother's deception to drive a wedge between them.

Perhaps if he'd been less good, he wouldn't have cared what was best for me.

Irene and David were blissfully happy together. It felt—suddenly—horribly unfair of them.

And after all, what did I really know of love?

Perhaps I was nothing but a clanging cymbal, after all.

I groped for my prayer book and remembered that I had given it to Una. Though I attempted to pray, I found no solace in it, and sleep escaped me.

The best thing would be to lose myself in a book for a bit, but I did not have one with me.

I determined to go down to the study to look for one. Not wishing to rouse anyone, I lit my way with a candle, shunning the house's plentiful electric lights.

Irene had assured me that the books in the study were not like those at Belle Mount. These books, at least, were provided for the purposes of *reading*.

I found the correct room—it was the one that smelt of cigars—and went in. I was perusing the shelves when I felt the air stir in the room, as if someone else occupied it besides me.

It sent a chill down my spine. I held the candle aloft. I could see no one, but there were several large wing-backed chairs in the room, with their backs turned to me.

"Reveal yourself!" I commanded, before a wave of fright could get the better of me. This was a wealthy household, with plenty to tempt a professional burglar.

There was a dreadful pause, then a masculine form unfolded from one of the chairs in an apologetic sort of way.

"I'm terribly sorry, Miss Worms. I didn't mean to frighten you," came a voice that was far more Oxfordian than I imagined a burglar's voice would be.

I quickly switched on the electric light. It revealed a familiar, good-looking man of about thirty with light brown hair. He wore a rumpled tie and an anxious expression.

"Oh! You're my grandfather's private secretary, aren't you?" I exclaimed. "I saw you at Belle Mount, didn't I?"

"Yes. I'm sorry I haven't had the pleasure of being introduced." He seemed as if he was the sort of person who was used to pleasing people. Hence the anxious expression.

"Do you live here?"

"Oh, no! I live in Brixton."

I raised my eyebrows. "In that case, do you mind me asking what you are doing hiding in a wing-backed chair in Piccadilly?"

"Very sensible of you to ask. Sir Joseph told me to meet him here tonight after he had dined, as he particularly wanted to look over some papers. He ended up needing me quite late, you see. And it's rather hard to get a hansom at this time of night, so I thought I would bunk down here. I'm to begin early in the morning, anyway."

"Surely the servants would have made you up a bed?" I asked in astonishment.

"The whole household was sound asleep by the time I decided not to go home. All except the scullery maid, to whom I bemoaned my fate, but she feared offending the housekeeper. And the footman I encountered was terrified of going near the linens for fear of what the butler would say."

I laughed. I could see rich households such as this would have their own troubles. "You might at least go and spend what's left of the night on a divan in the parlour," I pointed out, appalled at the thought of a grown man sleeping in an armchair.

He bowed. "I will do it for your peace of mind, Miss Worms, if for no other reason."

"Please do." It struck me that I did not know his name, but before I could ask it, it caught my eye that he was sheepishly slipping a book into a thin space on the shelves. The cover was an unmistakable, garish yellow. He caught my look. "I see I shall have to make a clean breast of it, after all. I was quite engrossed, and lost track of the time. I sniffed out my candle when I heard you coming so I wouldn't cause alarm." He slid the book back out and handed it to me, with something of the air of a guilty schoolboy.

"Gracious!" I exclaimed. It *was* a penny-dreadful: my latest novel. A spark of mischief ignited within me. "Shall I spare you the agony and tell you who did it?"

"Please don't! In this case I'd prefer to prolong the agony. The book is far too short as it is."

"Flattery, at this hour?" I squinted at him. "I don't suppose you were picking the lock on the safe, or something like that?"

"Oh, no. It would be quite absurd to attempt to pick the lock when I am in full possession of the combination."

I laughed. "Well, then. Goodnight."

"Miss Worms?"

"Yes?"

"Do *you* require assistance of any kind?"

"Oh! Not at all. I couldn't sleep and came down for a book. But I think I shall go to sleep now."

He bowed again—a small, secretarial bow. "I'm delighted to have been of service."

I went up to bed laughing softly to myself. The ridiculous encounter had lightened my mood, and I soon fell asleep.

CHAPTER TWENTY-ONE

On the next day, I went down to breakfast expecting to see my grandfather there.

I ran through possible explanations in my head for Penrith's enmity towards me.

Never mind sir, he merely tried to force me to marry his son because of the unique properties of my blood. Nothing out of the ordinary, you know.

Irene looked up from her cup of tea and read my expression.

"Sir Joseph never appears before lunch," she apologised.

"He must be very busy," I said.

"The war is keeping him even more so," David remarked, laying down his newspaper.

"Really?"

"We have business interests in Africa, you know."

"Oh. I'm sorry."

"Don't be," said David flatly. "At least, not on our account. War is good for business. Or so Father says."

It struck me how utterly opposite such a statement was to anything my own father had ever said about war.

"We're expected at Redfern's this afternoon, Edith," Irene reminded me as she poured me tea.

"I think I will be afraid to be seen there, in my shabby old clothes," I remarked, looking down at myself ruefully.

I had laid aside my mourning clothes, but my old clothes didn't seem to fit me as they had before. Dragon-keeping had exercised my body in ways that being a clergyman's daughter and secret novelist had not. And I was painfully conscious of the freckles that now bespeckled my nose from days on the moors. It really was trying to be the kind of person who freckled *in the rain*.

"Oh, no. You mustn't be. There's nothing a couturier likes so well as a true transformation!"

David looked at his wife. "Don't transform Edith too much. I like her the way she is. She's very...*her*." He looked at me uncertainly, as if he wasn't sure if he'd said something unpardonable.

I laughed. "Thank you, Uncle David!"

I wondered if Redfern's would feel the same when confronted with my calloused hands and freckled nose.

The door opened and my midnight burglar came in with an apologetic expression. "Excuse me, sir, but did the *Times* find its way in here somehow?"

This innocent question caused an unjustified amount of consternation in the room. David sprang up.

"Oh, here it is! Blast it—I've gone and opened it."

"Gracious, how on earth did it get to us first!" exclaimed Irene in dismay.

"I'm sorry, Tom. Can't think how it happened." David handed the offending newspaper to the secretary as if it were a viper he had nursed in his bosom.

"Never mind," he replied with a weak smile. "It must have been that new footman. I'll have a word with him." As he said this, he refolded the paper, smoothing out the pages painstakingly. Irene and David sat back down, and the tone in the room became genial again.

I must have been staring at this strange exchange, because the secretary looked up and caught my eye. There was a gleam in his, and for a moment I thought he would wink at me. But he merely nodded respectfully and withdrew with the controversial *Times* under his arm.

The breakfast was excellent, but my appetite was unusually poor. I was nervous and had not slept well. All I could think of were Simon and Cariad—when I wasn't worrying over my upcoming confrontation with Sir Joseph.

This would never do!

Before I could think better of it, I muttered something to Irene about getting a book to read, and a moment later I was tapping on the study door.

"Come in," called the secretary's voice.

I obeyed.

Sir Joseph appeared to be signing papers, while his secretary hovered at his elbow. A look of uncertainty crossed the secretary's face when he saw me. Sir Joseph looked up coldly, and I regretted my impulse to hasten the interview.

"Forgive me, I thought perhaps—"

"Of course, my dear, do come in and sit down," he said, putting down his pen. The secretary looked surprised. "Tom, leave us, please."

I sank into the chair closest to the desk as Tom made a quick exit.

My grandfather steepled his hands and gazed at me over them, waiting for me to begin.

"Sir, I don't know what you must have thought when I left Belle Mount so rudely."

"Don't you?" He considered me piercingly. "Then shall I tell you?"

I nodded.

"When you left Penrith—a man who is as notable for his wordiness as his arrogance—gasping for breath on my hearthrug after one word with you, this is what I thought: my granddaughter Edith is not a typical clergyman's daughter." I let out a choked laugh, but Sir Joseph did not smile. "She is, in fact, bone of my bone, and flesh of my flesh."

My breath caught. Once again, the revelation that he was pleased with me struck with a sharper joy than I could rationally justify.

"All the same," I stammered, "I thought you deserved an explanation."

"Do you want to give me one?"

"Well, to be honest, it's not a story I *enjoy* telling…"

"Then do not tell it. The older you get, Edith, the more you will understand this—" He leaned across the desk until, I, too leaned forward. "We all have secrets. And the more important things you do, the more secrets you have. They are valuable, Edith."

"You—you don't…mind?"

"That you have secrets? Not unless they threaten to hurt you. And if they ever do, well then, my dear…" He leaned back in his chair with a smile that clashed with the coolness in his eyes. "Then you must come to me. *And I will be sure to hurt them first.*"

Once at Irene's couturier, Redfern and Sons, I was made to stand on a plush stool and measured with gentle hands by two ladies with orchids pinned to their bosoms. Irene told me later that the attendants at Redfern's were distinguished by these expensive corsages. The tailor himself sat on a chair, scrutinised me with the utmost seriousness, and pointed a baton at the various parts of my person which were to be measured. He looked exactly like a conductor of an orchestra, who can't be expected to actually touch an instrument but directs the music nonetheless.

During this peculiar performance, my grandfather's parting promise was much on my mind.

What had he meant by it, exactly? Ought I to take it quite literally? Or was it merely an assurance of a normal level of grandfatherly loyalty and protection which I had simply never experienced?

I was released and Irene and the tailor put their heads together and murmured in hushed voices over drawings and fashion plates and fabric samples. Irene had begged me to give her the pleasure of choosing the stuff herself.

"It is unusual, Mrs Belmonte," the tailor murmured, "and the embroidery will be very difficult to achieve at the standard we demand. Most unusual."

"But not impossible," Irene finished.

"In Paris, it would be impossible."

"But this is not Paris, is it?" She smiled indefatigably at him. "And perhaps I will select my winter wardrobe in London this year, and not bother with Paris at all."

I slipped away from these baffling manoeuvres, finding a series of Redfern's newest fashion plates to look through. I was struck by a very smart-looking outfit consisting of bicycle bloomers and a fitted cardigan jacket that buttoned up the front. It was both useful and stylish, with neat lines that appealed to me. One of the orchid ladies was hovering nearby.

"Excuse me, I am quite taken by this design."

"Ah! Very popular with our more active clients."

"I—well, I have...an even more *unorthodox* conveyance...and I find I get chilled..."

An upraised hand stopped my explanation. "I have *just* the thing."

She took me into another room and drew back a curtain to reveal a most unusual outfit on a dress form. My mouth fell slightly open. I had never seen anything like it, and my feelings about it were anything but moderate.

"This was made for a lady—of course you appreciate I must be discreet about her identity—a very prominent lady, who has acquired the very newest machine for personal conveyance: a motored bicycle." She paused. "Of course, if this isn't suitable, we can certainly—"

"It's perfect," I interjected. "When can you have one ready for me?"

Once back in Piccadilly, the butler presented me with a calling card on a tray. I drew back my hand with a jolt when I saw the name:

DOCTOR NICHOLAS FARLEY.

"Hill," I said. "I'm not at home to this gentleman, at any time, ever. Do you understand?"

"Of course, miss."

Pulling off my gloves, I went up to my room with a pounding heart.

How did Farley know so much about my movements? Was I being followed? I ran to the window and peered anxiously down at the fog-dim street before I realised how irrational it was—Farley would be too clever to have Briggs follow me again.

For a moment, I had felt safe here. I shook myself. I *was* safe. Farley would not dare to do me violence in one of the wealthiest homes in London.

I will be sure to hurt them first.

The words brought a throb of relief. My grandfather would be more than equal to dealing with Farley.

Irene's maid, Claudette, had had my slate-grey dinner dress pressed, and she dressed my hair beautifully. I felt quite presentable until Irene rustled in. She wore a gown of persimmon damask with sleeves so puffed, they threatened to send her aloft if she were to step into a breeze. Diamonds glittered at her throat. Had I underestimated the occasion?

There was a discreet cough at the door.

"Sir Joseph asks if he may see you before dinner," Irene explained.

"Oh! Yes, of course."

Sir Joseph came in, in slimly tailored dinner attire, a diamond in his cravat, more distinguished than ever.

I really was letting everyone down.

"My dear, would you do me a great kindness?" He drew a jewellery case out of his jacket pocket. "I have here an heirloom of my wife's family. It would give me great pleasure if you would wear it this evening."

As he opened the case, I half-dreaded the glitter of some fabulous creation which would only show me up as the little rectory mouse I knew myself to be.

I didn't expect a dragon, coiled in a sinuous circle on the velvet within.

It had a long, serpentine body, exquisitely reticulated, so that when my grandfather lifted it out of the box, it curved on his hand as if alive—reminding me of Frances the moment she had hatched out of the fire.

Every detail—tiny gold fangs, green enamel scales, pearl eyes—was absolutely exquisite.

"*Oh*," I breathed.

He smiled in satisfaction. "Good." He gestured for me to turn, and I complied. He laid it round my neck while I watched in the glass. It lay on my skin with a pleasing coolness just above the collar bone, its head meeting its tail at the front, fastening to itself like the legendary ouroboros.

I no longer deplored the simplicity of my gown; it felt like the appropriate backdrop for such an ornament.

"The last time I brought this out, it was for my daughter to wear. I had intended to give it to her one day."

I turned round to face him, and as I did so I caught Irene, watching us.

"Shall we go down?" said Sir Joseph, offering me his arm. "I want to show off my granddaughter."

Irene's idea of a few friends for dinner turned out to comprise representatives from the Rothschild and Montefiore families, as well as many distinguished Gentiles, including a handful of peers of the realm and their wives, a bishop, the secretary of the Foreign Office, and a cabinet minister. Amidst this clutch of formidable strangers, I was delighted to see one familiar face: a serene white-haired lady who glowed with an inner light that rivalled the exquisite strand of pearls about her neck.

"Lady Battersea! How lovely to see you here!" I exclaimed.

"Miss Fairweather! Or am I to call you Miss Worms now?"

"Neither—you are to call me Edith," I answered.

I was taken in to dinner by the younger son of an earl. He seemed eager to please me, if rather inconsequential in his conversation.

I looked about for Sir Joseph's secretary. I had hoped he might make one of the party. However, as the Honourable Somebody-or-other next to me was very up to date on plays and operettas, we got on well enough.

The man seated on my other side turned out to be not just a Rothschild but an amateur naturalist. I felt immediately ashamed for all of my assumptions about bankers. I had just confessed my ignorance of high finance to him when somebody across the table teased him, saying, "Oh, Charles would far rather spend the day chasing butterflies than totting up figures in his father's office."

"Oh! You sound like my little brother," I said. "He has thoroughly terrorised the insect population of both the East Midlands and the Yorkshire Dales."

"You must bring him to visit us at Tring, Miss Worms. He can help my older brother catalogue his million moths."

"Million!" I gasped.

"Do tell Edith the story of Natty and the cassowaries,"chimed in Lady Battersea.

"My father is very occupied with business, you see, Miss Worms, and he does not always notice the extent of his sons' animal collections. My preferred species are rather small, thankfully, but my brother is more ambitious. He has a good many cassowaries in his menagerie, and for a time they were allowed to wander about the park freely. One day, my father was out riding when one of the creatures conceived a violent prejudice against him. This alarming giant bird from New Guinea, with its brilliant blue crest and savage mien, pursued him with frightening persistence. He managed to evade it, but only narrowly."

"Are they dangerous?" I asked.

"I'm afraid they are possessed of a truly murderous claw on each foot, no less than five inches in length. Since that time, I assure you their movements have been restricted. When you come to visit, you need have no fear." He smiled at me.

Feeling a sudden comradeship, I wished that I could confess my own role in the preservation and study of rare animals.

"I, myself, have an interest in the fauna of Yorkshire. I do hope I will be able to take you up on your invitation one day, Mr Rothschild."

The brassy voice of the cabinet minister seated near my grandfather now intruded upon our attention.

"The war will be over quickly. Buller will see to that. Our men are better trained and better armed, not to mention better bred!" he said. "It was madness of them not to accept our terms when they had the chance."

"All the better," my grandfather pronounced coolly. "When next we set the terms, they will be more favourable to us."

"And Her Majesty will add another province to her beneficent rule," someone said, and a few of the men chuckled approvingly.

"Do you think the war is morally justifiable?" I asked my dinner companion.

"Oh, justification can always be found for gold!" he said with a chuckle. "Those who are not blessed with the Midas touch by their race have to find it by some other means, you know."

So it was here, too, even among all this finery—that little syllable, unspoken yet still heard: *Jew*.

There was something in the way he glanced up the table at my grandfather—as if he was convinced that if the world was put right, their positions would be reversed.

"Midas was sorry about it in the end, after it afflicted his family," I replied. I didn't like his tone, and it occurred to me that the younger son of an earl might well be on the hunt for an heiress. "But I have never been turned into gold, nor do I ever expect to be."

"An affliction some of us would be only too happy to suffer!" He sipped his wine and gave a little grunt of appreciation. "Some men have *all* the luck, eh?"

All of a sudden, I missed Simon terribly.

Irene suggested that we withdraw and leave the war to the gentlemen. David's eyes flickered to Irene's with a momentary panic, soon replaced by the glassy dullness that his face had worn throughout the dinner so far.

In the drawing room, Irene beckoned me into the cluster of ladies talking about literature, where I felt myself on solid ground, but they moved onto other subjects of less interest to me—someone called Podge (who turned out to be the speaker's husband) had bought a motoring outfit for someone called Alphonse (who turned out to be a lapdog). The conversation darted between German, French, and English without batting an eyelid. I lost the thread and gave up.

Lady Battersea, seeing me grow quiet, came and sat with me.

"We are a feminine Tower of Babel, are we not, Miss Worms?"

"My father would love it. But why have I not heard any of the Jewish language your ladies in the East End spoke together?"

"Ah, but your family is Sephardic, my dear." At my blank look, she expanded: "My family—Charles's and mine—is from

Frankfurt. Yours is from Southern Europe. They escaped the Inquisition and came to England—oh, at least a hundred years before mine. So you have the advantage of me, you see."

"Is there much difference?"

"The practise of our religion differs on small points. And you Sephardim have a beautiful language of your own—a language of love and poetry, though it is not much used in England."

"But why?"

"The old Hebrew families of England do not choose to distinguish themselves in quite that way."

"I have so much to learn," I admitted.

"But you *wish* to learn, my dear. To say *I don't know* is always the beginning of learning." She looked me over, a sharper edge to her gaze than I had seen before. "You might be an excellent influence on your grandfather, if I'm not mistaken."

"I? What influence does he require?"

"Sir Joseph is of the old order—the ones who don't approve of my work with our brethren in the slums."

"Why ever not?"

"The old order made a great many sacrifices to establish their place in this country. And now they turn round and find a hundred thousand Ashkenazi on their doorstep!"

"Like a horde of disreputable cousins?" I suggested. I certainly could not imagine Sir Joseph welcoming Janushek and Hanna into his bosom.

"Exactly so," she answered with a tight smile. "What *will* dear Mother England think of them?" She lowered her voice a little.

"And while we are speaking of my work, I want you to know I did as you asked. I had Farley's name removed from all my charities after what you told me."

"How did he react?"

"I've no idea! He simply vanished from society. I haven't heard anything of him."

I was relieved to hear that Farley had not clawed his way back into any corridors of power, after all. "You said once that you knew my mother. Did you know her well?"

She patted my hand gently. "Enough to know that she would have exerted the kind of influence I hope you will on this family, had she chosen to stay in it."

As I could not imagine how I could hope to influence my grandfather more than my mother had, the remark confused me a little.

We chatted about her reform work until a footman approached me, murmuring that my grandfather wished to see me in his study. I was most surprised at this, as I had understood my grandfather to be enjoying his brandy with the gentlemen in the dining room.

Nevertheless, I excused myself and went into the study. The room appeared empty; there was no fire in the grate and the room had grown cold.

I turned to leave and saw a face I had hoped never to see again. Blocking my way to the door was a tall, dark-clad man with a ghostly face, cold green eyes, and bright copper hair.

I backed away from him. "Where is my grandfather?" I demanded.

"I would apologise for the deception," said Doctor Nicholas Farley, "but you don't mind a little deception, do you? You like things to be...exciting."

The desk now impeded my backwards progress. I glanced behind me for a weapon—I would feel much more comfortable with a nice sharp letter opener in my hand—but he closed the space between us in a heartbeat and put one hand over my mouth and the other on my bare shoulder.

"I won't hurt you—not now. I'm here to frighten you." He bent to speak in my ear. The inhuman calmness of his voice reminded me of the laboratory and paralysed me for an instant—just as he had paralysed me once with an antipodean poison. "You came to my laboratory and destroyed my work. Give me what I want. Or I will come and take it. And perhaps I'll destroy something you care about, just to even the score. And it will be a great deal more than merely exciting, I assure you."

There was a noise at the door behind him, and his grip on me released. I darted away and put a chair between us.

"Farley, what the devil is going on here?" my grandfather demanded, in a voice that was even more terrible than Farley's.

"Sir Joseph, I came to see you about an important matter."

"The important matter of insulting my only granddaughter?" He pointed at the door. "Get out of here!"

Farley blinked, then made for the door. Sir Joseph stopped him on the threshold with a gentle voice that was somehow more terrible than his ferocity.

"Farley?" Farley stopped instantly. It was most gratifying to see him being ordered about for a change. "Don't let me see your face here again."

Farley left swiftly without another word.

Sir Joseph stretched out his arms to me, and I went to them instantly, as a child might. He had never embraced me before. He smelled of cigar smoke and eau de cologne and the clean starch of his crisp collar.

"Did he hurt you?"

I shook my head against his immaculate shirt front, rumpling my coiffure.

"What made you come to the study, Edith?"

"A footman said you wanted me."

"I'll dismiss him immediately."

"Perhaps it was just a mistake."

"One which will not be tolerated. How *dare* Farley insult you like that, right here in my house! What did that guttersnipe want? Or perhaps it was obvious..."

"Oh, it was nothing like that!" I flushed, then made myself look up at him. "It's only that I've made a lot of enemies, Grandfather," I confessed.

"I have a few of those myself," he said drily. He looked at me with his penetrating gaze and spoke very softly. "I can protect you, Edith. Will you let me? No one ever has to hurt you again."

To my own surprise, I burst into tears.

Chapter Twenty-Two

I had a strange dream that night. There was water—lots of water—but then it disappeared and in its place was a desolation of mud flats. The mud, for some reason, filled me with horror. It stretched as far as the eye could see. It smelled of death. There was no reason why a vista of mud should inspire so much dread as that which filled my sleeping breast.

Waking, I found it hard to shake the lingering feeling of warning. It must have been Farley's startling appearance that had made me feel this way.

But there was something very strange about the encounter. If he really planned revenge, why warn me about it? It made no sense, unless he was bluffing and merely wished to frighten me. I had to acknowledge that if that was his aim, he had succeeded.

I shuddered as I remembered how close he had come to me. His sudden appearance in a place I had felt safe had quite unnerved me. When he spoke in my ear, his breath had touched my neck—the very place where his greed for my blood had left a mark.

And it had almost killed both of us.

A breakfast tray arrived for me, and with it, a letter from Violet.

Dear Cousin Edith,

I have tried provoking Simon to pine but I have failed. He just looked at me very ~~solemly~~ solemnly when I spoke of your letter from London, and did not go into a jealous rage when I told him that you had many ~~bows beaus~~ beaux at your feet there. (I know that was not <u>strictly true</u> *but there is a poet who said all is fair in love and war, Aunt Emily told us so.) So I don't think he wants to marry you after all.*

You should come back and take Janushek before it is <u>too late</u>*. He is mooning after Lily now. I don't think she likes it, but she may weaken if much time passes, because she has no oth-er ~~prospecks~~ prospects here.*

I thought you ought to know.

We have put G.S. back into the river as he was becoming very troublesome to all. Una did not cry, and Pip made her a portrait of G.S. to remember him by. She decided to let him go, I did not make her.

Your Devoted Cousin

Violet

P.S. Aunt Emily does not know I am writing. I will ask Janushek to post this.

P.P.S. I will not tell Janushek what I wrote in it.

I laughed over the letter, but it hurt a little all the same. I missed Ormdale already, even though it had done its best to break my heart.

London was not the refuge I had hoped.

Irene came in as I finished my breakfast.

"How is your headache?" she asked.

That was how my grandfather had explained my disappearance from the party.

"I feel much better," I reassured her. "I'm sorry I spoiled your evening."

"Oh! But you didn't! Everyone was delighted with you. The Honourable Roland is ready to propose marriage, but really—you can do better. And Connie is convinced you are exactly what this family needs. I don't disagree! I must say, *that* doesn't look as if it would help you sleep."

My hand followed her eyes to the scaly necklace around my neck.

"How odd! I hadn't realised I had it still. What am I to do with it?"

"I'll get Tom to put it in the safe when I see him. Do you have plans for the day?"

"Yes. I'm visiting my cousin, in the City."

"Oh, as it is Monday, you might take the motor with David. He goes to synagogue in the City on Mondays, for the Torah reading."

"And Sir Joseph?"

She shook her head. "Sir Joseph retains his customary habits. David has become more devout over the years. It's been so good for him. It steadies him. Oh, Sir Joseph has asked to see you this morning, as soon as you feel enough recovered."

We parted. I was relieved to not be going alone to see Gwendolyn—the encounter with Farley had shaken me. After I dressed for the day, I went down to find Sir Joseph. A footman (not the one who had erred last night—he had disappeared, never to be seen again) directed me to the garden.

I felt a little shy approaching him after I had gone to pieces all over him last night. But then I remembered how he had stroked my hair, and knew he hadn't minded.

I found him pacing in the arbour. I'd never seen him pace before.

"Good morning, Grandfather."

"Your mother never lived in this house," he said, rather abruptly. "But if she had, she would have loved this spot." He turned away from me. "It must seem strange to you that I do not speak of her. Our family used to be very happy. It has never been the same since she left." He turned, his face strangely soft. "Edith, I want to give you what would have been hers."

I stared. "Sir, I don't understand."

"Your mother's inheritance."

My hand went to the necklace which I still wore. He waved his hand.

"That? A mere bauble. I would give you so much more. I want you to take your rightful place, as my granddaughter."

I bowed my head. "I am deeply honoured to be acknowledged as your granddaughter."

He held up a hand in refusal. "Not just that. I want to make it official."

This startled me. "Official?"

"I am a man of business, Edith. I've had my lawyer draw up a document. I want to bequeath Miriam's inheritance to you." He took my hand and pressed it between his. "Humour an old man who is afraid of losing you as he did her mother before her."

"I don't know what to say."

"Say you will accept. I will send my secretary to you with the papers. Please forgive my haste, but seeing that man touch you last night... No one will dare to treat you that way when you are mine, Edith." He kissed my forehead. "I will leave you now."

I sat down on the garden seat, whirling with new thoughts and questions. I was amazed by the feelings of security and significance that my grandfather's words inspired, but I was bewildered by the idea of being made some kind of heiress, and what responsibilities that might entail.

None of it seemed real.

"Did he ask you?" Irene's voice startled me. Dressed in a light gown of muslin instead of her usual silk, she had appeared noiselessly just outside the arbour. Had she been there all along?

"Yes."

"I wondered if he would have the courage."

"Courage?"

"Sir Joseph is so different with you. More uncertain than I've ever seen him."

"Really?"

What had Lady Battersea said—that I would be a good influence on him?

"And David was so at ease with you from the first. We're so fond of you, Edith," she said, in a little rush. "Having someone younger about the house—it makes everything feel so hopeful. And you do like us a little, don't you?"

"Of course I do!" I struggled to clear my head. "But I have a life in Yorkshire, Aunt Irene, and obligations to fulfill. People I care about. People who need me."

Surprisingly, I thought first of Una.

"I rather think," said Irene slowly, "that Sir Joseph would try to ease the loss. Where he makes a request, he also grants. If there's anything your people in Yorkshire need—I'm sorry, it's *so* hard to speak of without being crass and commercial."

"Never mind that, Irene, I've a crass and commercial mind myself," I said with a rueful laugh. I had come to believe that Ormdale no longer needed me—but what *did* they need? "Of course I'll think it all over very carefully. How could I not?"

"I suspect Sir Joseph is uncertain with you because he can see you don't want anything from him," reflected Irene. "I don't think he's used to that. From anyone."

Was she right? Did I want something from Sir Joseph, in my heart of hearts? Had I come here because I wanted something from the Belmontes? It was an unpleasant thought.

Irene took a quick breath and stepped closer to me. "I promised myself I wouldn't say this, but—please—*do* say yes. I think things would be better...I think David and I..." She cut herself off, playing with her bracelet. I had never seen her like this. She was out of kilter, like a clock that hasn't been wound up properly.

"Is there something wrong, Irene? Please, do be frank with me."

"Nothing wrong, exactly. But I always thought that there would be...if we were to have children...that we might set up our own household—that Sir Joseph would recognise David as a grown man at last. But it wasn't to be." Her eyes glinted with tears. "Did I tell you, David even went to the Holy Land, and prayed at Rachel's Tomb for the blessing of children?"

"I'm sorry," I said quietly.

"Yes. We all are. Belle Mount hasn't seen a child in its corridors for more than twenty years." She shook herself. "You must have time to think. I shall leave you."

She hurried out of the garden.

What had I come for? I hadn't come looking for an inheritance, of that I was certain. At first, I'd come for answers about my mother. But this time? Had I come back to them only for a dress?

I already had family, friends, and financial independence as well. I didn't *need* the Belmontes. I could live without them. I had lived happily in Ormdale, unaware of their existence.

But I wanted them. *You are bone of my bone,* my grandfather had said, and something in me, some string tuned to the same temper, felt and acknowledged it.

I had been happy back in our East Midlands rectory, avoiding parish busybodies and feverishly writing every chance I got. I had not needed Frances when she tumbled out of the fire and opened my heart to Ormdale and all its creatures, but now I wanted her—and Gwendolyn, and every one of the friends I had made since then.

That first tentative unfolding of my heart to another creature had changed me, and I was changing still.

Perhaps this time in London was another confusing chrysalis from which I would emerge with new and startling colours.

Gwendolyn! Today was to be my day to visit her. I checked my watch and found it was almost time to leave with my uncle.

I went upstairs to my room and put on my hat and gloves. I opened the door and went down the passage to find Sir Joseph's secretary lying discreetly in wait for me. He gave a gentle cough.

"Pardon me, Miss Worms, but I've come for the necklace. It's to go back in the safe."

"Oh, I forgot again!" I fumbled with it, but I couldn't see the clasp and I was worried about damaging the delicate teeth that made the connection, especially with my gloves on. "I'm afraid it doesn't seem to want to let go of me," I admitted.

"Quite understandable," he said smoothly. "Allow me?"

He set the document and jewellery cases he was carrying down. I averted my eyes so I wasn't staring into his as he un-clasped the serpent's teeth with careful hands.

I suddenly wished I had an engagement ring to warn this young man off. Then I remembered with a wave of despair that I had no right to an engagement ring.

Oh, Simon.

"I still don't know your name," I admitted to the secretary, groping for a polite remark to make to him.

Having now unloosed me, he stepped back, and the serpent slid easily into my hand.

"Oh!" He opened the jewellery case. "It's Barrington."

It slipped through my fingers to the floor. We both made a dive for it where it glittered on the carpet, and there was an awkward moment where we scrambled about, bumping into each other.

"Sorry," I mumbled.

"No harm done," he declared cheerily as he snapped the case shut. "I see you're going out? I'll bring these papers for you later, then."

He tucked the document case under his arm casually. Some-thing about the way he did it made me very certain that there was nothing casual about them at all.

I forced myself to smile even as my heart hammered in my chest.

"Thank you," I said, and went quickly down to the waiting motorcar.

Barrington.

The name of the man who was the next link in the chain that led to Ormdale's shadowy nemesis. I told myself that Barrington wasn't an unusual name. Cousin Stephen had said he knew at least three gentlemen of that name.

Let it not be him! I thought desperately.

But it was like hearing a footstep in one's bedroom at night. If I hid under the counterpane, I'd never sleep again.

But I could not say what might be more terrible: the darkness, or whatever the light would reveal.

Chapter Twenty-Three

Gwendolyn was overjoyed to see me and did not seem to notice my subdued spirits.

"Oh, Edith! What a dream it is to see you! You can't think how many times I've imagined you visiting me here!"

Gwendolyn beamed as she bustled about setting up the tea things on an alarmingly small table. If one of us sneezed, all would be lost.

Her lodgings at Coburg Square were just as cramped as I remembered. This time there were signs of her personality, mostly suffrage posters, and an anatomical diagram which I avoided looking at too closely. Back at the abbey, her room had seemed like a nun's cell, apart from her collection of Inspector Green novels. I was oddly vexed to find them not here.

"I got a high distinction on a test yesterday. Millicent says I've become a swot. Do you know that's a sort of affectionate insult, and means I do nothing but study? As if there were anything I preferred to do! Such glorious leisure!"

There was a knock at the door and a young woman's head poked in.

"You on for tonight, Gwen? Oh, sorry," she added when she noticed me. "Only remember, it's at the vegetarian restaurant this time."

"Yes! See you there, Ivy." The head disappeared. "Anyway, I still wake up every day and can't believe my luck. I don't have to do *anything* but *study*! Can you imagine?"

Another cursory tap and another head poked in.

"Gwen, don't forget about the meeting. Oh—sorry to disturb you—only we've changed the place—it's at—"

"The vegetarian restaurant," the three of us finished together.

"Sorry," said Gwendolyn, as the second visitor retreated.

"Well," I said drily. "It seems you do get up to *something* other than study. I don't suppose you all study en masse at this establishment?"

"One has to eat occasionally," defended Gwendolyn.

"Yes—but does one have to eat *vegetables*?"

Gwendolyn went slightly pink. "It's a meeting about suffrage. The vegetarians have been very friendly to us."

"I suppose they are hoping you'll extend the franchise to livestock." I winced at myself. The words grated horribly on my ear. "I'm sorry. That was ghastly. I'm out of sorts today. I had a shock."

"You?" she asked incredulously. "Had a shock?"

"And what is that supposed to mean?"

"Edith, all the things I've seen you go through, and you never so much as turn a hair! What on earth have the Belmontes been getting up to in Piccadilly?"

I paused, reluctant to speak of this painful new suspicion. I decided to work up to it. "Farley appeared last night."

"What!"

"Sir Joseph threw him out—rather beautifully—but it frightened me," I admitted.

"That must have been horrid. I'm so sorry you had to see him again, after what he did to you."

"Yes. Well. And it's not just that. My grandfather wants to give me something."

Gwendolyn's eyes narrowed. "What sort of something?"

"My mother's inheritance. I haven't the least idea what it comprises."

"Will you say no?"

"Can one say no to such a thing?"

"I suppose one can say no to anything one doesn't want or need. Unless one feels *obligated*."

She said the word as if obligation were the worst thing that could happen to one. How to explain why I felt it so hard to refuse? Her eyes searched me.

"I don't want to hurt him," I said at last.

"Ah. You *do* feel obligated."

"He lost his wife and his daughter. He doesn't want to lose me, too. I wish you'd seen him with Farley. He was very protective."

"Protective? Yes, men can be very protective of things they consider their belongings."

"Gwen! Why would you say that?"

"It wouldn't be very surprising if he thought he could have anything he wants," she said simply, "he is tremendously rich and powerful, Edith."

"And Jewish—don't forget that—so I suppose what everyone says is right and he can't have any real feeling, can he?" I said bitterly. I certainly could not tell her about Barrington now.

"No!" Gwendolyn set her teacup down in dismay. "That's not what I meant at all!"

"The Belmontes are humans, Gwen, just like us, just like anyone else, even if they are rich."

"Of course they are! That's just what makes me wary."

"What do you mean?"

"Well, your mother left a position of privilege for one of obscurity. A woman has to have a very good reason to do that. What were her reasons?"

"She was in love with my father!" I objected.

"Yes, I'm sure. But was that all?" She took a deep breath. "Have you seen anything peculiar?"

"Peculiar? Nothing to compare with wyverns in the wine cellar," I retorted. "Really, Gwendolyn, people in glass houses, you know!"

"Edith, I know you think you're terribly worldly-wise, but you haven't known what it's like to live in the kind of family where—where every word must be carefully chosen. Where every step could spring a trap. Where shackles creep up around you so slowly, you don't see them until it's too late." Gwendolyn shuddered. "Heaven knows, I'm glad you don't. But be careful. Watch out for anything that doesn't feel right. And for heaven's sake, don't make any hasty decisions."

"I won't. His secretary has some papers he wants me to sign, but—"

"You mustn't sign them without reading them very closely. Perhaps we ought to have Millicent look at them—she's terribly good with financial things—or Ivy! She's studying law, you know, though of course they won't let her actually practise—"

I cut her off. "No, I'll read them myself. I may not be as *worldly-wise* as Millicent, but I'm quite—"

There was another tap at the door.

"We already know it's at the vegetarian restaurant!" I snapped, almost wild at being interrupted again.

The door opened and Miss Rivers looked in.

"I was only popping my head in to see if you needed sugar," she said mildly. "Good afternoon, Miss Worms."

"I think we have sufficient sugar, Milly," Gwendolyn said, and Miss Rivers disappeared like the others.

Milly. Once again, that bitter stab of jealousy. I'd wanted an intimate chat with my cousin—the kind we'd been used to during months of living together with almost no one else to speak to—and instead I found Gwendolyn positively besieged by friends.

Gwendolyn poured a fresh cup of tea. "Edith, I see this is not a very good time to tell you—but I don't know if I can make it to your soirée."

I gulped it too quickly and the tea burned my throat. "Another meeting?"

"No, an early lecture the following morning. It's rather important, or I wouldn't dream of missing it."

"Of course," I replied stiffly. "Please don't feel obliged to attend."

We persisted for half an hour but both of us were now trying too hard. I was relieved to have the excuse of meeting my uncle.

When she embraced me at parting, I dropped my guard and clung to her for a moment.

"Gwen!" I said impulsively. "You will come home for Christmas, won't you?"

"Christmas? Of course," she said with an unconvincing smile. "Where else would I go?"

This did not reassure me.

Once back at Piccadilly, the butler, Hill, intercepted me trying to slink upstairs. "Sir Joseph is waiting for you, Miss Worms."

I glared at him. The study door was ajar, and Sir Joseph appeared instantly at it upon hearing Hill's voice.

"Ah! Here you are at last. What have you been doing all day?"

I turned reluctantly to him. "I went to visit my cousin, sir."

He waved his hand. I realised that he had never shown even the barest interest in my other relations. It was as if they did not exist for him. They would not be brought into orbit. But after this afternoon, I could not imagine Gwendolyn and her suffragist cohort orbiting Sir Joseph, even for a single visit.

"I have something here for you." Reluctantly, I followed him into the study, where he indicated a large, flat package on his desk. I tore the wrapping to reveal a slash of startling aquamarine. Inside was the lake painting he had shown me at Belle Mount.

"I had it reframed for you."

The new frame was elegant but featureless.

The dragons were quite gone.

"Thank you," I said, hiding my regret. How long had the old frame been in the family, and how much longer might it have survived had I not foolishly commented on the picture?

"Barrington says he tried to give you the papers this morning."

"Yes, sir, he did. I have not had leisure yet to peruse them, I am afraid."

"Pshaw! A signature will suffice."

"Is it your custom, sir, to affix your signature to papers without reading them?" I asked quietly. "It is not mine."

He blinked. For a moment, I thought he might be angered, but then he laughed shortly and crossed his arms in front of him.

"Didn't I say you were every inch a Belmonte?"

"I seem to remember that you did pay me that compliment."

He leaned back on his desk and considered me for a moment, his eyes bright and cold. "Tell me what you want done with Penrith."

"I beg your pardon?"

"Penrith. One of your extensive collection of enemies. What do you want done to him?"

"I'm afraid I still don't see—"

"I collect secrets, Edith." This brought me up short. "I collect them until the time is right. I have plenty of Penrith's, all lined up and waiting, in a safe place. I could use one of them to ruin him tomorrow."

I inhaled sharply. "Ruin him?"

He nodded. "Circumstances have so arranged themselves that, financially, the man is entirely in my hands." He held out his hands, palms upward, representing a scale. "A feather's weight would do it, Edith."

The power of life and death is in the tongue, King Solomon had said. Perhaps King Solomon had been a little like my grandfather.

"Well?" he prodded.

"To ruin a man—how could it be right?" I stalled.

"Is the man a villain?"

"Yes."

"Does he presently occupy a position of power?"

"Yes."

"Would it not be right to remove him from that position?"

"I think it would be. Yes. But, sir, why should I be the one who orders the *coup de grâce*?"

He let out a breath of air—almost a laugh, but not quite.

"Shall I tell you why?"

I nodded.

"Because, my dear, I wish to do you a favour. A very great favour."

A moment passed in which we held each other's gaze and the clock measured out the seconds. I thought for some reason of the silent clocks at Drake Hall.

Love doesn't think so much of what is owed, I had told Simon.

Perhaps because love had always been free for me, I had never before understood why anyone would pay for it.

"I see," I managed to reply at last. I stood up slowly. "Please give me some time to think about it. It's a serious thing. In the meantime, I'll read the papers."

I stretched out my hand to him. For a moment, nothing happened.

Then he smiled in a grandfatherly sort of way. "Not tonight, Edith. You are tired from your visit. I'll send my secretary to you tomorrow."

I thought of objecting, but I *was* tired. "I'll go up now, then, and see you this evening."

"I'm afraid I've been called away unexpectedly. A business matter in Zurich. I'll take the late train tonight and be back in a few days."

"I pray you travel safely."

He kissed me lightly on the forehead, and I was already out of the door when his voice came after me quietly. "I'll give you until the soirée, Edith. To consider my offer."

To which offer did he refer? The ruination of Penrith, or the inheritance? But before I could ask, he had shut his door.

Once in my room, I sat on the bed, taking stock of my position. The room no longer felt like a gentle refuge—it was beginning to feel like a room besieged.

I must settle the matter of Barrington at once. It was unbearable to be in this state of uncertainty. I must with all haste confirm his identity by taking a look at his handwriting. And if he was the same Barrington who had hired Rivers, I would have to question him.

I sensed that Sir Joseph would not care for his private secretary to meet privately with his granddaughter and prospective heiress. But I had an idea that Barrington was ambitious, and he liked me—I could be sure of that. I must accomplish this quickly, while my grandfather was in Switzerland.

A shiver went through me at the coolness of my own calculations.

You are bone of my bone.

I'd always thought myself substantially my father's daughter. But the Reverend George Worms would not slip as naturally as I had into such intrigues.

As I sat at the writing desk in my room, I was amazed at my own composure. I was attempting to arrange a clandestine meeting with a young man I had just become acquainted with. Silently, I apologised to Simon.

I could remain in the dark no longer. I wrote the note with a firm hand.

Mr Barrington,

I have something to communicate to you, the nature of which necessitates the strictest confidence.

I hope I am not mistaken in believing that I can trust in your discretion.

EW

I was worried that Barrington might disappear since my grandfather was gone, so I hung about the next day, keeping my ear out for his voice. I daren't trust the note to one of the servants.

I was beginning to worry that all of my intriguing would come to nothing when Barrington entered the parlour the next afternoon to discuss some social engagements with Irene. I slipped out of the room and stepped behind a decorative urn in the dim passage to wait for him.

"Good day, Mrs Belmonte," came his light voice, and I heard the door shut behind him and footsteps as he approached.

My heart was pounding. I had bearded a quetzalcoatl in his den, but that was nothing to ambushing an attractive young man with the aim of forcing him into a clandestine correspondence.

I stepped into his path.

"Oh, I'm terribly sorry, Miss Worms!"

The apology was quite gratuitous, for how could it be his fault if young ladies sprang on him from behind the *objets d'arts*?

Not daring to look him in the eye, I crumpled the note into his hand, whispering, "Please do me the goodness to read this."

At that moment I heard footsteps and glimpsed the butler, Hill, over Barrington's shoulder. Was I imagining things, or did his glassy gaze grow suddenly sharp?

Barrington's face, meanwhile, was absolutely calm.

"Certainly, Miss Worms," Barrington said, a trifle loudly, erasing all vestiges of a tête-à-tête between us. "I shall be happy to check on this title at Hatchards. I'll be passing by there later today. And I'll have the papers ready to sign after your fitting this afternoon."

With a polite smile, he put the note in his pocket and went on his way down the passage. Hill had disappeared.

But I was not yet finished with my sneaking.

I had the impression Barrington had been instructed to positively stand over me while I signed those papers, and not to let me look at them alone, and that did not suit me at all.

While Irene was resting in the afternoon, I crept down in my stocking feet to infiltrate my grandfather's study.

As I put my hand on the doorknob, I almost hoped it would be locked. But the door opened, and as I stepped inside, the smell of cigars and eau de cologne brought back sharply the moment my grandfather had held me and stroked my hair.

The document case lay before me on the desk. I had only to remove the documents and slip away.

What had David said? That he needed books of information because he couldn't understand what novels were trying to say? Was my head so stuffed with wild scenarios that I saw deception and intrigue behind every wingback chair?

The loud tinkling of a bell close at hand shocked me nearly out of my wits—had I activated some kind of mechanical burglar alarm? It seemed to be coming from the desk drawer!

I opened the drawer to investigate, but as I did so, my eyes fell on the source: a gleaming steel and black skeleton on the desktop.

At first I thought I would let the telephone ring out, having little idea of what to do with the thing, but the sound might draw the attention of a servant.

I picked up the part that detached, fumbling with the cable. All the while I could hear a distant crackling punctuated with an insistent voice repeating a phrase I could not make out. At last, I realised which part corresponded to my ear and which to my mouth.

"Hello? I do beg your pardon..."

A voice spoke in German in my ear. This was a different voice than what I presumed had been the telephone operator a moment before. For a moment, I couldn't make out the words.

"I'm terribly sorry," I whispered into the thing, "I oughtn't to have picked it up at all—"

"Tell Herr Marzano the doctor here in Zurich says it was a false alarm. There is no need for him to come. All is well."

In Zurich! Was I really hearing these words through an underwater cable? "I'm terribly sorry, sir, but I think that you have been connected to the wrong line..." Heavens, how unnerving to speak to someone without seeing his face! How did people behave in such a situation?

The voice ignored my feeble attempts to communicate, repeated the same message in German, and then rang off. I have no idea whether the speaker heard me at all.

Flustered, I replaced the telephone receiver with care.

At that moment my eyes fell on something in the drawer I had pulled open.

It was a press clipping—a pile of them, in fact—mostly in Italian. There were photographs with them, of the same defiled landscape I had seen in my dream. Again, I was filled with an overpowering sense of desolation. I picked up a clipping. It showed a curious fossilised creature uncovered by the draining of the lake.

Could this be another clue to the dragon-linked heritage of my mother's family?

Then I glimpsed something that made a shiver run over me.

There was a tintype photograph, face down, further back in the drawer. It was the distinctive mark of the photographer's studio which had drawn my attention—because it was very familiar to me.

I turned it over. It showed a willowy young woman with a serious mouth and wide eyes. At first glance, she looked as harmless as a doe, but upon further inspection one might note a certain firmness about the jawline.

I knew this photograph, for my own copy of it was numbered among my dearest possessions. But the thing that chilled me was the other person in it: a fat baby in a floppy bonnet. It was me.

My grandfather had known about me, and he had lied to everyone about it.

I replaced it face down and shut the drawer

You didn't grow up in a family where shackles creep up around you so slowly you don't see them until it's too late.

But it wasn't too late.

I took the papers.

At my dress fitting that afternoon, Irene sat flipping through a magazine while I played the role of dressmaker's dummy. A breathtaking quantity of pale champagne silk was being painstakingly pinned and tucked into shape about me. At any other time, I would have been amazed at how quickly the thing came together, but today, my mind was racing with unanswered questions.

Why had my grandfather lied? It wasn't that I thought him incapable of suppressing a correspondence. I just couldn't understand his motive. He claimed to have longed to enfold me to his bosom, yet all my life he had been ignoring my existence.

"They have a man with brandy at the top of the mechanical staircase, in case anyone requires revivification," Irene said idly.

"Did you require it?" I asked, though I hadn't the least idea what she was talking about.

"At any rate, I felt it was *comme il faut.* And it was a very fine brandy. Come to Harrods with me and try it for yourself."

For a moment, I dallied with the idea. I hadn't actually told Stephen that I planned to visit him and Sylvia. They might not be home. And I dreaded to face it.

It had been on the tip of my tongue to agree, but instead I said, "It sounds lovely, but I'm afraid I must call on my cousins this afternoon."

"*More* cousins?" She looked up in surprise. "Is the metropolis full of your cousins?"

"Jammed. Do you like animals, Irene? Why don't you keep one as a pet?"

"Yes, I like them. Sir Joseph doesn't."

"Or footmen who make mistakes," I observed.

"Ah, well, he has very high standards for domestics. Fortunately, he also recompenses them at a higher rate than is usual, otherwise it would be quite impossible to keep the household properly staffed."

"What about his private secretary? Has he replaced him recently?"

"Oh, no! Tom's been with us for...it must be almost seven years, I suppose. Thank goodness! I don't know what we'd do without him."

"He's surprisingly charming for a secretary," I ventured noncommittally.

"He is, but I won't settle for less than a viscount for you, you know, my dear, and not for a few years, anyway."

"And if I prefer secretaries?"

"Then find another," she said with a dry laugh. "Or wait for a viscount with a secretarial air." There was a gentle warning in her voice now. "Tom knows where his bread is buttered, and it's certainly not anywhere near you, my dear."

"No butter at all?"

"None. Now, would you like me to drop you with your cousins before I go shopping?"

"No, I'll take an omnibus."

Irene raised her eyebrows but did not argue.

"Well, I'll see you this evening, then," said Irene.

Once Irene departed, the lady with the pins coughed delicately. "Miss Worms, the special ensemble you ordered, there are one or two adjustments. If you have time now...?"

"Yes, a little," I said. "And I was wondering—" I hesitated. "An acquaintance of mine, Mrs Cohen, mentioned having a motoring outfit made for her pet..."

"Ah, yes." She lowered her voice. "Redfern's does not accommodate such requests *officially*—as it is considered beneath their dignity. But one of the ladies here has been known to help with such accessories from time to time." She glanced over her shoulder, then handed me a card and a pencil. "Here—if you will write down the breed of your companion, please."

"Well, you see..." To what could I compare Frances?

"The animal is of indeterminate heritage?" she offered tactfully.

"Quite so."

"Then the dimensions, as near as possible?"

I had measured Frances for the ill-fated waistcoat, and happened to remember them. As I jotted them down, I thought that Redfern's might be Tailor to Her Majesty and consider domestic animals beneath their dignity, but the *couturier* had certainly never made an outfit for a creature so rare as my salamander.

Once released from Redfern's, I caught an omnibus in the direction of Bloomsbury. As I avoided a seat where an unspeakable mishap provoked by the motion of the vehicle had recently occurred, I realised that I felt disproportionately relieved to have escaped the new world of privilege I had lately inhabited. It was as if I had been in a very close and stuffy room without noticing it.

Watch out for anything that doesn't feel right. That's what Gwen had said.

What else, I wondered, had I completely failed to notice?

When I arrived at Brunswick Square, the scene of my summer adventures, the new housemaid took me out to Sylvia's tiny studio at the bottom of the strip of back garden. I was a little disappointed not to see the housemaid Lucy again, but it seemed that she had been so relieved at Michael's recovery that she had promptly married him and taken him away to open a shop somewhere far away from London.

"Edith! How delightful!" Sylvia was draped in a bespattered smock and had a dab of paint on her nose. Her hair was slipping out of its chignon, as usual. The effect was somehow charming. "The children are at school. It's a simply marvellous one—co-educational you know—I insisted upon it, though Stephen tried to talk me out of it. I won't have a son who thinks women are a different species. I may not be a natural mother, but even I can see all that was never a good idea! As for Stephen, I hardly see him anymore *at all,* since this hideous war began, so I can't tell you how *he* is."

"Oh," I said. "I was hoping Stephen could look at some legal papers for me. But if he's so busy—"

"I'm sure he'll do it for you, Edith. You know he has a soft spot for you. We'll go in and bother him in a moment. Where are you staying, while you are in London?" she asked as she put away her paints.

"With some relations of my mother's, the Belmontes."

She stopped cleaning her brushes for a moment. "How familiar that name is to me...it gave me quite a chill when you said it. I wonder..."

Bless Sylvia for not caring about society one whit!

"You probably heard it from my father once," I said. "Do tell me all about your latest series of paintings." I indicated the canvases propped all around the studio. Her eyes brightened.

Here, at last, was a subject she found engrossing. Sylvia was working on a series of landscapes based on plein air studies and sketches she had done years ago in Italy. I tried to listen to her, but my mind kept circling.

Sylvia was saying something about Italian aspects and light and the impossible colour of wisteria in April.

"Edith?"

"Yes?"

"You're not listening to a word I'm saying."

"Wisteria?" I hazarded. "I'm afraid that's rather more in Mother's line than mine. She really buries herself in the garden every time she comes to Yorkshire. I expect to find her coming out in leaves herself one of these days."

"Dear Emily—has she *finally* rebelled?"

"Rebelled!" I exclaimed.

"I've been predicting it for years—ask Stephen." Sylvia wiped her brushes briskly. "Nobody can go on being so good. It's not human. You see it now and then—they usually burst out and take up phrenology, or go up in a balloon. Perhaps for her it *will* be leaves."

"Well, she has been ordering a lot of seed packets," I reflected.

"Ah! You see?"

"What about you?"

"Me? Oh, I'm never going to burst out. I've never been as good as Emily, you see."

"And Crispin? How is he?"

"Poor old Crispy! Yes, he told me you were rather a dear to him in the summer. You must have thought it was too cruel of me to leave him. But he doesn't get on with the outdoors like Penny, and it's so trying for both of them. She swims like a fish, and gets as brown as a nut. Never has a chill or a cramp or a twisted ankle or anything—it's quite unfeeling of her, really. I was hoping Crispin and his father might—I don't know—form some sort of masculine alliance, with the females out of the house."

"Did they?"

"Who can say? Men are such mysterious, changeable creatures. Don't you think?"

"I thought they were the same species," I replied.

"Ah, but I went to a girls' school. So to me, they remain a mystery—as elusive as a creature of fairytale. Let's go find my own mysterious creature, shall we?"

"My own!" Sylvia shouted at Stephen's door, rattling the tea tray. For such an ethereal woman, she always made a shocking amount of noise. "You must stop bullying the Boers for half a minute. We have a visitor."

"Sylvia, I've told you—"

"There are *buns*."

There was a crucial pause. Sylvia elbowed me for a contribution.

"There will be no buns for you except on terms of the most abject surrender," I threatened.

Another pause and then the sound of Stephen padding over to the door. A key turned and it opened an injudicious crack. Sylvia pushed her way in with a crow of victory.

"Good heavens, it's the Lady Detective herself!" declared Stephen.

"Don't let him call you such things, Edith," Sylvia said, putting down the tea tray with a clatter. "Though it's nothing to what he calls me, I assure you, in the privacy of our own apartments—"

"My *love*!"

"But over such things a veil, as they say, is drawn."

"The veil might be a great deal thicker," Stephen protested.

I began to laugh helplessly, collapsing into a chair.

"Oh, help me," I murmured. Suddenly they were both looking at me fixedly, and I found I wasn't laughing anymore, but crying.

"Oh!" said Sylvia, looking from me to the plate of buns. "I see we are going to need more of these. I'll go for reinforcements."

She disappeared.

"I'm so sorry, Cousin Stephen," I said into my handkerchief. "I don't think I realised how my nerves have been weighed down until…"

"Until the two of us began larking about?"

I nodded.

"No, *I'm* sorry, Edith. Your father wrote to me and told me you were in London and that I should look out for you, which I plainly haven't done. Very stupid of me to assume that you would need no looking after in the lap of luxury in Piccadilly. Eat a bun."

I chewed on one obediently.

Sylvia came back with another plate. "Now. Tea." She began to make a racket with the spoons. "I don't remember if you have sugar, but here it is anyway." She handed me a steaming cup.

I took the papers out of my back and pushed them towards Stephen.

"I don't pretend to know what's going on," said Sylvia, "but if those Bellmott people aren't treating you properly, you must come here."

Stephen looked at me as he unfolded the papers. "She's right, you know."

I drank some very sweet tea and sighed. "Tempting. But I'm in the thick of something, and I feel I ought to see it through.

I've brought this here so you can tell me what sort of something it is."

There was a fulsome pause as Stephen paged through the document. He raised an eyebrow at me. "The thick of something, you say? Yes. Quite. I see that." He went back to the papers. "Most people would give their right arm to be given a choice like this, you know. It would make you an heiress of the first rank."

"But?"

"But we all know that you, dear cousin, are *not* most people."

"And thank heaven for that!" declared Sylvia. "Where would one be without one's individuality? It's absolutely the last thing one should ever consent to lose."

Stephen cast a glance at his wife. "No fear for you, my darling." He looked back at me. "Do you trust them? These new relatives of yours? The formidable Sir Joseph?"

"Why do you ask?"

He tapped the papers. "Because he doesn't trust you. It looks as if he's afraid you'll slip through his fingers, Edith— power of attorney, legal name change." He paged through them. "It's been a few years since I practised law, but this... Just look: conditions, conditions, and more conditions."

"There is nothing I hate more than a gift with conditions," Sylvia said with fervour. "It's simply not a gift anymore, is it? That's why I married you, Stephen."

"Why is that, my love?"

"Because there weren't any," she said simply. "Conditions, I mean. Wait!" cried Sylvia, making me jump. "I've just remembered."

"Remembered what?" I asked.

"Why that name gave me a chill. It was the lake."

"The lake?" Stephen repeated. "Sylvia, you did remember to open the window of your studio while you were painting today, didn't you?"

"Oh, stop it, Stephen, I'm no more addled than I always was. Fucino—the lake—my parents used to take me there when we went abroad. I've never seen somewhere so charming. Everyone thought he wouldn't be able to pull it off, draining that enormous body of water. Such a ridiculous idea, really! People laughed at him."

"Everyone thought *who* wouldn't be able to pull it off?" Stephen asked in confusion.

"The local princeling—Torino or Torlonia or someone. But at the last moment, a financier stepped in and put up the funds. Edith. It was *him*."

"Sylvia, this hardly seems fair," Stephen objected. "What are you accusing the man of—precisely? The removal of a charming body of water?"

Sylvia ignored him and fixed her gaze on me disconcertingly. With her light eyes and loose wrapper and her hair falling round her, she looked like some kind of modern Bloomsbury sybil. "It was a crime, Edith. A devastation. You mustn't trust him, Edith. Really. You simply mustn't."

Chapter Twenty-Four

B ack at Piccadilly, I found a brown paper package from Hatchards waiting for me. Tearing it open revealed all three volumes of *The Count of Monte Cristo*. I raised my eyebrows. What an extravagant form of secret communication Mr Barrington had chosen! A single volume would have suited our purposes just as well.

Within the front cover I found a short note.

Dear Miss Worms,

I believe the weather will be delightful tomorrow afternoon. Shall we say Regent's Park, by the lake, 2 o'clock?

Your obedient admirer,

T. Barrington

It took only an instant's glance to convince me that the writer of his note was one and the same as the writer of the other. I sat on the bed.

"Oh, *cholera*," I said under my breath.

I had hoped against hope itself that there might be some other explanation. But it was impossible to believe that Tom Barrington had any personal interest in collecting dragons. The thread of clues drew ever closer to my grandfather.

I could not imagine why Sir Joseph would hire Rivers to offer to buy dragons from my Yorkshire family. And what had Rivers's violent attempt to steal the Drake's treasure had to do with any of it?

It made no sense. But the fact remained that Sir Joseph hadn't just lied about my mother. There was something more. He had some designs on Ormdale which I could not fathom.

The thread continued on, and I must follow it to the end.

There was a handful of war protestors with a banner at Regent's Park. They looked uneasy and were regularly jeered at by passers-by. It seemed the war was thus far reasonably popular with the man on the street. I supposed the prospect of threatening a few Dutch colonists into giving up their gold mines wasn't too hard a scheme to sell to the British public.

I didn't have to wait long on the bench by the lake before a slim, well-dressed young man sat down next to me. Barrington had dressed with particular care; there was a fresh pink rosebud in his buttonhole.

"Lovely weather we are having, Miss Worms," he commented mildly.

Prolonging this would be torture for both of us.

"Would you please be so good as to explain this, Mr Barrington?" I said in a tight voice, handing him the torn note he had sent to Rivers.

He went very still. "Explain it? Whatever for? It's a note to a lawyer I had some business with."

"What business precisely?"

"This is why you wanted to meet me?" His voice was very flat.

"Yes," I confessed, my eyes alighting on the rosebud. For a moment, I felt rather beastly about it.

He began to laugh, but it wasn't the pleasant laugh I'd heard from him before. "I didn't see it before."

"I beg your pardon?"

"How like your grandfather you are. What a fool I am."

"Please do not evade my question."

"My private business can be of no interest to you, Miss Worms."

"I only wish that were true. However, you were responsible for hiring a man who brought mortal danger to my family, and I must know why."

There was a silence. Perhaps he was surprised by the 'mortal danger' bit. I hoped he was—I very much hoped that Rivers's violent actions had been his own initiative and not his employer's.

"I am Sir Joseph's confidential secretary," he said at last. "I will not betray his trust."

"Haven't you just met his granddaughter, unchaperoned? Didn't you write her a note, arranging a meeting? Wouldn't he view that as a betrayal of trust?"

He went pale. "You'd really tell him?"

"He can find another secretary. He only has one granddaughter."

He stood up and paced two or three times, before stopping in front of me.

"All right. But you can't hold this over me. If I tell you what you want to know, will you return my note to me?"

I nodded. "Of course. But there's something else I want."

"And what's that? My life's savings?"

"Of course not!" I cried, a little stung. "I don't need money. I just want you to open my grandfather's safe. Where he keeps all his secrets."

For a moment, there was no reaction. Then he loosened his collar. "I'm not sure I can do that."

"I'm quite sure you can," I corrected him. "You told me you knew the combination, remember? The night we met?"

"Blast you, I did, didn't I?" He gave a wild laugh. "Are you going to steal the family jewels and run away to South America?"

"Not at all. A tropical climate wouldn't suit me. I just want a very little secret. It's a small key. It has no monetary value. So perhaps I am not exactly like my grandfather," I faltered.

"Ah, that's where you are wrong," he said softly. "People always make that mistake about Sir Joseph. It's not about the money. It's never about the money with him, you know."

I stored this away for future reflection. "When can I see inside the safe? You can stay with me, to make sure I don't steal anything."

"Can I, indeed? Well. Best get it over with. When the household has gone to bed, we can meet in the study tonight."

"All right. Now, tell me about Rivers," I said firmly. Barrington sat down again, further away from me than before. I was relieved that all signs of partiality towards me had now vanished.

"I was lunching with a member of the club when I overheard a conversation between some members about an entail in Yorkshire, having to do with the Worms family. I'd been instructed to keep an ear out for anything to do with that family. So I wrote to the lawyer concerned in the matter. That's the note you have there."

"You had been instructed by whom?"

"Who do you think, Edith? He keeps watch on everything that belongs to him."

"I don't believe I gave you permission to call me by my Christian name. What instructions did you give Rivers?"

"Instructions? I merely arranged a meeting."

"Between my grandfather and Rivers?"

"Yes."

"And were you present at that meeting?"

"No, I was not. Sir Joseph can be—secretive."

"Do you know anything about what he was instructed to do in Yorkshire?"

Did my grandfather hire a man to lure my beloved brother into a cave and leave him for dead?

"No, but whatever Rivers did in Yorkshire, I cannot believe Sir Joseph meant *you* to be in harm's way, or anyone else, for that matter, since you mention mortal danger."

I looked at him sharply. He wasn't being sympathetic or trying to comfort me. He was just stating a fact.

"All right. Until tonight," I said, rising.

He stepped in front of me. "When will you return my note?"

"The moment you open the safe. I promise."

"Then I'll see you at midnight, *Miss Worms*."

He tipped his hat and strolled off. A crinkled pink thing on the path caught my eye. He had cast off the rosebud.

At five minutes to twelve, I ventured from my room. Though I was grateful for the rich pile of the carpets which muffled my midnight activities, I felt stifled by this house.

Wealth might be a protection, I thought, but it could also turn into a cage.

They don't trust you, Stephen had said of my new family.

Well, that makes two of us, I thought grimly.

Once in the study, I dared to strike a match and light the candle I carried.

"Good evening," said Barrington from where he sat behind the desk, almost startling a shriek out of me. If, as I suspected, he enjoyed doing it, I did not blame him. There had been that rosebud, after all.

I leaned on a chair for a moment to recover. "Let's get this over with, shall we?"

"Are you quite sure?" he said quietly. "Quite sure you know what you are doing?"

"Yes," I replied.

He got up and pressed a hidden mechanism, then swung out a section of the shelving to reveal the door of a safe.

It sprang open and Barrington stepped back to allow me access to it. I peered inside. There were a lot of papers and a jewellery case. I took out the jewellery case and opened it. There were smaller cases inside, containing several beautiful objects, including the dragon necklace and the diamonds I had seen on Irene. But not the key I sought. Crestfallen, I put it all back.

"Well. It's not here after all." I held out his note to him. "I'm sorry for troubling you, this must have been beastly. I don't ask you to forgive me, but I'm sorry all the same."

"No need to apologise." I couldn't see his face very clearly in the candlelight, but I thought something flickered there. "I deserved it for sheer stupidity. I should have known you'd never go for a fellow like me. They'll have you set up with a banker or a peer in no time."

"It isn't like that," I said quietly. "I've already *gone for a fellow,* you see—and he's neither a banker nor a peer."

Barrington stared at me for a moment. Then he took my hand. Before I could think to pull it back, he had guided my hand into the interior of the safe and placed it on a small metal object. It was cool to the touch, and fixed to the ceiling inside with some gum arabic. I pulled it out. It was a diminutive, Rococo key with a frayed scrap of ribbon tied to the handle.

Now it was my turn to stare.

"You—you knew it was there the whole time?"

"I always wondered what it was for," he admitted.

I opened my mouth to answer, but he cut me off.

"Don't tell me," he said briskly. "The less I know about it, the better."

He held the note to the candle flame and watched it curl into ash.

"Thank you," I said, putting the key in my pocket. "And thank you for the books."

"Ah, the dear old Count. You've read it before?"

"No." We really did find the oddest times to discuss literature. "I was raised in a rectory. My stepmother let me read pretty much anything, but *French* novels were a bridge too far, I'm afraid."

He looked at me with an unreadable expression. "Do you think you are prepared for whatever you use that key to unlock?"

"I don't know."

There was a silence. He brushed ash off his hands and picked up his hat from the desk.

"Goodnight, Miss Worms." The last words were uttered so much below his breath that I almost did not catch them: "And good luck."

Chapter Twenty-Five

Sir Joseph returned the next morning—which was also the day of my soirée. I had dared to hope he would miss it, for I could no longer feel comfortable in his presence. Had I ever really felt comfortable, I wondered, even when I'd felt the thrill of his approval?

"Edith, do look at this," said Irene, indicating a newspaper article at luncheon. "Isn't this about your nemesis? *A prominent Welsh industrialist has been ruined due to speculation on the stock market and lost his extensive property.*"

I gasped.

David looked over my shoulder. "You mean Penrith? But he's here—right now. I saw him go into Father's study just an hour ago."

Hill coughed. "I do beg your pardon, Miss Worms, but Sir Joseph has requested your presence in the study."

I stared at him. Did he want to force a confrontation with Penrith? With a rising sense of dread, I followed Hill into the passage.

The study door opened at the same time.

A diminished man now trudged out of the room, staring at the carpet. There was the same curly white hair, the same features—though they were almost unrecognisable now with an expression of absolute defeat.

As Hill helped him into his coat, Penrith looked up and our eyes met for the first time.

All the fire was gone from them. He turned away and went out the door.

My hand went to my heart.

"Edith," came my grandfather's voice. He was watching me from his study door.

I turned to him, stricken. "What will happen to him now? What will happen to his family?"

"He won't be absolutely homeless, if that's what worries you. He is going to the United States. His wife has abandoned him. Come—both of us know he is no loss to England."

Nor to Wales, I added silently. But that *look* he had given me!

"I didn't—I didn't ask you to do this," I forced out.

"But you wanted it, didn't you," he said softly. "It's as I told you, secrets are all very well—until they threaten to hurt you. And then you must act first. But if you let me protect you, you'll never have to worry about them again. I can protect you, Edith. Do you see?"

Protect you—or control you? Gwendolyn's words echoed in my head.

"I must rest before the party this evening," I murmured, and ran upstairs.

The gown from Redfern's was of pale champagne satin which caught the light like the interior of a shell. Tiny beads of pearls, glass, and silver picked out the embroidered lilies on the skirt.

As I stood before the glass, marvelling at it, the thought settled on me slowly that I did not feel entirely myself. It felt ungrateful to admit the fact, but as exquisitely as the dress fit my body, it did not quite suit my character. I could not get over the idea that it had been designed with someone else in mind.

The feeling of standing in for someone else and of failing in a thousand little ways prickled at me uncomfortably like a burr in my stocking.

If only Gwendolyn were coming tonight. If only I had a ring on my finger from Simon. I felt a pang of loneliness and out-of-placeness.

"*Enfin, le petit serpent,*" murmured Irene's maid, Claudette, as she held up my grandmother's necklace, lithe and green in her deft fingers.

I held up my hand, stopping her. The request to send it back to Sir Joseph was on my lips; the memory of my difficulty getting it off—tangled up with the end of my feelings of safety in this house—was on my mind.

But then I remembered the vanished lake. The creatures that existed now only in mud and memory. Perhaps this necklace was all that remained of my grandmother's people. I dropped my hand and nodded.

Claudette looped it round my neck, and I looked once more in the glass. Now, the girl with red hair, pale bare shoulders, and a gown the colour of pearls, had a fierce dragon at her throat: a dragon that bit hard and did not let go easily.

And here was something else that remained of my flame-haired grandmother and her lost world.

Me.

There was only a little left of the thread to follow—I could feel it, taut in my questing grasp.

Soon it would end, and I could go home.

I straightened and went down to meet the Belmontes.

"Doesn't she look charming?" Irene exclaimed, as I descended the stair.

"Quite perfect, my dear," my grandfather said with satisfaction. "Exactly as I imagined."

I noticed that Irene looked relieved, as if she'd been waiting for a verdict from him.

I remembered the moment I had met him—and how I had felt like a gem being examined by an expert for flaws. There was no warmth to the satisfaction in his voice. The pronouncement

came as a statement of fact—the conclusion of a lengthy valu-
ation.

He had tested me, and set my value. The fact that he had set
it high did not comfort me at all.

It was a chilly evening, and I wore an opera cloak over the
gown which had arrived from Redfern's the day before. I had
never worn something so precious, and once arrived there was a
heart-stopping moment to get clear of the carriage wheel, even
with the footman's expert help.

We had just been welcomed in the vestibule by my publisher's
wife, Mrs Lee, when the last voice in the world I had thought to
hear called my name.

This gentleman had no need to raise his voice—decades in
the pulpit had taught him the trick of being heard without
shouting.

"Father!" I cried, the warmth of his voice sending a flare of joy
through me, smoothing down my frayed nerves. If the butler
hadn't been taking off my opera cloak, I would have run to him
like a child.

The moment I disentangled, I went to him, hands outstretched.

"Oh, Father, I'm so happy you are here!"

Then I realised the Belmontes were just behind me.

"Father, I must introduce—"

I broke off. Father was staring at my gown in a stricken way. He dropped my hands as if they had burnt him.

"There is no need, Edith," said my grandfather crisply. "Though I have not seen this man since he was employed as a tutor in my house more than twenty years ago, I remember him clearly."

Father gave a slight bow. "Sir Joseph," he said in a guarded voice.

I recovered enough to murmur an introduction to David and Irene, but only Irene replied. David looked sick, and I saw that Irene was gripping his arm tightly. When I met her eyes, they fell away from mine, as if she was ashamed. But why?

"Shall we go in?" Sir Joseph said, and taking my arm, he swept me past my father into the hum and clink of the party with triumph in his eyes.

There have been times when my experience as a clerical appendage has stood me in excellent stead, and this was one of them. If I hadn't had years of practise nodding at people and sealing away my more objectionable sentiments, I would never have survived that evening.

Though my mind was furiously at work upon my own affairs, I was quite capable of making agreeable small talk with the journalists, authors, theatre impresarios, and who knows what else my publisher had invited to come stare at me.

The publisher himself, Mr Lee, took me round and introduced me to them all as if I were his own favourite child.

I was told by one woman wearing electric purple that now it was known I was a female, I had better retire Inspector Green and write fairy stories for children, as "that was all the public would accept from a lady writer."

I replied that I had a much better opinion of fairy stories than to attempt to write them myself. This confused her enough to allow me to escape further conversation.

Then the editor of *The Strand* found me.

"Miss Worms, won't you allow me to persuade you to write something for us? Or are you exclusive with Lee?"

"No, not exclusive, Mr Newnes. Only—please don't say you want fairy stories," I said faintly, veiling my excitement at meeting the editor of the Holmes stories.

He laughed. "Not quite. I'd be very curious to see what you might do with—a lady detective."

"A lady detective? That *is* an intriguing idea. And you don't think your readers would be too scandalised by such a thing?"

"The New Woman provides new openings for stories, Miss Worms. The trick is to scandalise them just enough to keep them reading, but not enough to cancel their subscriptions. A little like a clergyman's daughter who writes detective stories—or a minister's son who publishes them." And he winked at me in a companionable way that I did not consider impertinent.

When I was introduced to the handsomely bearded Irish author, Mr Stoker, and his astonishingly beautiful wife. I was tempted to say one or two things to him about blood transfusions, but in the end, I could get him to talk of nothing but the actor Henry Irving, who had been recently knighted. Stoker produced an anecdote of Sir Henry's most celebrated role, the Merchant of Venice.

"Sir Henry was so distracted on the way to The Lyceum for the show that he underpaid the cabbie. He was rushing in when the cabbie began to abuse him, saying it was all well and good for him to play the Jew *inside* the theatre, but outside, it was quite another matter!"

His wife gave him a quelling glance—undoubtedly, she had seen who escorted me into the party.

I finally managed to catch my Father's eye across the room. He was attending an older lady who had been rather ignored. Good old Father! The parable of the ninety-nine sheep might have been about him.

I asked a servant to direct me to the washroom, and a moment later, Father joined me in the quiet passage.

Together, we sank onto an upholstered bench screened by a potted palm. It was something we had often done during social occasions—slipped out together for a moment to sit quietly and restore ourselves before going once more unto the breach.

"Just what are you doing here, Father?"

He drew out an invitation from his pocket. "I was invited, I'll have you know! Did you really think I would miss your debut as a celebrated author?"

"And are you enjoying yourself, Father?" I asked.

"I'm very happy to see all these people appreciating your work, Edith," he answered tactfully.

"Father, what Sir Joseph said earlier—"

"Is true," he finished. "And it's my fault you heard it so abruptly. I was hired to tutor your mother in ancient languages. She was very gifted. That is how we met. I'm sorry I didn't tell you before."

"Did you...how did..." I struggled to put my question into words.

"Did I steal her away from her family? Is that what Sir Joseph said?"

I looked away, ashamed of my own doubts.

"Edith, your mother was as strong and true as sunlight. No man could have made her do anything against her conscience, however small. Whatever you think of me, you must understand that about her."

How like Father to be unconcerned with defending himself, but only her!

"More meetings in dark corners, after all these years?" Sir Joseph's voice was lightly taunting as he stepped around the palm.

I got up hastily. His eyes glittered in the light from the wall sconces. "Edith, your guests are waiting for you."

Father pressed my hand for a moment, then released it.

There was not a breath of compulsion about the gesture. Father trusted me. He trusted me to do as I saw fit, even in the bosom of people who hated him.

As I picked up my skirts and brushed past my grandfather, I heard his voice—not directed to me, but to Father, and his tone chilled my blood.

"Did you think I had forgotten, Worms?"

Chapter Twenty-Six

"Come, Edith, I have called for the carriage. It is time to leave." Sir Joseph's hand was on my elbow, guiding me, almost before I realised it.

"Where are Irene and David?"

"They went home an hour ago. David doesn't care for such things—no doubt you have noticed."

I nodded. "I'm sorry you had to wait for me, Grandfather."

"I shall be glad of the time alone with you, my dear," he said, as we made our goodbyes to the host and hostess.

As we rattled through the chill night, the fog crept even into the carriage, and the interior light cast an unsettling, milky glow. The thick curtains were shut, and the world had constricted to comprise only the two of us.

Against my hopes, the thread had led me here.

"You are very quiet, after your triumph," he remarked, his jewelled hand resting on his cane.

"My triumph?" I asked quietly. "Are you sure it was mine?" He raised an eyebrow but did not reply. "This gown—it was modelled after one of my mother's, wasn't it? You asked Irene to arrange it all."

He gave a little shrug. "I had a fancy to see you dressed after my daughter's fashion. I knew you wouldn't mind humouring an old man."

If he thought I would let him play that card, he was much mistaken.

"But it wasn't really for you, was it? It was for my father. You made sure he was invited, didn't you?" He looked at me impassively. "Why? Why was this important to you?"

"It was the last time I saw her," he said roughly. "At a party, wearing a dress of lilies, and the scent of lilies. She kissed me goodnight, and in the morning, she was gone—gone with *him*." His face contorted. "I will never forgive myself for bringing that man into my house."

"So you knew who she had gone away with all along. Why did you lie to David?"

"How could I tell him she had disgraced us by eloping with her own tutor? How could I tell him that the sister he adored had turned her back on her people? Had rejected our family and our faith? And all for what? The off-cast son of an obscure and declining house!"

I waited until this burst of resentment had dissipated. "But that's not quite true, is it, Grandfather? She never rejected her family. She wrote to you," I continued. "Did she write to David as well? Did you keep the letters from him?"

"He was too young to understand."

"And now? Oughtn't he to know what really happened?" He did not answer. "What about my grandmother? Did she know?"

"The grief of it drove my wife out of her senses. *Emotional exhaustion*, the doctors said, but to me it seemed a kind of madness. I paid for the very best care possible, and yet she died with strangers." His hand twitched on his cane—the hand that bore the ring with his wife's hair in it. "I have never ceased mourning for my daughter. Or for my wife." His voice was very hollow. Then he gazed at me. "Until the day you finally came to me. Then, at last, I thought I might put off my sackcloth. David has been a great disappointment to me. It was only in Miriam that the true vigour of our line was carried on—carried on to you. Your father never told you, did he?"

"Told me what?"

"That I would have raised you. After Miriam died. That I offered to take you." I stilled. This—I had not expected this. Was he telling the truth? "You would have had *everything*."

For an instant I remembered the darkest days of my childhood, when my mother's scent and warmth disappeared, and bread and coal had been scarce, and the prayers my father taught me seemed to go unanswered.

I allowed myself to imagine it, for a moment: Sir Joseph coming in his carriage to fetch me; perhaps bringing me the wax doll with black ringlets which I had longed for; the ponies and dresses and sleigh rides. Later, all the books I had coveted, and the quiet luxury of time to read and write undisturbed.

In the place of a younger brother, I would have had an older one. David and I would have been the best of friends. *She was everything to me,* David had said. And he would have said it of me, too. And my grandmother—would her story have been different, too? Would there have been no lonely death abroad, if a new daughter had come to gladden her days?

"You would have been a daughter to me, in every way as dear as she," he said. "Be that to me now, Edith. You can still have everything."

"Can I?" I asked. "You offer me a great gift, but you have placed so many conditions upon it, Grandfather, that it is hardly a gift any longer."

"You would have not only my name and my wealth, but my protection."

"Grandfather," I whispered. "Do I need protection by you, or *from* you?"

His fingers whitened on the knob of his cane.

"Don't be a fool, Edith. Don't make your mother's mistake. I will not sit idly by this time. Do you understand?"

My mouth went dry. "No. I don't understand any of it. Why did you send Rivers? What do you intend?"

My grandfather blinked, but other than that did not react to my question. The carriage drew up. The footman opened the door. All of a sudden the carriage was much too small, and I longed to escape it. I moved to do so, but my grandfather's hand shot out and gripped my arm. He was a strong man, but I felt his fingers tremble.

"Go back to *him*...and you will find out soon enough."

I shook off his grasp and ran into the house.

My grandfather had arranged a performance of sorts, with me as the unwitting lead actress. Whatever real grief he undoubtedly felt about losing his daughter, he had written his own tragedy. His sufferings—unlike Shylock's—were entirely of his own making.

I told you to leave, my great-grandmother had said.

I packed my things that night.

There was a cruel irony in re-enacting my mother's dramatic disappearance, which I did not intend. I sat a long while thinking of how I might explain it. In the end, I wrote a letter to Irene and David which I slipped under Irene's door so it could not go astray.

Then I scribbled the following words on the legal papers which I left on the dressing table:

Dear Grandfather,

What you want from me, in good conscience I cannot give.

Nevertheless, I remain

Your Granddaughter,

Edith Worms

When the maid came to make up my fire in the early morning, I was already dressed. Slipping her a coin, I asked her to fetch a footman and a hansom for me as quickly as she could.

I left the lily dress hanging in the room without a qualm. It had never really been mine. It belonged to someone else—someone who had, perhaps, never really existed at all.

I was half way down the stair when I heard Irene's voice.

"I'm sorry, Edith."

I looked back. Irene was above me on the landing, her hand on the banister, an incongruous froth of lace around her sad face.

"About the dress," she finished. "I didn't understand what it meant until I saw your father's face."

"I'm sorry, too," I said simply. "I'm sorry I couldn't stay—and help you with—all this. I'll write to you."

Her complete stillness made my heart sink. Somehow, I already knew.

"But I don't suppose he'll want us to see each other, will he?" I said. I might try to make peace, but he was bent on war.

"No," she said flatly. "With Sir Joseph, it is all or nothing."

"Then I'm afraid it will be nothing," I said quietly. "God bless you, Irene."

I escaped into the waiting hansom before anyone else awoke.

Inside my muff, a little key lay in my palm. There was a detour to make before I could go home to Wormwood Abbey: one last secret to unlock.

It wasn't until I was halfway to Belle Mount that I realised the key wasn't the only thing I had taken from my grandfather's London house, for I still wore the necklace.

Irene must have seen it, but she had said nothing.

As I had expected, Belle Mount was shut up for the season.

I went round to the gardener's cottage. On my visit a month ago, I had chatted with the man about getting seeds and cuttings for the garden at the abbey. Now, while he gathered up some things for me, I told him I would go into the house to rest before I caught my train to Yorkshire.

"I'll just go up to my mother's room," I told him. "No need to disturb anyone, I will be quite happy there."

I still had the key to the round room which Irene had given me when I first came.

I opened the bright room, and, pulling up a chair, I sat by the desk. The key was warm from my hand as I slid it into the ornate lock. There was a tiny click and the lid opened, releasing a faint scent.

A memory washed over me along with the fragrance, making me shut my eyes to hold on to it as long as I could: soft dark hair falling round me and the rich hum of my mother's alto voice.

When I opened my eyes, the first thing I saw was a stack of photographs. They must have been gathered from around the house and exiled here. I found one of Miriam and David as children and put it aside.

The inkwell, pen wiper, and a small Greek New Testament caught my eye next. All were of interest, but not what I had come for.

Moving it all aside, I found it at last: a stack of letters in my mother's hand, addressed to several members of the family. They had all been diverted and hidden here—closed up in the room Miriam had escaped. Her final communications with her family had been suppressed with a coldness that shocked me.

I put my face in my hands and allowed the anger to wash over me for a little. Then I looked at the photograph of the brother and sister.

"Well, Mother. I suppose it is better late than never," I murmured, tucking the stack of letters into my pocket with a sudden feeling of gratitude.

I did not mean to make war with my grandfather, but if peace required it, then I would not falter.

The gardener was waiting for me when I came downstairs. He had ordered the pony-trap to take me to the station. After I got in, he handed up a box to me.

"They're lily bulbs, miss, your mother's favourites."

This startled me a little. "I thought you didn't know her?"

"No, I didn't have that honour. But I know this garden like the back of my own hand, miss, and she left her mark. You can get to know someone by their garden."

"Can one really? Thank you. I will take these to my step-mother—she is a very keen gardener."

"They had that in common, then, miss," he said, pleased. "Do you think you might take it up yourself?"

"Perhaps I might," I said with a smile.

Thus I left Belle Mount with something I had come looking for, and something I had not—a gift from my first mother, to my second one.

The trees were showering dying leaves on the avenue. My great-grandmother was sitting in a basket chair in the front garden outside her Tudor house, watching the little eddies in the air.

"Good morning, Nonna," I called as I came in the gate.

Her rheumy eyes focused on me, then shifted to the glitter of the snake at my throat as I approached.

I knelt down on the grass by her.

"I'm Edith. I've come to give you something. You see, Miriam did leave, just as you told her to."

"Miriam?" The wrinkles on her forehead deepened.

"Yes. She listened to you. She married, and was happy. She wrote you this letter to tell you about it." I took the letter from my muff and set it in her lap. "Yes. I'm sorry I'm not her."

Slowly, her hand went out to touch the necklace. Did she understand me at all, I wondered?

"She made a life for herself," I went on. However brief, I thought, it was hers, and it *had* meant something. The woman who had sent her father that picture had risked much, and loved much, and had stood by her choice. Perhaps I would never understand every choice she had made, but I knew she had gone to God with a clear mind and a true heart. "Is there anything I can do for you, dear Nonna, before I go?"

She laughed suddenly, her eyes crinkling up in mirth. "Why would I mistake you for Miriam? She was tall. Not like you at all."

I blanched. She chuckled.

"Well," I said, but before I could rally, she glanced about her furtively, the laughter gone.

"I kept it, *bambina*."

"Kept what?"

"I never showed it to anyone. I knew if I did, he would stop it." She leaned close and whispered. "I have it with me still."

"May I—may I see?"

She indicated the walking stick propped next to her. I took it in my hands and she fumbled with the head of it until I unscrewed it for her. It was hollow. I inverted it and a rolled piece of paper dropped out onto the lawn. Had my mother managed to get a letter to Nonna after all?

"Mrs Marzano?" called a voice, and I looked up to see the nurse coming down the path.

I put the paper in my muff.

"I'm afraid I have a train to catch. But I'd like to come see you again, Nonna, if I may."

In answer, she took my face in her hands and kissed my cheeks, one at a time, all her haste and caution forgotten. There was a spark in her eye that I could not quite define. I was only relieved that this time I had not upset her.

"*Mia cara*," she crooned at me, "I am so glad you are free."

I kissed her in return and went back to the hired pony-trap, walking down the path to the sound of the old lady chuckling to herself.

As the trap set off, I unfolded the paper she had given me.

Mamma,

They won't let me have books. They won't let anyone speak to me. They take even pen and paper from me. I have given the nurse one of my rings for this. She promises to send it. I don't know if she will keep her promise. Do not leave me here a moment longer, I beg.

Then the letter veered into Italian.

It was nonsensical—Nonna was not isolated or deprived. She must have written this in a moment of mental confusion. In all likelihood she would not understand my mother's letter to her. But it had been right to deliver it, all the same. Tucking Nonna's ravings sadly into my muff, I remembered how she had stared at the necklace which had been hers. It occurred to me that I really ought to have returned it to her.

Unconsciously, my hand went to my throat...and found nothing. The necklace was gone.

I gasped. So that was why Nonna's eyes had gleamed at me so when she kissed me goodbye!

A chuckle escaped me, then a full-throated laugh, as I thought of the old woman gloating over the little sea-beast, which had been returned to her at last.

CHAPTER TWENTY-SEVEN

The first thing I did when I got to the abbey was make for the stables. Cariad was in the stable yard, drinking from the trough. When she saw me, she bounded towards me. I reached out for her. She extended her wings and curved them round me as I buried my face in her neck. I felt like a bee shut inside a crocus.

An equine snort and stamp from behind her made her lower her wings. I exclaimed in surprise to see Portia.

My heart beating high, I looked around for Simon, but saw only Pip, crossing the stable yard with a bucket of mash.

"Pip! Is Mr Drake at the abbey?"

"No, Miss. Mr Drake stabled his mare here while you were gone, for company for the dragon, seein' as it were lonely."

"Have you made a friend, Cariad?" I asked her in surprise.

As if in answer, Cariad turned towards Portia and huffed in a fond way, as if to say, "Look what I found."

She reminded me of George and his moth.

"Canst thou draw out leviathan with an hook? Will he make a covenant with thee? Wilt thou take him for a servant for ever?"

There was only one person who quoted scripture in just that way.

"Father!" This time, I *did* run to him and throw my arms around him, surprising him enough to make him stagger back a step. "What are you doing here?"

He drew back to study my face. "More to the point—what are *you* doing here? Was there a quarrel? Did they send you away?"

"No, Father," I said. "I'll tell you all about it, but first—this is Cariad, from Wales. She saved my life." I took his hand and held it out to her to smell. "Cariad, this is Father. He is very good, and so you must be very good to him."

She snuffed and nuzzled his hand.

Father gazed at Cariad, reaching another hand to touch her horns in wonder. *"Wilt thou play with him as with a bird? Or wilt thou bind him for thy maidens?"* he murmured to himself.

I drew him to the bench against the stable wall. It was in a sheltered little nook, nestled between the stable wall and the wall of the abbey. We put our backs against it and felt the lingering warmth from the autumn sun. Then I rested my head on his shoulder like a child. I wasn't sure how long we'd have, just the two of us, and there were things that needed to be said.

"Father, I must apologise. I doubted you."

"Entirely my fault, Edith. I should have been more forthcoming with you. I always intended to tell you more about how your mother and I came to marry, but the right time never seemed to come. Until, I suppose, the time had passed, without my knowing it."

"Some things are hard to tell," I said, thinking of Simon. "Sir Joseph never let the family see her letters. He let David believe that she never cared enough about him to say goodbye. But I found them all, and I'm going to give them to everyone who is still alive to receive them. And I brought you this."

I handed the Greek New Testament to him.

Father was silent for a moment, gazing at it. He opened the cover and there was written, firstly, *George Worms*, and secondly, in a different ink and hand, *Miriam Belmonte*, and *Luke, chapter one, verses 52-53.*

"I gave her this. I wasn't part of the household, the way Sir Joseph made it sound. I came every Tuesday and Thursday to give her lessons in ancient languages. She was a year older than me. I thought her far above me in every way, Edith. But she didn't see it like that."

"How did she...how did she come to change her religious ideas?"

"Oh, my dear, how I wish she were here to tell you herself."

"Was it—for love?" I asked.

It had been true of Irene, but how desperately I wanted it to be untrue of my mother.

He looked at me seriously. "Of course. The strongest love of all. *For I am convinced that nothing shall separate us from the love of God, which is in Christ Jesus.*"

"Then it wasn't for you? She didn't convert for you?"

He looked a little confused. "For me?" Then he blinked. "Ah. So that is how Sir Joseph explained it to himself. No wonder he hates me so." He took a breath. "She was always a princess in a tower to him—a jewel in a casket. Something to be locked up and kept under guard, for fear of being stolen. But she was never that. She was fearless. Her mind was as sharp as a diamond—nothing but a diamond can write on a diamond. You understand?"

"But you taught her, even so?"

He laughed a low laugh. "Not for long—she left me in the dust."

"That's why you tried to teach me Greek, isn't it?"

"Yes." He took my hands in his and spoke firmly. "You are Miriam's daughter, and you are every bit her equal, but you are your own woman, Edith."

With these words, pieces that had fallen out of me went back into place.

Father could see me, trust me as I really was, but Sir Joseph could not. And perhaps even Miriam had felt the same way—that she was an idea to him, rather than a person. Perhaps if her father had really known her, she would never have run away. Perhaps the gift of being loved in this way was what Father had offered her.

"But I must ask, Edith. You didn't know your mother, but you know me. Do you really think I would have accepted such a sacrifice from her? Even if she had offered it to me?"

"I'm sorry. I should have known you wouldn't."

Father took a long breath. "And now I must make a confession to you in turn. After Miriam died, Sir Joseph wrote to me. He wanted—"

"He wanted to adopt me," I interrupted. "I know. He told me. But if you were going to apologise for not saying yes to him—*don't*. Being locked in a tower wouldn't have suited me anymore than it did my mother."

"I'm afraid that's not what I wanted to apologise to you for." His voice lowered. "I must apologise—because I very much wanted to let him."

Father had wanted to give me up?

"I was frightened, Edith," he said heavily. "I was frightened of not being able to care for you. Miriam died so quickly, when she was in my care—"

He struggled for a moment. I put my handkerchief in his hand, and he crumpled it, blinking fast.

"The only reason I didn't give in was because on her deathbed your mother pressed me to give my most solemn promise—that I would be the one to raise you, no matter how hard things became. God help me, I almost didn't keep it. I went so far as to write to him the winter after she died, but I never sent it. It almost killed me not to. I was a coward, Edith."

"But you *kept* your promise," I insisted. "You kept me— just as she knew you would. You kept faith with her, even though you were afraid! That wasn't cowardice, Father—that was courage."

This wasn't the kind of thing one got to say to one's father everyday, and I sensed how important it might be to him, so I waited a moment before I said it: "Thank you for keeping me, Father."

I reached up and gently lowered his head to my shoulder this time, and something about the movement released the tears at last.

We stayed there until the stone wall at our backs cooled with evening, and the dragon and her horse went back into their stalls.

The next morning I woke early. My heart was pounding with anticipation. I had unpacked last night and put my parcels from Redfern's on my dressing table.

There was no rich gown inside, but a pair of thick bloomers (rather like the jodhpuri breeches which had become so famous recently) and a double-breasted jacket in chocolate-coloured leather which fit me exactly, yet gave me a full range of movement. The outfit was finished with a warm high-necked cardigan jacket, a flame-coloured muffler, a pair of motoring goggles on my head, my Dragon-Keepers' belt about my waist, and my stoutest boots.

I crept out of my room and shut it very softly behind me, hoping to avoid being seen by the household at this early hour.

Turning, I saw two open-mouthed faces staring at me from Una and Violet's bedroom door.

"Oh. Good morning," I said, flushing. I straightened my jacket self-consciously. "Is it too…"

"Marvellous," Violet blurted, her voice husky. "It's too marvellous is what it is."

I looked at Una. She shut her mouth and nodded.

"What does it feel like?" asked Violet.

"The clothes? Or the flying?"

"Both!"

I reflected.

"It feels like me," I said, with pleasure.

I flew Cariad once again as the moors sparkled with frost under the morning sun. If this ever palled on me, I thought, then I would be utterly dead to earthly joys.

There was smoke coming from the shepherd's hut where the meadows met the lower fells. That was the home of Jacob, the old man who had walked all the way to the abbey with a groundling attached to his leg, and became our test subject for the antivenin.

Something stirred in my memory.

Ask them in Ormdale what happened.

Farley had said that to me from his hospital bed. And Jacob would be the right person to ask.

I felt a flash of dread. Did I really want to know? Did I want to uncover yet another dreadful family secret?

But I'd watched Gwendolyn run away from her history, and while I understood her, I knew that I didn't want to spend my life closing my eyes to the truth about my family—either part of it.

A redwing flashed past, wings spread, and my heart caught.

Ormdale had suffered through centuries of lies and secrets, and yet there was still such joy, such beauty.

A phrase came back to me.

We ascend.

It had been my grandfather's motto, but perhaps it could mean something quite different to me. Could I hope to wrestle with every secret in my chequered family history until it blessed instead of cursed us?

Mother had taught me something as a child: *I am, I can, I ought, I will.*

I directed Cariad towards the shepherd's hut.

I left Cariad outside with the large, meaty bone I had brought in my satchel, and I found Jacob inside his cottage, tending a ewe with a broken leg. The dark cottage smelled of peat smoke and wool. He showed no surprise at my appearance, but offered to share his breakfast of oatcakes and sheep's curds.

"Jacob, may I ask you about some Dale history?" I asked as I ate with him. "I especially want to know about anything really tragic that happened, about thirty years ago."

"A generation ago. Let me see... There were a sad death at the time of Master Simon's birth, and very unexpected," he added. "One of the servants up at the Hall died in childbed. A hale one, she was, and nobody expected it."

I recalled the crunch of yew berries underfoot. "Was that Anne Forrester? I saw her grave in Ormby."

He nodded. "Her bairn and Mrs Drake's were born within a day, and one died, and t'other lived. And t'werent the one you would have thought, what with Mrs Drake being so delicate."

"No, this story would involve a little boy, not a baby. A boy with red hair, even brighter than mine. Perhaps you'd remember that?"

He looked into the peat fire. "Aye."

My heart jumped. "Tell me," I said firmly.

"The family was sent out." His voice was grim.

"Sent out? You mean expelled from Ormdale? Who expelled them?"

"Your grandfather, lass."

"Why?"

"For destroying one of the beasts. 'Twere the only reason folks were ever sent out."

"Why did they destroy it?" I asked.

"It was the mother, and one of the bairns, that died of being bitten. They couldn't find the Mercy in time. I don't recall that every happening before or since."

"Who survived?"

"The father and the boy. His hair was like a copper that's just been shone. He were a bright lad—bright hair, and a bright mind."

"Yes, I can imagine that." I put my hand to my forehead in despair.

"Now, lass, tha munna take on so."

"It's just...there's so much *wrong*, Jacob. How am I ever to mend it?"

"Tha's not to mend all," he said firmly. "If tha set out to mend all, you'll mend nowt. See here." He pointed at the sheep. "If I thought on every sheep that'd take ill and perish in my lifetime, I'd lie down on ma bed and not get up again. But this yow—she needs help with 'er leg now. So I won't lie abed and mourn for those that canna be helped while she sickens. Mend what falls to tha hand, lass, and leave all to God."

I left, oddly at peace. The tragedy of Farley, —the little boy that had been Farley—was beyond my reach.

But other things still lay within it.

When I used to help Mother with the mending, I had bewailed the size of the pile, rifling through it in despair. But

Mother had always said, "Just start at the top of the pile, Edith, and go from there. You'll find it will lessen before you know it."

And what lay at the top of the pile right now was something that had stood out from Jacob's stories.

Anne Forrester.

I could still picture the words on her headstone.

There is nothing hidden, that will not be revealed.

I felt as if I had bumped up against something in the dark and was groping for a light. If only I could speak with someone reliable who had been there at the time of Anne's death.

With a start, I remembered someone who had been an intimate witness to all the tragedies of the Dale. The fact that he was dead did not stop me consulting him—because his journal lay waiting in my study.

Once back at the abbey, I changed quickly into a frock and went to my study. With pounding heart, I opened the doctor's journal given to me by Mrs Worthing and leafed through the entries the year of Simon's birth. When I found it, I had to sit down.

CHAPTER TWENTY-EIGHT

Minutes later, I was on my way to Drake Hall, running with the journal clutched in my arms. The grass was slippery with dew and I slipped once. The distance between the houses had never felt so far.

This was not my secret to keep. This was not my curse to break. But the means to break it was within my reach, and I would not stop until I had given it into the right hands.

"Forrester!" I shouted heedlessly as soon as I got into the house. It had always felt like a desecration to make noise in this house—until now. Now I was ready to shout enough to wake the dead.

Forrester stepped into the passage, a polishing cloth in his hand.

I stopped short. "Forrester! I've found proof. Of who Simon is! I have to show it to him!" I thumped on the journal for emphasis. "*Please*. Anne would have wanted it, wouldn't she? The truth."

His shoulders loosened, and he gave the smallest of nods.

"Where is he?" I asked breathlessly.

He gestured toward Helena's door. Running up the stairs, I rapped on the door and let myself in without waiting for an answer.

My words tumbled over each other before my eyes adjusted to the dimness of the room.

"Oh, Mrs Drake! I didn't understand, and I'm sorry for what I assumed. But this can't be kept from him a moment longer."

A tall figure rose from the chair by the bed. Simon. He was holding a book in his hand, and there was a light in his eyes at seeing me, shadowed by concern.

"Edith, are you quite well?"

I held out the journal to him. "This is for you."

Helena's voice came, reed-like but clear, from the bed curtains. "Simon, dear, won't you get me a drink? My throat."

Oolong had been sitting at Simon's feet, and now he ran to nudge my ankles.

"There's a drink by your bedside, Mother," Simon said quietly, and came toward me.

Helena's aged lapdragon, Mr Darcy, stood up on unsteady legs, and looked back and forth between us, conscious of something momentous.

"Simon! Please. Be so good as to leave me alone for a moment with Edith."

He paused. Still I held out the journal. What if he refused it? What if he wouldn't break his curse? What if it was just too late?

"Simon—if you love me—do not take up that book," Helena said.

Simon's eyes met mine. Was he waiting to see if I would range my pleas against Helena's, like an opposing army?

I closed my lips. No. I would not hinge my love upon his obedience. He'd had enough of that for a lifetime.

"No, Mother," he said gently but firmly. "Edith says this matter concerns me. I shall see it out."

He took the book from me, and I felt as if he'd taken a great weight from me. Helena gave a faint gasp.

He examined the book. "What is this, Edith?"

"Old Doctor Dunstable's journal."

"Our old doctor?"

"Yes," I said. "I've marked the place."

It fell open to the ribbon.

"This is dated the day after my birth," he said slowly.

A strangled sound came from Helena.

"Mother," he said, "is there something you wish to say to me?"

But she covered her face with her hands and said nothing.

It was horribly quiet in the room as he read the entry. Mr Darcy looked anxiously at Helena. There was a furrow on Simon's brow that deepened.

"This entry says, '*yesterday, Mrs Drake was delivered of an infant son, perfectly formed, but dead upon birth*.'" He looked up at me, puzzled. "And yet, here I am. Quite alive."

Once, I had questioned the choices that had made up his adult life, and the shock of hearing my rather harsh judgement had provoked a wild fit of bitter laughter.

We had both grown up quite a lot since then. Still, I did not know how he would react.

I could only whisper, "'*Perfectly formed*', Simon."

He stared at me, then looked at his left hand. His eyes darted to Helena, his breath quickening.

"I'm not yours." There was no particular expression to the words. "Then...who am I?" he asked simply.

I hoped Helena would tell him. She ought to be the one to do it—she was there when it all happened. On my part it was mere detective work.

"Madam, I beg you to tell me, who are my parents?" This was addressed to Helena, with a strained note of formality.

I think it was hearing this tone in his voice that made her begin to sob. Simon was calmest when he was afraid.

"Edith?" Simon was looking at me now.

"In the following entry, the doctor writes that the next day a woman employed as a maid in this household died of childbed fever, but that her infant son survived her. If you read on, you'll see the doctor's notes."

Simon went back to the journal. After a moment, he said, "Yes. I see now. *Missing the first digit on the left hand*. Yes, that is me. Not perfectly formed, like the other."

He turned towards the bed and gave the ghost of a courtly bow. "I am sorry, madam, that you lost your son."

Simon turned to me as if he didn't see me, but someone else. "What was her name? My real mother?"

"Her name was Anne Forrester, Simon. You are the son of Peter and Anne Forrester."

Almost before the words were out of my lips, Simon was on his way out of the room. As he brushed past me, his fingers touched mine for an instant with a fierce pressure. And then he was gone, noiseless as a shadow.

The sound of Helena's sobs was unbearable. I went to her side and gathered her in my arms and held her.

And so I found myself inside Helena's world for the first time, shrouded in the dark curtains of her bed, and as I gazed at the weave of the fabric with its pattern of leaves, it stirred a quiet horror within me.

What a small thing this was—to fill a whole life.

The little lapdragon shuffled closer to Helena and laid its head on her knee. After the sobs stopped, Helena became very still. Oolong pawed at the door but Mr Darcy glared at his fellow dragon until it stopped and settled on the rug.

Finally, when I thought Helena must be asleep, she spoke. "He'll hate me. Now that he knows. He'll hate me."

"Why would you think such a thing?"

"He only loved me because he thought it was his duty, because he's so good," she said with a dull finality. "He's the only person who ever has loved me, and now it is all over. He'll love his real mother now, instead of me."

"What a dreadful thought! But love isn't like that at all, Mrs Drake. It's not a plate of buns without enough buns on it for everyone who came to tea. It's a teashop, stocked with all the things to bake buns forever and ever."

She made a broken little sound. "Oh, Edith. Why is it always *food* with you?"

I flushed, and then bit my lip. "Do *you* love him, Mrs Drake?"

She caught a sob in her throat and swallowed. "I'm not sure I've ever really loved anyone in my life."

Love does not grow in a cage, I thought, and believed her. My grandfather had locked my mother in a cage, too.

But her confession fanned an ember of hope within me. Because I was sure my grandfather would not admit the same. For him, love was whatever he willed it to be. He would confess no lack, no failure.

"Perhaps you haven't," I admitted. "And perhaps you can start now. Perhaps today is the day of your salvation."

She gave a great sigh. "No, Edith. It's too late for that."

"Indeed, ma'am," I said firmly, "you will never convince me it is ever too late for salvation."

After that, she did sleep for a while. I made up the fire and left her when her maid came in.

Chapter Twenty-Nine

Exhausted, I lay myself down on my own bed and slept. The pattern of Helena's drapes writhed with snakes and hissed at me in my dream. I woke to someone gently gripping my arm and saying my name. I looked up to see Mother.

"You were having a nightmare. I'm sorry, I wasn't sure whether to wake you, but it is teatime and I know how much you like parkin, and I'm so afraid the children will simply vanish it..."

I cut her off by catching her in my arms for an impetuous embrace.

"Oh! My dear!" said Mother softly.

"I do like parkin," I mumbled into her shoulder. Then I jumped up. "And I have something for you. They're lilies. Or at least they will be when you plant them, and don't kill them, as I would undoubtedly do."

I pawed through my drawer, a little muzzy from sleep.

"Why, I was just wanting lilies for the cloister," Mother said in a pleased sort of way. "It will look perfectly Rossetti, don't you think? What kind are they?"

I found the box and handed it to her. "Um, the lily-ish kind?"

"Where did they come from, Edith?"

"They came," I said slowly, "from my other mother."

She looked up, startled.

I sat down again. "And the gardener at Belle Mount. He was very pleased at the idea of you having them, and so am I. And I think she would be, too."

She looked down at the bulbs again. "How very extraordinary." Her voice was watery.

"Mother, are you crying?"

"Don't mind me."

"I don't mind one bit. Though it does seem as if people have been crying on me rather frequently of late. Perhaps I ought to come with a warning of some kind. *Tear-inducing.*"

Mother laughed into her handkerchief.

"It's only...you know, I was only twenty-five when I married your father—very close to your age now. And I was so terrified of getting it wrong. I felt I was always a few steps behind."

"I don't believe it!" I cried.

"No, it's true. I used to look at the photograph of Miriam with you as a baby and wonder what she'd say to me if we met. And now...well, now there's this—when I was feeling rather low. Thank you, Edith."

I put my hand in hers, and then placed my other one over it. "Why do you feel low? Is it something to do with Father and the war?"

"I'll let your father tell you about it."

"Well, let's go before all the parkin does."

Amidst the clink and chatter of teatime with the children, Mother caught Father's eye and gave him a nod.

"Well, children, Emily and I would like to talk to you about something."

They quietened, wiping crumbs off their mouths.

"George, you asked this morning when we were going back to the rectory. The fact is, I'm not sure we will ever live there again."

"Why, sir?" asked George.

"Well," said Mother, "do you remember what I said about loyal opposition?"

"You said if someone in a position of authority is doing something that betrays their office," said George, "one must stand up to them for the common good."

"Like Brutus!" added Violet, picking up the cake server and jabbing George with it.

"Well, preferably without making the senate floor run crimson," said Father, "or, indeed, the tea table, but yes—that's the idea."

"Who exactly are we stabbing this time, Father?" I asked. "And what sort of trouble are you in?"

My parents exchanged a glance.

"Oh," I said. "As bad as that?"

"I have been asked by my bishop to retract an observation I made regarding the waging of a just war."

"What was your observation, precisely?"

"That the only defensible war is a war of defence."

"Oh, Father! You trundled out St Augustine to condemn the British Empire!"

"Not the entire Empire, Edith," Mother said quietly.

"But where was your sense of self-preservation, Father?"

"That seems a particularly ironic remark coming from you, my dear," Father said.

"Well, apples and trees and all that, you know," I murmured.

"Leaving apples aside, we are at a crossroads. I may seek another ecclesiastical position in another parish. Or I may give it all up."

"All?" I looked at them both. "Do you mean you'd hand in the collar? For good? Are you really considering it?"

"It has occurred to me since Michaelmas that I might serve God just as well without a collar. And we have a home—even if it is a rather chilly one—here." He turned to the children. "I wanted to hear what they had to say."

There was a small silence.

And then the children started cheering.

"Now, children, Father hasn't made a decision yet," Mother reminded them. "He's been a clergyman for ever so long, you know. It's not easy for him to just leave it all behind."

"I must consider," he said, "where my duty lies. But I cannot continue in a situation which does not allow me to exercise my God-given conscience."

Conscience. I sensed an opportunity and plunged. "I've become terribly averse to secrets of late. So while we are confessing shocking opinions, I probably ought to tell you all that—well—I've been a suffragist since July."

They fell silent.

"*Women's* suffrage specifically—though now we are talking about it," I went on, gathering momentum, "I don't see why poor men shouldn't get the vote as well as middling and rich ones. And I'm joining the Women's Tax Resistance League. I mean, I haven't actually *resisted*, and probably I won't ever, but taxation without representation does seem unfair—like that ghastly Stamp Act, which our colonial cousins protested so memorably a hundred years ago. And look how well they're doing now—at least on the money front, anyhow."

I held out my teacup to Mother, who stared at me and made no motion to pick up the teapot.

"I'm not planning to toss the tea onto the carpet, just to be clear," I added.

"Oh! I know about that one!" cried Violet. "Aunt Emily read it to us!"

At that, Mother rallied and poured tea.

"Mother?" I asked at last, a little nervously. "Have I shocked you?"

"Yes. You've completely shocked me," she admitted in a pale sort of voice. "I never thought you took in any of it."

"Any of what?"

"Well, the Stamp Act, for one! Your eyes always glazed over completely whenever political science was mentioned. I'm astonished that you remember anything about the American Revolution at all. It wouldn't have surprised me if you thought they still sang God Save the Queen."

George chortled. "Do you know I asked Eddie once about the Magna Carta and she said it was the biggest map ever made?"

"I never!" I cried. "Well, if I did, it was just to stop you asking me any more questions." I turned to Father. "Well, what about you, Father? What do *you* think about it?"

"I think," said Father, slowly wiping his spectacles which the tea had steamed up, "that if you do ever decide to *resist*, as you say, that I'd like to see the look on their faces if you showed up at the polling place on the back of a dragon."

I grinned. "What was Mother always trying to teach us, George?"

Catching his eye, we said it together:

"I am, I can, I ought, I will."

Halfway through Violet and Una joined in.

When I looked at Mother, she was blinking at her teacup. All our smiles vanished.

"Oh dear! Did we say it wrong? Or have I really upset you, Mother?"

She sniffled and straightened. "It's just—I didn't think you were listening. As you know, I've never cared very much about the franchise. I've always believed there's so much for us to do without it. But I'm quite ready to wear the purple ribbon with you, Edith—and I'll invite the Bishop's wife to tea when I do it!"

At this last remark, a little fire kindled in her eye, and I remembered Sylvia's prediction.

"Now that I would *very* much like to see," said Father heartily.

I had hoped that Simon might come see me that day, but he did not appear. While I was disappointed, I knew that he must have much to contemplate and much to say to Forrester. And I knew he had not forgotten me; that touch of his fingers on mine as he left the room had been a sort of promise.

I went to my study late in the evening and found to my surprise the old doctor's journal on my desk. There was a faint smell of wet dog. Simon and Pilot had been here, and had gone.

I went to the kitchen, hoping that he might be there.

"Was Simon here?" I asked.

Hanna looked up from kneading dough and shook her head. "I see no one."

Her salamander poked its head out of her apron pocket, as if to underscore her answer.

I looked round the quiet kitchen. I could hear the thump and splash of the tweenie scouring pots in the scullery.

"Do you miss the city, Hanna? Janushek told me once he missed being able to lose himself there."

"Lose himself? No." She sprinkled flour on the board. "Here is good now."

"Just now? Not always?"

She looked at me very seriously. "I stay now. I stay until you have five or seven babies, and then I go."

"Five or seven?" I squeaked. Then, overcome with curiosity, I added, "But not six?"

She shook her head. "Twins. I nurse them."

"Well!" I said, and got very quickly away.

I got my book from the study and went up to my bedroom. I had forgotten my candle, and the night was coming earlier now, so I had to grope my way a bit.

As soon as I went into the room, I knew I was not alone. There was a faint ember-glow from the dying fire; nothing else. Then I heard a faint whine of greeting and the thud of a tail on the hearth rug.

Someone was in the chair by the fire, and he had brought with him the smell of rain on the moors—and a very large dog.

"Simon," I breathed. I reached for the matchbox.

"Wait," came Simon's voice, very low.

"All right." I sat down opposite him and waited.

The wind sighed outside. How natural it was to be quiet with him, and how utterly safe I felt.

It dawned on me that this is how it might feel to be married to him—the two of us, sitting quietly in the dark together, with the fire burning low, and Pilot on the rug, and the wild weather outside making things all the more snug within.

"I'm sorry, I wasn't thinking," he said softly. "Did I frighten you?"

"Never."

"Edith, I came to return the journal, and to talk with you, but I found the map sitting on your desk. And all of a sudden—I had to go see them. I'm sorry I didn't tell you first. I wasn't thinking clearly."

"Them? But whom do you mean?"

"My ancestor's compatriots."

Suddenly it dawned on me what he meant. I couldn't speak for a moment. Simon had visited the dark lair of his ancestors' beast, and had apparently escaped unharmed.

"Simon, you didn't—you didn't—but—they might have eaten you!"

"They didn't," he said dryly.

"Did they maim you?" I cried. "Is that why you don't want me to put on the light?"

At this, he laughed. "No."

"What on earth possessed you to do it?"

"I'm not quite sure." He reflected. "It's been rather a day."

"Yes, it has, hasn't it," I agreed.

"Edith—they didn't hurt me at all. And they want to get out. They've been caged up for so long."

He said it gently, but there was a determination beneath it that quickened my pulse. I took a long breath.

"Unimaginably long. But are you quite sure...that it isn't *you* who wants to get out?"

"I don't know." He let out a shuddering breath. "That's exactly it—I don't know what I want."

I felt a stirring of dismay. Would all of this change Simon? Would he become someone different? I forced myself not to panic at the thought.

"I expect it's not a question you've really ever let yourself ask, is it?"

"No. It isn't."

"Well. Then you must give yourself a little time over it. Perhaps after sleeping."

He gave a movement of discomfort.

"What's wrong?"

"I don't want to go back—there. Not yet."

"Well, let's find you somewhere to sleep here at the abbey, then. May I light the lamp now?"

"Yes."

I struck a match and kindled the lamp. He looked a bit muddy and blown about, but underneath was a new kind of stability. It was like lifting an old carpet to find good strong oak beneath.

"You look as if you've been dragged through a cave," I said.

He looked down. "I'm sorry."

"It suits you. But I'll have hot water brought up to you first thing in the morning, and clothes fetched from Drake Hall."

He stood up and looked around him, as if he had suddenly become aware of where he was for the first time.

"I shouldn't have come in here. Forgive me."

"No need."

I held out my hand to him. His fingers closed over mine. I led him out the door into the passage.

"Gwen's room will do. You know the one?"

"Yes."

He took the lamp from me. He hadn't taken his eyes off me since I'd taken his hand.

The lamplight fell on something round his neck. It was a gold chain threaded with tiny shells, a few beads of turquoise, and an iridescent feather. He saw me looking at it.

"My father gave this to me," he said. "It has been passed down in his family—our family—for generations."

"From the valet?" I said, ashamed not to know his name.

"Yes. I wore it into the caves. And…it really seemed like the creatures recognised me in some way. I wonder if it was the necklace that did it."

Might such long-lived creatures have memories as prodigious as their antiquity? Wasn't it said that elephants and crows remembered everything?

"Edith?" he said, interrupting my thoughts. "You don't—you don't mind, then."

"Mind?"

"About who I really am?"

My mouth trembled with suppressed laughter. "Do I mind that you're not descended from the most piratical family in Yorkshire after all?"

He made an indescribable sound deep in his throat.

"But that's not even the best part, you know." I leaned towards him and whispered, "The best part is—we're not related in the least."

I started to slip away, but his hand went round my waist.

"Stop. That wasn't the whole truth just now. When I said I don't know what I want."

He was close enough that his breath stirred my hair, and along with it a deep joy and relief inside me. I knew exactly what he was going to say, and the happy certainty of it was like watching the sun rise.

"Because I've known what I wanted since the moment I saw you coming down the stairs of the great hall last spring. The light caught your hair around your face like a halo. I thought at first you were a sort of saint."

Well. Perhaps I hadn't known *exactly* what he was going to say.

"And you don't mind about who *I* really am?" I said. "That I'm not a saint after all?"

"No," he said with his warmest smile—the smile that had first made me reassess my judgement of him. "You're more than anything I could have imagined."

He must have remembered how muddy he was, though I didn't care in the least, for he let go of me abruptly.

"Goodnight, Edith."

"Goodnight," I said.

He went down the passage and I went back to my room. Both of us were smiling like babies.

CHAPTER THIRTY

Very early, I sent to Drake Hall for a change of clothes.

Then I tried to go about my morning business, but I could not keep my mind on any task, and I kept jumping like a cat every time a door opened in case it was Simon. Plighting one's troth was all very well in the dead of night when hearts were high, but how was I to behave when I saw him again by the unforgiving light of day?

Approaching the dining room at breakfast time, I heard the low tones of Simon's voice mingling with those of my parents and the children, and my heart failed me utterly. I could not face the prospect of seeing him for the first time after last night in the company of my entire family. Had he said anything to them?

I backed away, and, seizing a bit of bread and jam from the kitchen, I went up to my room.

A bracing morning ride over the moor would put some sense into me. I put on my new dragon-riding ensemble and ran down to the stables...only to scrape to a sudden halt at the stable door.

Simon was leading Portia out.

"You're not—leaving?" I asked in dismay.

"Just taking a ride to clear my head," said Simon.

"Oh! Yes. Me too." Then I realised what I was wearing, and flushed crimson. "I had this made for me in London. It's very practical. It gets rather cold up there."

He looked me over slowly and nodded. "It looks warm."

"It is."

I had skipped breakfast for this? Meeting in the dining room couldn't possibly have been as bad. *Nothing* could be as bad. For heaven's sake, I was wearing *trousers*!

He put his foot in the stirrup and swung up effortlessly, then looked at me with a sparkle in his eyes.

"Race you to the Great Rock?"

He turned his horse.

"Wait a moment!" I cried. "You've got a head start!"

"You can fly," he flung back over his shoulder. Then he touched his heels to Portia's flank and was off.

I let out an indignant shriek. To my surprise, Cariad sprang forth from the stables and was instantly at my side, holding my riding harness in her teeth.

"You *dear*!" I said appreciatively.

A moment or two later and I was in the air.

I was surprised by how much ground he had covered, but he was right—I had a distinct advantage. Portia had to jump fences. Cariad had only clouds to contend with.

Simon was below us now, galloping across an upland meadow. I placed my hands on Cariad's neck and pushed gently downwards. She responded by descending rapidly towards him. Our speed was the same now, and she drew abreast of Portia, her feet skimming the grass, then furled her wings and ran alongside her for a moment, shoulder to shoulder. Portia's hoof beats thundered, throwing up clods of turf.

Simon turned and grinned in delight to find me so close.

Shyness forgotten in one wild impulse, I leaned to the full extent of my harness and grazed his cheek with a clumsy kiss.

I instantly regretted it, for he almost fell off.

I cried, "Up, up!" to Cariad and got myself out of his way before I could cause a mishap.

By the time he and Portia picked their careful way across the fissures of the Great Rock, Cariad and I were sitting on a huge stone, listening to the sound of the river below.

I didn't dare look at him, and mumbled an indistinct apology.

"But Edith," he said, dropping down next to me on the rock, "I thought we were done apologising for kissing one another."

I looked up to find him looking rather intently at me, and I thought he might be about to try out another reason to apologise.

"Wait," I said. "Here's something I'm really sorry about. I kept a secret from you—a very important one. I thought I was keeping Helena's secret, and Forrester's, but I should have found a way out of it sooner. I'm sorry."

He reflected on this. "Father says he made you promise not to tell me. I'm not sure what you could have done differently. I knew you had something to tell me. Do you remember asking me if finding out I was someone quite different than I thought would change anything?"

I nodded.

"It's changed everything," he said simply. "Do you know what is the strangest thing to me now? Despite all the lies I knew about—all the lies I saw the Drakes tell each other—I trusted them to tell me the truth about myself. Why did I? When I felt so out of place and wrong all the time, why did I think it was *my* fault?"

"It's in the nature of a child to trust, Simon. That's why it's so beastly when someone takes advantage of it."

Simon looked at me. "Every day of my life, I've been trying to make amends, before God, for simply being born. Until yesterday. It's as if someone tied a burden on my back when I was small, and every year it grew heavier, and all the time I thought that's just what growing meant. And now it's gone. I feel as if I am flying all of a sudden. I feel as if I'm up in the clouds, right there with you. It's only when I look down, that it gets dizzying." He took a deep breath. "I haven't decided what to do next. But I won't pretend I'm someone I'm not. I've done that long enough. I'm the child of two servants. I'm descended from someone who was little more than a slave. What that means for my future, I have no idea."

His left hand was on the rock next to me. I put my hand over it. When he spoke again, his voice was rough with emotion. "You're the only person who ever thought what I wanted was important. You said I should take time to think about it. But I don't need to take any more time to tell you—that I want this." He turned his hand, palm upward, under mine. "I want this. I don't know what else I want yet, but if you don't mind being patient with me—I suspect I have a deal of growing to do ahead of me still. But there isn't anything of me, or whatever I might turn out to be one day, that wouldn't be yours—if you wanted it."

He looked at our hands, his abbreviated thumb next to mine. Very timidly, I touched it with mine, just to tell him that I *did* want him—every bit of him, perfectly formed or not.

"I can be patient about most things," I said very solemnly, "but there's something I want from you very soon."

"Yes?" His brow was furrowed in deadly seriousness.

"Firstly, you must play Chopin with me, and let me take the second part sometimes."

He raised his eyebrow.

"Secondly, if you wouldn't mind, please provide a ring as soon as is convenient. You wouldn't *believe* the number of young men I've had to fend off in London," I said, remembering Violet's letter.

"Oh, wouldn't I?" he said in a low voice, and gently tilted my chin upwards so I looked in his face.

And that was the end of talking for a little while.

This time, there were no apologies.

The days began to slip past more quickly. There was still a bittersweet little space where Gwen and Frances were missed, but I'd never had so many people I loved together in one place, and my heart was very full.

I sent Irene a letter but heard nothing in return. I began to believe that my grandfather's cryptic threat had meant nothing after all, and that he had scared Farley off conclusively.

Simon had his most needful possessions brought over from Drake Hall and lived with us at the abbey. He went on walks with Forrester, and sometimes he came to my tower room to talk about them, though just as often he would go off riding alone afterwards.

I was true to my promise to be patient with him. He had spent his whole life being someone he wasn't. It would be understandable if it took him a little while to sort things out.

The weather became harsher, and we all drew inward a little—a little closer to the fire and to each other. It was delightful to watch Simon unbend in our family circle, and each person in it seemed to make a facet of him sparkle a little more. He discussed history and languages with Father, poetry and plants with Mother, natural history with George (God bless Simon), and books and dragons with me. In the evenings we took turns reading aloud from *The Count of Monte Cristo*. We all wept for the unjust imprisonment of poor Edmond Dantes, and cheered when he finally found a means of escape.

It was now well and truly winter, and it became more of an effort to get out of bed. As I gathered up my courage to brave the chill each morning, I made it part of my routine to read a few pages of Doctor Dunstable's journal after my morning prayers—at least the parts that pertained to life in the Dale. In his notes about Helena, he called her condition *nervous exhaustion*. The cures he talked about prescribing—no books, no conversation, complete silence—sounded almost as bad as the disease, in my opinion.

What had my grandfather said? That he had sent his wife to Switzerland for treatment for something similar. I hoped her treatment had been kinder than Helena's.

Simon had not spoken of going to talk with her, and I chose not to prod him about it. I remembered my own horror at being asked to see her, and her deception of me had been far less deep.

When I thought of those moments I had spent within the curtains of her bed, I prayed. To me, her fate seemed as awful as that of the quetzalcoatyls.

Simon said no more about them, either, but I fancied that he had visited them again, for twice I found my treasure map put back in a slightly different place in my desk than I remembered keeping it, and once he came back from a ride looking as if he had been caving again.

One Sunday morning in church, I slipped my hands into my muff for the first time since my trip to Belle Mount. Something papery crinkled inside. I remembered the rambling note from Nonna. My mind wandered terribly during the homily, and it was all too easy to discreetly slide out the paper and read it again.

Mama,

They won't let me have books. They won't let anyone speak to me. They take even pen and paper from me. I have given the nurse one of my rings for this. She promises to send it. I don't know if she will keep her promise. Do not leave me here a moment longer, I beg.

As far as I could make out from my Latin, the Italian merely rephrased the English portion.

But then there was this this, which I had overlooked before in the events of the day on which I had received it:

Please get word to David. Ask him to bring me home. As you love me, don't let this fall into Joseph's hands.

The note distressed me, though I did not know why. I had seen for myself that Nonna was not ill-treated. However distressed her mind might be at times, she enjoyed periods of tranquillity.

With a wheeze, the organ sounded and everyone stood up for the final hymn. I folded the paper and stood to join them. But as I did so, I saw the name at the bottom of the paper.

Judith Belmonte

That wasn't Nonna's name. Her family name was Marzano—the nurse had said it.

Judith was Nonna's daughter. The woman who had died far from home, in a sanatorium in Switzerland. My own grandmother. Could this be her last letter? A plea to be brought home?

After the benediction, I wandered out to the cemetery. I was dimly aware that my parents were speaking with the curate. Simon was standing by his mother's headstone, holding his hat. He looked up and caught my eye.

"What are you thinking?" I said, as I drew close.

"I'm thinking how strange it is that she rests here with the real Simon Drake. And that after all, my mother did give her life for me."

The words gave me a chill. I looked up at him, worried. While he didn't look cheerful, he didn't look morbid, either, or as if he was blaming himself this time.

The truth really had set him free.

"Did Forrester tell you how it happened?" I asked, slipping my arm through his.

"He was stunned at the loss of his wife, and they took advantage of his grief. The Drakes offered his motherless child a higher position in life. He realised his mistake too late, and then he was afraid no one would believe him. He chose to stay and keep watch over me."

"It must have all happened so fast, for the switch to have been effective. Perhaps your father wasn't the only one taken advantage of, all those years ago," I ventured. I was thinking of Helena, who had lost a baby, and had no time to mourn.

"I'm not sure I can think of her yet, Edith," he said, divining my meaning. "Not yet. I'm still mourning this mother."

"Of course you are," I said.

We stood for a little by the grave, and when he was ready, we walked back to the carriage.

"What were you thinking of during the service?" Simon asked.

I took out the note from my muff. "This note from my grandmother. She died far from her family, in Switzerland. It's such a lonely letter."

Simon took the note. "But Edith, you told me she died in the eighties."

He showed me the letter again. I had not noticed that it was dated.

March, 1895.

I stared at it. "But it can't be! That's only four years ago." My arm tightened on Simon's and I looked at him in horror. "You don't think—that he would have lied to people about his own wife dying?"

Simon's jaw tensed. "It wouldn't be the first time your grandfather lied about something, would it?"

A gust of wind stung my eyes, and I suddenly recalled the crackle of a voice over the telephone in my grandfather's study, and the book Barrington had chosen for me.

The Count of Monte Cristo.

The story of an innocent, imprisoned for decades.

Had my own grandmother suffered such a fate? Might she yet be alive, suffering still, praying for someone to rescue her?

Simon bent close to me. "*Whatsoever ye have spoken in darkness shall be heard in the light.* Remind me, what's the rest of that text?"

I swallowed. "*And that which ye have spoken in the ear in closets shall be proclaimed upon the housetops.*"

"So. No more secrets." He smiled suddenly, a grim, determined smile I had not seen on him before. "Perhaps I should adopt that as my motto. I don't think the Forresters have one. But in the meantime, what are we to do with this letter?"

"It was meant to be given to my uncle David." I took a breath. "But I don't trust my grandfather's servants to deliver it."

"Then trust me," said Simon.

CHAPTER THIRTY-ONE

Simon left the next day. His plan was to wait at the synagogue to meet my uncle after the Torah reading.

After seeing Simon off at the station, I paid a call on Dr Worthing.

"Oh, Miss Worms!" Mrs Worthing greeted me with a surprising amount of relief. "And I thought you'd forgotten!"

"Forgotten?" I repeated.

"The charity bazaar! You were to call on me to discuss the details. It's in five days, you know."

"Yes, of course." I had, in fact, forgotten entirely.

Mrs Worthing began to convey a lot of information to me while I struggled to recall if I had promised to donate anything. Despite Mother's unfailing encouragement, I have never excelled at handiwork.

"And you're quite sure you can bring him?"

Him? I thought helplessly. Had I promised to donate something masculine?

Then I saw the glance she gave my gloved left hand, in case there might be a little bulge on one particular finger.

"Oh, *Simon*!" I exclaimed in relief, folding my hands discreetly in my lap. "Yes, yes, of course."

But as soon as I said it, I realised I had no idea what Simon's feelings on charity bazaars might be, and I wasn't sure what kind of claims might reasonably be made upon the time and energies of one's sweetheart, having never before had one of my own.

Dr Worthing came in to boast about Gwendolyn, waving about her latest letter. How often did she write to him? It looked longer than any of the letters she sent me.

"She's doing quite marvellously, you know," he said. "I knew from the first she was exceptional. Really exceptional."

His wife and I exchanged a smile. Mrs Worthing had been instrumental in opening her husband's eyes to the *exceptionality* of Gwendolyn.

"Dr Worthing, do you mind me asking—have you ever attended Mrs Drake?" I asked.

"I have not had that honour, Miss Worms."

"From what I understand, her last course of treatment was quite ghastly." Mrs Worthing glanced at me sharply, recognising that I had read the old doctor's journal. "I believe your predecessor diagnosed her with nervous exhaustion. Would your treatment differ from his?"

"It would be impossible to prescribe a treatment from a distance, Miss Worms, but if you are speaking of what is commonly known as 'the rest cure', I think that in its insistence on treating the *mind* of the patient, it fails to take into account circumstances which may be affecting the patient's body. An unhealthy situation may account for much."

"What sort of unhealthy situation?"

"I could not venture to say, having not had the opportunity of examining Mrs Drake's surroundings."

"Of course," I said. "I'll do my best to persuade Mrs Drake to consult you herself, Dr Worthing."

When I arrived back at the abbey, my parents were seeing off a visitor of their own. Mother's face had a pinched look. I waved at the irritating little curate as cordially as I could, but he rattled obliviously into the distance, stiff-backed in his gig.

George's head popped out the front door behind Father and Mother. "Is the coast clear?"

"Clear," sighed Father.

"Release the dragon!" George called back, and Una and Violet issued forth with Hanna's salamander, who did not look particularly ferocious.

Violet made up for it. "If he ever comes again, we'll release all the dragons we can find on him—and we'll release *Janushek* as well!"

"What did he come about, anyway?" I asked, getting down from the carriage. "It can't have been for the enjoyment of our company."

Mother walked inside abruptly. Father handed me a clipping from a society magazine, a passage circled in red.

A recent shock in the world of the shilling shocker has been the identity of the popular author E. W. Fairweather, long supposed to be a man, and now revealed to be a member of the fair sex. Miss Edith Worms of the Yorkshire Worms has been revealed as the true author of these sensational mysteries. That a member of the landed gentry should amuse herself with writing yellow back novels is not shocking in itself, but that the daughter of a clergyman should demonstrate a thorough acquaintance with the proceedings of our criminal courts is more surprising. Perhaps the Rev Worms has not himself been informed. Perhaps he has been too busy performing his clerical duties to notice his unmarried daughter's literary activities.

"Oh, Father," I said. "This, *and* the dreadful war? I'm so sorry."

"Don't be. If a sparrow cannot fall without providential notice, then a visit from an envious curate cannot escape it either. Excuse me, I must go back to the library." And off he went.

"Violet," I asked, "what did you mean about releasing Janushek? Is he a weapon?"

"He's an anarchist, isn't he?" she retorted frostily. "And they shouldn't be allowed to meddle with explosives."

I looked to George for further explanation.

"He's been unloading and storing explosives, for the lime-works," said George. "Janushek's quite all right, of course.

But he won't let us near the explosives, and Violet's cross about it."

"I told Dugdale, but he didn't listen to me," said Violet. "I won't mind an explosion or two, when they come. Everyone will see I'm right, then."

And she looked suddenly cheerful about the prospect.

Going to the kitchen, I found our friendly anarchist at the table with Hanna, peeling parsnips while she read aloud to him. She had tethered her salamander to the kitchen table with some string, and it sat by her feet, watching its twin jealously.

For Janushek's salamander, having outgrown the cap, was perched on his shoulder.

"*And a certain woman, which had an issue of blood twelve years, and had suffered many things of many—many—*"

"Physicians," said Janushek, holding up a piece of parsnip, which disappeared into the salamander.

"*—physicians, and had spent all that she had, and was nothing bettered, but rather grew worse, when she had heard of Jesus, came in the press behind, and touched his garment. For she said, If I may touch but his clothes, I shall be whole.*"

"What are you doing with the Gospel of St Mark!" I exclaimed.

"I am teaching English with it, Rusalka," Janushek said acidly.

There was an almost imperceptible sidelong glance from Lily, who was putting on her shawl as if she was about to go out.

Janushek shifted in his chair. "Miss Worms," he corrected him-self.

"Miss *what*?" I cried.

"If you do not approve of Mark, we will change to *Marx*," Janushek said irritably, reaching to take the book from Hanna.

"I want to know the rest," said Hanna, grabbing hold of it.

"He dies," snapped Janushek.

"For shame!" This from Martha at the larder door, hands on hips. "You just had to go and ruin it for her, didn't you?"

Janushek went pale and surrendered the book. "I—I apolo-gise. So. We will continue—with Mark."

Hanna smiled. Martha went to stir something on the hob, waving at Hanna to continue.

"*And straightway the fountain of her blood was dried up; and she felt in her body that she was healed of that—*"

"Plague.*"

"*And Jesus, immediately knowing in himself that virtue had gone out of him, turned him about in the press, and said, Who touched my clothes?*"

Lily put the shawl over her hair and slipped out through the scullery. I went to my study. A phrase kept echoing in my head.

If I may touch but his clothes, I shall be whole.

If only Helena could do the same.

Something stirred in my mind, like a curtain lifted by a draft that came from a window you didn't know was open.

When Janushek appeared at my study door, I was hunting through my notes to find the ones on poisons.

"Were you looking for me before?" he asked.

"Janushek, what do you know about chemical dyes?"

"More than I want to know. I was the supervisor in a dye factory."

"The apocryphal dye factory?" I recalled with surprise. "I thought that was just one of your—stories."

"I only wish it had been," he replied.

"They make people ill sometimes, don't they?" I asked. "You might have fabrics, or textiles, or wallpapers—for simply years and never know what they're doing to you?"

He nodded. "When you work with them every day—you soon find out."

"What do they do to people? Would they cause fatigue, and headaches? Stomach aches? Heart palpitations? Nausea?"

"Yes, all of that—and worse."

"Worse?" I stilled, horrified.

He looked away. "Worse."

"Which was the most dangerous?"

"The arsenic ones. Arsenic is—"

"I know. I had to read up on poisons for my books. And Father's about to lose his job because of it. But never mind that now. If you saw a fabric that had been dyed with that—would you recognise it?"

"Yes." And then his eyes went very hard. "Green."

"Green?" I whispered.

"Scheele's Green, and Paris Green. They were the worst. Some of the workers even turned green. And not just their skin."

Janushek squinted at me. "What is this about, Rusal—Miss Worms?"

"I have a hypothesis. But it may be wrong." I sat down and took a deep breath. "Why are you calling me that, anyway?"

He shut his eyes in frustration. "I am trying to be more... respectful."

"*You*—respectful?" Then I had an idea. "Did Lily ask you to do it?"

"She did not *ask*. But I have seen her face when I call you the other name."

"Ah." I bit my lip. How to tell him that Lily might feel a little tender about any special familiarity between us? Years of watching her employers had made her observant, and like as not she had put two and two together long ago (and probably even before I did). "Janushek...are you quite sure it's anything to do with being respectful? Might it be something quite different?"

"What else could it—" Light broke over his face. "*Idiota!*" he cried. Then he darted off.

Janushek had given me all the information I needed, so I gave up on my notes. I paced the room.

Perhaps I ought to wait until Simon returned. But equally, Simon had asked for patience about confronting Helena, and it would be unfair for me to do anything that might force his hand.

And the same God who ordained the fall of every sparrow as well as the visit of every spiteful curate had ordained that I would discover this clue at this moment.

I put on my own coat and headed to Drake Hall.

"It's Edith," I called softly at Helena's door.

"Come in," she answered.

The room seemed darker than it ever had before. But of course, I had never seen it as the year waned. My friendship with Helena had begun in the spring and had ended in the summer. Could it be reborn as the year grew dim and old?

"I brought you a book," I said, going to her beside. "It's absurdly long. This is only the first volume. But I think you'll like it."

I tried to keep from staring at the bed curtains. Could I be right in my suspicions?

"Are you still writing, Edith?" she asked, to my surprise.

"Simon told you?"

"He's very proud of you."

I flushed.

"He's not coming back to me, is he?" Helena said very quietly.

"I don't know," I admitted. "I don't think he knows either—yet. He's gone to London for a few days."

"It doesn't frighten you?" she asked quickly, the old, sharp Helena once again.

"What?" I stalled.

"Ah," she said softly. "I see it does. Brave Edith."

I took a moment. "I'm not brave. It's just—this place— Ormdale—to some people, it's a cage. I don't want it to be a cage for him. Because I know that even then he'd stay for me. So the door must remain unlocked, you see, even if it *does* frighten me."

"A cage. Yes." She adjusted the lorgnette on the chain about her neck. "I tried to run away once, when I was a young woman, about Violet's age. I took some of the Drake silver and hid in a farmer's cart. I planned to pawn the silver and seek my fortune. I dreamed of becoming a gypsy." She laughed, but it turned into a cough. "They fetched me back, of course. They needed their Marsi, didn't they?"

I took a slow breath. "Helena, what would you say about seeing the new doctor, the one that has helped Gwendolyn? You don't have to answer straight away. But I think he might be able to help you."

"Oh, *doctors.*" She waved a hand, and then she spoke very low. "I never felt like a real mother. I didn't even want Simon when they gave him to me. But my husband had to have an heir, and the old doctor said the baby would give me something to do." Her fingers plucked at the bedclothes. "After a while, Simon made me feel—important. Loved, even. And he's all I've ever had. But whether he ever wants to see me again or not," she said slowly, "I'll do my best to make things right for him. As right as they can be." She lifted her grey eyes to me. They made me think of empty rooms. "I think if anyone knows what that is, it's you. So I'll do whatever you say, Edith."

Chapter Thirty-Two

I was making my way up the river path when I heard voices ahead. I stepped behind a thicket out of instinct. It was still a possibility that Farley might send someone after the antidote.

They were coming closer.

"We both have scars." That was Janushek's voice.

"But I can see thy scars, Brik. Mine, tha canna see them."

Upon identifying the voices, I had been about to step out of my hiding place when I was so surprised at hearing Lily call Janushek by his Christian—or rather, non-Christian name—that I froze.

I could see her now. Lily had a basket full of willow tips to make tea for her grandfather's rheumatism.

"Not just on the outside, Lily," Janushek answered softly, and his tone startled me. "I told you. Be warned. If anything, it's worse for me on the inside than on the outside." He made a helpless gesture at his face.

I knew he wore a layer of defiance with me as a way to prove that he didn't care about the difference in our stations in life. But even when that layer had been at its very thinnest—in London, at the coffee-house—he had never spoken in this way to me. It was as if every last one of his weapons had been thrown down, leaving him quite defenceless.

Lily went still, so she must have heard it too. The way she held herself was like a doe poised on the edge of a clearing, trying to decide whether she'd sensed a hunter or one of her own kind.

Bother it! I should *not* be hearing this, but I was reluctant to startle Lily and curtail such an interesting conversation. With any luck, they would keep walking out of earshot, and then I could get out of their way entirely.

I tried to conjugate Latin verbs in my head so I wouldn't hear anything more.

Teneo, tenere, tenui, tentum...

"There's some as deserve better," she said hoarsely, as if every word cost her something.

His shoulders sagged. "You're right. So, then. I'll stop bothering you."

"*Bothering* me?" The deer was completely gone now— her face was as flinty as her tone. "Shut thy cake-oil, Brik Janushek."

Then she dropped her basket, took his face in her hands, and dropped a number of kisses on his scarred cheek.

I could not have told you how to conjugate anything at all—not even *amo*, not to save my life.

I'm not sure who was more shocked—me, Janushek, or the salamander on Janushek's shoulder, who had an unrivalled view of the proceedings.

A gasp must have escaped me, for Lily stopped kissing him and peered into the thicket that concealed me.

"I didn't see *anything!*" I shouted wildly in their direction and stumbled off as fast as I could.

When I got back to the abbey, George was waiting for me.

"Edith, something's up," he said.

"Good heavens, what *now*?"

"Father told me to fetch you and Mother to the library."

"All right, I'll go. Have you fetched Mother?"

"I daren't. She's crying in the garden."

I found Mother sitting on the bench, dry-eyed now.

"Father says we're to come up to the library," I said.

"Yes," she said, standing up. "I'm quite at peace now."

We made for the library together.

"Mother, I'm so terribly sorry I've added to all this."

She put her hand on my arm. "No. You've done nothing amiss. I've had my cry, and now I'm ready to be strong again. It's all for the best, you know. Whatever parish is willing to take us next, we'll start out fresh, with nothing to hide. Do you know, I'll enjoy having a famous daughter. I'm sure people will bring me reviews, and ask me all sorts of amusing questions."

We went into the library together.

Father was gazing at a document through his strongest spectacles and George was gazing mournfully at his moth jar on the window sill. For a moment, they looked exactly alike.

"Ah ha! There you are at last!" cried Father.

"Yes, Father—we are come to hear the doom you will pronounce."

He stared at us over his spectacles. "The what?"

Mother sat near him comfortably. "I hope it's not to be very far from Yorkshire, for I'd like to visit Edith often. Please don't say we're to be sent to the Outer Hebrides."

Father looked at her with a slightly puzzled air. "Have you been reconciling yourself to being cast out of your Eden, Emily?"

"Don't you think Eden was significantly warmer than Yorkshire?" George asked. "After all, our first parents didn't wear any clothes."

"I'm sure it was, George. And I've always known we would leave," said Mother to Father. "Perhaps that's made it all the more—prelapsarian. Happily, there will be no cherubim barring the way back with a flaming sword."

Her tone was light, but we could both sense the sadness behind it.

George and I looked at each other.

"You ought to know that I wrote to the bishop earlier today," Father said carefully, "to resign my office as a clergyman of the Church of England."

Mother stared at him. "You *what*?"

"Emily, I can't think why you are so surprised. We discussed this."

"We discussed the fact that you had to perform your duty to God!"

"And I thought you knew what I was talking about—that my unexpected but undeniable position here in Ormdale requires my presence and attention, and only mine, while there are many young men eager—all too eager, in some cases—to fill every pulpit in England several times over."

Mother still stared, but slowly, her eyes began to fill with tears.

"And even if the bishop were to write and beg me to return, which he certainly will not, I wouldn't do it." He took both her hands in his. "I can be dense, Emily, and it took me too long to see how tired you've become, but as soon as I'd seen it, I couldn't ignore it. And you can rest here. You've been strong long enough, Emily. Let me be strong for a while."

"Good job, Father!" said George.

"Oh, Father!" I burst out joyfully. "I could just *kiss* you!"

"Never mind, Edith, I'll take care of that myself," said Mother firmly. And she took Father's face in her hands and did just that, most capably.

George blushed and stared at his moth, and I fled—for the second time that day.

I did not go to bed that night alone, for Simon had asked me to keep Pilot with me. The dog was quite dry this time, so I was not given an olfactory reminder of his presence in my room. But I could hear his steady breathing, and it was a welcome reminder of Simon's care.

I wondered how he was faring in London. I prayed my uncle would give him a fair hearing and would know what to do with the letter.

I tried not to imagine my grandmother imprisoned in a featureless alpine sanatorium.

It was around two in the morning that Pilot woke me, hackles raised, growling deep in his soft throat.

I lit the lamp. "What is it, Pilot?"

He began to scratch urgently at the door. I let him out and he ran baying down the passage.

I flung on my dressing gown and went after him. By now I could hear the movements of others as they woke and stumbled about, looking for shoes.

I ran down the stairs and straight into Janushek, clothed and carrying a gun.

"What are *you* doing here?"

"Drake asked me to stay while he was gone," Janushek answered shortly.

"Where's Pilot?"

"I don't know."

We jumped as we heard him snarling outside.

Janushek unbolted the door and ran out, with me close behind, but there was no moon tonight, so we only heard the pounding hooves of a horse fleeing, with Pilot snapping at its heels.

Janushek whistled and Pilot returned to the small circle of illumination provided by my lamp.

"Did you get a look at him?" I asked Janushek as I knelt down and patted Pilot appreciatively.

"No," Janushek said. "Cover your ears, Rusalka." He fired a warning shot in the air, as a parting message to our intruder. "He won't come back tonight," he said grimly, shouldering the firearm as if it were second nature to him.

No one slept much the rest of the night. Janushek was waiting for me before breakfast.

"Did you find anything?" I asked eagerly.

"I found the open window where he got in. It was in a disused room, under the bedrooms. And he left you something."

He held out an envelope marked *Edith Worms* in sharp, familiar lettering.

I no longer felt eager.

"You know this handwriting?" I asked him as I took it.

"Yes." He paused, then shrugged. "Also, I already opened it."

I shot him a narrow glance and read it myself.

Edith,

You are a fool for thinking yourself safe from me here.
Farley

Chapter Thirty-Three

After breakfast, Dugdale came over from the lodge and everyone gathered solemnly in the sitting room. Everyone except Violet—who gathered, but did not seem to know what solemnity meant.

"Do we all get weapons now?" she asked, bouncing in her chair. "Can we rig booby traps? George gave me a book that tells you how to make traps for bears."

Mother shushed her. "Let's hear what Janushek has to say to us, dear."

Janushek stood to address us all. "Last night, there was an intruder, chased off by Pilot. He left a note. It was written by Farley."

There were a few intakes of breath. Janushek passed round the note. His eyes rested on me.

"Are you bothered by the same thing that I am?" he asked in a low voice.

"Do you mean, what does he gain from leaving me threatening notes? Wouldn't it be better to surprise us?"

"Exactly, Rusalka."

Janushek's eyes flicked to Lily. She returned his look with a small, reassuring smile. I tried not to notice.

"Which makes me wonder," began Janushek, rubbing the scar on his cheek unconsciously.

"Yes?" prodded Father.

"If his aim was not the antivenin at all," he continued, looking at me, "but just to frighten you."

"But how would that serve his purpose?" I asked.

Janushek shook his head.

Violet saw her opportunity. "What if he wants us to think it's the antivenin he's after but really it's something else? What if he wants to kidnap Edith and drain her blood?"

George kicked Violet. Una looked ill.

"No," I said. "He only wanted my blood to make himself immune, and that didn't work, Violet. So that's not something we have to worry about. And if he is trying to continue his plan to make chemical weapons, then he really needs the antivenin, because it gives him an advantage over any other scientist that tries to copy his weapons."

"Does he want them to use on the Boers?" asked Violet. "The newspapers say—"

"Did you get the newspapers out of the wastebasket again, Violet?" asked Mother. "I've told you—those people will print anything. Lily, make sure you burn them next time."

Father looked thoughtful. "Edith, what about that matter of the Rivers fellow? Did you ever clear that up? I wonder if there's anything else we might be dealing with here."

"Anything else?" The time was fast approaching when I must divulge everything I had learned in London, and I dreaded it.

Dugdale nodded. "Aye, it would be helpful for us to know as much as we can."

I gave a sigh. "Well. Yes. There is something else. I'm afraid it turns out Rivers was hired by my grandfather, Sir Joseph Belmonte, to come here and investigate our dragons and then, rather absurdly, to offer to buy some from us."

This was met with general surprise.

"Buy them?" repeated George. "Is he a naturalist?"

"Not at all! And he is no admirer of the Worms family, so it couldn't be to our benefit."

Janushek crossed his arms. "How far would he go? Could there be a connection to Farley?"

"I don't see how," I answered frankly. "My grandfather threw Farley out when he came to the house in London to threaten me."

"Farley was there? In the house? And he knew exactly when you would be alone?"

"Yes, but—" I broke off. "Wait."

I thought rapidly. I went over it all again—the order of things. How my grandfather had offered to protect me. The way he had accomplished Penrith's downfall just to put me in his debt. How a footman had told me my grandfather wanted me in the study, when it was Farley who awaited me there. The footman who was dismissed before I could question him.

"Give me the note again," I said. Someone handed it to me and I read it again.

Edith,

You are a fool for thinking yourself safe from me here.

My head swam. What had been my grandfather's last words to me? *Don't be a fool, Edith. Don't make your mother's mistake. I will not sit idly by this time.*

Was this threat meant to prompt me to seek protection from my grandfather? Had he dictated it to Farley?

Had Farley ever before called me by my Christian name?

I put my head in my hands.

"I'm afraid I'm endangering us all," I said when I regained the power of speech. "My grandfather warned me that something terrible would happen if I came back here. I didn't take it seriously at the time. But looking back—I wonder if Farley was following instructions. He could have hurt me that night in London, if he'd wanted to. But he didn't. He even told me he was only there to frighten me."

Father's brow was knotted with concern. "So, could Violet be right? Is Farley really just acting as an agent of Sir Joseph, and not seeking the antivenin at all?"

"I'm sure he is seeking it. He's totally focused on his work, and with war declared..." I glanced at Violet. "Well, I imagine this is his best chance to interest the War Office in his weapons again. But I think Sir Joseph is involved, and perhaps he has been keeping Farley on a lead—telling him how far he can go."

It was horribly plausible.

"But surely Sir Joseph wasn't behind that violent attack on you in the laboratory, Edith!" exclaimed Mother.

"No." I shook my head decisively. "Farley wouldn't have dared to do that to Sir Joseph's granddaughter—he was careful to experiment on people—" my eyes fell on Hanna for a moment "—people who wouldn't be missed. I'm sure he wasn't aware of any connection. I'll hazard a guess that the two of them met in the last three months. Farley wriggled his way out of trouble with the police rather easily during that time. And Sir Joseph's connections are of the highest. His secretary, Barrington, says he's been watching me. Watching us."

What was it he had said to me about *collecting secrets*? Of course he would have been collecting my secrets, too.

"So perhaps he became aware of my entanglement with Farley and questioned him about it. He must have realised he could use Farley to frighten me. I wish I'd asked Barrington about it, but I didn't suspect anything about this when I spoke with him."

"Who would ever suspect their own grandfather of behaving in such a way?" Mother exclaimed. "And why would he do such a thing? How could it possibly benefit him? I can't understand it at all!"

"It's never about money with Sir Joseph," I said, remembering Barrington's words. "Sir Joseph wanted me to join his household. Change my name. In effect, he wanted to lure me away—just as he believes Father lured *his* daughter away."

My eyes met Father's. He went a little pale as he took in my words. We were all silent for a moment. Then Mother laughed.

"Lured her away?" she repeated. "My darling, gentle husband? But that's patently absurd! From what George told me, it was entirely Miriam's idea. And I don't doubt it for a moment."

"Well," Father said humbly, "perhaps we ought to get you to explain it all to Sir Joseph, Emily."

"I don't think anyone can change his mind once it's made up," I said sadly.

"But what about the treasure?" asked my brother. "Did Sir J. send Rivers after that?"

"No, I'm sure he didn't." I shook my head. "What was it that Rivers said to you, George, about finding the map in some archives somewhere? Rivers heard Cousin Stephen talking about the entail at his club and offered his services. He must have had that map already and been looking for an opportunity to poke about here in Ormdale. And Barrington was there having lunch that day, heard the name *Worms*, and followed his orders—which was to stay close to anything that concerned us."

He keeps a close watch over everything that belongs to him, Barrington had said.

"He arranged a meeting between Rivers and Sir Joseph. The thing I still don't understand is what my grandfather could have wanted with our dragons. Why offer to buy them? I can't make head nor tail of it."

Dugdale cleared his throat. "It seems to me," he concluded briskly, "that regardless of who is behind it all, there are three things Farley and any ruffians he sends here may want from us: our antivenin, our beasts, and our Marsi." He looked round at us. "And since we are not handing them over anytime soon, the next order of business is sending them packing, if and when they show their faces again after Janushek's warning last night."

The children's eyes were enormous.

"But see here," objected my brother, "they jolly well can't besiege us and issue demands—like some sort of shootout in a cowboy story, can they? We're in England, not Wyoming!"

"Drake and I have already made a plan to protect us," Janushek answered.

"It doesn't involve shooting, does it?" asked Mother.

Dugdale weighed in now. "No ma'am. You can ask Squire, he knows all about it. We're peaceful folk here, and we'll defend ourselves as peacefully as we may. I'm to alert all the tenants and the people of Ormby to be on their guard against outsiders. Which—if you'll excuse me—I'll do now." He stood up.

"But oughtn't we to notify the authorities, Dugdale?" Mother asked.

"It's a wild story, Mrs Worms," Dugdale said with a doubtful shake of his head. "Even if there were police closer than Skipton, I doubt they'd take it seriously. Antivenin and mad scientists and millionaires? And from what we've just been told, the people who are coming after us have some of the authorities on their side." Mother looked a little deflated. "Don't you worry, ma'am. There'll be time to involve the authorities once we've caught 'em red-handed. It'll sound less wild when we have an intruder or two locked in the cellar."

"I have something to add, before we all go about our business," I said. "For many of you, there is no necessity to be caught up in this affair at all. Hanna and Janushek have already suffered at the hands of Dr Farley, and may have no wish to repeat the experience. Lily, I don't think it fair to endanger you and your family. Mother and Father must decide about the children themselves, but I'd like to give the rest of you the opportunity to leave, if you wish, until this crisis is over. I've no idea what Farley is planning, but speaking from experience, it won't be pleasant."

There was a little rustle as people looked at each other.

Then Lily spoke up. "Excuse me, miss, but this is the only home I've ever known. And as Brik can tell you, if it comes to a fight, I'm not half bad at defending what I care about."

Her eyes went to Janushek, and again, there was that quiet warmth from her amber eyes. He smiled, and I think at least three of us were remembering that moment when Lily had felled him with a spade.

"What about you, Hanna? You've more reason than any of us to avoid another confrontation with Farley."

"I have good shooting, if you give me gun," she replied, disconcertingly off-handed about it.

Then Una took hold of Father's jacket and tugged gently. He leaned down to listen.

Una spoke only to him, but we all heard her quite clearly. "Please don't send me away, Uncle George."

Father's eyes twinkled with delight. "These Britomarts and La Pucelles put the rest of us to shame!" He took her hands in his. "However, I hope, with Janushek and Drake's excellent defences, and, above all, God's help, we won't have need of any displays of Amazonian bravery. And I have found something that may help us."

He took out a worn leather cylinder with a flourish, and I saw that look of gloating in his eyes which was familiar to me—a look he wore whenever he came across some piece of historical arcanum that particularly delighted him.

"I've just been showing Emily. I found it in the library, shelved most inappropriately with the works of Isidore of Seville."

"What have you got there, Father?" I asked, trying not to chuckle at his excitement. "How is Isidore of Seville's friend going to help us this time?"

Father removed a parchment from the container, then unrolled and held it up. A large wax seal dangled from it.

"It seems that we may have someone else we can call to our aid, if things become desperate. I mean, one suspects this sort of thing is purely ceremonial, but still!"

As I stared at the document, I felt my own eyes grow round as the children's.

George came close and scrutinised the seal. *"Elizabetha dei gracia Anglie Francie et Hibernie Regina Fidei Defensor,"* he read slowly. "But that's—"

"Yes!" Father almost shouted. "The second great seal of Elizabeth Tudor!"

"But Father," said George, his expression of bewilderment mirroring mine, "what does it mean?"

"It means, my dear, that anyone who wants to steal a dragon from Ormdale may wish they had never heard of them," Father said with relish.

Chapter Thirty-Four

The next two days were rather tense. The children were required to keep Pilot with them, and windows and doors were carefully barred each night. I felt that all would be well as soon as Simon returned, and I longed to know what had come of his meeting with my Uncle David. Surely he ought to have returned by now?

Helena had given me permission to bring Janushek to meet her. So I took the first opportunity of a break in his duties to take him with me to Drake Hall.

I was worried that Lily would not want him to walk with me, but she gave us a quiet smile when we passed her in the kitchen.

When we passed the place I had spied on them, I flushed. "I'm dreadfully sorry about—the other day."

He laughed. "Two important things have now happened to me on this riverbank."

"Oh! This was where I threatened you with a knife, wasn't it? Did you—did you clear it all up with Lily, then?"

He broke off a twig thoughtfully. "Perhaps not all. But we care about each other enough to go on clearing it up. And now I hope again."

"That sounds like something St Paul said. *Love bears all things, believes all things, hopes all things.*"

"Are you trying to preach to me, Rusalka?" he teased.

"Apparently I don't have to," I retorted. "You're already reading the gospel of St Mark."

"It is a very good story," he admitted. "I've told Lily that if we have children, I do not mind that they will be Christian."

"You don't *mind*?" I stared at him. "But—wouldn't you want your children to believe the way you do?"

"Believe?" He looked thoughtful. "For me, religion is more tradition than belief. And with our people, the child's religion is that of the mother. But you knew that, of course?"

I stopped walking. "What do you mean?"

"I mean that I am Jewish for the same reason that you are—because my mother was."

"But I'm only half! Not the real thing, like you."

"No, no, no, it doesn't work like that." He stopped and faced me. "Is that really what you thought?" His eyes were puzzled but kind. "You *are* Jewish, Edith, and your children will be, too. With our people, there is no half. I thought you knew that, back in July when you said you would be *schvesstar* to me."

I felt strangely overcome. I had always felt, deep down, that being half of something was rather an uncomfortable thing to be. At the same time, I realised that I'd been afraid of losing

Janushek's friendship. And now it turned out he had accepted me as a sister long ago.

For a moment, I was dangerously near using his collar as a handkerchief again.

I gave myself a little shake. "All right. I'll have to think about all this later. Let's keep on."

Janushek whistled and told me jokes about Russians the rest of the way, which I appreciated more than I would have under other circumstances.

When we got to Drake Hall, I made him wait in the passage while I went into Helena's room.

"Mrs Drake, I've brought Janushek, just as I told you. Will you see him?"

She put down her book and nodded, her face taut.

I turned back to the door and called him.

He came in, and I was happy to see him take off his cap for once. He glanced round the room, then his eyes stopped on the bed curtains and he went still.

"Janushek?" I prodded, my heart thudding fast.

He gave a small nod.

"Are you quite sure?" I asked.

"Yes."

It took all of my self-control not to rush out of the room—a reaction I had not anticipated. My eyes met Helena's and I saw on her face the terror of lying beneath the very shadow of death.

There was a strong possibility I would be sick on the rug.

Then a voice came from behind me—a voice that instantly steadied me.

"Edith?" asked Simon in concern. "Are you all right?"

I would have tottered as I whirled round, but he caught me in his arms. He had a coal-smut on his cheek from the train.

"The bed curtains, Simon," I choked out incoherently.

"Arsenic," said Janushek grimly. "It's an arsenic dye, Drake."

"It's hurting her?" Simon asked quickly.

"Not immediately, but over time…" Janushek trailed off, and their eyes met.

Time. There lay the horror of it. How long had she been in this room?

Simon spoke in my ear. "Edith, will you let Forrester take you downstairs?"

I nodded. Forrester, who had followed Simon into the room, led me gently away. Over my shoulder, I saw Simon gathering Helena up in his arms as easily as he had carried me over the moor when I was ill.

"No, Simon," she protested, her hand crumpling his lapel. "Let me die here."

"Death has already taken one of my mothers," he said in a low voice, "I won't let him claim another."

With a great shuddering sigh, she stopped struggling and laid her head on his shoulder.

Forrester gave me tea in the kitchen. Gleaming with copper pans and blue and white china, it was far cosier than the cavernous kitchen at the abbey. Oolong padded in and patted my knee until given pride of place in my lap.

"I had a room made ready for her at the abbey this morning, just in case," I said, holding the pleasantly-hot teacup in my hands. "Do you think she'll agree to go there for a while? I shall ask Dr Worthing to come see her, in case anything can be done to counteract the effects. Do you think she'll see him?"

"I think Simon will be very firm, miss. He was very firm with me about several things."

I could tell from the way he spoke that he was pleased about it.

"You know, it's a little awkward—you calling me 'miss'," I ventured. "I'm fairly confident you're going to be my father-in-law."

His lips twitched a little as he cut me some bread and butter. "Aye."

"I think your son would like it if you called me Edith. And as you say, he can be very firm," I added.

"Has he spoken with you about the name?"

"The name?"

"He wants to go by Forrester. I can't talk him out of it."

"Oh!" I thought for a moment, then smiled. "As you know, my name, presently, is Worms, which unfortunately makes most people think of little wriggling things rather than dragons. Forrester will make a very nice change."

Simon came in, holding Mr Darcy, and I drained my teacup to hide the fact that I had turned crimson thinking he might have overheard my words.

"Janushek says there's nothing dangerous in the sitting room, so I've put her in there, Father," he said to Forrester.

"What ought we to do now?" I asked.

"Janushek told me about Farley's note. If you don't mind, I'd like her to stay at the abbey. It's sensible to have just one place to defend." He handed Mr Darcy to Forrester and touched my shoulder. "Are you feeling better now?"

I nodded. "It was just—the horror of realising it."

"Yes. If only I'd known years ago," he said quietly.

My eyes searched his face. He did not seem downcast, but galvanised. There was a straightness to his shoulders and a set to his face that made me a little shy of him.

I put my hand over the one resting on my shoulder. Forrester busied himself feeding Mr Darcy out of a chipped Spode saucer.

"You must invite your father to dine at the abbey," I said. Simon looked at me in surprise. "I don't think he's met my parents properly. They'll have so much to talk about."

Forrester nodded and fed the lapdragon as if this conversation was a perfectly normal one.

God bless butlers, I thought. *How restful it will be to have one as a close relation.*

Forrester straightened and cleared his throat. "Now. I've something to show you both." He looked at Simon. "It's something more from your ancestor, lad."

"Do you know his name?" I asked.

"Aye. His native name was lost, but Ignacio is what the Spaniards called him," said Forrester.

"And the Drakes called him Ignatius," finished Simon.

Forrester opened a cupboard behind him. There amongst the brooms and mops, was a similarly-shaped object wrapped up in layers of sacking.

He held it out to Simon.

Simon unwrapped it slowly. It was a staff, something like a shepherd's crook or bishop's staff. Simon looked at it closely. "Cedar wood," he said.

He traced the curling part with this right thumb. It was pock-marked, as if it had once been decorated with precious jewels, long since looted. Simon spun it upright next to him, holding it comfortably by a sort of hilt one-third of the way down the shaft. It was as tall as he was.

"Shouldn't it—shouldn't it be in the British Museum?" I suggested timidly. "Instead of the broom closet?"

The two of them looked at me.

"I went to the British Museum while I was in London, Edith, and I saw the Aztec antiquities," said Simon slowly. "It seems to me that they have...quite a sufficiency. Besides, they wouldn't know what it's for." He stood tall, gripping the staff with a confidence that sent shivers down my spine. "And I do."

Chapter Thirty-Five

The next day was devoted to packing up necessities for Helena and installing her in my bedroom. Simon was resistant at first to my giving it up, but I was quite satisfied to bunk in with Violet and Una for the time being, and I think it relieved Mother's mind a little to have the three of us in the same room while there were intruders creeping about at night.

"You're exhausted," I said to Simon when he came out of Helena's room. "Come ride with me?"

He brightened. "When you say *ride with me*—what exactly did you have in mind?" he asked. "Because I've often thought that the first time we rode together, it was not under pleasant circumstances."

He was right—a breakneck gallop to save the life of an envenomated child had not been an auspicious introduction to horse-riding.

"You want me to give horses another chance?" I asked. He nodded hopefully. "Only for you, Simon," I said, taking his arm, and we went down to the stables as if we had always walked together so.

When we ambled out of the stable yard on Portia moments later, I was riding in front, with Simon's arms about me, which felt both the safest and most adventurous place to be at the same time—a delightful combination.

"I must tell you about London," he said.

"London? Oh! London," I stammered, distracted.

"I liked your uncle," he said.

"I thought you would. What did he say about the note? Did he recognise the hand?"

"Instantly. It was his mother's, just as we suspected."

I swallowed. "Will he confront my grandfather?"

"He planned on going directly to Switzerland before Sir Joseph caught on, which I thought was wise."

"Can my grandmother really be—alive?"

"Who can tell? The note was from four years ago. But whatever he finds awaiting him, the truth is always better than a lie. Which brings me to another subject." He guided Portia toward the bridle path that skirted the sheep meadows on the way to Talbot's Farm. "The feathered serpents. I did some research in London, at the British Museum. I learned that the Aztecs didn't depict their Quetzalcoatl as harming humans. In fact, it was portrayed very benevolently—a patron of renewal and agricultural abundance, if you will."

I opened my mouth to object—for I had not felt either patronised or renewed when it chased me out of its lair—but I shut it again. After all, the creatures had not hurt me. And I owed Simon a little trust by now. More than a little.

"Next time I go visit them, I'll take the staff," Simon said. "I believe it was used to handle them." He paused. "I've given it a great deal of thought, Edith, and I've come to believe we can release them safely, without endangering anyone." He paused. "But if it frightens you, I won't do it."

"But Simon, how can you say they are safe, when my uncle and cousin were killed in the caves by these creatures?"

"But they weren't."

"What!" I cried. "Gwen told me you found their bodies, defaced by beasts."

He shook his head. "I lied to her. I told her Gwen we'd found the bodies, but it wasn't true."

"But why? And what happened to them, really?" But as soon as I'd spoken, I remembered there were many ways to perish in an unmapped cave system. I'd imagined perishing there often enough myself.

"I was afraid she'd order people to keep searching, and there was no hope by that time of them remaining alive. And I did not want to lose any more lives. If I hadn't told your uncle that the legend about the Drake dragon was true, they'd never have gone after the treasure." He took a deep breath. "When I went up to London, I told Gwen the truth, and she was kind enough to forgive me. Do you remember how harsh I was to you, that day at the caves, when you wanted to send a search party in for Rivers?"

"You mean, when you gave me brandy so tenderly? That's all right, I understand now. At the time I was just happy to have my prejudices against you confirmed," I added mischievously.

"Ah! I thought you didn't like me at first. When *did* you begin to like me, then?" he asked, a little anxiously.

"Perhaps it was when first I saw your fine house at Pemberley," I said as seriously as I could manage.

"And as it turns out, Drake Hall was never mine," he said wistfully. "I'm sorry about that, Edith."

"Simon, I wouldn't mind if you lived in the pele tower."

"Now, there's an idea," he said.

I let out a breath. "So, in the absence of incriminating evidence, it seems your pets have been absolved!"

"Then the answer is...yes?" he said hopefully. "About releasing them?"

He sounded so much like a child pleading for his puppy that I couldn't help laughing.

"You aren't going to stop asking me, are you? Wait!" I cried. "Is that why you came riding with me? So you could utterly distract me and get me to agree to unleashing giant serpents on Ormdale?"

I felt the laugh that welled up in him even before I heard it.

"Well. When you put it that way, it does sound a little unsportsmanlike," he confessed. "But back to riding—are you ready for a canter?"

"Is that the one that rattles your teeth in your head?" I asked.

"No, that's galloping," Simon said. "Cantering is like a nursery rocking horse, but faster. I think you might like it. Lean back a little and hold onto the pommel."

He touched Portia's sides with his heels and she leapt into a thrumming gait.

The Dale was stark in winter, but the sky bloomed with the sun's last warmth, and I have seen no more beautiful sky than one finds in Yorkshire, up on the fells.

Perhaps there was something to horse-riding after all, I admitted to myself. And perhaps I'd like almost anything if I could do it with Simon.

After a bit, he slowed Portia and turned her about where we could overlook the abbey—a crumbling relic of time, with its tower, parapets, ruined church, chimney stacks, and outbuildings.

"Any better than last time?" Simon asked.

The chill air made my cheeks glow as I caught my breath. "Much better, thank you! But I do wish I could take you riding up there with me." I looked up wistfully at the colouring sky.

He let out a long breath, which ruffled my hair. "You take me up already, Edith," he said quietly, "just by looking at me the way you do."

Abruptly, I twisted round in the saddle to confront him. "Not like a treacle tart?"

He blinked. "I beg your pardon?"

"Something humiliating Mother said. *Do* I look at you like that?"

He reflected on this before he answered. "Before you, I only ever experienced love as a hunger that I couldn't fill. But—what did you say?—*love is something that fills, and warms, and makes you more yourself.* You do that for me, and you make me feel—as if I might do it back." He finished a little bashfully, like the old, shy Simon whose gentle selflessness had first won my trust. "In short, I don't mind being a treacle tart."

I laughed and settled back to face the path. He began to nudge Portia back down towards the abbey. A solitary window had kindled there, glowing as a terrestrial twin to the the evening star above us.

For the first time, I relaxed in the saddle. My head rested on his collar, and a feeling of deep contentment settled over me despite the increasing cold.

"Simon, it falls to me to inform you that the most onerous test of devotion is almost upon you."

"I'm ready," he said gravely.

"Don't you want to ask what it is?"

"I feel sure you are going to tell me."

"It's very, very bad. You are to stand with me all afternoon at the stall of a charity bazaar, persuading people to buy ugly things they don't need—pen wipers and d'oyleys and antimacassars."

"If that is the worst of it, Edith, I'm not sure it compares to watching you compete for the hand of another man."

It took me a moment to think what he was speaking of, but when I did, I let out a groan of regret. "Oh! I completely neglected to think of it from your perspective. I *am* sorry. And I'm trying to do better. Are you sorry that I gave them the antivenin?"

"No. The children oughtn't to suffer for the sins of the parents. And—well, I liked them," he admitted. "I was there for three months. Picked up a bit of their language. They taught me about their dragons. Under different circumstances, it would have been rather a splendid time."

I laughed. "Different circumstances than being shot, held hostage, and poisoned?"

"Exactly so."

"Oh, Simon! You are too good-natured by far. I suppose that is why I am not—we balance each other out nicely. I have a far more suspicious nature."

We both laughed. Then Simon spoke slowly.

"I've thought about what I want, Edith. And what I want—is to believe that there's something good here. In Ormdale, and all the Dragon Families, and in what we've protected together, however badly it's been done. Something worth all the years I gave it. And I think—I think it's not just my good nature, as you call it. And I hope it's not childishness, or fear of change."

Knowing how he felt about me, and how quickly things were changing for him, I hadn't wanted to sway him, but I was relieved that he felt as I did about the legacy we shared.

"Fidelity isn't childish. And about the Dragon Families—well, I've something to show you back at the abbey. Something Father found in the library."

"But Edith, what about you? You really like it here, don't you? It's not just duty for you?"

I nodded. "I stayed first because I was needed. But now I want to stay. *There are things I love here.*"

I wondered if he remembered saying those words to me at the end of a spring day, when he first showed his heart to me a little.

I suppose he did, for he took my hand off the pommel and raised it to his lips.

With Simon at my side, Janushek's bullet in the night felt very far away.

It was hard to convince myself that a villain lurked, readying himself to strike, when we were all so very cosy.

So, two days later, on a clear winter day in the second week of December, Simon drove us in his gig to Embsay for the charity bazaar.

"How was Gwen when you looked her up in London?"

"Happy." He gave me a sidelong glance.

"Hmph," I said. "She promised to come for Christmas, but I expect her to write any day now and tell me she's going to friends in Kent or somewhere."

"I believe her friend Ivy did invite her to her family's home in Cornwall," Simon replied, and my heart sank. "But she told Ivy she couldn't miss your first Christmas at Wormwood Abbey."

"Did she really?" I faltered. My spirits leapt at the prospect of Gwendolyn completing the family circle. "Of course, I want her to be happy..."

"Of course," he said mildly, "just not *too* happy."

We both laughed.

As we drove by the station, I glimpsed a thin figure, scanning all of the passing traffic with an uncertain expression.

"Aunt Lavinia!" I cried. "Simon! It's Miss Birtwhistle!" We drew up alongside her. "You remember Simon, of course?"

"Dear Mr Drake," she said fondly.

"What a happy surprise this is!" I said.

The smile that had lit up her gaunt face upon seeing me faded. "Oh. Then you didn't get my note."

"Never mind that, I'm delighted to see that you've come for your visit at last!"

Simon handed me the reins, jumped down, kissed Miss Birtwhistle's cheek, and went to fetch her bag.

"And you are just the person we want today, anyway."

Chapter Thirty-Six

As soon as we arrived at the school where the bazaar was being held, Simon was stolen away to lift something which had been deemed too heavy for the feminine frame. Miss Birtwhistle and I acquainted ourselves with the contents of our stall.

"And which of these things did *you* make, Miss Worms?" Miss Birtwhistle asked tactfully, inspecting a beaded napkin ring.

"Absolutely none," I confessed. "I know it's dreadful of me. I'm sure I'm only here because people want to get a good look at the new squire's daughter."

I caught a glimpse of Simon fixing someone's framed sketches to the wainscotting, surrounded by the admiration of an appreciative cluster of ladies, and wondered if he was forever lost to me.

"How bad is it?" I asked, turning back to her. "Be frank."

"Well, the chair-backs are not very elegant, but these bed socks and pin cushions might do the trick. All the little things; Christmas gifts for the unprepared." Her eyes ranged about the room. "I do think our chances of success will improve materially if Mr Drake is returned to us."

"Then pray for me," I muttered, and squared my shoulders.

Simon was obviously trying to extricate himself politely when I arrived, and completely failing.

"*There* you are!" I cried loudly, as if Simon had been a kitten that had got itself lost, which quieted everyone. With as proprietary an air as I could manage, I took him by the arm and led him back to our stall. I could feel everyone's eyes measuring the very few inches between the two of us.

"Edith. Did you just make some sort of ritual public claim upon my person?" Simon said in a *sotto voce* of suppressed delight.

"I did indeed," I said. "One has to be very firm in situations like these. These women would have had you running errands for them all afternoon! When I *particularly want you*."

Just for good measure, I picked a non-existent bit of lint off his jacket. Suddenly, he took up my hand and kissed it quickly.

I sensed a general intake of breath from all onlookers.

"Gently does it!" I warned him. "I need you to be eligible enough to sell all these gimcracks."

That afternoon, our behaviour towards each other was just outrageous enough that our stall boasted an ever-replenishing queue.

Meanwhile, Miss Birtwhistle did a steady business. "Wouldn't you like one of these charming little carved boxes to go with your pincushion? Yes? And you must take one of these chair-backs, we're just giving these away, you know."

"Splendid, Miss B! We're almost there!" I whispered. "If we keep on like this, we might get home before dark."

My spirits were very high. Cavorting with my almost-fiancé over the napkin rings had made the hours simply fly by. The benefits of having a sweetheart had not been quite so overstated as I had always assumed.

"Mr Drake, please wrap these d'oyleys—*without crumpling the paper, mind you!*"—I scolded playfully, rapping him on the arm with the scissors—"while I fetch more string from Mrs Biddle."

I went to one of the stalls near the entrance for the needful supplies for our final assault upon the purses of Embsay.

I was taking some out of a box when I caught a glimpse of a figure through the open door, walking by on the other side of the street. I went cold all over.

It was Briggs.

I could not follow him and see where he went, for Briggs would recognise me.

I ran back to Simon. Taking the package from him, I said in a low voice, "I've just seen one of Farley's men in the street. He has an eyepatch and he was walking that way."

Simon was gone almost instantly.

"Well, Miss Birtwhistle," I murmured as I tied up the package. "You *have* come at an interesting time. We've been expecting some trouble, and it looks as if the trouble may be upon us at last."

Miss Birtwhistle looked at me for a moment. "Dear me," she said simply, and sold the last stack of d'oyleys.

Simon returned twenty minutes later.

"Your eye patch fellow is one of a group from London, staying at the Elm Tree Inn. I've advised the landlord to keep an eye on them, and I've spoken to the local magistrate. Unfortunately, no one has committed a crime yet, so we cannot detain them. But they'll be closely watched. Well done spotting him, Edith."

I nodded, thinking fast. Simon and Janushek had their plans, but could there be something I might do to stymie the villains?

What had Simon said to me? That he wanted to find some good in the dragon families? Here was a chance to do it conclusively.

"Simon, I must nip out to the telegraph office."

"I'll pack up here and meet you there," he said.

Half an hour later, I walked out of the telegraph office and squeezed into the gig with the two of them. Simon had picked up heated bricks from the inn for our feet and he tucked us up snugly in a travelling blanket against the evening chill.

"Mrs Worthing said we sold out before any other stall," said Miss Birtwhistle as we set off on the road to Ormdale. "She seemed very pleased."

"I should think she would be," I said, "for it was entirely her idea to enlist Simon. Did you speak to her, Simon?"

"Yes," he said, "and thanked her for giving you the journal. She said she hadn't been entirely sure what was the right thing to do under the circumstances."

"What did you tell her?"

"I told her that as far as I am concerned, the truth is always the right thing to do. Edith, do we even know what that bazaar was benefiting?"

"I believe it was the Fund for the Amelioration of the Daughters of the Country Clergy," said Miss Birtwhistle.

"Well, I can tell you," I said as I put my arm through Simon's, "this clergyman's daughter is feeling the benefits already!"

As soon as we got home, Miss Birtwhistle and I thawed our extremities in the warm kitchen, our chairs pulled close to the range, and had our supper while Simon went to the lodge to speak with Janushek and Dugdale. Mother came and met our new guest, asking her questions about her journey.

"I'm very sorry to arrive unexpectedly and put you all out," Miss Birtwhistle apologised.

I turned to Hanna. "Hanna, I was thinking the east bedroom might be best—"

Mother touched my arm. "I've arranged it all with Lily."

"Oh," I said. "Well, then." Up until that moment, I had never really thought of Mother as the mistress of Wormwood Abbey.

Losing that responsibility felt like coming into a warm room and taking off a muffler. The muffler had suited me, but I found I was lighter for having taken it off. Things were changing again around me, but this time I didn't mind.

It felt like the dance at Michaelmas. We took turns, changed places with each other, and the shifting patterns it made were as beautiful as the seasons.

Later, I tracked down Mother and handed her the chatelaine Gwendolyn had given me months ago.

"You outlived it, then?" Mother asked. "The charity bazaar?"

"Oh, yes. Simon and Miss Birtwhistle together made it pass by like a dream. I'd no idea it could be like that."

"When something is done for love, it changes everything," said Mother, brushing my cheek with a light finger.

"Yes," I mused, "it's like the opposite of King Midas, isn't it? It's a metamorphosis. Speaking of which, has George's moth hatched?" I hadn't seen him with the jar lately.

"George is in mourning, my dear. He has kept the chrysalis as a relic, but he says all hope is gone."

After doing my duty so beautifully, I was ready for the sleep of the just, but I was not, alas, to be thus rewarded.

Before I'd been asleep an hour, I awoke to a little scuffle and a feminine cry of alarm from the direction of Simon's room.

I had a lamp ready, which I lit with all haste and carried out with me into the passage.

Pilot lay outside the door, thumping his tail on the floor as if nothing was the matter.

"Gracious!" I exclaimed as the circle of light fell on the person I least expected to see standing in the passage of Wormwood Abbey: Meredith Falconer, the sharp-tongued beauty I had sparred with in Wales.

She clutched a small carpetbag defensively.

"It is not as it looks!" she said.

"How *does* it look?" I cried in utter confusion.

At that, I heard Simon laughing and a familiar female voice scolding him.

"Gwendolyn!" I shrieked, and rushed into the room.

I thrust the lamp onto the bedside table, averting my eyes lest I see Simon in his nightshirt, and threw my arms around Gwendolyn joyfully.

"What on earth are *you* doing here?" I demanded.

"What am *I* doing here?" she repeated indignantly. "In my own bedroom? Imagine my absolute horror upon creeping in here, thoughtfully trying not to wake you all, and finding a *man* in my room!" She waved a hand in expressive horror. "Of course, it turned out not to be a man at all, only *Simon*—thank heaven!"

Simon had his back to us, trying to discreetly clothe himself, and his shoulders heaved with laughter.

"All right," I acknowledged, "this is your bedroom, after all, but how on earth is Miss Falconer here—with you? *She's* not a vegetarian!"

We both turned to see Meredith looking rather uneasily at Pilot in the passage.

"Good dog," she murmured.

"My train was delayed and I came across her at the Embsay station, asking how to get to Wormwood Abbey," Gwendolyn said lowly. "I found a boy who grew up in Ormby to drive us here."

At that moment, Janushek appeared at the other end of the passage with his rifle and lantern, very groggy.

"What on earth are *you* doing here at this hour with a rifle, Janushek?" Gwendolyn asked in amazement, taking in the firearm.

"Very little," he said, rubbing his eyes.

Now it was Mother's turn to appear, looking like Florence Nightingale with her lamp.

"Dear Gwendolyn, won't you introduce us to your friend?" asked Mother, taking her for a schoolfellow.

"No, this is Miss Falconer, Mother," I put in. "I told you about her. It seems all our security measures are dubious at best if people can just walk in at all hours."

I made this last comment for Janushek's benefit. He yawned.

Violet and Una's tousled heads popped round the door-frame of their bedroom. Oolong padded out from their feet and stretched, making Meredith start.

"Security measures?" repeated Gwendolyn, staring round the suddenly crowded passage. "What is going on? And why are there so many people here?"

"Excellent question," I said. "Let's start with the newest arrival. Why have *you* come, Miss Falconer?"

Meredith cleared her throat. "I have come," she said, with as much dignity as could be summoned under the circumstances, "to retrieve Aunt Lavinia."

And with that, she put her carpet bag on the floor with a thump. She looked tired and very young. For once, her garments looked a little rumpled.

Mother nodded as if all this brouhaha was to be expected. "Let's go down to the kitchen and put on the kettle, shall we? I expect it won't take much to get the fire going."

Mother touched Meredith reassuringly as she passed to lead the midnight procession to the kitchen. "Welcome to Worm-wood Abbey, my dear."

It was at that moment that I realised: Mother had quietly undergone her own metamorphosis. She had become the Lady of the Manor.

Chapter Thirty-Seven

Mother sent Violet and Una to bed, but the rest of us had cocoa round the kitchen table while Gwendolyn was apprised of the most vital recent developments.

"But Gwendolyn," I asked at last, "how on earth did you two sneak back in when poor Janushek has spent hours going round locking and barring every ingress?"

Meredith's eyes darted back and forth between us with an expression of guarded puzzlement as she sipped her cocoa.

Gwendolyn snorted. "Every ingress? You really think anyone could stop *me* from getting into Wormwood Abbey? I was toddling about the cellars on the hunt for groundlings while Janushek was still—well, doing whatever Janushek was doing as a juvenile. Stringing aristocrats up from the lampposts, probably."

Janushek stretched and scraped his chair back noisily.

"I'm going to bed. Show me in the morning how you got in." He gave Gwendolyn a familiar pat on the arm as he passed. "It's good to have you back." And he was gone.

"Well!" Meredith murmured when no one rebuked him for his unservantlike behaviour.

"I suppose Miss Falconer and I will have to camp in the east room tonight," Gwendolyn conceded, "since Simon seems so snug in mine."

"No good, I'm afraid—Mrs Drake is in the east room," I said.

"Mrs Drake!" Gwendolyn stared at Simon. "What's happened at Drake Hall?"

Simon and I looked at each other. Mother began to clear the mugs away.

"That," I said slowly, "would require a good deal more cocoa to cover."

Gwendolyn shook her head numbly. "For years I was terrified that everything would come undone here, and now it's happening. And I don't know what to think except that I'm terribly glad that none of it—at least as far as I can tell—is my fault."

I took her hand across the table and Simon put his arm round her shoulders.

"But it's not coming undone, Gwen," I said, "not like we joked about back in April. It's not the Fall of the House of Worms, or anything."

Then I caught my breath, for a thought had struck me with startling force, even as I said the words.

"What is it, Edith?" asked Mother, turning round from putting away the cocoa tin.

"I—I think I've worked it out at last," I said. "Never mind tonight. I need to sleep on it to make sure there's any sense in it." I got up. "Gwen, you ought to sleep in the room with your sisters—it will be a treat for them. Miss Falconer and I will slip into Miss Birtwhistle's room." I turned to Meredith with a reckless gaiety. "It will be just like old times!"

"How jolly," she said in a tone that reminded me of tea that had gone cold.

Simon stood up himself. "The two of you must take Gwen's room," he said. "I'll sleep in the sitting room."

I opened my mouth to object.

"No, Edith," said Simon gently. "You know Miss Birtwhistle oughtn't to be disturbed."

Gwendolyn's eyes widened. "*No, Edith*?" she repeated. "Well, *those* are two words I never thought to hear in a sentence together from Simon Drake."

"Simon's getting very good at saying no to me—*and* saying yes," I added mischievously. And just for good measure, I stood on my tiptoes and kissed him on the cheek. It was the sort of thing I would be happy to do every evening for the rest of my life.

Then we all went up to bed, Meredith following after me.

"So," she said dryly as we got ready to get into bed, "this is your *happy single life*, then."

"Well, I wouldn't give this as a specimen of a normal evening," I admitted. "And I'm ashamed to admit the single part didn't last quite as long as I intended."

We were lying in bed now, just as we'd done in Wales when I'd told her about my life at Wormwood Abbey.

"You're very lucky, Edith," she said softly, facing away from me.

I waited for it—the barb, the pointed comment. But it never came.

"Shall I put out the light?" I asked.

"Yes," she said.

My mind was whirling, so I didn't fall asleep for a little while. At one point, I was sure I heard Meredith give a little sniffle.

Oversleeping, I woke alone. I quickly dressed and hurried downstairs to find everyone getting on quite well without me.

Mother was showing Miss Birtwhistle the children's nature journals. George and Pip had their heads bent over some paper, creating a mysterious diagram and whispering. Gwendolyn was telling Violet and Una tales of modern life in London, while Meredith looked on at a frosty distance.

I wasn't sure which vignette had provoked her disapproval.

A distant boom sent the children running to the window.

"It's the blasting for the lime-works," Mother explained to Miss Birtwhistle. "A good deal louder than I expected, I must admit."

I beckoned to Gwendolyn and she followed me into the passage.

"I've something to show you. You remember how I always said we weren't just Dragon Keepers, but Royal Dragon Keepers? Well, Father found something that backs me up. Come up to the library."

Once there, I took out the parchment from its ancient case and spread the document carefully on the desk.

"How's your Latin these days, Gwen?"

"Medical," she said.

"Well, I'll cut to the chase. According to Father, it says that the Sovereign bestowed a hereditary position in the Royal Household on Benedict Worms and all of the heirs of his body in fifteen eighty-six."

"A hereditary position in the Royal Household?" Gwendolyn repeated. "But...we've never even been to court!"

"Yes, but it's ceremonial. Like the Keeper of the Swans, you know—*he's* never been at Court."

"What keeper of the swans? What are you talking about?"

"George explained it to us. All the mute swans in the Thames by rights belong to the sovereign. There's still a fellow who keeps track of them. Apparently, they make a bit of a party out of counting them once a year. No idea how they tell if they're mute or not—I do hope they don't poke at them."

"Edith, would you please stop digressing and tell me what this means for us? Really, you are worse than some of my lecturers!"

"It means that unless the position has been absolutely abolished—and I can't believe anyone's bothered—my father is the Dragonmaster to the Queen."

"Dragonmaster?" Gwendolyn's face was blank.

I nodded. She swallowed and sat down.

"All right, Edith, I'm going to try very, very hard not to laugh. And I'm going to listen while you tell me why this is *not* the most ridiculous thing I've ever heard in my life."

"I'm not sure it isn't ridiculous, in its way, but perhaps some of the nicest and best things in life *are* a bit ridiculous. Falling in love, and cream buns, and—I don't know!—babies, and singing, and the monarchy itself, for goodness' sake! And dragons and detective stories!" I waved my hand helplessly.

"That's it?" she asked flatly. "I mean, I'm trying to be fair, Edith. I know I've been impatient with you in the past, and I've let you down. But that's all you have to say about it?"

I took a deep breath. "It *is* ridiculous to have a Royal Dragonmaster in eighteen ninety-nine. But then—we've got dragons, haven't we? And people trying to steal them from us—so I suppose they're Dragon Hunters. And there's a hidden Spanish treasure, and babies being swapped in bedpans, and the deity of the Aztecs is caged up down in the caves—only Simon wants to let it out and make it his pet! I know you want life to be rational and orderly and modern, like one of your textbooks, but this is real, Gwen. I didn't invent it! This is life in Ormdale.

For better or worse, *this is our family*. And sooner or later, we all have to come to grips with it. And perhaps if you do, you can help decide what happens in the next part of the story."

Something of this must have sunk in, because she said, "All right. But how does this help us? What next? Do we get a pension or something out of it?"

"Really, I've no idea. But Father thinks it ought to guarantee us—and the dragons—some sort of special protection, beyond the normal English common law right of private property."

"Protection? How could it? And what about the others—do the Falconers know about this?"

"No. They don't," said Meredith's voice, startling us by stepping out from behind a bookshelf with a dusty tome in her hand as an alibi. "Believe me, if my parents knew there were any royal connections, I would have heard of it long ago."

Gwendolyn and I exchanged glances.

"What about Wales and Cumbria?" I asked.

Meredith shook her head, pushing the book into an empty space nearby. "I'd have heard. I know you probably don't trust me, but you might consider that I've no reason to lie about this." She slapped dust off her hands and grimaced.

"While we're all being honest—why did you really come, Meredith?" I asked. "Surely you could all muddle along without your aunt for a few weeks, at least. You can't be so mean-spirited as to deny her a brief holiday."

"Mean-spirited?" Her mouth worked. She turned away for a moment, then spun back. "Aunt Lavinia just—*left*! She left us—without even a by-your-leave! She left *me*!"

We stared at her. She poked a finger at me.

"You ruined Wales for me—I almost *had* him, and then he sent me away! As if I meant nothing! And now you want to take Aunt Lavinia too! Don't you understand what will happen when she's gone? I'm the next in line! The next in the line of sad and miserable spinsters who live only to *serve*! And I won't do it, I tell you! It's not fair!"

And with a stomp of her foot, she began to cry.

Gwendolyn and I looked at each other, and then, to my intense surprise, Gwendolyn went to her and put her arm round her.

"And you're all so *happy* here! I didn't believe it until I saw it," she said through gritted teeth. "I thought that sort of thing was just a sham. I hate you. I absolutely *hate* you," she sobbed into Gwendolyn's shoulder.

Gwendolyn and I looked at each other over her fair head. If I had ever bet anything in my life, I'd have bet five pounds Gwendolyn would have hated Meredith on sight, but now I understood: Gwendolyn knew all about being trapped.

"It's no good, you know," Gwendolyn said, patting her on the back. "I tried to dislike Edith once, but she'll have you in the end."

Meredith's spine snapped upright and she took a step back.

"We're not friends," she said with a concluding sniffle, dabbing her eyes with her handkerchief. "Are you going to do it, then?" she said abruptly.

"Do what?" I asked.

"Blow the lid on this whole thing. That's what it comes down to in the end, doesn't it? Honestly, the only reason it's gone on so long is because of the sheer blinding stupidity of *people*. They only see what they want to see." She took a little mirror out of her pocket.

Gwendolyn's eyes flitted to me, then she went still.

"Oh," she said. "You want to reveal the dragons, after all these centuries." Her voice was perilously steady. "That's what you meant by *the next part of the story*."

"Gwen," I said gently, "the people who dreamed up that oath of secrecy you took when you were a child—they lived in a world with thicker shadows. They didn't have trains and tourists, or cameras and electric lights and telegraphs to worry about. You know that world now—from London. It's not here yet, but it's coming. With Dugdale's lime-works, and with Hanna, and Janushek, and even Dr Worthing—it's drawing closer every day. Can't you see it?"

Gwendolyn wrung her hands and turned away to look out the window.

I remembered something Helena had said to me once. "We've always lived in a thin margin here in Ormdale, but now it's shrinking to a sliver. Wouldn't it be better to make the choice ourselves while we may?"

Meredith looked up from applying something to her nose (it may have been powder, but I oughtn't to conjecture). "If you ask me, revealing ourselves to the world might materially improve our prospects. After all, they could hardly be worse! I say, won't you set me up with a doctor, Gwendolyn? Not a country doctor, of course. The kind that has a nice little practise in Harley Street would suit me very well."

"You can afford one who has a practise in Harley Street?" I asked, confused.

Meredith stared at her, indignant. "No, you numpty! I am in *perfect* health. I want to marry one."

Gwendolyn made a choking sound. I took her by the arm and moved her towards the stairway. They had hit it off far better than I could have hoped, but, in my experience, a little of Meredith went a long way.

"Yes," Meredith said thoughtfully, trailing after us. "I'll trade you Aunt Lavinia for a doctor. She doesn't eat very much, and she's very good at sewing and making ends meet. I don't suppose you happen to have any coming as houseguests for Christmas, do you? Because if you do, you might just lend me a frock, Gwendolyn—it won't be as lovely as mine, but I like a challenge, anyway—and I'll sort him out right away and be done."

Gwendolyn looked at me helplessly and I gave a little shake of my head. Once Meredith got something into her head, argument was futile.

"Meredith, I'm sure Mother is wondering where you are."

I waved her towards the sitting room.

"All right, but I warn you," Meredith said a little sternly, "I expect to be included in any more secret conferences." And off she went.

"All the single doctors I know are women," Gwendolyn said, looking after her.

"It would be cruel to tell her," I said, taking her arm and walking down the passage with her. "Gwen—one more thing. I know you don't want to be the one to end the way things have been done for centuries. But you're not on your own anymore. There's me, and Father and Mother, and Simon, and George and Violet and Una. Heavens, it seems even Miss Falconer is joining the family now, at least until she realises the most eligible man for miles is Dugdale! I don't think any curses will fall on us. I think the clouds will break with blessings instead. But either way—we'll face whatever comes next for the Worms family together."

Gwendolyn lifted her dark eyes to me. "You're a writer, Edith. You said we can decide what happens in the next part of the story. How would *you* write it?"

"Well, if there's one thing I've learned, it's that I don't write this story on my own, Gwen. If things are going to get better, they must get better for everyone."

We had reached the Great Hall, and Gwendolyn stopped still.

"You took away the tapestries," she said in shock.

"Yes. We had a Michaelmas feast, and I thought the guests might like to see the frescoes."

Gwendolyn began to laugh a little wildly. "You thought the guests might like to see them? Frescoes of human sacrifice? At a feast?" She flung a hand at the section in question.

"Frescoes of human sacrifice *ending*, Gwen!" I pointed at the abbot with his unconventional footstool. "You can't only see the darkness! What about the light?"

"I've never been able to see it." Gwendolyn shook her head. "Why? What's wrong with me?"

I took her hands in mine with a sigh. "It's no fault of yours. Our family lost the thread, somewhere along the way. I think each generation must choose to take it up—freely, of their own will, or things go rotten. Love doesn't grow in cages, and secrets are the worst kind of cage."

Suddenly, we heard feet barrelling across the floor above our heads, shouting at the window, and a great commotion outside. Exchanging glances, we ran for the door, unbolted it, and stepped out into the sunlight.

Nothing could have prepared me for the sight that met my eyes.

Simon was on Portia, and he had the long staff of his ancestor in his hand. He was holding Portia's reins tightly and she had a blindfold round her eyes. She was walking backwards, while in front of him, not six feet away were two giant figures, their bodies extending another ten yards or more. At first, my mind could not fathom what I was seeing.

"Is that—is that—" choked out Gwendolyn.

"The feathered serpents," I replied, my steady tone belying my racing pulse.

Chapter Thirty-Eight

The silken ripple of mighty muscles under the dark scales was breathtaking in the daylight. One—presumably the male—bore a spectacular ruff of teal and scarlet feathers, iridescent in the sharp winter sun. The female's decorations glowed a lustrous amethyst.

If one turned aside, Simon would gently touch the tip of his staff to the side of its head to redirect it.

Simon dismounted, tucked the staff under his arm, and very slowly led Portia closer to the serpents step by step, speaking reassuringly to his horse all the while. They kept their eyes fixed on him, their heads bobbing gently. I had never before thought Portia was small.

"Oh, look," I whispered, "he's introducing his friends to each other."

Gwendolyn's fingers dug into my arm. "Are you quite certain you want to marry *that*?"

"Never more so," I breathed, gripping the door frame.

"He's not 'too Heathcliff' for you after all, then?"

"No. Not a bit."

Gwendolyn's voice lowered. "Don't you dare ask me to be godmother to your children, do you hear? I don't want to be responsible for whatever heredity will do with them."

"And we'd already planned to name one of the twins after you," I said plaintively.

She froze. "Do you know what they say about me at medical school? They say I have no nerves at all. No feminine qualms. It's all your fault. You've shocked them all out of me with your escapades. And now you've turned Simon into"—she made a small helpless gesture towards him—"whatever he is. That is not the shy boy I grew up with!"

At this point, Portia and the two giant creatures drew very close to each other. Portia gave a whinny and tossed her head. Simon spoke to her and she calmed. He slowly let go of her bridle, then reached up one hand to each of the serpents. They lowered their heads so that a hand rested on each muzzle.

Portia nuzzled at Simon as if she were looking for him. She got as far as his ear, then stopped, scenting the dragons again. There was a slow moment where all four of them seemed to be in silent communication; a strange heraldic knot of man, serpent, and horse.

Now, first one, then the other quetzalcoatyl gently—oh so gently!—arched their necks and stretched past Simon to make a gesture of unmistakeable protection over the horse.

"I haven't turned Simon into anything," I said, when I was able to breathe again. "He's realised who he was all along."

Simon looked over his shoulder, inviting me closer.

Taking a deep breath, I walked slowly to meet him. He stretched out his hand to me and I took it gratefully. He drew me into the strange congress of creatures, until I was overshadowed by them. Up close, each glossy scale had an oily sheen that made an individual rainbow in the sun.

"You did say that you liked surprises," he said very softly in my ear, and then he took my hands and carefully placed them on each warm muzzle. I could hear the faint clink of the shells at his throat.

Simon noticed the tear on my cheek before I did. "Is something wrong?"

"It's just—this is the most beautiful thing I've ever seen," I whispered. They had been his words to me in the moonlit forest in Wales. "How do you expect to surprise me ever again after this?"

The was a smile in his voice when he answered. "I have just one more for you. Then I might have to save them up for a few years."

There was a whistled signal from behind the creatures.

"Ah," said Simon. "Dinner time. Hold Portia for me?"

I took Portia's bridle. Simon coaxed them away to be fed.

Janushek and Forrester were waiting at a distance, each with a cart containing a deceased cow.

I heard voices above me and glanced up to see the children hanging out a window. Above them, Lily was poised at another open window, the old blowpipe at the ready. Beside her was Hanna, who held an uncocked rifle very comfortably.

Simon had been thoroughly prepared for every eventuality. I turned back to point this out to Gwendolyn, but she was gone.

A moment later, Simon joined me.

"The egg is safe?" I asked.

"We protected it from the blast. They'll be able to come and go now from their nest in the caves."

"However will we afford to feed them?" I wondered.

"They don't seem to get hungry very often. George tells me it's normal for reptiles to eat once a week. I thought it best to reward them for their good behaviour."

"Namely, not eating me and Portia?"

"Exactly," said Simon. He took off Portia's blindfold.

"But Simon, there's something I don't understand. Just now, with the serpents, you didn't seem the least bit nervous. But when the same thing happened with Cariad, you trembled. It was the first time I'd ever seen you really afraid."

"Oh." He looked down.

"Simon?"

"It wasn't fear. Not exactly." He looked up sheepishly. "You don't remember what else happened at that moment?"

"What else happened?" I repeated, thoroughly bewildered.

"You held my hand," he said simply.

There was a little landslide inside me. The only thing to do at that moment was to hold his hand again.

The serpents coiled into contented spirals and appeared to be going to sleep.

"Is this where they're going to live from now on?" I asked. "Because it will be hard to explain to visitors—as rare as they are here at Wormwood Abbey."

Simon's face crinkled in puzzlement. "I wasn't actually intending for them to go to sleep here. I was going to drive them back to the caves."

Just then Janushek appeared from round a gigantic coil.

"Drake! We've got a visitor on the way."

Simon and I looked at each other.

"One of the Ormby boys just came up to tell us they stopped someone on the road through the woods."

"Don't tell me you've turned Robin Hood now, Janushek?" I exclaimed. "Do you have a band of merry men?"

Janushek gave me an odd look and went on talking to Simon. "He came from Embsay in a hired gig he's driven himself. I sent word back to let him come up."

"Hadn't we better find some place to put the serpents first?" I suggested as Simon's face furrowed further.

"No need. It's an old friend of yours, Rusalka." Janushek's lips quirked. "And he already knows all about dragons."

I gave a cry of delight and spun on my heels to run back into the house.

"Edith?" called Simon. "Where are you going? And who is it?"

"It's a representative from Cumbria! And I'm going to go tell Cook we're having another guest to lunch before she has my head!" I called back as I ran off.

When John Tallantire stumbled into the Great Hall a little later, his hair stood up and his freckles stood out even more than I remembered them doing previously.

"I have come—to honour our families' ancient agreement," he stammered.

His announcement was a little overshadowed by the enthusiasm of Father, Mother, and George upon meeting him.

"I say," said George, pumping his hand. "Very good of you to help save my sister from that villain in London!"

"Oh, that was just good fun, really, and I only came in at the end," he said, looking round in confusion. "But see here. Do you normally have—*those*—out front?" He waved a hand behind him.

It was Father's turn to look confused now. "What do we have out front? Emily, have you planted something particularly alarming?"

Mother laughed softly. "Simon and Edith have been training some of their creatures this morning and they've fallen asleep in a prominent position. I'm sure they'll tell you all about it later."

"Ah! I apologise," said Father. "I was buried in books this morning, but I will be more sociable for the rest of the day, I promise you. It seems to be the calm before the storm at the moment, Mr Tallantire, and I was enjoying a moment of peace in the library."

"*Peace*?" repeated Tallantire, with a backwards glance towards where the serpents were slumbering.

"If you'll just come through to the sitting room, it's ever so much more comfortable there," said Mother, leading the way. Tallantire's eyes darted about as he tried to make sense of it all.

Father fell in beside Tallantire. "You must tell me all about this ancient agreement. I think you may be interested in a fascinating document I found from the late Elizabethan period. I think it sheds some light on the history of our family, and possibly yours, as well."

"Can I help with your case, Mr Tallantire?" asked George. Tallantire had a decent-sized case with him, but George's attempts to help were politely rebuffed. "All of the bedrooms that don't leak are full-up. So you'll have to stay in my room. I hope you don't mind insects. Or amphibians."

Tallantire looked unmoored, and threw me a helpless glance.

I smiled. My family might be odd, but they were thoroughly delightful.

We encountered the Derbyshire contingent in the sitting room.

"I think you may already know Miss Falconer and Miss Birt-whistle?" I asked. "Mr John Tallantire, of The Scalehouse, near Renwick."

Tallantire gave a little swerve on the carpet and changed colour when he saw the Derbyshire beauty.

"Oh! Uh, yes, uh, we have met. Years ago. Miss Falconer won't remember me at all, I'm sure." His nervous laugh made me doubt it.

"What a delightful surprise," she said, extending her hand to him with a blinding smile. If there was anything odd between them, she wasn't admitting it. "This is turning into quite a party! There's nothing I like more than an impromptu party—it saves so much planning and fuss!"

Martha stumped into the doorway—looking as dark as one of Odin's ravens—just in time to hear Meredith's words.

"Luncheon is served!" she shouted at us all and disappeared, slamming the door.

"I wonder if we'll ever see her again," I said.

We went through to the dining room and Simon now appeared, come back from taking Portia to the stables.

"Oh, Mr Tallantire, this is—"

"Simon Forrester," Simon said without a pause, shaking his hand. "Very glad to meet you at last. Welcome to Ormdale."

Tallantire was looking round the table hopefully for one face in particular.

"Shall we wait for Gwendolyn?" I asked Mother quietly as everyone seated themselves.

Mother shook her head. "She's not coming down. I expect she needs some time to rest after last night."

"Now if we only had someone from Wales, we'd have all the Dragon Families represented," I announced as we began on the soup.

Meredith gave a delicate shudder. "I should think we're better off without them, aren't we? I was never so glad to escape a place." She turned to Tallantire. "How relieved you must be that none of your sisters made the journey. It all ended in utter disaster, you know, when a lake beast stupidly mistook me for some kind of human sacrifice!" A hand fluttered to her bosom. "Thankfully, it removed all possibility of a match between Derbyshire and Wales."

I looked at Miss Birtwhistle, who unfolded her napkin.

"A lucky escape for both of you, then," observed Mother with no hint of irony. She always knew the right thing to say.

Pip and Hanna served the simple but pleasing meal of parsnip soup followed by a rabbit pie, rich with gravy, and dark brack cake with cheese.

"Hanna, do please apologise to Cook and tell her I don't expect such miracles," Mother murmured to Hanna. "If we have unexpected guests again we shall be more than content with a cold collation."

I saw Meredith's look of surprise at this exchange.

As the meal drew to a satisfying close, I began. "I hope I won't give you all indigestion, but I have some information to impart."

"Oh yes?" inquired Father. "What fresh revelation is this, Edith? I'm beginning to expect them at regular intervals now."

"Yes, but first—a question for our guests." I turned to them. "Has anyone ever offered to buy your dragons, to your knowledge?"

Meredith stared. "Buy our dragons? Never! Who could possibly want them?"

Tallantire looked very serious. "You mean like Farley? For experimentation? No."

"That rather confirms my suspicions. I think I've finally realised what my grandfather is after."

"Your grandfather?" repeated Tallantire, eyebrows shooting up.

"Yes," I confirmed. "He's—well, he's not your average grandfather."

"You haven't met mine," Meredith muttered.

"Out with it, then, Edith," said Father. "We're all concerned in this business now. And we're all custodians of the same secrets."

"He wants..." I took a deep breath. "The Fall of the House of Worms."

The words fell into silence. Everyone was staring at me. It sounded so absurd after a lovely meal on a rare sunny winter's day in the Yorkshire Dales.

"Well! How terribly Gothic!" burst out Meredith.

"He's been watching us long enough to know we have dragons," I went on, "and that the Worms family has always done their utmost to keep them secret. And if he can find the thing you care about—then he knows where to strike." I played with my fork. "I expect it was he who made sure my name got into the society papers. I wouldn't be surprised if he's been behind some of the pressure about your political views, too, Father." I looked across the table to him. "He warned me not to come back—to you, Father. He wasn't...entirely reasonable about it."

"Then this may all be laid to my account," said Father regretfully, putting down his glass. "I must apologise to all of you. Many years ago, as a very young man, I unintentionally made a formidable enemy—one with a memory and a hoard as considerable as that of any dragon of legend, I'm afraid."

"I can't imagine it was your fault at all, sir," said Tallantire.

"But still, the problem remains," insisted Father, looking at him. "He may not seek your downfall, but if he reveals *our* dragons to the world, the eyes of the blind will be opened. People will go looking for them, and they will find us. It will change everything."

"Then let it," said a voice at the door, and we all looked up to see Gwendolyn, her hand on the doorframe, her face like flint. "Things have stayed the same for too long. I'm ready for a change, and I'm not the only one. What about you, Miss Falconer?"

Meredith's demure, girlish demeanour cracked slightly under Gwendolyn's piercing gaze and I caught a glimpse of the Meredith I'd known in Wales—someone who took risks, and wanted things deeply.

"Yes," she said very quietly, then again more firmly, "*yes*. I think I am."

"What about you?" Gwendolyn asked, her eyes shifting to Tallantire.

He looked back at her like Sir Galahad laying eyes on the Holy Grail.

"I'm quite ready to follow Miss Worms—I mean, Mr Worms's lead here. My family will understand this wasn't a choice you made lightly."

"Simon?" Gwendolyn said.

"You already know what I think, Gwen," he said softly.

"Yes. You were the first of us," said Gwendolyn affectionately, and her gaze rested on me. "After Edith."

Did she feel she'd been forced into this? I began to stammer an apology. "I'm sorry, Gwen—"

"No. *I'm* sorry, Edith. While I've been running away from our family secrets, I've been expecting you to keep them for me. That wasn't fair. Especially when because of you—and Aunt Emily and Uncle George—my sisters and I are not alone anymore." She stood behind her sisters' chairs and put a hand on each of them. "None of us are. We'll come out of the shadows together."

Then Gwendolyn sat down in an empty chair and seemed to become her normal self again. "Is there any cake left?"

Chapter Thirty-Nine

That afternoon, Simon and Janushek briefed us. In the unlikely event that intruders evaded the men of Ormby (who were guarding the road to the abbey) and breached our defences, we were to fall back to the Muniments Room, which was the most secure room in the building. Janushek had stocked it with food and water. Knowing Janushek, he had likely also stocked it with weapons.

If it all happened in the middle of the night and we could not reach it safely, we were to lock ourselves in our bedrooms and refuse to come out under any circumstances.

The children were instructed to stay close to the abbey until we had confirmation from Embsay that Briggs and Co had taken a southbound train out of the Dales.

After our briefing, I felt sorry for the children being confined on such a lovely day, and I noticed that Mother looked tired.

"How about a game of hide-and-seek, children?" I offered. "Mr Tallantire and I will seek."

I motioned at Mother, who slipped gratefully away.

"What fun!" Meredith said, with an exaggerated edge of wistfulness.

"You needn't squint at me, Gwen," said Violet, "of course we'll let your friend play. But she mustn't complain if she gets dusty."

"Oh! I never mind a little dust," answered Meredith. "And anyway, these are Gwendolyn's clothes."

Violet looked at her consideringly for a moment. "I've got a good hiding place for you," she said, and seized her hand.

"We'll be waiting for you, Mr Tallantire," Meredith flung over her shoulder tantalisingly.

Tallantire's teeth appeared briefly in what must have been an attempt at a smile.

As soon as the children (and Meredith) scattered, Tallantire turned in relief to Gwendolyn and me, the only people remaining.

"I thought we'd never get rid of her! When I got your telegram, I wasn't sure exactly what sort of help you needed, but I've brought something from the Scalehouse."

He squatted down by his case. I now saw that it had been pierced with air holes.

"Do you know the history of our family? My ancestor was honoured for defending Renwick from a cockatrice. They were building a new church and they found the creature hiding when they were demolishing the old one. My honoured ancestor felled it with a rowan branch—or so they say—but I suspect he just waved the branch around and drove it home. My family were already Dragon Keepers by then, and had been since King James at least."

"Did you bring one? A real cockatrice?" I cried in excitement as he opened the clasp. "Oh, I've been wondering what—"

The words died on my lips as I laid eyes on the unspeakable creature inside.

Gwen came closer to look over my shoulder.

"Gwen—" I choked out to warn her, but it was too late.

"*What the dickens?*" she cried. It was the most unladylike thing I had ever heard her say, and must be put down to the coarsening effects of medical study.

Tallantire beamed up at us. "It's the Renwick Cockatrice, don't you know! Ah. You don't know," he concluded, from a look at our stricken faces.

"Would you—would you mind—" I waved my hand incoherently until he shut the case. Then I took a deep, restorative breath.

"I've dissected a cirrhotic liver, and it had nothing on that," remarked Gwendolyn grimly.

I was ready to feel sorry for Tallantire but he actually seemed pleased by the effect his creature had on us. He stood tall.

"It's our cockatrice. Otherwise known as a basilisk. The pride of the Cumbrian Worm Warden. We've kept them alive for centuries, you see, for such a time as this."

"Just how do you expect it to help us?" Gwendolyn asked, impressed by his unquenchable spirit.

"Well, they don't really turn you to stone when you look at them, but they're jolly intimidating, don't you think? King James was so pleased with my ancestor removing it from public view that we still don't pay taxes hundreds of years later."

"You don't pay taxes?" I cried.

"Do you mean you really think it will strike fear into the hearts of our enemies?" Gwendolyn asked, ignoring my look of envy.

At that moment, Janushek came in. "Dugdale just got word that they've left Embsay."

"They are on the way here?" I asked, heart pounding.

"No. It looks as if they've had a change of heart and gone home."

Tallantire looked at us with palpable disappointment. "It's all over, then? The great peril?"

"I suppose it is," I said in amazement. My grandfather must have had a change of heart and called off Farley—it was the only explanation!

Gwendolyn put her arm round me. "Well. This has been a very trying few days. Go have a rest—eat something, read a book. Mr Tallantire and I will entertain the children."

Despite the occasional scuffling of feet and distant muted shrieks of the children's game, I fell into a deep sleep. At one point, I heard Pilot barking, but I was too tired to rouse.

I woke confused and groggy. It was dark. I groped for a light. As I did so, I heard stealthy footsteps in the passage. Thinking it must be the children continuing their game, I struck a light.

The footsteps stopped immediately.

But hours must have passed while I slept. They could not still be engaged in the same game.

Instinctively, I put out the light, then I cursed myself silently. If this was an intruder, he would surely know now that I was aware of his presence. It whispered closer, then stopped again. I fancied I could sense the rhythm of his breath at my very door.

I couldn't bear it any longer. "Who's there?" I cried.

No answer.

Now—the very worst sound imaginable—there came a scrape at the keyhole. The jangle of a set of lockpicks. I recognised it from my encounter with Janushek, but this was not *my* thief (he would have asked permission before picking my lock).

Intruders had penetrated the abbey.

I gathered a breath to scream for help.

But now there came a distant whistle. This was met with a muttered oath from the fellow at my door, the sound of the lockpicks being stuffed into his pocket, and then heavy feet thudding away as stealth was abandoned for haste.

This was my chance to get out and join the others before whoever-it-was returned to make another attempt on the door.

I snatched up Oolong, unlocked the door, and raced down the passage. All of the bedrooms were open and empty except for Helena's, which was locked. I scratched on it and hissed, "Mrs Drake!"

It was Hanna who opened the door to me, dimly illumined by the light of the fire. I slipped inside.

I looked for Helena and found her—frail-looking by the light of a single candle at her bedside. Removed from her stately surroundings at Drake Hall, she might have been anyone's invalid mother.

"What's happening?" I asked Hanna.

"I sit with Mrs Drake," Hanna answered. "Then I hear strange voices and I lock door."

"Did you hear a struggle? A fight?"

"Running, an hour ago."

"And the children? Where did you see them last?"

"After supper, everyone was together in the sitting room, I think."

I sighed in relief and put Oolong down. "Oh, good. Then hopefully they made it safely to the Muniments Room. There was a stranger up here a moment ago, trying to get into my door. I was foolish enough to cry out, which means they will come back again."

I glanced at Helena, then back to Hanna. She nodded—we could not leave Helena alone.

"This house has many ways—I can creep and spy," offered Hanna.

"I'm not putting you in harm's way, and I know those ways too." I chewed my lip thoughtfully. I couldn't stop thinking of the trick Miss Birtwhistle had helped me play back in Wales in order to escape. "The intruder heard my voice. If he comes back, it will be because they expect to find me up here. What if we trick them?"

"*Tak*, but how?" asked Hanna.

I began to unbutton my cardigan. "Like this."

In order to fasten the back of her housemaid's dress on me, Hanna had to lace my waist more tightly than was my habit.

"Too many honey cakes," she said under her breath, with a little chuckle.

"You bake too many!" I retorted.

The swap done, we assessed each other. Hanna had arranged her hair as much like mine as possible, while my own was covered with her scarf.

"Well, how very unnerving," I said at last, while Hanna muttered something in her language.

"Take this," said Helena, startling us both. She drew a small revolver out from under the coverlet and held it out to me by the barrel.

Well, perhaps she wasn't just *anyone's* invalid mother.

I hesitated, then shook my head. "I haven't the least idea how to use it. You're better off keeping it here."

I turned to Hanna, and put a hand on her arm. In the dim light, it was strangely like talking to myself.

"God bless you," I said.

"*Gei gezunderheit, shvesstar*," she murmured, and kissed my cheek.

Instead of taking the main staircase, I crept down the tiny spiral stair designed for servants. This route was perilous in the dark, but I was certain that the intruders would not know of its existence. Indeed, I had asked the servants not to use it until the steep treads could be repaired, for they were slick as glass with wear.

I reached a door that I knew was almost completely hidden in the panelling on the other side, and led to the dining room. I reached out to feel for the latch, when I heard a clinking sound. It reminded me of the afternoon I had spent hidden in Farley's laboratory in London. This stopped me at once.

Soon, I heard footsteps in the dining room.

"They're all holed up in that tower, doctor." This cockney rumble belonged to Briggs. "They say that they've provisions for as long as we care to stay, and they won't come out no matter what we threaten. What's more, they claim help is on the way and we'd better get out while we can. We can't find any laboratory equipment. It must be inside with them."

"Is *she* with them?"

A shudder ran down me at this voice—Farley, himself, had come.

"I don't think so. I didn't hear her," replied Briggs. "And I think she'd be talking if she was in there with them. She likes the sound of her own voice, doesn't she?"

I bristled.

"Find her. She's here somewhere."

"You told us we couldn't hurt her."

Something in his voice made it sound as if he'd like to test that limit.

"And they don't know that," Farley said with a touch of impatience. "We will use her to bargain for the antivenin."

"Smollett says there's someone up in those bedrooms—a girl. It might be her."

"Then go get her." Footsteps began to creak obediently away. "Briggs?"

"Yes, sir?"

"Remember, you are to tell me at once if you find any of the creatures, you understand?"

He grunted and left.

I couldn't move. I heard nothing from Farley now, which meant that he was still standing—sitting?—in the dining room, with only a wall separating us.

I could picture him, pale face and bright hair, like a moth at dusk. Waiting for me.

I remembered how those green eyes had seen through my deception about the laudanum in the tea. Would he sense me crouching behind the panelling?

I forced myself to breathe deeply and reflect on what I'd learned.

It was evident that the intruders had come by a different road than the one we guarded. Evidently, Farley's memories of the Dale had been clear enough to bring them over the fells.

So far, our plan of defence had worked, but if they got their hands on me and used me as a hostage, things would change for the worse.

If they got their hands on *anyone*, things would change for the worse.

They had been told not to hurt me, but I had no surety that they would not hurt others. And others might be concealed in nooks and crannies about the place besides myself.

Even now, Briggs was going upstairs to search the bed-rooms—eventually he would break into the room where Hanna and Helena were hiding. Thankfully, they had the protection of a gun, but they would not be able to hold out indefinitely.

I heard the sound of voices drawing nearer. One of them was female. My heart sank.

"I found someone!" This time it wasn't Briggs, but some other myrmidon. "It's a lady—I found her in the linen cupboard."

"What in heaven's name is going on?" cried Meredith's voice. "I fell asleep playing hide and seek with the children and awoke to this ruffian looming over me."

"It's not the ginger that you're after, doctor. What do you want done with this one?"

"You're a doctor?" asked Meredith, brightening. "Are you one of Miss Worms's medical friends come to visit?"

"Perhaps," replied Farley cautiously.

"I'm Meredith Falconer—*Miss* Meredith Falconer."

"Miss Falconer, we are here for two things: the antivenin and a dragon. Both in just repayment of things that were stolen from me. If you can help me to achieve these things, then I can be on my way without troubling you all further. And you will have my gratitude."

"The place is simply crawling with dragons, I keep tripping over them," she said. "There's one sleeping in the corner of the linen closet, as quiet as the grave. Will that one do?"

I bit my lip. Was she telling the truth?

"Go get it, Hodge," said Farley, and the other man left.

"I can send you some antivenin myself if you supply me with your address. Or perhaps I could visit you myself to deliver it. Do you have a practise in London? In Harley Street, perhaps?"

Was Meredith actually trying to flirt with *Farley*? I repressed a snort of disbelief.

"It looks as if you are going to be very useful indeed," he said appreciatively. "I have a score to settle here. Miss Worms and her friends took something from me, something very valuable. You will make a valuable bargaining tool."

"I wouldn't advise using me as a hostage, if that's what you mean," she said. "They don't like me much."

"You astound me," said Farley tonelessly.

She gave a sigh. "Shocking, isn't it?"

There was a scuffling sound in the passage.

"I got it!" shouted the man called Hodge. "I got the little blighter!"

"What is its appearance?" demanded Farley.

"Mostly black, with some gold bits, a blue tongue, and a tail like a ruddy little arrow."

My heart thudded in horror. Frances had been hibernating in the spare linens near the warm kitchen all along? If only I had known, I could have protected her!

"Excellent. I have not seen that kind before. We now have one of our objectives, and a female hostage as well. This creature will make the perfect addition to my laboratory."

Something inside me exploded at his smug tone—something as potent as the dynamite that had released the quetzalcoatyls from their subterranean imprisonment.

My hand found the latch and pushed it open.

Chapter Forty

The three figures in the room were lit with a reddish glow from the dying fire.

Farley had his back to me, and the myrmidon Hodge was occupied with a very agitated sackful of dragon. Thus, it was Meredith alone who saw me emerge like a ghost from the wall where the shadows were deepest.

She let out a high-pitched shriek.

Farley spun round, his black coat flaring out to reveal a waistcoat bristling with strange vials that glinted and clinked as he moved.

I had acted without self-regard, in just such a way as a mother might behave if her infant were threatened, but upon seeing the face of the man who had almost killed me, I pulled up, speechless.

It was this that saved me from the consequences of my rashness.

"You!" he exclaimed in surprise. Then he lowered his voice. His eyes glittered in his pale face, and he took one threatening step towards me. "Tell me where she is." It took me a moment to realise that he was—unaccountably—speaking in German. "If you do not take me to her, I will hurt you. Nobody will care. Your life is cheap. Do you understand?"

At first, I was stunned, then I realised: he had recognised me—as Hanna Kapler, his one-time test subject. I had thought to trick from a distance, not at close quarters.

I bowed my head to shadow my face and spoke shakily in German, hoping he would not recognise my voice.

"I will show you," I said.

Meredith had sensed her moment and disappeared. Hodge saw it at the same time as I did and let out an oath.

"Never mind," said Farley. "She is of no consequence. Come."

As I edged past him towards the door, he took my upper arm in a pincer grip. I recoiled, frightened that he might recognise me by sheer proximity. But he did not look at me. Perhaps he had never really looked at Hanna's face, or any of the subjects he had mistreated, even under the bright gaslights of his laboratory. Perhaps he had only looked at the parts of them that were useful to him.

"Now," he said. "You will take me to her."

Farley produced a smuggler's lantern to light our way, and I led them up the great staircase to the bedrooms, his fingers digging into my arm the whole way.

Once, I had thought him ambitious and cold, but not wantonly cruel. That idea had been formed by his behaviour towards E. W. Fairweather—a well-connected *lady*.

Now, I was Hanna, a poor migrant, and with every step, the viciousness of his grip warned me that there was a side to Farley I had not seen yet.

Was he armed? What were the strange clinking objects under his coat? Janushek had destroyed all his poisons. Did Farley intend to take my blood after all? Just how mad had he become? He had told his men not to hurt me, and I had thought it was because of a promise made to my grandfather, but now I wondered if it was because he longed to hurt me himself.

My thoughts threatened to spin away from me into darkness, but I clung to the important ones: if I could get him to where Hanna and Helena were, they could force him at gunpoint to let Frances and me go free.

There would be a chance to use *him* to bargain with his confederates and gain the upper hand.

We had arrived at the door. He nodded at me, squeezing my arm until I gasped. Hodge waited close by. Frances had stopped struggling when she heard my voice and gave him no more trouble.

I knocked on the door softly.

"Miss Ee-dit," I said, hoping Hanna would forgive me for mimicking her accent. "It is Hanna."

I heard the door unlock and footsteps recede quickly across the room. Good, she had remembered to stay in the shadows. I prayed he would not get too close to her.

"Open the door slowly," he whispered in my ear, drawing something from his pocket.

I obeyed.

We shuffled inside the room together, Hodge following.

A small young woman in a white blouse, dark blue woollen skirt, and amber cardigan stood on the opposite side of the room, near the armoire, her face just outside of the circle of candlelight. Her russet hair glinted in the light from the low fire, and her hands were clenched at her sides. The little black arrow shape of a salamander head peeped out between the buttons at her front.

"Well, Miss Worms." I felt Farley's body relax. "Here you are. And once again, you've managed to make everything so much more painful than it ever needed to be."

She did not answer.

"You thought that all my poisons were destroyed by your Polish lover, didn't you?" (My *what*? I darted a glance at Hanna, but she seemed sufficiently sobered by the peril of our situation not to laugh aloud—as she no doubt would later, if we survived this.) "But you were wrong. I keep samples of them in a separate storage location, which is how I was able to continue my work over the last few months. Yes, I *continued* my work! Every time someone tries to destroy me, I become stronger. This poor woman, Miss Kapler, is afraid of me, you see. She understands what you do not—that some people are predators, and some are prey."

Were my eyes playing tricks on me, or did the woman before us stand straighter at these words?

Farley went on. "There is no divine readjustment of the scales. No reward for the poor and meek, as you so quaintly believe. There is only strength and the will to wield it. Everyone who chooses weakness regrets their choice in the end."

He held up something metallic.

"This is an invention of my own—a venom gun. Thanks to you, I was able to secure the funding I needed to develop it to its fullest potential."

He pointed it at her for a moment, and my heart leapt.

"But it would do nothing to *you*. You are immune to the poison inside it. Shall I demonstrate it on someone else?" He held the barrel against my neck, and despite the nasty feeling of the cold metal, I was relieved. "In my laboratory, you told me that you would never allow those less worthy to suffer for a higher good. But I wonder if it's true. Let us conduct an experiment."

He swivelled the barrel towards Hodge and pulled the trigger.

Hodge let out a yell and dropped his sack.

"Here now, that *stings*! What do you mean by it?" He plucked out and threw away a dart about six inches long from his midsection.

"I am testing my hypothesis, Hodge," said Farley. He turned back to the silent young woman. "He has now been envenomated with a new concoction of my own—a mixed solution of coral snake and monocled cobra." He made it sound like a recipe of great taste and refinement. "How do you feel, Hodge?"

"Are you having a joke?" he asked, rubbing at his waistcoat resentfully.

"Let us see which he will lose first—vision or movement."

"Now wait a minute!" the man objected quite reasonably.

"What a shame I don't have an antidote to spare him these sufferings. If only there were someone here who cared about poor fellows such as he."

"Stop the joke, guv'nor," Hodge whined, but his face was tight and his forehead damp.

"Will he have permanent nerve damage, I wonder? Just how effective is your antivenin, Edith? I can't wait to find out. Or rather, I can wait. But can you? More to the point, can Hodge?"

This wasn't what I had anticipated, but it gave us an opportunity to continue the charade, and Farley had gambled rightly—we couldn't allow the man to die.

As a signal, I gave Hanna the smallest nod I could manage. Her shoulders sagged, and she hid her face in her hands. Then she whispered in a choked voice of defeat that masked her accent, "I'll get it."

Farley jerked his head towards the door. "Go with her."

Hodge took her by the arm and fairly rushed out the door with her.

Now only the two of us remained.

I could hardly believe it had worked.

Farley let out a breath through his nostrils and let go of me. "You see? Those who are too principled to choose power, Miss Kapler, have only themselves to blame when they find themselves in the hands of those who are not."

I bent and gathered up the sack with Frances into my arms, and then I moved across the room into deeper shadow. Farley had his back to me, watching the door. I worked at the knots holding the hessian sack closed.

He began to speak in a reflective way, almost to himself.

"If I had not intervened, you would have been sent to a brothel in South America. Did Miss Worms tell you that?"

I said nothing. The longer before he realised who I was, the better. And if I could get Frances out of this sack, I could count on her protecting me as she had protected me from Rivers long ago in this very room.

"The truth is, she is using you, just as I did," he said reflectively, almost as if speaking to himself. "But what other purpose have you, after all? No education, no skills, no position, no advantages. When they've profited by your vigour in domestic labour, when you are old, they will send you to a workhouse."

"No," I said without thinking.

Then I realised he had been speaking to me in English since Hanna left the room. He thought I could not understand him.

He turned slowly. "No?" He squinted into the shadows, and the look of satisfaction on his face slid away. "You are not Miss Kapler. Who are you?"

"I am weakness," I whispered. "I am mercy. I am the finger on the scales." My voice rose. "I am everything you despise and everything that will be your undoing!"

He pointed the venom gun at me, stepping back.

I laughed. "Your venom can't hurt me." I tore Hanna's scarf from my hair and stepped into the circle of light.

"*You!*" he hissed. Realisation flashed through his eyes and he made for the door to stop Hodge.

A low woman's voice spoke from the bed.

"Drop that and put up your hands, please, Doctor."

CHAPTER FORTY-ONE

Farley froze, pointing the gun towards the voice.

"I have a gun myself with a perfectly average bullet in it," said Helena in a voice as dark as night. "As I understand it, *death* also deprives one of sight and movement."

"I'll shoot you first," he managed.

"I've no doubt you would!" said Helena with a dry laugh. "But you now find yourself surrounded by people who cannot be harmed by your outlandish weapon."

He lowered the gun.

"I imagine that even now that misused minion of yours is telling his confederates how the doctor shot him and was willing to watch him suffer in agony," Helena went on. "I expect that any moment, he will be gratefully receiving a treatment of antivenin from my son and will listen very carefully to our terms of surrender."

Farley hardly seemed to hear her. "Show me your face," Farley demanded in a hoarse voice.

There was silence as she carefully kindled the light by her bed while keeping the gun trained on him.

"I know you," he said, with a calm that stopped my breath. "Do you know me...*Mercy*?"

Perplexed, Helena shook her head. "No. I don't."

I stopped working at the knots. Something was happening that I had not foreseen.

And then Farley began to tell us a story, very quietly. "The child was bitten first. And then the mother, when she pulled the groundling off him. But the older boy wasn't scared. There was the Mercy at Drake Hall—she would keep them safe. The magical young lady. The father carried his wife the whole way. The boy had to carry his brother. But he still wasn't frightened. When they arrived, everything was in disarray. The Mercy had run away, and they couldn't find her. Then the boy could see his father was scared, but the boy believed he could heal them, himself." He gave a bitter laugh. "It was the hair, you see. People in Ormdale with red hair were treated like they were special. People used to leave little gifts for them. They would rub their hair for luck. They were magic." He looked at her, momentarily a bewildered boy again. "But I wasn't magic enough. Why did you leave us that day? Why did you let them die?"

"I didn't mean any harm," she whispered. "I was just a girl. I was so young. I never tried to leave again—never! Forgive me."

"Forgive you?" he repeated. "No. *No.* Why should I? Why should you live?"

He straightened. In his black coat, he suddenly seemed an executioner.

"I've only been half alive myself for thirty years," she said, bowing her head as if waiting for the stroke of judgement. "Half of me is in that graveyard with your family."

"Half is not enough, and you know it," he said hollowly. "I'm the last one in my family you haven't killed, and you have me at gunpoint. Yes, I see just how sorry you are."

The gun in her hand wavered.

In that moment, I could see the whole story writing itself on the page in front of me.

Helena, in her profound feelings of remorse, was going to give up that gun, and Farley—he might end her life before he thought better of it.

I had physically struggled with Farley once before, and I knew I was no match for his savage strength. Surprise was my only hope.

It was time for a twist in the story, and there was only one I could think of that might work.

"Here's an experiment for you, doctor!" I cried out, and threw my dragon, sack and all, directly onto the burning logs.

Farley looked. The flames flared up and consumed the sack in a matter of seconds, revealing Frances, speckled with colour, serenely basking in the heat, her neck curved back in the strange posture in which I had first seen her as a hatchling.

It had not been a lively fire, but it quickly waxed hotter, as if Frances herself was feeding it. And her colours began to glow and change.

We stared open-mouthed, all else forgotten, at this wondrous creature that burned and yet was not consumed.

Her skin wrinkled and cracked, and she wriggled it off and cast it aside so that it rolled onto the hearthrug like the pilgrim's burden.

And still she grew.

The flames leapt higher. They were rising up the chimney now, and I could hear a distant roaring. The room was filled with a pungent smell, but the air was clear as clear, and once again, she outgrew and discarded her skin, and it seemed that every iteration of Frances glowed brighter and hotter.

Farley staggered back, and I held up my hands to shield my face from the blistering heat, but neither of us could wholly look away.

I think we might have let it go on and on, until the abbey itself was bathed in flames and we perished in them together, but at that moment Helena's little lapdragon jumped up on my washstand. Standing on its hind legs, it pushed the full pitcher of water so that it tipped over into the fireplace.

The fire hissed and crackled and grew dim. Frances awakened from her trance, surrounded by broken crockery.

Her body was now the size of a Labrador retriever.

She pulled herself easily over the grate, looked at me, then looked at Farley, and opened her mouth. A greenish gas puffed out, rather anticlimactically.

Farley and I both stared at it as it wafted towards him. Then Frances shook her head with a snap and sparks flew off, glittering as they drifted through the air like embers.

They were fiery scales.

A few of them hit the cloud of gas, and it burst into flame with a *whoosh*.

I blinked and staggered. When I opened my eyes, the door was open and Farley was gone—like a magician exiting the stage.

Frances rolled onto her side and flicked her tongue in my direction.

"Show-off," I choked. I reached out, testing the air around her for heat. No heat came from her, so I gently stroked her belly. "Thank you for not basking uselessly this time."

The roaring kept on, but I couldn't see the source.

"I think the chimney's on fire," I said, going to Helena quickly. "Can you walk?"

At that moment, I heard running in the passage and Simon and Father appeared at the open door with Pilot at their heels.

"Thank God!" Father breathed when he saw us both.

"Frances chased Farley off," I explained. Their eyebrows lifted when they caught sight of her.

"*That's* Frances?" asked Father, crouching to look more closely. "My—how you've grown!"

Simon came to me and put his hands on my shoulders, his own sagging with relief when he saw me unharmed.

"I think she also set the chimney a-fire," I said.

While Pilot sniffed Frances all over, Simon went and craned his neck to look up the chimney.

"You're right. I'll get up on the roof and put it out. Farley's men have surrendered to us. They're secure in the cellar with Dugdale. We needn't worry about them for now." He came to the bedside and bent down to help Helena put on her slippers. "Let me see you both out of here first. All present and accounted for? Dragons as well?"

"Mr Darcy," Helena whispered.

I looked round. "What happened to him?" I asked.

"He's gone." Helena said bleakly. "Farley took him."

My heart sank. How had I missed Farley taking him?

"Where's Oolong?" I asked suddenly.

"He hid as soon as Farley came in," said Helena.

While Simon lifted her out of the bed, I crawled under the bed.

"You poor thing! The horrid man's gone now," I whispered.

Oolong came to my arms, and we all went downstairs, Frances and Pilot following behind.

"We've yet to find Violet, Pip, and Miss Falconer," said Father on the way, "but the list is getting smaller. I'll go check the kitchen."

The sitting room was a cheering cacophony of voices and activity, bright with candles and a well-fed fire.

Mother embraced me with exclamations of relief. Gwendolyn had her arms round Una and nodded at me over her head.

Simon put Helena down on the settee and Miss Birtwhistle tucked a blanket round her.

Tallantire and George were talking enthusiastically over his basilisk-case, which was, thankfully, shut. George gave a cry of excitement when Frances threaded her way through the room to nose at it.

"...And then while Gwendolyn gave that poor man the antivenin," Mother was explaining to my half-listening ear, "your father—well, he was quite marvellous! You should have seen him *bid them halt in Queen Victoria's name*! He told them all about being the Grand Royal Dragonmaster, or whatever he is, but I don't think that alone would have been quite enough to deter them, except then Mr Tallantire piped up very helpfully and offered to give them *his* dragon, only when he passed it out the door to them they all screamed and blasphemed. One of them fainted dead away! His friends had to carry him down to the cellars, in the end. Apparently not all of them even made it to the abbey to begin with. Some of them ran off the moment they saw Simon's creatures out on the lawn."

Over Mother's shoulder, I saw Simon step out into the passage and intercept Janushek, who as at that moment passing by, to tell him about the fire. Janushek threw me a wink and a grin through the doorway to show he was glad to see me safe before he headed off to handle the fire.

Martha and Hanna came in with trays—I smelled honey cakes. Steam wafted merrily from the big brown teapots. In the light, the resemblance between Hanna and I was less striking, but she was still wearing my clothes.

"Ee-dit!" she called out comically, echoing my imitation of her accent.

"At your service," I said, bobbing a curtsy as I took the tray from her. Then I grew serious. "We won't send you to a workhouse, you know," I said, forgetting that Farley had said those words to me, not to Hanna.

"I know," she said cheerfully. "My honey cakes are too good. But after your babies, I marry handsome farmer with many sheep."

Hanna's salamander streaked out from under her skirts and scuttled over to Frances.

"Hanna, look!" I gasped.

Some mysterious filial communication must have passed between the two salamanders, for the little one was now riding comfortably on its mother's back as if they had never been parted.

I glimpsed Simon outside in the passage, looking for me over everyone's heads. I returned the tray to Hanna.

"I'll be back in a moment," I promised her, heading for the door.

"Martha, you must take something down to our guests in the cellar..." I heard Mother say as I left the room.

Oolong just managed to slip out and hide in my skirts before I shut the door behind me. Simon and I were alone in the passage.

"You're going after him, aren't you?" I said to him.

He nodded.

"Then I'm going with you," I said, putting my hand into his.

The lid of the old oak chest next to us creaked open and Meredith sat up, a cobweb decorating her hair.

"Is it all over?" she asked.

"Almost," I said. "See here—you gave away my dragon." It rankled, though in the end it had turned out very well to have Frances at my side.

"Did I?" She blinked at me a little nervously. "I didn't know it was anything special."

"They are *all* something special," I said with great dignity. "They belong to the Queen, and they are *Royal*." I handed Oolong to her solemnly. "Take better care of this one while we chase down Farley. And go have a honey cake, everyone's looking for you."

"Dare I ask if you have a plan?" asked Simon as I snatched up a macintosh on our way towards the door, Pilot sticking close to us.

"Me? Do I ever? You're the one who plans ahead, Simon. You tell me how we're going to catch him!"

"Do you have anything of Farley's to track him with?"

I considered this. "Well, he manhandled me enough—would this apron have his scent on it?" I turned my back to him, indicating he should untie it.

At this, Simon stopped dead. "Are you all right? Did he hurt you?"

"Why?" I asked, remembering my grandfather the night Farley had threatened me. "Are you going to call him rude names and offer to thrash him?"

Simon seemed faintly abashed as he untied Hanna's apron. "No. I was going to ask if *you* needed anything—a cup of tea or a lie down—"

"Bless you!" I spun round, stood on my tiptoes, and planted an awkward kiss somewhere in the vicinity of his chin, then drew back, just as awkwardly. "But no—what I need is to get our dragon back."

"The *Queen's* dragon, you mean?" he said dryly.

"Well, I thought that would impress Meredith. We shall have to find out if the Queen even cares about them at all once we're through all this."

"Do you know," he said earnestly, "if you warn me when you want to kiss me, I might bend down to meet you..."

"It just—comes over me all of a sudden," I confessed, going pink.

Just then, Lily rushed in, a crinkled sort of look on her face. "Have you seen Pip?"

Simon shook his head. "He and Violet must be together."

"I'm sure they're somewhere safe," I said. "They both know every crevice in this place. Any moment they'll realise it's all over and come out."

She nodded, but I didn't think I'd really relieved her at all. "Do you know where Brik is?"

"I sent him up to the roof with your father to put out a chimney fire," Simon said, then looked back to me, hesitating, as Lily ran up the stairs to find him.

"I can't imagine anything has happened to them—after all, you rounded up all the ruffians, didn't you? Wait! What about Briggs? I heard Farley send Briggs to find me, but I didn't see him again."

"I haven't seen him at all," admitted Simon.

"Perhaps he ran off when all his comrades were taken to the cellars?" I guessed hopefully.

Gwendolyn came in, holding Una's hand.

"Edith," she said. "You must hear this before you go anywhere."

Una swallowed. "I know where they are. At least, I know what they're doing."

Just then, Pilot began to paw at the front door, making excited floppy jumps and looking back at us like we were being fools to worry about anything else but going after Farley and Mr Darcy.

I looked at Simon in anguish.

"Even though he's got a head start, he won't go fast," Simon calculated. "The moon is full, and you can spot him from the air on Cariad. I'll be on Portia, with Pilot to guide the way. We'll be faster, and we know the Dale better than he does."

"You're right," I said. "Well, Una, what has your sister gotten up to this time? And where exactly has she taken Pip?"

"To light the beacons," she said.

"The *what*?" Simon and I exclaimed at once.

"Your blessed beacons, Edith," said Gwendolyn, in a sore voice. "It was news to me that they really exist. It would be polite to at least *try* to keep me updated about these things, you know."

"Gwen, if you only *knew*—!" I said, throwing up my hands.

"Una," said Simon with tremendous patience, "are you telling us that Violet and Pip have gone off to the fells alone to look for the Pele Tower?"

"Oh no," she said, and we all gave a sigh of relief. "They already found it. Go and look." And she pointed towards the door.

Simon released all the bolts and pushed it open and we spilled out. The great shapes of the quetzalcoatls on the lawn looked like cloud shadows, but there were no clouds in the clear night sky, only a great round moon, and pale stars.

I scanned the horizon.

"It looks like they did," said Simon in amazement.

And then I realised—that brighter low-hanging star wasn't a star at all.

It was a blazing signal fire, far off on the fells.

CHAPTER FORTY-TWO

"But—but—how on earth—" I stared at Simon. "*Cariad?*"

I ran for the stables. But I didn't have to go far, for Cariad had heard my voice and appeared with a rush of wings before me. She was wearing the riding harness.

"The children must have flown her there!" I exclaimed to Simon and Gwendolyn, who had both followed me.

"And back?" guessed Simon. "And it must have been hours ago—that's quite a blaze."

"Then where are they now?" asked Gwendolyn.

There was the sound of shouting voices from the roof.

We looked up to see flames leaping above the abbey.

"Simon, would my chimney fire do that?" I whispered.

"No," he said. "It's coming from the other side." And he set off at a run round the abbey.

I got on Cariad and buckled myself into the harness. Gwendolyn went back inside to warn the others.

Beacons, Una had said.

More than one? But of course! There would have to be one up on the fells, to signal for help, and one closer to the abbey, to light the way to it for any allies who answered the call.

Why hadn't I thought of it before? It seemed the children had.

As soon as Cariad rose into the air, lifting me above the roofline, I saw that the leaping flames came from a bonfire on top of William's Tower. The tower was made entirely of stone, so it should be safe. There was a much smaller fire coming from my chimney, quite far away. I directed Cariad to circle the abbey so I could look for Pip and Violet.

There were men on the roof near my bedroom chimney, with buckets of water at the ready, but they seemed quite laissez-fair about the whole thing. One of them took off his cap and waved at me cheerfully, a salamander silhouetted on his shoulder.

I flew as close as I dared and shouted at Janushek as I went past, "Lily's looking for you!"

Then I flew over the abbey again, scanning the dark maze of chimneys, gables, towers, ridges, crenelations, and narrow walkways for any sign of the children, but I was feeling less worried by the moment. It seemed as if they had returned from their astonishing feat at the pele tower to light the signal fire here on the abbey tower. But where were they now?

Although I was privately impressed that Violet had gained Cariad's trust, I would certainly have words with her about riding my dragon without permission—and for bullying Pip into dangerous escapades.

Then I heard a shout from the other side of the great kitchen chimney stacks. That was Violet, and there was a desperation in her voice that gave me pause. Spotting a relatively level spot on the roof, I landed Cariad, unbuckled and slid off. Careful not to slip on loose bits of roofing, I edged round the chimneys as quickly and quietly as I could towards the sounds of a scuffle.

"Let go of him!" came Violet's voice.

"Shut your trap," hissed Briggs, "or I'll push you off!"

I could see them now, a little below me, lit by the blaze atop the tower. Briggs was dragging Pip down the incline of the roof towards the exterior stair that led down from the muniments room.

Violet kicked at him, then darted out of reach. "You're going to be surrounded by dragon keepers from all over England any minute, and they *eat* pirates!" she shouted.

He made a grab for her but she ducked behind a chimney pot shaped like a wyvern, ghoulish in the firelight.

I stepped out from my hiding place before he could grab her. "Stop, Briggs! The game's up."

He jerked round. Pip's neck was locked in his beefy arm.

"It's over," I said to them both, holding out an arm to Violet. "Farley has fled and all the rest have surrendered."

Violet scrambled up to me and I put my arm round her.

"You're bluffing," Briggs growled.

"No, Briggs—she's not," came Janushek's voice. He was a silhouette on the ridgepole nearby. "All you'll get docked for is breaking and entering. Don't make it worse."

"No! I'm not getting docked for anything." Briggs shook his head emphatically. "I'm taking this lad with me. Once I get safely away from here, I'll let him go, without a scratch on him. Get it? Don't you get any closer! And don't try anything!"

"All right," Janushek said, sitting down on the ridgepole calmly and holding up his hands to show he didn't have a weapon. The salamander wandered down his waistcoat to perch next to him on the roof.

And then I spotted Lily, just out of Briggs's sightline, completely still against a crenelation, nearly invisible in her grey housemaid's dress. She had the blowpipe at her lips, and looked like she was carved from the same rock as the stones that built the abbey.

I forced my gaze back to Briggs, lest he notice her.

"Violet, look at me," Janushek warned.

It was too late—Briggs had followed Violet's gaze to Lily, and as the dart whistled through the air he jerked towards the head of the stairs, which was a short drop below where he was. But in doing this, he swung Pip out over the edge, two stories from the gravel walk below, and Lily made a sound of desperation.

Janushek slid down the roof at a dizzying speed and landed on his feet, grabbing for Pip, but Briggs blocked him. Janushek and Briggs tussled, until Janushek hooked his foot in the back of the bigger man's knee, scooped Pip into his arms, and tossed him onto the roof away from the edge.

Briggs recovered and retaliated with a vicious slug to Janushek's chest that sent him reeling back, catching himself on the incline of the roof.

Briggs was advancing to hit him again, a nasty slur on his lips, when an unearthly scream—almost like an eagle's—pierced the air and a wyvern chimney pot smashed over his head.

Briggs collapsed to his knees, felled by Lily, who stood over him, fair hair blowing out behind her, eyes flaming, a shower of sparks from the tower fire gilding her like a figure from myth.

"Get away from here!" she screamed, shards of the chimney pot falling from her fingers. "And don't *ever* come back, hear me? We won't stand by while you hurt *peaceful folk like us*!"

Grasping Violet's hand, I ran to Pip and put my arm round him.

Though I did not see it myself, I was told later that at that moment, a bit of the guttering gave way beneath Briggs and he started sliding off the edge, dislodging masonry as he groped wildly for support. If he'd only swung the right way, he'd have landed safely on the stair, but his missing eye played him false, and he did not judge the distance correctly. Panicked, he caught a fistful of Lily's skirts.

As Lily jerked down after him with a cry, I looked up to see Janushek grab hold of her arm. Now the only thing keeping all three of them from falling to their deaths was Janushek's other arm, wrapped round a downspout.

Everyone was yelling, in Cockney, Polish, and broad York-shire. Even the salamander was chittering from his perch on the rooftree.

Violet wrenched out of my grasp and scrambled down to-wards the stair.

"What are you doing?" I shouted.

"I'm going to bite the pirate's fingers!" she shouted back.

I turned back to get the harness off Cariad—if I could get it in time, I could secure Janushek to the chimney stack—

The yelling stopped abruptly.

To everyone's amazement, Briggs was rising up in the air with a look of utter confusion on his face—on the back of a Welsh dragon.

He was level with me and Violet now. A hooded figure held him round the waist on the pommel of the saddle.

"Told you!" Violet called out to the white-faced Briggs.

Simon appeared from behind me. He shouted in Welsh to the rider and waved at him. The rider nodded in reply and flew off with his prisoner, rejoining a second Welsh dragon which I could hardly make out against the dark sky before they both disappeared behind the abbey. Two of them!

I laid my head on Simon's bosom and allowed myself to breathe to the rhythm of his heartbeat for a moment.

"I've sent them after Farley," he said. "Are you ready for your comfortable chair now?"

I laughed into his waistcoat. "Close. But I'll never forgive myself if we don't get Mr Darcy back." I looked up at him and slowly gathered the lapels of his greatcoat in my hands. "Consider this a warning," I said softly.

He bent down to meet me.

Everything was very quiet for a moment.

"No, no! What are you all doing? There's no time for *that*!" came Violet's frustrated voice.

I lowered myself from my tiptoes and resurfaced. Lily and Janushek were in a familial huddle with Pip and the salamander at the centre, and they paid Violet no heed. The two of them murmured softly to each other, and Janushek's hand cradled Lily's cheek.

"We have to capture the mad scientist *now*!" Violet insisted.

"Violet, you are going down to the sitting room to show your family you are safe," Simon said severely.

"That's right! Simon and I are the ones going after the mad scientist," I said.

Gwendolyn's head appeared as she ascended the very stair above which all the events had occurred moments earlier. She surveyed the scene before her.

"What did I say about keeping me updated, Edith?" she said a little severely.

"As soon as things stop happening for half a minute, I will!"

She crossed her arms and waited.

"All right." I took a breath. "Briggs took Pip hostage, and Lily shot him with the blowpipe but somehow the beacons worked, and the Welsh came and caught Briggs when he was falling before he could drag everyone off the roof to their deaths."

Violet let out a howl. "You left out everything about *me*!"

"And now you two are going after Farley," Gwendolyn concluded.

We nodded.

"Well, I'm coming with you," she said grimly. "Once the world catches onto what's going on here in Ormdale, we're going to need lots of little Dragon Keepers to shoulder the work, and I don't intend to have any of them myself. So *someone* with sense has to make sure you and Simon survive long enough to produce them."

"Gwen, please moderate your language!" I cried in distress over Simon's laughter. "This isn't medical school."

Moments later, Gwendolyn was holding on for dear life behind me on Cariad as we swept over the moor, scanning the ground for Farley.

I could see no sign of him. In the distance, over the fells, I caught sight of a Welsh dragon soaring, silhouetted against the full moon. Who was the rider, and what had he done with Briggs?

Then I saw Pilot below us. I pushed down gently on her neck and Cariad swooped to follow him. I let her have her head.

Gwendolyn made a strangled sound as Cariad levelled out abruptly a few yards from the ground.

"Think of those the little Dragon Keepers!" I flung back at her merrily.

"I *am* thinking of them, you lunatic!"

"Come now, this can't be as bad as an afternoon at the dissecting table."

"I'll take a tumour over this any day."

"Watch out—she's headed into the trees! Hold on!"

"What do you think I'm doing *now*?"

Cariad followed Pilot into the hidden wood. We had to crouch close as she dodged the bony-fingered branches.

Then she slowed and stopped on a patch of riverbank I didn't recognise. Was that an overgrown ruin, where the ground rose a bit? I could make out a half-fallen chimney. Pilot was at the water's edge, growling softly.

Gwendolyn slid off and I followed, looking for footsteps in the muddy bank.

"He must be following the river to try and get out of the Dale," I said. "The water will be confusing the scent."

Gwendolyn seized my arm and spoke low. "She didn't lose him."

I followed her pointing. There, on the other side of the riverbank, staring into the water with a bundle under his arm, was Farley.

CHAPTER FORTY-THREE

He looked up at us. I couldn't be quite certain of his expression in the moonlight, but his posture had a look of resignation about it.

Was he ready to surrender at last?

"It's gone," he said.

"What's gone?"

"The cottage I was born in. I always pictured other people living there, but they must have thought it a place of ill luck and abandoned it. They were always superstitious. I should have thought of that." He gave himself a little shake. "Do you know why I sent the Pole instead of coming myself? It was because I promised myself I would never come back here." He looked at Gwendolyn. "Your family rejected me—sent me away to die without a second thought, when I was a mere child. Did you know that?"

"No. I'm sorry," she said quietly.

The bundle he held under his arm wriggled. He had wrapped Mr Darcy tightly in his coat to protect himself from being bitten. The little phials attached to Farley's waistcoat gleamed in the moonlight like some dark wizardry.

"Sorry for what, precisely?" he asked acidly. "Sorry that all my family either perished here in poisoned agony or were sent out to die of starvation and cold? Or perhaps you're sorry that I was adopted by a city doctor and won a scholarship to study organic chemistry? Be honest—if I'd died along with them, or eked out a short life in a factory, you wouldn't be sorry at all. None of you even noticed what happened to my family."

"We're trying to change all of that," said Gwendolyn humbly. "Or at least—Edith's trying."

He looked at me. "All those people back there—doing your bidding. What is your hold on them?"

"They don't do my bidding," I said ruefully, glancing at Gwendolyn. "Sometimes I wish they did. But they're here now, when I need them, because—because—"

How could I explain to him that when I demanded least from people, they gave most?

"Because of love," finished Gwendolyn. "They're here because of love."

"Love," he said thoughtfully. "That's useful."

Then he drew out a second venom gun from his pocket. Pilot barked and bristled.

"Thank you for explaining. Now you are going to get me out of here."

"You said yourself that gun can't harm me," I objected. "And if you shoot my cousin, we'll fly away and heal her."

"This one isn't a reptile venom," he said, his voice like surgical steel. "It's the one I tested on you. Yes, I see you remember it. How do you feel about doubling the dose?"

"You promised my grandfather you wouldn't hurt me," I insisted, but I went cold all over. "And if you do, you'll have to reckon with my dragon, as well as everyone in the Dale, in addition to whatever Sir Joseph does to you."

"Yes. But you see, it's your cousin I'll shoot. I think that will hurt you quite enough, and fulfil Sir Joseph's requirements."

I stepped in front of Gwendolyn. "It was she who saved your life by calling an ambulance to your laboratory!"

He ignored this. "In precisely ten seconds, I'm going to start drowning this dragon or shooting your cousin—or both, whichever option is most viable—unless you agree to fly me out of here on that." He pointed at Cariad.

I gaped at him.

"And if your beast tries to hurt me, I'll shoot it, too, and make the best of it on foot. I've got more than one bullet. Make up your mind. Perhaps this will help you decide."

Keeping the gun pointed at me, he dropped the dragon bundle into the shallows of the river and held it under the surface with his foot. Air bubbles erupted around it.

Cariad came up behind me, snuffling in alarm. I held out my arm to stop her, knowing he'd shoot her if she threatened him. Pilot ran up to higher ground and began to bark at us, as if urging us to follow him.

A great rushing sound and crashing of branches was our only warning for the surprise that came next.

A great ribbon of darkness with two gleaming eyes tore a passage through the trees and undergrowth of the riverbank, spattering our clothes with mud, and slithered to a stop a few yards from us, rearing up high in the air, a frill of feathers flaring out.

A voice from somewhere above our heads spoke with just a touch of Yorkshire in it, and more than a touch of laughter. "Whatever poison you've put in that, Doctor—I don't think it's enough for this beast."

"Simon?" I cried out in amazement, squinting upwards at the silhouetted form of a man atop a quetzalcoatyl.

"It's enough for you," said Farley, and he pointed it at Simon and fired.

It was too dark to see clearly what happened next. Something zipped downwards from the heavens, smashing the phials on Farleys' chest, and he clutched at himself with a scream of pain.

Dimly, I was aware that the rushing sound had never stopped.

Then there was water, water everywhere, knocking us off our feet. We were waist deep in it already and our skirts were dragging us under. I grabbed at Gwendolyn's hand but it was slippery, and the water tore us apart before I could get a firm hold, and Pilot was barking in an exasperated way because he had warned us but we hadn't listened.

Where had it all come from so suddenly?

"Cariad!" I called.

Something slid under me in the water and lifted me up out of the flood, but it wasn't Cariad. I groped around for something to hold onto and found fins.

A river dragon!

But where was Gwendolyn? I shouted for her in a panic.

A strong hand found mine in the dark—I knew instantly it was Simon's—and hauled me up onto the serpent's back.

Simon was unharmed—the paralysing bullet had missed him in the dark. But I had no time for relief.

"We've got to find Gwen—the river—I couldn't hold her!" I babbled.

The water level was rising quickly, and I was disoriented. Where had I last seen her?

Now Cariad appeared, swimming alongside us against the merciless current, which seemed to have no effect on the giant serpent. Indeed, its body was temporarily damming up the rising water.

Cariad nuzzled my shoulder insistently. And then I spotted something pale among the black branches of a willow, like a kite caught in a tree.

"There's Gwen!" I shouted. "She's climbed above the water!"

"I'll get her. Go with Cariad and get safe and dry," Simon urged.

He lifted me by the waist and I managed to get my leg and sopping skirts over my dragon's back.

"We'll be just behind you," Simon promised.

As Cariad flew upwards, I looked down and saw a boiling torrent of white water below me.

A dark figure was clinging to the bank.

"Farley!" I shouted.

Before I could act, the figure was swept away with no more fanfare than a dead leaf in the current.

I steered Cariad downriver, but I could see no trace of him and my hands would soon be thoroughly numb. I had to get home while it was still safe for me to fly.

There was nothing I could do to help Farley.

I sagged and clung to Cariad, shaking in the cold night air, as she winged toward the abbey.

Once, I opened my eyes to see the faintly iridescent form of the quetzalcoatl slithering along the ground below me towards the abbey, two figures on its back.

What had become of poor Mr Darcy? If he was as much a creature of water as Oolong, I had my doubts as to whether he could be drowned. And where on earth had this torrent come from when it hadn't rained in two days at least? Was it possible the little dragon had called it up himself, just as Oolong had summoned water from the pipes in the laboratory?

And what had smashed Farley's phials like that?

Cariad landed outside the abbey in a patch of light cast from the open front door. Someone with foresight had started a fire in the Great Hall fireplace. Cariad walked right in and sat down in front of it.

I rolled off her back, dripping profligately, and huddled as close to the fire as I could.

A moment later, Simon and Gwendolyn stumbled in, almost as wet as I was, followed by Pilot.

"I'm not going to hug you," Gwendolyn said, teeth chattering. "You're too wet."

"I love you, too, Gwen," I chattered back.

She dumped a very cross-looking little creature onto the floor. He shook droplets off.

"Mr Darcy!" I cried joyfully.

There were Welsh voices at the door, and Simon looked up with a very mixed expression on his face. Cariad looked up, too, and her body tensed.

"Drake!" a voice I had never wanted to hear again called out in a cheery way that grated on me. "We tied up that ruffian in the stables. Very odd fellow—he kept asking us not to eat him."

Three cloaked figures stood in the doorway. The speaker alone had his hood thrown back, revealing dark curls and a dimpled grin, while the others remained shrouded, as if uncertain of their welcome.

"And who is this now?" asked Gwendolyn in exasperation.

"The Welsh Worm Warden," said Simon.

I had determined to forgive Arthur for the good of my immortal soul, but the indignation that filled me on seeing him on my doorstep made me doubt its eternal welfare.

"Cariad is looking well!" He eyed her a little nervously. "May we come in?"

"I don't know," I said. "I'm trying to think if we can just leave you standing there."

"*Of course* you must come in!" cried Miss Falconer, coming in from the passage with a stack of blankets. She tossed them carelessly to Simon and crossed the floor to Arthur, glowing.

"Your Highness! I'm so relieved to see you fully recovered from your dreadful injuries last summer. The fall from such a height while you were out searching the Welsh mountains for Miss Worms after she got lost—it's nothing less than a miracle you survived!"

"Fall?" I asked, perking up my ears as Simon wrapped me in a blanket and sat me on the oaken settle.

The two other riders came inside but still remained hooded, as if only too aware that my welcome had been inconclusive.

Cariad padded past us all and out the door, probably to visit with her kind.

Arthur took Meredith's hand with less enthusiasm than I expected. Was he afraid I'd call him to account for his sins in front of everyone?

"Yes!" said Meredith. "The prince had a fall when he was recapturing the female dragon—just after you left, Edith. It was only his extraordinary stoicism that enabled him to withstand the pain enough to remount his beast and return safely home with both of the dragons."

"What a shame there was no one there to help him back into the saddle in his injured state," I said, nestling deeper into the blanket so I didn't have to look at him.

"Ah!" He laughed nervously, as if he wasn't quite sure how to play this scene. "I didn't mention your part in it, Miss Worms, because I couldn't have my father sending someone else after you. I couldn't let him know I helped you, of course."

"You helped her?" asked Meredith in surprise.

Arthur made a little self-deprecating sound.

I fumed inside my blanket. How could he stand there in front of my friends and act as if he hadn't treated me abominably?

But perhaps I oughtn't to say anything. Hadn't Simon said he hoped there was something good about the Dragon Families? And hadn't the proved it by coming to our aid? What if Arthur's past greed and fear were to drag us all down into a sordid tangle of recriminations from which we might never extricate ourselves?

But I had reckoned without Gwendolyn.

"You would have been a great deal more helpful if you hadn't chased her and tied her up," she said, "and then left her in the wilderness to find her own way home across England."

There was an odd sound behind me of the air going out of someone's body, and then an impressive thud. I turned round to see Arthur laid out on the floor and Meredith gasping down at him.

It took me a moment to realise that it was Simon who was responsible for Arthur's abrupt recumbence.

Arthur rubbed his jaw and made no move to get up.

"You might have warned me, Drake," he groaned.

"You lied to me," said Simon, standing over him and dripping water on his feet. "You told me Edith got away safely."

Arthur pointed at me wildly. "She's safe, isn't she?"

Simon peeled off his jacket and laboriously rolled up his wet sleeves as if going about a distasteful chore. He spoke to Arthur as if he were a reprobate adolescent that required a speedy lesson. "On your feet, Pendragon. You get a free hit this time because I didn't warn you first."

I stared at him in confusion. *This time*?

"Simon, you—you told me you weren't a fighter!" I protested.

He looked at me for a moment. "I meant that I don't like fighting—not that I *can't* fight."

"Can't fight?" Arthur snorted, getting to his feet and backing away. "He fought off a handful of my best men when he came back looking for you."

"As he jolly well should have!" Gwendolyn said.

Things were getting out of hand. What would happen to our fragile alliance if Simon beat the stuffing out of Arthur the very first time he came to help us?

"Wait! You needn't fight for my honour, Simon," I told him.

"I'm not fighting for your honour, Edith," he said very seriously. "No one thinks it's anything but perfectly unspotted."

"Unassailable," Arthur interjected, nodding vigorously.

Simon threw him a killing look.

"The reason I am fighting him," Simon explained, "is because of how he behaved. He endangered you, deceived us all, and escaped unscathed."

"Unscathed!" Arthur cried. "Well, I like that! I was in bed for weeks in *great pain*, as you well know, Drake! You even read aloud to me!"

"You read to him?" said Gwendolyn, offended.

"I was very low!" Arthur said defensively. "The fact is, Drake doesn't know it, but I never fell. Tell them, Miss Worms—tell them how I got hurt, and how serious it was!"

"You *want* me to tell them?" I asked in disbelief.

"I want Drake to know I was thoroughly punished, even for his bloodthirsty tastes! Please—for the sake of my beautiful face, if for nothing else." And he gave a weak smile, as if suddenly doubtful that this was the best tack to take with me.

It wasn't.

"All right." I turned to Simon. "Cariad saw him trying to take me back by force, so she threw him across a glen and cracked his ribs."

"I see," said Simon, very calmly. "And is that all, Edith?"

I looked at Gwendolyn helplessly. She gave me the slightest shake of the head, as if to say, *I won't make you tell.*

For a moment, I wished Father were here so he could decide what happened next. The squire of Ormdale, the one who had sat in judgement in this very hall at Michaelmas, he would know just what to do.

What right did *I* have to mete out justice?

But I knew what he would say. Arthur held a position of authority in the Welsh dragon-keeping community—therefore, as many people as possible should know the worst about him.

If any good was to come from the Dragon Families in the future, it must start with truth.

I let out a breath and nodded to Gwendolyn. She cleared her throat.

"Not quite all," said Gwendolyn. "He told her she would be forced to stay in Wales until she'd provided him with a child."

For a moment, everyone was silent.

Then Meredith laughed nervously. "But of course! You needn't put it so crudely, Gwendolyn—the aim of the whole party was to select a bride for the prince—a princess of Gwynedd! There's nothing indecent in that! And of course the prince thought Edith was there because she'd consented to the whole thing. I was the only one who knew she'd been hoodwinked into attending! It was all a dreadful mistake, and it ruined a very pleasant party."

"Tell them," said Simon to Arthur, in a quietly terrifying way. "*Now.*"

"Oh, right, then," muttered Arthur, clearing his throat. "The fact is, I've brought the Princess of Gwynedd with me."

And he held out his hand to the smallest of the cloaked figures.

She threw back her hood.

"Angharad!" I cried. I had not expected to see the beautiful weaverwoman again.

"I am pleased to see you," Angharad said, giving us a queenly nod, "and you, *dewin dreigiau,*" she said this to Simon, with a warm smile.

"You spoke English all along?" I wondered.

She shook her head and indicated Simon. "The *dewin* has taught me."

A look of fond friendship passed between them.

"Well!" murmured Meredith. "It sounds as if Mr Drake's captivity in Wales was a good deal pleasanter than anyone imagined."

"Just what are you implying about my wife?" asked Arthur with impeccable timing.

"Your *what?*" I gasped.

His dimple wavered uncertainly, perhaps remembering the regrettable circumstances under which I had advised him to marry Angharad, who was already the mother of his children.

"I didn't marry her to please *you*, Miss Worms. It was entirely to please myself."

He took Angharad's arm in his, as if presenting his bride to us at a garden party.

"You should know," said Simon to the rest of us, crossing his arms, "that the two of them have been married for years."

I stared at Arthur. "You had a wife *all along?*"

"Well, our marriage was a little on the morganatic side," said Arthur with a rakish wink that did him no favours with anyone present, "but I'm reliably informed it was legal."

The final hooded figure revealed himself now. It was Emrys.

"I can attest to that," he said.

"Are you a priest?" demanded Meredith.

"A dissenting minister, Miss Falconer," Emrys answered. His eyes darted to me, then dropped in shame, no doubt thinking of how he'd failed to warn both of us of our false position in Wales. "Or used to be. It's been a long time since I've been worthy of such an office."

"We had to keep it a secret from my father, of course," said Arthur breezily, as if that excused everything.

"But...he would have *bigamised* one of us!" I objected, and Meredith and I shared a look of utter horror.

"And that's why I thrashed him the first time," said Simon flatly, "when Angharad told me they were already married. Holding a bride competition was bad form to begin with—doing it while already married was criminal."

"Simon," I said solemnly, "I could just *kiss* you."

"Is that my warning?" he asked in a pleased voice, stepping closer to me.

We were interrupted by the sharp report of someone's ear being boxed.

I looked up to see Arthur rubbing his other cheek.

"And I missed it *again*!" I said in disappointment.

"I saw both of them," said Gwendolyn, "and they were glorious. But not *nearly* enough."

"I'm inclined to agree with that," said Simon darkly.

"To think I might have wasted myself on *you!*" Meredith hissed, wiped her hand on her skirt, and sailed out of the room.

Arthur looked at Angharad balefully as if to ask why she let all this happen to him.

"You deserved that," she said quietly. Then she looked at me, and her eyes were full of sadness. "I do not ask you to forgive us, Worm Warden, but please—will you let us rest and water our dragons? We can sleep in the stable."

Arthur seemed about to object, but I saw Angharad grip his arm.

Simon spoke very quietly to me, as if no one else was present. "You decide, Edith. Forgiveness doesn't mean pretending everything is all right. You taught me that."

I took a deep breath and turned to the three cloaked figures.

"You hurt us both—Simon and me. And it's God's mercy that both of us recovered as well as we did." Angharad and Emrys bowed their heads, and Arthur shifted uncomfortably. "But you got rid of Pendragon, and you sent me Cariad. We asked for help, and you came. You stopped my friends from tumbling to their deaths. And it seemed as if it was a crossbow bolt that struck Farley and stopped him shooting at us."

"Oh, that was my shot," Arthur interjected. "Pretty neat, wasn't it?"

"What you've done tonight doesn't excuse what's been done in the past," I persisted, ignoring him. "But repentance means change. And change—I suppose it takes time and patience. We've had quite enough fighting for one evening." I straightened. "The Yorkshire Worm Warden welcomes the representatives from Wales, and thanks them for their aid. Let no one say we turned aside a Dragon Keeper on a winter's night."

Chapter Forty-Four

The three of us left the Welsh contingent to Mother in the interest of not catching our deaths.

Lily insisted on having enough hot water brought up to the bedroom to fill the old tub. I did not like to order such a luxury when the kitchen was so far away and the servants so overworked (a sponge bath would have sufficed), but in my current state, I was too weak to resist. I went first, and then Gwendolyn had her soak while I sat by the fire.

With a cellarful of ruffians safely locked up several floors below, and Frances lying nearby, and Cariad sleeping in the Great Hall, and everyone I loved nearby, I felt that God was in his heaven and all was right with the world.

"Gwen," I said, "I know what you're thinking."

"Do you indeed?"

"That it would have been much more restful to have gone to Ivy's house in Cornwall for Christmas."

"It *would* have been more restful," she reflected. "But it's like you said—this is our family. Dragons, and floods, and sieges—all of it. I was terrified to come back, but it's not so bad, really—not now that we're all in it together. Do you want to know what I was really thinking of? I was thinking that the only thing I want right now is a new Inspector Green novel to curl up in bed with for the day."

"Oh! Well, I have been rather busy..."

"I know. But when everything calms down a bit, after you and Simon get married—and I'm not unreasonable, I don't expect you to write on your honeymoon!—you might think of your readers again."

I smiled. "I think I have an idea for the next story. Would you like to hear it?"

Gwendolyn took herself off to bed, but I was restless. I didn't know what had become of Meredith, and I was famished.

I crept down the stairs in my dressing gown as quietly as I could, on the off chance that anyone had managed to get to sleep after all. When I arrived at the kitchen, I found a charming little supper laid out on a tray—a piece of rabbit pie, a slice of bread (admirably buttered), and a dish of blackberry jam.

"There you are," said Simon, materialising from the shadows.

"What are you doing in the kitchen at this hour?" I asked.

"Waiting for you. Here!" He had positioned an armchair close by the kitchen range—I recognised it as the favourite chair from my study. "I've just put the kettle on."

"*You've* put the kettle on?" I repeated in astonishment.

"Yes." His lips quirked. "I'm quite able to make a proper cup of tea, in case you were worried. I am the son of a butler, after all."

He led me to the armchair and I sat down in it. He brought the tray and set it on my lap. The kettle whistled just as he whisked it off the hob and poured a little steaming water into the teapot.

"How long have you been waiting for me?" I asked in wonder.

He swished the water about and spilled it out again before filling it properly. He was warming the pot. (When he said he knew how to make tea, it was no idle boast.)

"Oh, a few hours."

"A few *hours*?"

"You still don't know what I'm doing?"

Since my mouth was full of pie, I shook my head.

"Someone told me once, very memorably, that she liked adventures, but she wanted a soft chair and a hot cup of tea afterwards."

A choked sob escaped me, surprising even me.

"Is something wrong?" he asked anxiously, setting down the cup of tea he had just poured for me.

Covering my face, I shook my head. There wasn't anything wrong, it was just that I'd unexpectedly begun to cry while my mouth was full. I reached for the tea and gulped some.

"I've made myself choke, that's all. I told you I'm a very earthly sort of creature!" I snuffled.

He knelt down near me.

"I've thought of how I want to say this, and I hope you won't mind that it's not original. I'm not an artist like you."

He took a deep breath, and then he spoke the entirety of the Shakespeare sonnet he had quoted to me many months ago in the dining carriage of a train.

"When, in disgrace with fortune and men's eyes,
I all alone beweep my outcast state,
And trouble deaf heaven with my bootless cries,
And look upon myself and curse my fate,
Wishing me like to one more rich in hope,
Featured like him, like him with friends possessed,
Desiring this man's art and that man's scope,
With what I most enjoy contented least;
Yet in these thoughts myself almost despising—"

He looked up at me, and I'd never realised that his eyes weren't just dark, they were black as the quetzalcoatyls, black as the caves under the Great Rock. And they were full of a mysterious beauty that I wanted to spend my life trying to understand.

"Haply I think on thee, and then my state,
(Like to the lark at break of day arising
From sullen earth) sings hymns at heaven's gate—"

He smiled at this, and I remembered the dawn ride.

"For thy sweet love remembered such wealth brings
That then I scorn to change my state with kings."

After that, I had to pick up the napkin on the tea tray to staunch the flow of tears. As I did, something small and heavy rolled out.

A gold ring, formed in the shape of a dragon's wing. It would curl round my finger like Cariad's wing curved over me.

"It's made of Spanish gold—well, from the New World, really, from Ignacio's country," he said. "I had it made in London. I couldn't take a ring from the Drakes, but I thought I might use just a little of the gold that was taken from my ancestors to make one of our own."

"Yes," I said softly.

"Yes?" he repeated, then paused. "About the gold? Or about marrying me?"

"Both. Every kind of yes."

Young ladies are not supposed to feel hungry when they are receiving a young man's declaration. Alas, I am but an earthly creature, but after I finished this welcome repast, we went out to see the sun rise over the Dale, leaning our backs against the kitchen wall and listening to the birds singing hymns at heaven's gate.

"*Did* you beweep?" I asked. "Your outcast state? In those first days, when you found out who you really were?"

"That first part of the poem is how I've always felt. But when I found out Forrester was my real father—everything about my life began to look different. He loved me, and stayed for me, even without any return."

Then you will begin to know something about the love God bears towards His children, Father had said.

"All the time I thought heaven was deaf to my cries," Simon said in wonder, his fingers threading with mine, "it had already answered them."

"Look!" I said.

The three Welsh dragons were winging riderless through the sky in the distance, their wings edged with fire, cavorting together in exultation. We watched them in silent wonder.

After a little, we could hear the sounds of the household waking up behind us.

"Simon, I saw Farley swept away in the current. Do you suppose there's any chance..."

"I'm off to Ormby now to see if he washed up anywhere downstream."

I nodded. "And I'm going to find out what happened to Meredith."

Conveniently, I found Meredith and Gwendolyn together when I went up to get dressed.

I was about to announce my happy news when I realised that Gwendolyn looked a little guarded.

"I've just been asking about Mrs Drake," Meredith said. "Will she get better now? Or is it too late, after all this time? Well? You can be honest with me, you know."

"It's hard to say," Gwendolyn said hesitantly. "She was never allowed to exercise or live a healthy life, and the loss of her child, followed by the influenza infection, took what little strength she had. It isn't just one thing—like a torn sleeve that needs mending. It will take time to see."

"But you have some idea of what might help her," Meredith insisted. "A change of scenery, perhaps?"

"Sea air? Perhaps. It certainly wouldn't hurt."

"Meredith—am I to understand that you—*like* Mrs Drake?" I was struggling to come to grips with the idea of Meredith and Helena as anything but potential nemeses.

Meredith gave a little sniff in response. "I spent a few hours with Mrs Drake yesterday evening, and she is far and away the most elegant person I've met in Yorkshire—which isn't saying much, I'll grant you. However, she seems to feel it would be best for everyone if she got out from underfoot and made herself scarce for a while, especially with a wedding fast approaching." She glanced at my ring—what sharp eyes she had! "I must say, Mrs Drake is uncommonly thoughtful for an invalid. My grandmother could learn a lot from her. So—what if I take her away for you?"

"Take her away?" I repeated. Meredith was talking about Helena as if she were an unruly pet.

"Yes. To the seaside. I'd be her companion, you know. I think she'd pay me a dress allowance, as well as a salary—I can see she likes to have pretty things about her."

"Why?" I asked baldly. "Why are you doing this?"

Gwendolyn cast me a quelling look and put her hand on Meredith's. "You told me you want to get married, and have your own household. Are you giving up on all that?"

"Heavens, no!" exclaimed Meredith. "I'm not giving up. I'm strategising. Look." She shifted in her seat and gave us both a level gaze. Her hands were folded in her lap in the traditional attitude of contentment, but there was a contained energy about her that reminded me of something. "Any simpleton can see that things are about to change for our families. And when things change, there's a chance they'll change for the better—or the worse. Well, I'm not going to wait around for worse."

It came to me. Hers wasn't a pose of resignation, but waiting—to spring, to pounce on anything better that life might offer. I couldn't help but admire it.

"It won't be forever," she said. "I'm still young. I'll help Mrs Drake settle in, but I won't stay with her forever. Watering places are excellent places to find husbands. A widower, or a wealthy gentleman with a nice, tragic disease like tuberculosis. They'll see me taking care of Mrs Drake, and they'll see what a beautiful ministering angel I make." She dimpled. Was it the first time I'd seen her really smile? Not a smile to persuade, or dazzle, but just a smile between sisters, at a private joke? "And I will, you know. I'll be a perfect angel."

Remembering what Father always said about how terrifying God's angelic messengers really were in the scriptures, I could honestly nod my head in agreement.

Chapter Forty-Five

"Where are the revolutionaries?" asked Meredith when we got to the dining room, which was much less populated than I expected. Tallantire was alone there, scarfing bacon and eggs with the air of a man pursued.

"Well, Janushek and Hanna eat in the kitchen…" I offered.

"Not them, I meant the *radicals* who came last night."

Tallantire swallowed so quickly, I feared for his digestion. "The Welsh are in the library with the squire. If you hurry you can be gone before they appear."

"You're hiding from them!" Her eyes narrowed. "Why?"

He flushed and kept eating.

"Perhaps you heard of the Welsh Warden's ungentlemanly behaviour?" I suggested.

"Criminal behaviour," muttered Gwendolyn.

"That's it!" Tallantire said, relieved.

"If only I were a man!" Meredith sighed. "Then I could have really given him a shiner, as my horrible little brother says. Is there marmalade?" She peered into a jar. "Or only sticky toast crumbs?"

"Would you really want to be a man?" asked Gwendolyn, with a curl of her lip. "Most of them are so...self-involved."

"Sorry, the crumbs are *my* little brother's fault," I said, offering her jam instead. "But he's not awful, just a little exhausting sometimes. And I do think you're unfair, Gwen. Father isn't self-involved, and neither is George—he hardly ever notices himself. If you were to open up his heart it would flutter away like a moth, or run up into a tree. I'd put Simon on the same list but you told me two nights ago he wasn't a man."

"That was before he rescued us and knocked a miscreant over."

"Ah, so it's knightly deeds that hold the key to your heart? I *am* surprised!"

I glanced at Tallantire—sure enough, he was listening with all his ears.

"Who did Drake knock out?" he said.

"That horrid little Welshman you're hiding from," said Meredith.

"Oh!" Tallantire looked shocked. "I'm all for thrashing cads in general, but you can't strike a Worm Warden—even a Welsh one. That's not cricket at all."

"Did someone mention me?" came a roguish voice and the three of us ladies gave a groan and became instantly fascinated by our toast and tea.

Tallantire slumped, taking cover behind the tea service.

Arthur swept the room with his sparkling blue eyes. He looked a little disappointed at his reception.

"You are all summoned," he said with a sweep of his arm.

"Summoned?" repeated Gwendolyn.

"To a solemn gathering of Dragon Keepers. Ah! Good morning to you, Cumbria."

"Morning, Wales," Tallantire grunted.

Arthur peered at him. "Wait a minute—you're not John!"

"Not John?" I stared at Tallantire. "Then who are you, if not John?"

"Of course I'm John," he said, straightening in his chair.

"No, no, no! Your brother is John. You're one of the other ones, with the silly names..." Arthur snapped his fingers. "Ethelbert or Egbert or someone..."

"Cuthbert," said Meredith suddenly, setting down her teacup.

The colour of Tallantire's face testified to the truth of it.

Arthur's eyes glinted and Meredith laughed.

"But we all called you Custard instead," Meredith went on, "because you ate so much at the nursery tea that you were sick all over your trousers, and then while they were drying outside, my brothers went and—"

"What's this about a meeting?" interrupted Gwendolyn in a tone that brought both of them up short.

Tallantire, who had gone from red to pale during Meredith's story, glanced at her gratefully.

"In the library," Arthur said.

Finishing our toast quickly, we got up to join the others in the library. As we were going up the stairs, I heard Tallantire's voice behind me, talking quietly to Gwendolyn.

"It wasn't a lie. All of the boys in my family have the name John—but I do have another name, a dreadful one which my family uses at home, and my oldest brother goes by John."

"Cuthbert isn't dreadful," Gwendolyn said.

"You don't think so?" he said hopefully.

"I think it's a man's actions and not his name that counts, Mr Tallantire," she said crisply, stopping outside the library to give him a piercing look. "You're wrong about thrashing a Worm Warden, Mr Tallantire, but you are right about one thing—some things *just aren't cricket.*"

Then she walked in, leaving Tallantire wondering whether he had been taken up or down a peg—or both at once.

To my surprise, Helena was already in the library, along with Emrys and Arthur and my parents, while Miss Birtwhistle sat at the desk with pen and paper.

"Miss Birtwhistle has been so good as to agree to take notes for us. Well, then," said Father, "are we all here?"

They had arranged the chairs in a circle, and I sat in one.

"Except Simon," I said. "He's gone to see if Farley survived the flood."

"Yes, the flood. Simon told me last night that it may have had something to do with the blasting he and Janushek did in the caves to let out the quetzalcoatyls."

"The what's-its?" asked Arthur.

Helena answered him. "Meso-American dragons. They were walled up in the local caves by the Drakes centuries ago."

Arthur's eyebrows rose. "And you let them out?"

"I was not responsible for the action," Helena said, "but as the representative of the Drake family at this meeting, I lend my full weight to the decision."

Arthur muttered something about 'insanity' and 'English.'

"It seems," continued Father, "that the blasting altered the structure of the caves, and over the following days, the underground river altered its course and finally built up enough force to burst through an obstruction. Thankfully, I've received word from Ormby that no damage was done to the village. The river level has risen much higher before in the past, so they were prepared for such an eventuality, especially in winter. One family lost a cow, and they will be speedily recompensed."

Father's eyes met mine in a way that made me wonder if the cow had in fact been lost to something rather more carnivorous than the river.

"Edith, I have shown the Welsh Warden and his steward the documentation from Queen Elizabeth, and I've shared with him my wish to seek to reinstate the Royal status and Crown-protection of all English dragons."

The sentence took my breath away.

"Pardon me," Father said abruptly, "I should have said English and Welsh."

Arthur inclined his head graciously, even though Father had looked at Emrys, not him. "British will do," Arthur conceded.

"British dragons, then. I will first ask if any of you have questions. Then I shall open to objections."

"I have a question," said Meredith. "Does it mean we won't have to hide anymore?"

"I cannot foresee what the consequences of this revelation will be, Miss Falconer," Father said very gravely. "I cannot promise your lives will be any easier. It may well be that, if we do this, in a generation our children will ask us why we chose to let the genie out of the bottle."

"I understand that. But—perhaps we might travel. Perhaps we might marry outside of just a few families." Meredith's gaze went to Mr Darcy, which Helena was cradling protectively in her arms. "And perhaps we might even take our dragons with us into the world, without hiding them."

"Yes," said Father. "Many things will change. And with change comes opportunity to makes things better. There are people in this room who have shouldered an almost unbearable degree of responsibility. I hope the coming change will bring a kinder distribution of duties."

I looked at the person in the room who I felt had borne the cost most heavily. "What do you say to the idea, ma'am?"

Helena's grey eyes were as bleak as the winter sky.

"I chose to give up my right to make decisions for Ormdale, Edith. You know how I misused it in the past." She glanced at Arthur, as if for the first time she truly understood the situation she had put me in, then back to me. "I'm here at this meeting only at your father's request. My only wish is to retire somewhere, at a distance from Ormdale, and leave it in better hands. If I could take my own dragon with me, as Miss Falconer suggested…" Her voice failed for a moment. "It would be a great comfort."

We were all quiet for a moment, and then Father said, "Are there any other questions?"

Gwendolyn spoke up. "How can we be sure that the authorities won't use our dragons in just the way Farley intended?"

"I'm afraid we can't be sure," said Father. "The government of this country is legally bound not to use chemical weapons, which is why Farley was working in absolute secrecy. It is my belief that bringing the dragons into the open will only make any double-dealing of this kind harder, even on the part of the government."

"I've been wondering about the beacons," I said, turning to Emrys. "It seems an impossible distance, and how could you be sure it wasn't just some winter bonfire you saw?"

"We have a viewing point in Gwynedd," said Emrys. "It's two standing stones, and between them, we can see the point where the signal fire should appear."

"All the way to Yorkshire?" Gwendolyn exclaimed in disbelief.

"Oh, no!" put in Arthur. "It was the Derbyshire one we saw."

"You never!" cried Meredith.

"And when we landed at the tower in Derbyshire, there was a very dirty boy who told us he'd seen the Yorkshire fire and done his ancestral duty. He seemed to expect us to make a great fuss over him."

"Was he frightfully ugly, with giant ears and a missing tooth here?" asked Meredith. "Why, that's my little brother, Charley! It's the first useful thing he's done in his whole life, then! He's the most famous stinker. What?" She looked round at our expressions. "If you don't believe me, ask Aunt Lavinia!"

Miss Birtwhistle gave a sigh. "Regrettably, my niece is truthful on this point." And she went on taking notes.

"He showed us a telegram from Miss Worms," continued Arthur, "and pointed out the marker for Yorkshire."

"Well, good for Charley the stinker!" I declared. "And may his fame increase for better reasons."

"What's this about a telegram?" wondered Meredith.

"Tell them about the telegrams, Edith," said Mother.

"Yes," I said. "Simon gave me the idea of sending them. I knew there was an old agreement about helping in times of danger—both Arthur and Tallantire had told me about it. I thought it was worth a try, so I sent them to all the Dragon Families the day before yesterday, when we found Miss Birtwhistle in Embsay and caught sight of Briggs on the street. I had no idea the children were going to light the beacons, but I suppose that added a certain urgency to my request."

"We didn't get a telegram," said Arthur. "It'll be waiting until one of my men pays a visit to Ogwen Cottage, I expect."

"I got ours," said Tallantire, "and I came straightaway, before the beacon."

"So all the Tallantires sent was a younger son and a freak of nature?" said Meredith heartlessly.

Tallantire drew himself up. "The Renwick Cockatrice, Miss Falconer—"

"Was very useful, indeed, Mr Tallantire," finished Mother. "It's just as I always say, not all of God's creatures are pleasant, but all of them are—useful."

She didn't say *beautiful* this time.

"Meredith, you must admit it did have an unexpectedly useful effect on the intruders," reminded Gwendolyn.

"I'm so glad you all like it," said Tallantire, beginning to beam again. "Because young George is completely fascinated with it. He says he needs longer to study it, so I've promised he can keep it."

"What!" I said, and Gwendolyn started in her chair.

"How very kind of you," managed Mother.

"That brings me to a special report," Father said, rubbing his hands. "I've asked two experts to join us."

Father nodded to Miss Birtwhistle, who went to the door and opened it as the rest of us exchanged baffled looks.

"They are ready for you now," she called into the passage.

George and Pip shuffled in, carrying something hidden under a cloth. They set it on the desk.

"Good morning, Dragon Keepers. Thank you for allowing us to present our proposal," said George. If I had ever seen his hair so carefully combed or his collar so pristine, I did not remember it. "I will be brief. When the dragons are made public, people will go tramping all over our lands looking for them. And even if we receive Crown protection, people will come, and, with all respect, we won't be able to fight them off forever. But we have a plan. We are going to give them what they want, *and* protect the dragons at the same time."

Pip plucked the cloth off, revealing a model hothouse, with an atrium two stories high. Inside were paper model dragons, beautifully drawn and stiffened with paste, hiding amongst little plants made of cloth scraps as well as rocks and bits of moss.

It was beautiful, a tiny world full of hope. Pip's face shone with pride.

"Years ago, there was a private menagerie at Wormwood Abbey with a collection of dragons," George explained. "Mrs Drake has kindly told us all about it. Why shouldn't we rebuild it, but open it to the public this time?"

"You mean like the museum at Tring? The one the Rothschilds opened to such great success? Or so I've heard," I added when I sensed Meredith's interest. I wasn't ready for her to know that I was personally acquainted with one of the richest families in England.

"Yes, exactly!" George responded brightly. "A menagerie of English dragons. And a few foreign ones as well, like Oolong and Frances. I don't want to get ahead of myself, but it could be—well, it could be the pride of England, you know. We'd be the first nation in the world to have such a thing. Naturalists would come from all over the world to study them. They might stay in the village and—buy things, you know," he added doubtfully. George had never been much interested in business.

"Indeed they might," I agreed with a smile. George looked relieved.

"And any of the other families, if they don't want people knocking on their doors, might lend us a dragon for a special display, you know." He looked tentatively at the Welsh representatives.

"Lend?" asked Arthur, raising an eyebrow.

"Sell," I said firmly.

"We would, of course, provide remuneration for any dragons lent to the Ormdale Menagerie of *British* Dragons for study or breeding purposes," Father clarified.

"And when you open to the public," said Tallantire, positively glowing, "you'll open with a Renwick Cockatrice in your collection. It will be an international sensation, there's no doubt about it."

The door had been left open when the children came in, and I now saw a greatcoated figure quietly waiting there for a break in the conversation, a staff in his hand.

"Simon!" I said.

"I've missed something important again, haven't I?" Simon said ruefully.

"Wait a minute," objected Arthur. "I don't want to be mean-spirited, but in what capacity are *you* attending this conclave, exactly, since I've been told you aren't a Drake anymore?"

Helena stiffened, and I looked forward to seeing her demolish him.

But the blow came from another quarter entirely.

"Shall I remind you," said Father, looking at him owlishly through his spectacles, "that you yourself are present at this meeting despite all of our gravest misgivings as to your character, Mr...I'm sorry, it was *Penrith*, wasn't it?"

Arthur's smile faded.

But I had just had an epiphany and thus didn't care a fig whether Arthur was bested or not.

"I'll tell you why Simon is attending," I said, jumping to my feet with more excitement than dignity. "He is attending—as Ormdale's Head Dragon Trainer!"

Simon's eyes lit with a flash of recognition. He sat down in an empty chair, and set the staff down casually next to him.

"Aye," said our new Head Dragon Trainer, relaxing into Yorkshire as everyone looked at him with a touch of awe. "That I am."

CHAPTER FORTY-SIX

After that, there was rather a lot to do.

Simon had to drive the quetzalcoatyls back to the caves so that they didn't take up permanent residence on the front lawn.

The men in the cellar had to be delivered to the authorities in Skipton by Dugdale, and right away, or they'd be stuck with us for Christmas, and I knew Martha would never forgive us if we gave them any of her Christmas dinner. Tallantire went with them, to take the train home from there.

Farley's body had not yet been recovered, so he had to be reported as a missing person. I wondered if there was anyone who would mourn him—the man who had adopted him, perhaps, if he was yet living.

Father drafted a letter, with Miss Birtwhistle's assistance, to the Lord Steward of the Royal Household. It would, we imagined, be immediately thrown on the Royal Rubbish Heap as the work of a crank, but Father felt it ought to be done anyhow as a matter of politeness, since the Lord Steward was his direct superior as Royal Dragonmaster.

Meanwhile, I wrote a letter to the only man I knew who might both believe us and have the connections to begin the process of Father's reinstatement: Cousin Stephen.

I was just finishing this, when Mother came in with a glowy sort of look, as if a hyacinth had come up very early.

"Edith, I thought you might like to know that Simon's just gone to have a little talk with your Father."

"Oh?" I said absently, sealing the letter. And then, not at all absently, as I realised what she meant, "*Oh!*"

By then, Mother had crossed the room and put her arms round me.

"I didn't want to say this before, but I haven't ever met another man I thought would suit you nearly as well as Simon, and I'm so, so happy that this has come to pass after all."

I laughed joyfully into her shoulder. "Yes, handsome dragon trainers who like to read novels *are* rather thin on the ground these days, aren't they?"

We laughed damply on each other for a bit, then Mother drew back to look in my face.

"Mrs Drake has spoken with me of her wish to go away, and of Miss Falconer's part in the plan."

"Gwendolyn says it might help to restore some of her health after years of living in an unhealthy atmosphere. I'm a little alarmed at the idea of prescribing a holiday with Meredith Falconer to a recovering invalid. What do you think about it?"

"I think they are both ready for a change in more ways than one. And—it must be said—I can't imagine that either of them will let the other take the smallest advantage of her, and that is a strange kind of relief."

I found Angharad sitting in the leafless cloister garden. With her wool cloak and ancient beauty, she looked like a medieval supplicant waiting to give her confession to the monks.

We were to say goodbye to them that evening. If Charley Falconer proved faithful to accomplish the second useful act of this life, the beacons would be lit to light them back safely to Wales that night. I certainly hoped for it, as I had no desire to accommodate Arthur a moment longer.

"I wanted to thank you, Angharad," I said. "All the time I prayed that someone would be a friend to Simon while he was in Wales, and now I know my prayers were answered. What was it you called him last night, in Welsh?"

"The *dewin dreigiau*. It means one who makes magic with dragons."

That must have been what Arthur had meant when he asked if I was a dragon charmer. But it wasn't me after all, it was Simon. Had he inherited it, like I had my Marsi blood, from an ancestor? Or was it a matter of character, to be so trusted by dragons?

She patted the stone seat next to her. "I wish to ask of you a favour." I sat, and she searched my face. "My sons. I wish to send them here. It was the custom."

"Oh! Fostering, you mean?"

Dimly, I remembered that medieval lords in history books were always swapping children—an alarming custom. Had the Dragon Families practised it? I remembered a little curly-headed boy weeping over his dragon-bitten brother, both of them as beautiful and probably as vain and selfish as Arthur. I scrambled for a polite way to decline. "Well, of course they'd be welcome for a visit, perhaps in the summer, but Simon and I don't even have a home yet."

"In the summer, then," she said, nodding in satisfaction.

What had I just agreed to?

She must have seen the doubt on my face, for she said, "Simon was very good to them."

And I understood. Arthur cared for his children in some fashion—he had run to rescue them from the *addanc* when he was terrified of it himself—but he was not a good man, to put it mildly.

Anyone who had spent time with both Arthur and Simon could not help but see which one of them would be a better influence on fledgling manhood.

While I prayed for real change for the good in Arthur, I did not count on it, and neither, I now realised, did Angharad.

I put my hand on hers impulsively.

"We will look forward to welcoming them to Ormdale," I said, and meant every word.

The abbey's chill passages were rich with delicious smells from the kitchen. Dough bubbled in mixing bowls, ginger and cinnamon simmered with apples on the hob, and in the great ovens onions roasted and pastry crisped.

People were busy with Christmas secrets, and we had to stomp around loudly or risk being shrieked at every time you opened a door.

On Christmas Eve, I took Frances out for a walk. I did not bother with a lead—she was much too big for her collar, and she was happy to follow me without it.

The swollen river had receded, leaving branches and mud everywhere, but I found the little ruined cottage again quite easily, the place where I had last glimpsed Farley.

It was a dreadfully sad place, made sadder by the end of Farley's story. Watching the water swirl at my feet, I admitted that I hadn't been able to wrestle a blessing out of this part of our family legacy. But then again, it hadn't been my story to write.

Later, I would ask Father to say the burial service with me there, as we had done for Rivers.

As I turned to go, I saw something glint in the mud. I put it in my pocket.

My feet and hands were cold on the way home, so I stopped in at the lodge. I found Janushek smoking by the fire in a masculine midden of books and tobacco fumes, with muddy boots propped on the fender and wet socks drying. His salamander was licking at a half-drunk cup of coffee sitting on a stack of books.

"No, don't get up, I've just popped in for a moment," I said. "And don't stop smoking, I don't mind pipes."

"What makes you think I was going to offer to stop smoking?" he asked around his pipe.

"I beg your pardon."

"I graciously give it."

"I suppose you know Lily would have a fit at this mess." I moved pamphlets and crumbs off the other seat so I could sit across from him. "I'm looking forward to watching her take you very firmly in hand."

"Not as much as I look forward to it." The crookedness of his grin was emphasised by the pipe in his teeth.

I snorted and put my own wet boots on the fender. "The lines are fallen unto us in pleasant places, after all, Janushek," I said with a sigh.

He looked at me quizzically.

"It's from the Bible. The part we *share*," I said, when he began to shake his head. "The psalmist says it. You can't be more Jewish than King David, Janushek."

"I finished Mark," said Janushek.

"And?" I said.

"I would have read your Gospels a lot sooner if I'd known they said things like this." He picked up a book and opened it to a place he had marked. "*And Jesus looked round about, and saith unto his disciples, How hardly shall they that have riches enter into the kingdom of God!*"

"Hm," I said, taking out of my pocket the thing I had reclaimed from the mud and polishing it until it shone. I held it, round and gold, between my thumb and forefinger. "And what about this?"

He took the pipe out of his mouth. "Rusalka. Have you been disporting yourself with the river gods again?"

"How much did you find?" I said, nodding at his muddy boots and wet socks. "After the flood?"

He picked up the tobacco pouch on his lap. It clinked. "Enough that there is very little chance of me entering the kingdom of God."

"I'm not so sure," I said, eyeing him narrowly. "What is it for, Janushek?"

His eyes flashed. "Might it not be for myself?"

"No. Because you are not a thief anymore."

He tapped his pipe on the fender, not looking at me. "It is for a school."

I was perplexed. "A school? For Pip?"

He nodded. "For Pip. But also for more than Pip."

"You mean, a school for Ormby? For all the children of the Dalefolk?" I took a breath. "Janushek, you're right! After all they've been through, the gold should go to something that will really help them!"

"Stop!" He held up his hand. "You are making me sound *good*."

I laughed. "All right, Janushek. But all the same, I am glad it was you who found it. *You* are no Midas."

I looked into the fire, suddenly sad.

"You are thinking of your grandfather?" he guessed.

"*It is easier for a camel to go through the eye of a needle, than for a rich man to enter into the kingdom of God.* I don't know if there's any hope for him, Janushek."

He picked up the book again and read aloud. "*And Jesus looking upon them saith, With men it is impossible, but not with God: for with God all things are possible.*"

"But you don't believe that," I said in surprise.

"Do I not?" he said thoughtfully. "You told me once that it was a great comfort to believe in the stories that mothers tell their children at night."

"Then—has something changed for you?"

"My story has changed," he said simply, and I thought of Simon. "So quickly, I do not trust it yet. And so I wait for more evidence. More evidence that the goodness I find is real."

He went back to smoking. The old Edith would have tried to convince him, but for this Edith, it was enough simply to sit and wait with him.

As a detective novelist, I knew that the evidence was every-where.

When I got up to leave, he got up too.

"I don't know how to ask this exactly," I said, "but if you would like to share Christmas dinner with us, we would be honoured. And of course, we won't be insulted at all if—"

"You shared my shabbat once, Rusalka. I will gladly share your Christmas."

The dining room twinkled with candles on Christmas Eve. Simon and his father had come in the afternoon with a small fir tree for the children, and we had decorated it with Pip's paper dragons.

At the last moment, Violet had come in, dusty, with a box full of wood shavings.

"I found the angel!" she announced.

I expected a lady angel with golden hair, but instead she shook off the shavings to reveal a fierce St Michael holding a long spear. Much of his paint had rubbed off, and his expression was enigmatic, but when he had been placed at the top of the tree, he looked less like a dragon slayer than a Dragon Keeper, with a staff instead of a spear.

After supper, we sat by the fire and sang carols, while the little paper dragons that perched on every branch listened to us under the watchful gaze of St Michael, and the room smelled of beeswax and fir resin and Martha's blackberry wine, and flesh-and-blood dragons sat at our feet.

And what could be a better symbol of Christmas than a myth made real?

Call up the butler of this house,
Likewise the mistress too,
And all the little children
That round the table go;
For it's Christmas time, when we travel far and near,
May God bless you and send you a happy New Year.

It was a wassail song, not a song for the inside people like us, so well-fed and well-heeled, but the people outside. Of course the Dale children would be too frightened to wander up to the abbey with a song on their lips in hopes of sugar-plums for payment, but on that night, with St Michael at peace with the dragons on the little tree, I felt a deep certainty inside me that Ormdale's story, like Janushek's, had finally changed.

Father must have had the same thought, for he began to recite, as he often did on the nights when he took a glass of wine or port after dinner. I had dreaded he wouldn't do it now that he was a squire instead of a clergyman, but I saw my mistake—Father had worn the collar because of who he was, and not the other way round. And who he was had not changed, and never would.

"The wolf also shall dwell with the lamb, and the leopard shall lie down with the kid; and the calf and the young lion and the fatling together; and a little child shall lead them. And the cow

and the bear shall feed; their young ones shall lie down together: and the lion shall eat straw like the ox. And the sucking child shall play on the hole of the asp, and the weaned child shall put his hand on the cockatrice' den."

One day—one day soon—the children would come to the door, without any fear. And they would not be sent away hungry.

"George," said Una, pointing at the chimneypiece. "Look!"
We all looked.

Inside George's sad moth jar—swathed with black crepe for mourning—something was stirring.

Chapter Forty-Seven

The elm trees were still bare when I took Simon to the little house on the avenue to Belle Mount to meet my great-grandmother. The March rains and the weak spring sunshine after it had made the earth smell fresh and young as we walked up the path to her house.

Inside, Nonna took both of our hands and crooned over us, "*Grazie, grazie*! You have brought my *bella bambina* back." She wasn't wearing black this time, and she seemed light in spirit as well as in body.

I noticed she wasn't wearing the necklace—was it hidden in her cane?

Irene coughed behind us. "Edith, it's time."

A motor car was approaching.

Simon and Irene took Nonna out of the room.

I stood at the window and waited, trying not to glance at the folding painted screen on the other side of the room, behind which David waited.

David had dismissed the servants for the day, so we would be quite alone for the task that awaited us.

The motor car was outside the gate now. The chauffeur opened the door for Sir Joseph, while Barrington remained inside. As Sir Joseph came down the path, Barrington tipped his hat at the window in a gesture of complicity.

There were footsteps in the passage, then Sir Joseph opened the door himself. My heart jumped at being in the same room with him again. Was it fear, pity, or anger? I could not be sure.

"Grandfather," I said.

"Edith." His driving coat had a fur collar, and he held his jewelled walking stick in one gloved hand. As always, he radiated wealth and confidence, but there was a hairline crack in the polish—a mere feather's weight of vulnerability. Irene believed that little crack was made by me.

Could it be widened so much as a camel? That was not my purpose today, but it was my secret hope—that the prison my grandfather had made for himself would one day open enough for him to begin to see how far he was from the kingdom of heaven.

"I have come to make you an offer."

"Really. And what is this offer?"

"There are two things you care about. I'm going to let you keep one of them."

"You think you know me so well? Tell me, then, what the great Sir Joseph Belmonte cares about."

"Reputation. And power."

For a moment, he seemed surprised. Had he thought I would put my name on the list of things he cared about? But I knew him better than that. It wasn't *me*, in any meaningful sense, that he cared about—it was power only that he craved; my loyalty, my obeisance. Everything that he admired about me, he had appraised as a collector seeking to swell his own importance.

He relaxed a little and began to draw off his gloves. "I am intrigued how you expect to offer either of them without the other."

Something was kindling in his eyes as he took off his well-brushed hat and set it on a small table. He enjoyed it—the sense of going up against danger, and winning.

I knew it, because it was the sort of thing I felt too. But not today.

"I'm going to offer you a chance to keep your reputation, Grandfather."

"How good of you." His eyes were dancing now.

"You tried to destroy us, but you failed. You told me once your personal motto: we ascend. But it is you will descend, into the very depths, not the Worms family."

"And why would I do that, Edith?"

"Because otherwise you will be the fall of the house of Belmonte. *That* will be your legacy—not ascension, but ruin and infamy."

Now the light his eyes turned to coals of wrath.

"You are speaking nonsense."

"You once told me it would be right to remove an unworthy man from a position of power. Was that nonsense?"

"Penrith was unworthy because he was a fool," he spat at me in disdain. "Stop this idiocy, Edith. You know you can't hope to prevail against me. I am not a fool like Penrith!"

"No, I can't hope to prevail against you alone. But I am also not a fool. And I am not alone. You are not the only one to collect secrets, Grandfather. Come out," I said quietly.

David stepped out from behind the screen, very pale but calm.

Sir Joseph blanched, then his lip curled in contempt.

"You would take my son's loyalty? I told you, Edith, David has been nothing but a disappointment to our family. You can have him, for all the good he will do you. I would have given you *everything!* Did you really think to frighten me with—*that*?" he scoffed, gesturing at his son.

David's cheeks were burning as he lifted his eyes to his father's. Something in them made Sir Joseph pause.

"No, Father. We've got something far more frightening."

He stepped fully out from behind the screen, and as he did so, he gently drew by the hand another person from behind the screen.

I had now met her several times since David had brought her to England from Switzerland, but my insides still cramped with rage when I saw the woman who had been so mistreated by my grandfather.

Judith Belmonte was tall and gaunt, with a mass of silvering ginger hair. I had been afraid to look into those eyes that had seen so much suffering. But in them, I had found no resentment—only gratitude for the granddaughter she had lost and regained.

But today, my grandmother burned like Justice herself, unveiled and terrible, with a green snake coiled at her throat.

Sir Joseph made a sound deep inside his throat, then looked wildly round the room, as if he had to confirm the reality of his surroundings.

"Do not speak slightingly of our son. He is the man who rescued me, Joseph," Judith said. "My desperate pleas for freedom—which you ignored—found the ear of Adonai at last."

"You were ill—they told me you needed rest—"

"I did not need twenty years' imprisonment! And you told my family I was dead!"

"It was only to stop them from pestering you, so you could get better," he said in a soothing voice that made me want to scream. "You were unwell after we lost Miriam—I did my best with what the doctors told me, my darling—"

"No, Joseph," she said with deep sadness, "you told everyone I was dead because you wanted me dead."

"No! I just wanted you to stop holding me back!" he shouted, jabbing the floor with his stick.

The room went utterly quiet.

"I've had Mother's sanity tested and certified by four eminent doctors, Father, in Paris and Zurich," David said. "And I have copies with lawyers in several cities. And I spoke to them about Mother's patrimony as well. You had no right to touch her property in Italy. What you did in Fucino—you never had her consent to sell any of it. It was completely illegal." Barrington had been quite ready to help us find the paperwork we needed to prove it all, and David now retained him as his own secretary. "I may have disappointed our family, but you"—David's voice broke—"you have done everything you could to destroy it."

Slowly, Sir Joseph sat down. I didn't recognise his voice when he spoke—all of the polish was stripped away. "What do you want from me?"

David picked up a document case. "Edith and I had some papers drawn up. It's an agreement. It gives me control over the business."

"You?" He looked up in confusion, as if he had expected me to angle for the job.

"Yes, Father," David said patiently. "It means your legacy will be untarnished in the eyes of the world. Our family will not fall. Your business will pass to your own son—as it has in many another family like ours. There is no disgrace. We will say you retired because of your health."

"Reputation...without power," he murmured.

It hadn't been my idea—it had been Judith who had decided on this course. After twenty years of helplessness, she had earned the right to decide what happened next.

"You retain our properties on the continent. You can live a quiet life there, and you may do as you please, but you will not try to contact or interfere with any of us again," said David, "or I will make all of this public."

I took the documents out and handed him a pen, showing him where to sign.

"I am not given to signing things without reading them,"he muttered.

"You know that this is more than you deserve, Father," David said. "I would have called down fire from heaven. You may thank Mother for this mercy."

"And what do you expect me to do? With the rest of my life?" Sir Joseph said at last.

"Perhaps you might go to a sanatorium," I said. "You were happy enough to send your wife to one."

Clamping his teeth, he scrawled his signature and threw the pen down. Then he lifted his eyes to Judith reproachfully. "And our family? Will we never be together again?"

I held my breath.

"Ask me that question again—after twenty years alone," she said in a voice that made me shiver.

I had always wondered why the ancients depicted Justice as a goddess, when it was Mercy that was considered the more womanly virtue.

I wondered no longer.

Epilogue

MAY, 1900

On a bright morning of the first April of a new century, Simon and I were married at the crumbling little church in Ormby.

The Belmontes offered to put on a splendid society wedding for us, but neither Simon nor I cared for the idea. We did, however, care for their company, and were very pleased when they came all the way to Ormdale for the wedding, giving me the pleasure of introducing both halves of my family to each other. Somehow, George and David got onto the subject of carnivorous plants and became fast friends. My grandmother, Judith, brought me her wedding veil of Italian lace.

Hanna found lilies of the valley in a tiny hidden hollow in the woods, and wove me a bridal crown of braids and flowers. My mother had been a statuesque sort of lily, but the diminutive kind suited me better. And I belonged to a valley now.

As Judith arranged the veil over my hair, I contemplated the filmy lace. Did the repeating pattern look just like dragon scales, or was I imagining things?

"It seems we have much to say to each other, granddaughter," she murmured, her voice rich with things unspoken. "Soon, when the season changes, we shall have time for that."

"So we shall," I whispered back.

Gwendolyn wore lavender at the wedding, and was happier and more beautiful than ever. Though I suspect it was her joy at the prospect of another term of medical study after the Easter holidays that illumined her so, as much as the occasion.

Tallantire kept looking at her like she was the bride. We all find his lack of dissembling rather endearing.

All of us except Gwendolyn.

Gwendolyn says weddings are like measles, only far more deadly. There may be something in what she says, for I have caught Dugdale looking wistfully at Miss Birtwhistle. And of course it will be rather lonely for him in the lodge all by himself, now that Janushek has given up being a bachelor.

(Miss Birtwhistle, by the way, has become an official part of our household, taking on the position—the *paid* position—of Housekeeper of Wormwood Abbey. Harry Falconer came by in January to fetch her home, and was politely turned away.)

All the Fairweathers came to the wedding—even Crispin, who rubbed at his spectacles as if to confirm all the wonders he was seeing. Did I hear him mutter something about metaphors when Frances and Oolong followed me with Violet and Una up the aisle?

With our permission, Cousin Stephen brought along a friend of his—a private secretary to the Lord Steward of the Royal Household. So I expect any day we shall receive an answer to our letter after all.

Helena sent her warmest congratulations to us from her new lodgings on the seaside, but did not return for the wedding. She is comfortably settled now, and her doctor has advised her against trying her newfound strength with travel just yet. It has all lifted a great weight from Simon, and I cannot help being grateful for her delicacy in not trespassing on his good nature.

Meredith is with her, playing havoc with the male population in general and, I suppose, diseased widowers in particular. Helena has taken Mr Darcy with her, and keeps him within her private rooms—though she writes that with Meredith in such fine form, no one has spared him much attention so far.

In the end, the only people dear to us whom we missed at the wedding were Janushek and Lily—for the simple reason that they ran off to get married themselves.

Pip has got a postcard from them, with a photograph of a lovely place called Robin Hood's Bay. I am happy to know that Lily has at last fulfilled her dream of going to the sea, and it was Janushek who took her there.

He has been made head of the new Limeworks, which will open in a few weeks, and Dugdale is busy sprucing up the old cottage in preparation for their return. Pip is painting a lovely seascape for them to put over the fireplace, in memory of their honeymoon.

I thought Mother and I might cry during the service but it was Simon who almost lost his composure. And then I looked over to see that Father's and Forrester's faces were very stiff, as if a breath of wind would undo them.

If Janushek had been there, he would have blubbed, and that would have been the end of it for all of them.

Perhaps his absence wasn't so impulsive after all.

The scaled members of our wedding party alarmed the curate even more than we expected, and he had to be prompted through the liturgy by Father. The man must have been thoroughly shamed by his ecclesiastical failure, for afterwards he was never seen again in Ormby—a development which has only added to the joy of the occasion.

Father is acting as lay-reader until the parish finds another curate.

The wedding breakfast was held at the abbey, and my only regret was that I was too distracted by sheer happiness to do justice to the baked delicacies prepared by Martha and Hanna.

After the speeches, Simon whispered in my ear. "Ready?"

"Almost," I whispered back, and slipped out, touching Gwendolyn's arm. "Help me change into my going-away outfit," I said.

She followed me to my tower study and when she saw just what I was changing into, her eyebrows shot high.

"You're wearing *that*?"

"Well, I call that hypocrisy, coming from a suffragette who dissects bodies!" I replied.

"You'll never catch *me* in trousers, Edith," she said firmly, as she helped me with the buttons. "It's not dignified. And I think even men look better in skirts—you know, like the Scots."

I whooped softly. "Shall I tell Tallantire? I'm sure he'd be willing to wear anything. He'd give his body to be *dissected*, if he could be sure of getting your attention that way."

"Hush! I'm not at all interested in his body!" exclaimed Gwendolyn, and then covered her mouth. We both giggled like girls for a moment, and then suddenly both of us sobered.

"You know, Gwen, you told me once that friendship with you might be costly," I remembered as I buttoned up my cardigan and slipped the goggles round my neck. "But it occurs to me that friendship with *me* has been costly for *you*. In less than a year, I've undone everything your family used to live for."

She folded the dragon-scale lace with reverent hands and a grave expression.

"No, Edith. Love is costly, and the truth is costly. But I've tried living without them." She looked at me. "They are worth the cost—every bit."

Some would say it is not very considerate towards the nerves of her family for a young lady to leave her wedding breakfast on the back of a giant serpent—and in trousers, no less (me, not the serpent).

Thankfully, my family's nerves are made of sterner stuff.

There were only a few small screams and a good bit of applause when Simon whistled for his pets to emerge from the woods and take us to our new home at Drake Hall, where Cariad was waiting in the stable, heavy with her baby (an unlooked-for gift from the reunion with her mate at Christmas).

Drake Hall! Really? (I hear you ask.)

Well, it came about like this.

Cousin Stephen was extremely helpful in drawing up the papers for Helena to officially adopt Simon so he could inherit the property he had been raised to care for. It took several months of consideration for Simon to agree to this. I refused to attempt to persuade him.

Early in the new year, when Simon was still thinking it over, he took me on a walk through the rooms of Drake Hall, recounting memories of his childhood.

Not *all* of them were awful.

Then we played Chopin nocturnes together while Pilot and Frances listened, and the daylight faded around us.

Before we left, we went up to the old clock in the passage, unmuffled it, and wound up the mechanism.

I could almost feel the place emptying of ghosts with every tick of the clock, until finally, it chimed the hour. The homely sound made the house feel young again and eager for life, with all its wild and wonderful changes.

Simon let out a long breath and held me in his arms.

The spell, at long last, was thoroughly broken.

Tolstoy, I am glad to say, is quite wrong.

All unhappy families are alike. But happy families are each happy in their own way.

They all need love, and honesty, and freedom, and laughter, but some of us need other things too.

As it turns out, a few of us are made very happy—in the case of the Drake-Forresters, quite *ridiculously* happy—by dragons.

Next for Ormdale

Welcome to

The Gilded Age of Dragons

where ancient creatures and airships collide,
and a pair of sisters from Yorkshire may tip the scales of history.
The next generation of Ormdale will return
in a brand-new story

A Menagerie of Dragons

set ten years later in a world forever changed
by the discovery of mythical beasts.
Coming in 2025

Want to keep up with all the gossip
from the world of Ormdale's dragons?
Go to www.christinabaehr.com
to subscribe to
Christina's newsletter.

A Note on the Dragons

While researching the history that flows through *The Secrets of Ormdale* like an underground river, I found that whenever I lifted up a historical rock, there were dragons hiding beneath it.

Some examples?

There is an extraordinary prayer book known as the Rothschild *Mahzor*, currently held by the Jewish Theological Seminary. It was produced in Florence in 1492 and shows that Jewish artists of the Renaissance were just as fascinated by dragons as their Gentile peers. There is also a beautiful sea-dragon pendant in the British Museum, donated by the Rothschilds, which gave me the idea for the necklace in this story, although I ended up basing my design on a reticulated serpent, also of Victorian design.

Serpentine-themed jewellery was surprisingly popular among the Victorians, and perhaps originated with the engagement ring given by Albert to Victoria, which looked like a snake coiled round her finger (and contained a lock of her hair). While this would not be considered particularly romantic today, the symbolism conveyed was of long life and constancy.

Perhaps reptiles can be romantic, after all.

The Marzano/Belmonte family is entirely fictional. I have placed them in the same social circle as the Montefiores and Rothschilds because so much has been written about them that it made depicting an Anglo-Jewish family easier than it would have been otherwise.

The Fucine Lake (now the Fucino Basin) in the Marsica region of central Italy and its monumental draining—completed in 1877 by a debt-ridden Italian prince—are quite factual, as is the ancient belief that the people of this place (known as Marsi) could cure snakebite. Virgil has a beautiful description in Book Seven of the *Aeniad* about the death of a Marsi healer-priest who could tame 'river-serpents'.

Since many Sephardic Jewish people have family names taken from places, I chose to name the family Belmonte after a location in Portugal. Later, I realised that the name probably jumped out at me because it is in *The Merchant of Venice*. That play may have ridden a wave of antisemitic sentiment in the late Elizabethan era, after Roderigo Lopes, the Queen's Portuguese Jewish personal physician, was executed on suspicion of attempting to poison her at the behest of the Spanish Crown (a crime of which he was likely innocent).

Which brings us to poisons.

The character of Helena Drake was inspired by the many undiagnosed invalids in Victorian literature, many of whom likely suffered from diseases such as ME/CFS, POTS, and Fibromyalgia (which are still very poorly understood today). Reading about cases of 'emotional exhaustion,' I came upon what was known as 'the rest cure', a tortuous treatment which inspired a horror story by someone who endured it (*The Yellow Wallpaper* by Charlotte Perkins Gilman) and was roundly discredited during her lifetime.

I was also saddened to discover that one of my favourite nineteenth-century artists, William Morris, refused to believe that the arsenic dyes which produced new and beautiful greens during his lifetime were dangerous. While relatively benign in objects like book covers, when used in textiles and wallpapers they caused serious health issues, and of course, injuries to the people who worked with them.

All of this led me to wonder what it would be like for someone in the late 1800s to experience a trifecta of chronic illness along with environmental triggers and unhelpful experimental treatment.

The bleak, gothic sanatoriums built for tuberculosis patients that now stand empty in the mountains of Europe inspired me to imagine Judith Belmonte's internment. Though I wish I had invented this, it was all too common for women to be relegated to a sanatorium or mental asylum for indefinite captivity without appeal, regardless of their mental health. See Nelly Bly's exposé *Ten Days in a Mad-House* for a contemporary account of this.

In *The Florentine Codex,* I was overjoyed to discover a source for 16th century Aztec culture, fully digitised online by the Getty Museum. An extraordinary anthropological survey of the Nahua people compiled by a Franciscan friar with the assistance of Nahua elders and scholars and filled with indigenous artworks, this stunning document is worth a look for anyone interested in Mesoamerican cosmology.

I cannot resist sharing this excerpt:

...before the rain begins, there are heavy winds and dust clouds, and thus they said that Quetzalcoatl, god of the winds, was sweeping clear the roads ahead of the gods of the rains, so that they could come down with their rain.

My inspiration for Simon's family heirlooms came from the Codex's description of the garments of the Quetzalcoatl priest:

He had a gold necklace from which hung some precious little seashells. He carried on his back, as an emblem, a tuft of feathers fashioned like flames of fire; he wore some leggings from the knee down, made of tiger skin, from which hung some small seashells.... in his right hand, he held a scepter like a bishop's staff. Its upper portion was crooked like a bishop's staff and abundantly adorned with precious stones... The part where it was held looked rather like a sword's hilt.

While I was imagining and writing the appearance of the Quetzalcoatl, I was very excited to discover that the Mexican King Snake has black scales with beautiful rainbow iridescence.

As for the other Dragon Keepers, while there has never been (as far as I know) a Royal Dragonmaster, there still exists a Royal Swanmaster (as Edith describes), accountable to the Lord Steward of the King's Most Honourable Household, and that is what I have based this position on, though I have made my fictional position hereditary, for obvious reasons.

According to the Cumbria County History Trust, William Hutchinson's *History of the County of Cumberland* (1794) contains agricultural footnotes written by a surveyor called Housman, who gives us the earliest known record of the Renwick Cockatrice, which tells us that John Tallentire of Scalehouses enjoyed exemption from tithes 'derived from a circumstance which happened about 200 years ago, almost too ridiculous to be credited...an ancient possessor being said to have slain a noxious cockatrice'. Housman claims that Tallentire had an official exemption from tithes dating back to the time of James I, though he did not 'suffer it to be read by curious visitors' (I would have been one of them).

When I began to draft this book, the subject that gave me the most anxiety was beacons. I'm grateful to the online Tolkien fandom, who have done a lot of research into beacons and how far they can be seen by the naked eye (it's complicated), and to Suzannah Rowntree for telling me about the pele towers which are dotted all over England, just as I describe.

In large part, this is why I write historical fantasy: to remind us that we all live in a fantasy world.

As Chesterton says, all we have to do is sit still and let the wonders settle on us like flies.

Or, perhaps, like very small dragons.

Acknowledgements

They say that this section is the hardest to write, because however many people you mention, you will never to able to acknowledge everyone who helped you. Let's see.

Thank you to my friends and family. Thank you for your patience, encouragement, and for rejoicing with me.

Thank you to my beta readers, illustrator, and editor, and especially to Karen Scharff for her careful and generous discussion with me of Judaism throughout this series.

Thank you to all of my readers and reviewers, even the ones who (quite unaccountably!) did not like my books. Thank you for the gift of your attention. You could have done any number of things, and you spent time on my books.

I have avoided thanking God in my previous books, not because of any lack of thankfulness on my part, but because an acknowledgement in the back of a book does not seem sufficient to thank the maker of the very materials from which stories are made.

Still, I'd like to thank God for everything—but most of all for dragons.

www.ingramcontent.com/pod-product-compliance
Lightning Source LLC
Chambersburg PA
CBHW031730180726
48283CB00005B/1450